Born Out of Wedlock

by Lyn Gardner

Dedication

To Boni –

Thank you for shining a light at the end of a very long, dark tunnel. Through your smiles and your laughter, your encouragement, and your support, I found my way back to something I love to do. So, I dedicate this story to a woman who will always be a dear, trusted, and loved friend.

L.

Prologue

The sound of her screams urged him onward. Pressing the accelerator to the floor, he sped down the winding road, mindless of the torrent of rain drowning the countryside and obscuring his vision. The windshield wipers seemed out of control, moving so fast across the glass that his vision cleared for a blink of an eye before it was again obliterated by streams of water trying to get in.

The sky was black and then it wasn't. Ripped at the seams by arcs of lightning, cobwebs of brilliance snaked and danced their way across the heavens. False hope was given as the road became flooded with light, but then it disappeared, and headlights not nearly bright enough, fought their way through the onslaught.

Halfway between somewhere and nowhere, his only choice was to continue north, for the town behind them was farther than the one in front. He swore under his breath as a pothole steered the car toward an embankment, and gripping the wheel, he straightened the tires and drove on. She screamed again. He was scared.

Suddenly, he took a deep breath. Up ahead he could see lights. Faint images amidst the deluge, the tiny shimmering glare of incandescence signaling that safe harbor was within reach. He placed his hand on her knee to offer comfort and silent assurance that everything would be all right, but she didn't say a word. He dared not look away from the road, but he paled at the dampness he felt under his palm. Sticky and warm, he knew what it was and when he clutched the wheel again, his hand was dark with her blood.

Earlier that morning they had driven through the little town. She had called it quaint, but not their style, and he had laughed because it was true. He was born into a family where chauffeurs were the norm, and when she had become his, she had slipped into the role of an untitled princess without blinking an eye. He didn't mind. He loved her, and they both preferred silver spoons over plastic cutlery. There was something to be said for never having to do without…and normally, they didn't.

The day had started like most weekend mornings, enjoying their tea and scones in their upscale condo in the middle of London, but then she announced she was bored and wanted to get away. When he called for the chauffeur, she balked and suggested they go on their own, and while he usually preferred not to drive, he couldn't say no. He could never say no to her. He loved her too much for that. She was his life.

So they meandered that day. Heading south down back country roads, while he kept his eyes focused on his driving, feeling slightly awkward behind the wheel of a car, she amused him by acting as his tour guide. As they drove past billboards spouting sustenance ahead, she joked about the faded colors of the placards and the fact that she didn't find yellow and green food that appealing. She pointed out little pubs with crooked signs and petrol stations missing numbers in their pricing. Misspelled signage on store windows had brought tears of laughter to her eyes, and the fact that a tiny village barely a few miles long would feel the need to have a walk-in clinic had caused her to raise her eyebrows in surprise. It seemed so stupid at the time. Now it didn't.

He remembered every word she had ever spoken, so upon entering the little town, he knew exactly where he was going. Just a bit farther up the road on the left was a small building with a glass front, and as he approached, his hand pressed on the horn and stayed there.

Inside the clinic, it was quiet. Two nurses and a doctor watched the clock, waiting for it to strike nine. It had been another long and tedious day. One cold, two fevers from the flu, a broken finger, a rash from eating too many strawberries, and the village hypochondriac with his latest tale of woe had filled their day, but only just barely. With the storm wreaking havoc, the television in the waiting area had been turned off, so under lights flickering in time with the lightning, the staff sat silent. One sipped coffee, one scribbled aimlessly, and one read a magazine. Ten minutes and they could go home.

Their heads popped up in unison when the sound of the thunderstorm was broken by the blare of a car horn. The room filled with the brightness of headlights, and for a moment, they all felt dread. Believing the car wasn't going to stop, they scrambled to their feet, but just as quickly the thought left their minds as they heard the screech of brakes...and all was well again. A loud crash of thunder suddenly rocked the building. Cringing at the sound, for a split-second they forgot about the car, but then they heard the horn still honking for help.

The doctor, serving out his last days before retirement, flew past the two nurses, decades younger than himself, and pushing open the doors, he ran out into the storm. His light-blue surgical scrubs turned dark almost instantly, and mindless of the wind and blinding rain, he hurried to the driver's door and yanked it open.

"My wife! My wife! Please help my wife!" the man inside cried out.

Leaning into the car, the doctor saw the woman sitting in the passenger seat, and when the lightning flashed again, he paled. She was covered in blood.

"Get a trolley!" he yelled over his shoulder as he ran to the passenger side. "Get a trolley, *now!*"

Pulling open the door, he knelt in a puddle and took the woman's pulse. It was faint, but it was there. Hearing the rickety sound of the gurney being pushed across the rutted parking lot, he rose to his feet, and as the storm raged around them, the three trained in saving lives tried to do just that.

As the doctor barked orders at his staff, the husband tried to explain what had happened. Eight months pregnant with twins, his wife had gone into sudden labor only an hour earlier. At first, they believed they had time to get home. Back to the world they knew with modern hospitals, doctors smelling of cologne, and where everything money could buy could be bought, but they had been wrong. Within a few minutes after her labor began, she screamed she was bleeding, and her screaming didn't stop until the village had come into view.

Swinging doors with small panes of glass flew open as the trolley smashed into them, and rubber-soled shoes squeaked across the floor as the team of three rushed her to the largest examination room they had. They weren't prepared for this. They were a clinic not a hospital, and scrambling, the nurses filled cloth-covered surgical trays with everything the doctor shouted he needed. Behind them, standing in a puddle of water mixed with blood, the husband stood in shock. This wasn't happening.

Tomorrow was her birthday, and he had a surprise. This wasn't happening. This was *not* happening.

Thirty minutes later, he sat alone in a room smelling of disinfectant and blood. The stainless steel rail of the stretcher was cold on his arm, but her skin was still warm. Sheets of green and white were draped over her lower half, trying to hide the hemorrhage that had taken her life, and every few seconds a drop of blood could be heard as it hit the floor.

They had left him alone so they could attend to the living, but as far as he was concerned, *she* should have died, too. *She* was the reason he no longer had a wife. *She* was the reason he no longer had a son. *She* was a murderer, and he would never, ever forgive her...and he would make her pay.

Chapter One

Accustomed to the sounds of the city, the pigeons lining the iron fence surrounding the park cooed and burbled amongst themselves oblivious to the late morning drizzle that had two-legged beings hastening down the street for protection. A car horn in the distance caused a few to ruffle their wings, but it wasn't until the doors to the courthouse across the street flew open with a bang, when the flock rose to the heavens en masse, the beat of their wings reaching a quick crescendo before they scattered in the sky.

More than one passerby glanced at the woman dressed in black as she stormed from the building, but she couldn't have cared less. Rushing down the stairs, she took four long strides toward the 1984 Daimler limousine parked on the street, before she suddenly came to a stop and whipped around. Mindless of the misty rain and the fact that even more people were now milling about, she glared at the two women standing frozen on the steps behind her.

For a moment, no one moved and then the two women tentatively walked out into the rain. Shielding their hair with their handbags, they both swallowed hard at the sheer fury they saw in the other woman's eyes.

"They've ruined *my fucking life*!" she roared, pointing to the upper floors of the building. "This is bullshit, Fran, and you know it!"

"You need to calm—"

"Don't you *dare* tell me to calm down! Don't you *dare*! Those bastards just sentenced me to Hell, and there's not one *fucking* thing I can do about it!"

"There are still ways—"

"*I've run out of time!*" the brunette bellowed. "You told me two years ago we could win this. You said there was no fucking way the mediators wouldn't agree, but you were wrong. Those fucking bastards sided with him."

"But we *did* win," Francesca Neary said as she moved one step closer to her client.

Incensed, the woman marched over, stopping just short of plowing into her lawyer. Pointing her finger in Francesca's face, she leaned in until their noses almost touched. "You call *this* winning? Really? Winning is me walking away with everything I rightfully own and him not getting what he wanted, but that's not the case, is it Fran? Unless I do what those bastards insist I must, I lose every fucking thing I hold important. Everything I've worked for, everything that is my *birthright* to have, I lose, and you have the audacity to stand there and say that we've won? Tell me something, Fran. Just how many people did you have to shag to get that law degree of yours?"

A crowd had not yet gathered, but Francesca Neary could see that a few people had stopped to gawk, and more than one was whispering to the person standing next to them, pointing at the woman they no doubt now recognized. Although livid her abilities as a lawyer were being challenged, Fran knew better than to start an argument in the middle of the street. Lowering her voice, she spoke as calmly as her anger would allow. "I think that our best plan of attack is to go back to the office and discuss this. Talk about our options—"

"*What* options! You said it yourself...every bloody loophole has been sewn shut. Every particle of speech has been examined under a microscope, and there are no mistakes. It's airtight, and you know it."

"I'll keep looking. I won't give up."

"Oh, that's just bloody great, Francesca!" the woman said, waving her arms in the air. "You keep looking while I watch my entire life go down the toilet, but I have a question for you. Will you keep looking even *after* I cease paying you?"

"It's not going to come to that."

Disgusted with the conversation and the woman standing in front of her, Addison Kane cast an evil eye toward her personal assistant who was standing a few steps behind Fran. Repulsed by association, she curled her lip at Millie Barnswell, turned on her heel and strode to her awaiting car. As she approached the silver and black limo, Addison's agitation erupted again, and before her chauffeur could open the door, she kicked it as hard as she could.

David Turner didn't blink an eye at the indentation left by Addison Kane's boot in the polished panel of the vintage automobile. Opening the door, he waited for his employer to enter, and then quickly closed it and trotted to the driver's side. A minute later, two women were left standing in the rain.

Opening the umbrella she had been holding the entire time, Francesca offered protection from the drizzle to the older woman standing to her right.

Stepping under the wide black brolly, Millie watched as the limousine drove down the street. "Oh my," she said looking up at Fran. "Seems like we've been forgotten."

Letting out a long breath, Fran said, "Well, I don't know about you, but the last place I want to be right now is in the back of *that* limo."

"Yes, she did seem a bit upset, didn't she?"

"That's putting it mildly," Fran said, waving for a taxi. "How about you and I go get a drink? Give her some time to cool down before we go back to work."

Checking her watch, Millie said, "It's a bit early, don't you think?"

"It's either that or we go back to the office. Your choice."

Millie pursed her lips and thought for a second. "I believe there's a lovely little bistro right around the corner."

***

An hour later, Millie politely smiled as the waitress placed two more glasses of wine on the table. Waiting until the woman walked away, Millie said, "I really think we should go back soon. Addison will be wondering where we are."

"And what if she is?"

"Sorry?"

"Millie, she's out of control right now," Fran said, keeping her voice low. "We go back to the office, and all she's going to do is ruin something else, and I prefer it not to be us."

With a snort, Millie said, "She was *extremely* angry, wasn't she?"

"Yeah, but she was also right. We *are* running out of time."

"Surely there is some…some precedent somewhere."

"The problem is we're fighting a three-hundred-year-old tradition," Fran said as she picked up her glass of Chardonnay. After taking a healthy swallow, she said, "The courts don't like getting involved when it comes to changing a company's policies, no matter how antiquated they may be, and that's exactly what the mediators told her today."

"So, what *are* the options?"

"What?"

"You told Addison that you wanted to go back to the office and talk about the options. I was just wondering what they were."

"There aren't any, but people were beginning to stare, and I was trying to get her off the street. The way she is with publicity, if she wakes up tomorrow morning and sees her picture on the front of the tabloids, today's little tantrum will seem like a walk in the park."

"Oh," Millie murmured. "Will she truly lose everything?"

"No, of course not," Fran said through a grin. "This has nothing to do with her personal wealth. She'll still be one of the richest women in this country. Addison's private investments alone guarantee that, but you and I both know that's not what this is about. The only thing she cares about is Kane Holdings, and in a month, the board will have no recourse but to take it all away from her."

"Just like that?"

Fran emptied what remained in her glass, and placing it back on the table, she sighed. "Just like that."

***

Shortly after two o'clock, Millie rode the lift to the top floor of the Kane Holdings building. Taking a deep breath as the chime signaled she had reached her destination, she stepped out into the carpeted hallway, smiling at a few of the office staff as they strolled by. Walking to the end of the corridor, Millie pulled open one of the etched glass doors leading into the president's office, but as she entered, the sound of someone's sobs stopped her momentum. Bewildered, she looked at the two secretaries stationed to the right and left of the entry and saw the youngest, hired only a few months before, bawling her eyes out as she filled an empty box with picture frames and plants.

"What's this?" Millie asked, taking off her raincoat.

"I've been sacked," Phoebe McPherson said, sniffling back a tear.

"What? Why?"

"When Miss Kane came back, she told me to cancel all her appointments for the day. I didn't think that would include the Milborrow meeting since it's taken us so long to get it scheduled, so I reminded her about it, and she went into a rage. She called me incompetent and then tossed my day planner to Lydia, and told me to pack my things and go."

"Oh, I see," Millie said. Taking the time to hang up her coat in the small cloakroom behind the woman's desk, when Millie reappeared, she looked over at the other secretary, Lydia Patel. "So, did you cancel everything?"

"Yes, but the Milborrow people were *not* happy," Lydia said.

"No, I suspect they wouldn't be," Millie said with a frown. Turning her attention back to Phoebe, Millie reached over and placed her hand on the box filled with odds and ends. "There's no need for this. You're not sacked."

"But Miss Kane said—"

"Don't worry about what Miss Kane said. I'll talk to her and get this sorted."

"But—"

"Phoebe, trust me," Millie said softly. "I've known Addison for a lot longer than you, and she's had a rough morning. Now, I think the best thing for all of us to do is to forget about what's happened here today. You two take the rest of the day off, with pay of course, and I'll handle whatever incidentals come along. How's that?"

Phoebe exchanged a quick look with Lydia before responding. "Oh, I don't think we should—"

"I insist."

"Millie, are you sure?" Lydia asked as she looked at the stack of work piled on her desk.

"Yes, now get out of here," Millie said with a nod. "That's an order."

***

As Fran walked toward the president's office, she stopped mid-stride as Addison's two junior secretaries came out carrying their coats and handbags. Checking her watch, she shrugged off her confusion and went inside.

"Admin holiday?" she asked, seeing Millie sitting behind her desk at the far end of the room.

"More like getting them out of the line of fire."

"Oh?"

"It seems Addison's ill temper came back to the office with her, and she proceeded to sack Phoebe when the poor thing questioned one of her directives."

"What?"

Rolling her eyes, Millie said, "And I don't know what she's doing in her office right now, but I've heard at least three things hit the floor and another two bounce off the wall."

Fran's shoulders fell. "Tell me you're kidding."

"I wish I was."

Chewing on her bottom lip, Fran looked in the direction of the double eight-foot-tall cherry doors, behind which she knew lurked a very annoyed woman. "You know, maybe I should come back later. I wouldn't want to be the next head on the block."

"Throwing me to the wolves, are you?" Millie asked, the slightest of a twinkle appearing in her eyes.

"Hardly," Fran said with a laugh. "If there's one person around here with job security, it's you. I'm just her lawyer, but you're her right *and* left hand. She couldn't get through a day without you."

"You're also her friend."

"That's debatable."

"Is it?"

"At times," Fran said as she sat on the corner of Millie's enormous desk. "Don't get me wrong, I still like Addison, but she doesn't make it easy. I can't tell you the last time we had a conversation that wasn't about work."

A loud crash coming from the next room caused both women to jump, and with a snicker, Fran hopped off the desk. "Well, I'd best go in and see what I can salvage."

"I'm sure whatever she just broke can be replaced."

"I'm not talking about the furnishings, Millie," Fran said as she walked toward Addison's private office. "I'm talking about her life."

Fran winced as she quietly opened the door, holding her breath as she peered through the crack. The hand-woven Persian carpet was littered with shards of pottery, and as Fran stepped inside, she was careful not to grind any of the ceramic into the wool fibers of the intricately designed rug. Across the room, Addison stood in front of the credenza filling a glass with scotch, and by the shattered pieces of crystal amidst the multi-colored remains of sculptures and vases covering the floor, Fran assumed the glass in Addison's hand wasn't the first she had held since returning to the office.

***

Addison Kane was the president of Kane Holdings, a company that had been in her family for over three hundred years. It had begun as a tiny trading business, bartering for land and product, and as the decades passed it had slowly grown. Land bought for only a few pence had been sold for thousands of pounds and investments made on the new and unusual turned into gold mines. Visionaries, the founding fathers of Kane Holdings had been able to sit back and count their coin as the upper-class scrambled for chronometers, mechanical pencils, sewing machines, and perambulators. The money rolled in, and for over a century, although the company continued to dabble in real estate and innovations, for the most part, it was kept afloat by the interest earned.

Upon graduating Oxford with a bachelor's degree in Economics and Management, Addison was welcomed at Kane Holdings with open arms by her grandfather, Xavier Kane. His ancestors' vision had been passed down to him, and under Xavier's leadership, the company had begun to grow again. Unfortunately, the family's keen business sense had skipped a generation. The company had never held his son Oliver's interest. His biggest accomplishment was just getting to the office on time, but Addison seemed to thrive in the ways of the company. Spending her days at her grandfather's side, she absorbed every word Xavier spoke, every lesson he taught, and every trick he knew...and at night, she learned even more.

Sequestered in a room located at the end of a very long and dismal hallway, while the other occupants of the house slept, Addison did not. Behind a meager desk atop which was a lamp with a green shade, she'd sit in silence, poring over financial newspapers, business journals, and market studies. Riveted by what they contained, she'd watch trends, analyzing growth and eyeing companies on the cutting edge until the wee hours of the morning, and when it was time to return to work, she'd spend hours interrogating her grandfather in the ways of business until eventually, he threw up his hands.

Xavier Kane was not a stupid man, but he realized Addison's thirst for knowledge far outweighed what he could teach. Believing she would eventually run the company, Xavier convinced her to return to school at

Oxford, and much to his delight, less than two years later, Addison Kane had an Executive Master's degree in Business Administration.

Xavier's health began to fail shortly after she returned from school, and acknowledging his own mortality, he began to make plans for a future that would not include him. While it was true Addison had excelled in her classes, and when standing by his side, she could do no wrong, Xavier needed more. He needed for her to prove herself...on her own.

To show him she was strong enough, smart enough, and shrewd enough to one day assume the position of president of Kane Holdings, Xavier came up with a test. Opening a subsidiary company under the name of AK Investments, Xavier deposited one million pounds in the company accounts and told Addison she was in charge. She had one year to prove to her grandfather she would be able to take the reins of Kane Holdings when it came time for her to do so, and prove it, she did. Less than a month before he died, Addison walked into her grandfather's office with the audited financials of AK Investments, the one-year-old off-shoot company of Kane Holdings...now worth over five million pounds.

Four weeks later, Oliver Kane walked into the same office and took his place behind the carved walnut desk made by artisans centuries before. Finally rid of the man who had forced him to accept his daughter's existence, Oliver's plans were simple. Live off the dividends of his stock and disown the offspring he loathed. The only problem was Xavier had added a codicil to his will. Fully aware of his son's feelings, while the bylaws of the company were written in stone, one mere paragraph modifying the last will and testament of Xavier Alexander Kane had guaranteed his granddaughter would keep her job at Kane Holdings, for as long as she wanted.

Oliver was livid. Once again, he was forced to accept what his sperm had produced, and for the first time in his life, his interest in the company was piqued. Xavier's addendum to his will, while totally within his rights, hatched a plan in Oliver's twisted mind. For the next few years, while his daughter continued to add to Kane Holdings' portfolio of investments, he studied every syllable of the company doctrine, eventually hiring Maxwell Firth to ensure Oliver's last will and testament would be iron clad as well.

Known as one of the most cunning attorneys in all of London, Maxwell saw an opportunity he couldn't resist. By crafting an unbreakable will, there would come a day when Kane Holdings would be up for grabs, and he'd be there waiting with an open billfold.

Aware modern-day courts would undoubtedly balk at the prejudice of the archaic company documents stating only a male heir could inherit,

Oliver and Maxwell decided not to pick that particular fight. Instead, Oliver made it clear in his will that he was going against the company's bylaws by leaving Kane Holdings to his daughter; however, he made something else *very* clear. He stated that while he could not find it in his heart to follow *all* the mandates set down by his forefathers, Oliver believed the principles on which the company was founded were righteous, and he requested that those remaining ideologies be honored...to the letter.

Firth had spent every waking hour for over a month constructing his masterpiece, a means to an end for Addison Kane, but it was an end Oliver could never really enjoy. When the words of his will were finally known, Oliver would not be around to see the pain he had inflicted on Addison. Firth, having his own agenda, knew this was the chance he'd been waiting for.

The Board of Directors of Kane Holdings was made up of seven men, all of whom having taken their seats during the reign of Xavier. With the same mindset and morals as their dear, trusted friend, they knew the brilliance of Addison, and their dividends showed it. Time after time, Oliver had lost his battles in the conference room, but with two members about to retire, vacant seats needed to be filled.

The bylaws of Kane Holdings clearly stated it was within Oliver's rights to appoint the new members, so the seats were quickly filled with like-minded friends of Firth and Oliver. To add insult to injury, and to assure him many gleeful days watching his daughter answer to those who would always side with him, Oliver also hired Maxwell as the company lawyer.

***

Hearing the door latch behind her, Addison looked over her shoulder, her eyes narrowing at the sight of Francesca Neary. "What do you want?"

"I thought we could talk?"

"About what?" Addison asked, slowly raising the glass to her lips to take a sip.

"About what we're going to do."

"*We?*" Addison said as she strode across the room. Throwing herself into the high-back leather executive chair behind her desk, she glowered at Fran. "Exactly when did this become a *we* issue?"

"You know what I mean," Fran said as she sat down in a chair opposite Addison's desk.

"Actually, I haven't a clue, because those bastards this morning were fairly crystal in their explanation and trust me, I was paying attention," Addison said, slamming the thick-bottomed glass on the desk. "The way I understand it, and feel free to correct me if I'm wrong, I have just over a month before I will have no recourse but to sit back and watch my company get cut up into little bits and pieces and sold to the highest bidder." Regarding the woman across the way, Addison narrowed her eyes again. "Now, did I miss anything?"

"Only the fact that by changing what they did this morning, you now have an option."

Addison's nostrils flared like a bull about to charge. "*That* is not an option, and you bloody well know it!" she yelled, sitting forward in her chair.

"Why? It's a way out, isn't it?"

"Just because they agreed the company doctrine can't dictate *who* I marry since the law has been changed, that doesn't mean it's an option. I don't give a shit if it says man and wife, or wife and wife...it is still *not* an option!"

"Why not?"

"Because it's a fucking life sentence and one that I care not enter into, thank you very much," Addison growled. Grabbing her drink, she downed the contents and then threw the glass across the room.

Francesca had seen several of Addison's tantrums over the years, so she didn't blink an eye as the imported crystal met its demise against the wall. "It wouldn't be for life, Addison," she said calmly. "We could arrange that it would only last a few years."

"Oh...and how exactly are we supposed to do that? My ancestors were quite crafty when they wrote up the company's bylaws or weren't you paying attention?"

"You know I was, but nothing's impossible. We have a way out, and we should explore it."

With a snort, Addison shook her head. "You know there's a fine line between being an optimist and being an idiot, Fran, and right now you're leaning toward insanity."

"Maybe so, but it's a way for you to keep your company, and the last time I checked Kane Holdings was the most important thing in your life."

"*It is!*" Addison said, jumping to her feet.

"Well, then we need to find you a wife."

"Jesus Christ, you're not getting it, Francesca!" Addison barked. "The women I see, I see for only one reason, *and* for only one night. That's it.

Most are already married, and even if they weren't, I wouldn't ask them, not with the conditions I'm being forced to meet. I'd prefer to keep the digits in my bank account at the breadth they are now, rather than watch them dwindle down to zero because some tart believes she's worth more than she is just because she's got large tits."

"But if we could find someone—"

"I have an idea. What are you doing for the next three or four years?" Addison said, eyeballing her lawyer.

"Sorry, I'm taken, but nice try," Fran said with a grin. "What about Millie?"

"You're teetering on insanity again, and in case you haven't figured it out, I don't find any of this even remotely funny," Addison said, the timbre of her voice lowering as her annoyance grew.

"I know that, but it sounds to me like you're at least open to trying this. That is if we could find someone. Yes?"

"Exactly how do you plan to do that, Fran?" Addison said, crossing her arms. "Put an ad in the Singles Column? 'Wealthy woman requires a wife. Length of service yet to be determined. Must be willing to agree to—'"

"Addison, I don't know how we're going to do it, but if I know you will at least consider it, I'll do everything I can to make it happen. Just give me some time to come up with something. Okay?"

Addison let out a heavy sigh, taking one breath and then another until the need to kill left her thoughts. Sitting back down, she ran her hand over her hair as yet another long breath escaped. "I don't want to lose my company," she said softly. "And if this is the way to keep it, then I'll do it. I won't be happy...but I'll do it."

Opening her briefcase, Fran pulled out a pad of paper. "Well, then we'd best go over the details."

Raising her eyes to meet Fran's, Addison cocked her head to the side. "What details?"

"What you're going to offer this woman when I find her."

"First you find her, and then we'll talk."

"Don't you want to—"

"No, I *don't*!" Addison shouted, slamming her fists on the desk. "I've been through quite enough today without having to discuss what else I'll have to give up besides my name in order to keep the company I bloody own! You find the tart, and then we'll discuss details, and if I were you, I'd start looking in churches, because unless this bag's a saint, you and I will both be out of a job!"

Chapter Two

Lighting another candle, Millie Barnswell said yet another prayer. The house of worship was quiet now. The seven o'clock service had long since finished, but she had remained behind, enjoying the solitude of her church. Returning to a pew, she sat and glimpsed at her watch, sighing when she saw the time. She'd have to leave soon. Doors on churches were no longer left unlocked at night, but for a few more minutes, she watched as the flames of the candles danced in the drafty old sanctuary.

Hearing a small commotion at the back of the church, she turned around and smiled at the sight of a familiar face. Watching as the woman struggled to control the cleaning cart as she pushed it up the aisle, Millie said, "Good evening, Joanna."

Distracted as she tried to correct a misdirected wheel on the trolley, Joanna Sheppard nearly jumped out of her shoes when a voice broke the silence of the church.

"Oh, my God, Millie," she said, holding her hand against her chest. "You scared the shi...um...living daylights out of me."

"I'm sorry, dear. I thought you saw me."

Jerking the cart as it veered toward yet another wooden pew, Joanna said, "No, I was too busy trying to get this blasted wheel to go straight."

"Yes, it does seem to have a mind of its own, now doesn't it?" Millie said with a snicker.

"It most certainly does," Joanna said as she came to a stop. "So, what brings you here tonight? I usually only see you on Sunday."

"Yes, well work's been rather stressful this week, so I thought I'd stop by and light a candle or two. It always has a way of taking the edge off, if you know what I mean."

"Alcohol does that for me," Joanna said with a laugh. "That is when I can afford it."

"How's your father?"

"Oh, he's okay, but still as cantankerous as ever, I'm afraid. That's the reason I'm here tonight."

"Really? Why's that?"

"He apparently was quite a handful earlier this week, and one of the nurses said he ruined her shoes by pouring his lunch all over them. I had to buy her a new pair, and it wasn't in the budget."

"That's too bad."

"It's all right," Joanna said with a shrug. "As long as I can have him home with me, that's all that really matters."

"You do get some assistance, don't you?"

"Of course, but it doesn't take care of the debts he had. I'm still working to pay them off," Joanna said as she began to push the cart toward the altar. "And speaking of that, if I want to get home at a decent hour, I'd better get this place tidy. I still have an office to clean on my way home. Nice talking to you, Millie."

"Good night, Joanna," Millie said, getting to her feet. "By the way, will I see you on Sunday? I'll bring those books along that we talked about last week."

"I'll be here pushing my mop as always," Joanna said over her shoulder. "That is unless some rich doctor comes along and offers me a better deal."

***

Over the past forty years, there wasn't much Millie Barnswell hadn't seen or done as an employee of Kane Holdings. At the tender age of twenty-one, she had walked over their threshold as a temporary typist, and sitting amongst others like herself, she had done what they had not. She had followed the rules given her. She didn't chatter or gossip. She didn't paint her face or chase after the men hoping for a good catch. She did her job, and it paid off. When the other temporary workers left a few months later, Millie was asked to stay on.

After spending a few years in the typing pool she moved into research and development, and working as a junior secretary for the manager of the department, she paid her dues in more ways than one. Shy and reserved, Millie had never met anyone like Virgil Barnswell. Enamored by his good looks and muscled physique, one thing eventually led to another and shortly after she turned thirty, they were married.

Nine months to the day after their wedding their son Trevor was born, and Virgil couldn't have been prouder; however, before Trevor reached the age of two, he was diagnosed with cerebral palsy. Unable to accept the limitations of his son, before Trevor's fourth birthday, Virgil walked out and never came back.

So, with the help of family and friends, Millie raised her son without a father. Wanting to give Trevor everything she could, she began working even harder at Kane in hopes of obtaining a more lucrative position. Skipping lunches and taking breaks only when the need for a bathroom became great, her productivity was second to none, and as Millie had hoped, someone finally noticed...and that someone was Xavier Kane.

At the age of thirty-six, Millie Barnswell became the personal assistant to the president of Kane Holdings, and for the next fifteen years, she worked alongside one of the kindest men she had ever met. When Xavier died, there were not many at his funeral who cried more than Millie. Three years later, Millie attended another funeral after a lung infection took her son away.

After Xavier's death, Millie had accepted the position as Oliver Kane's assistant, and at first, she was disheartened by the lack of challenge and common courtesy, but after the loss of Trevor, she no longer cared. She went to work as she always did, punctual and professional, but the next few years drifted by as if she was in a trance. If Xavier had still been occupying the president's office, he would have noticed her sadness, but Oliver did not. When he died unexpectedly of a heart attack, Millie didn't even sniffle.

Having worked for Oliver for nearly nine years, Millie had become numb to boorish and standoffish superiors. So, when she was offered the position of personal assistant to the newest president of Kane Holdings, she accepted the job without blinking an eye. Addison was known throughout the company to be a brooding woman who rarely smiled, and having met her on numerous occasions when she worked alongside Xavier, Millie was well aware just how cold and curt she could be, but it didn't matter. She assumed there'd be no surprises working for Addison. It would be the same drudgery Millie had become accustomed to, and it would allow her to continue to mourn the loss of a son long since gone...or so she thought.

Addison was a driven woman, focused on only one thing...success. Unlike her father, she was diligent to the point of obsession, typically arriving at work in the early hours of the morning, and leaving long after the last employee exited the building. Her sedulousness surpassed even Xavier's, and Kane Holdings began to grow like it had never grown before. Although Addison Kane's ability to be cordial left a lot to be desired, when it came to the business of making money, she was downright brilliant.

In awe of the woman's intelligence, Millie began looking forward to going to work again. Since the death of Xavier and Trevor, work had become just that, but with Addison in charge, each day brought new projects and challenges. While Addison never asked Millie to work longer hours, she began showing up just after Addison arrived, and more than once, when the president of Kane Holdings left late in the night, it was Millie turning off the lights. On occasion, Addison would seem to lose her antisocial demeanor toward Millie, but it took nearly twelve months before the tide finally turned, and when it did...it turned for good.

One morning, walking into the office carrying two cups of coffee, the cardboard holder slipped from Millie's hand and fell to the floor. Dressed in her usual professional business suit, low-heeled shoes, and looking as prim and proper as any sixty-year-old woman could, without thinking twice, Millie muttered, *"Shit!"*

Unbeknownst to Millie, Addison had just walked out of her office and hearing the expletive fly from the genteel lady whose gray hair was coiffed in a chignon, Addison began to laugh. In one swoosh of spilled coffee, the dam was broken. Addison's austere exterior, at least when it came to Millie, disappeared, and that morning, the ice maiden and the PA became friends.

They never went on shopping outings or even had lunch at nearby cafés, but within the confines of Kane Holdings, a mutual respect had been born. They worked side-by-side, navigating comfortably through project after project, and as days turned into weeks, Millie found herself liking the woman more and more.

Most assuredly diagnosable as obsessive-compulsive, Addison had a strict regime she followed with every takeover, every land deal, and every investment. On numerous occasions, Millie inwardly sighed at Addison's constant questions to ensure things were in order, but as time passed, she accepted the woman's quirks for what they were...scars put there by a father who had berated Addison up until the day he died.

The rumors of Oliver Kane's hatred for his daughter had been spoken by many employed at Kane, and Millie had heard them all, but it wasn't until she came to be the woman's assistant when she saw the damage Oliver had done. Many a night, Millie would go home with Addison on her mind. It seemed such a waste for a beautiful woman who had an intelligence way beyond her years to be locked into a soulless existence that centered on success and *only* success. It was as if without it, and the company that had been in Addison's family for centuries, it would have somehow proved her father right...that her birth should never have happened. Luckily, Millie thought Oliver Kane was an arse.

***

As Millie schlepped into her house on Friday night, she debated on whether to walk to her neighborhood church and light a few more candles. The night before she had lit two, the first, like always, had been for Trevor and the second, for Addison. She had prayed for a way out for the woman who had become her friend. Some solution that would enable Addison to keep her birthright, but after spending the day listening to heated arguments between Francesca and Addison, Millie feared her prayers would go unanswered. Exhausted from her week of worry, she sighed and made herself some tea. Deciding a splash of port was also in order, she headed up the stairs with tea in one hand and a small glass of sweet, red wine in the other, knowing that God could hear her prayers, whether they be in a house of worship or at the side of her bed.

A short time later, as sleep was taking hold, a thought popped into Millie's head, jolting her from slumber so much that she sat upright and stared into the darkness. The smallest of grins appeared on her face when she realized her prayers may well have already been answered.

***

"I thought I saw your car in the garage," Addison said, standing in the doorway to Fran's office. "What are you doing here on a Saturday?"

Looking up from her computer, Fran said, "I'm researching singles' websites, trying to find you a wife."

The mere mention of the word caused Addison to set her jaw. "Do you honestly think you can find someone on those stupid things?"

Since returning from the courthouse on Wednesday, Fran had spent every waking minute of her time trying to find a solution to Addison's problem. She was tired. She was worried, and she was fed up with Addison's spoiled, rich kid attitude. Glaring at the woman in the tailored Zegna suit, Fran said, "I don't know, but it's the only thing I could think of. Why, do *you* have a better idea?"

"No, but then again, I thought *you* could do your job."

"I *can* do my job!" Fran yelled, getting to her feet. "But every fucking time I went to file the papers, every sodding time I tried to fit this into your goddamned schedule, you kept delaying. How many meetings did you cancel? How many bloody times did you push this aside and find other projects where you thought I was needed more? In your infinite, goddamned wisdom you thought you were smarter than he was. There was no *way* the mediators wouldn't find in favor of the *great* Addison Kane, but you were wrong, Addison! You may be one hell of a businesswoman, but your father, the son-of-a-bitch, fucked you from the grave!" Pointing at the door, Fran said, "Now, get the *hell* out of my office so I can try to find some fucking way to get *you* out of the mess *you* created!"

Somewhere over the years, their friendship had been lost to contracts and workload. Addison had forgotten about the nights they had spent studying together. The times when Fran forced her to leave the school in search of pubs and parties to show her life actually did exist outside ivy-covered buildings and libraries rich in tradition. Having never had any friends in her youth, the concept was foreign to Addison, but as she stared back at Fran, the lawyer's dark blue eyes blazing with fury, Addison knew she had wronged one of the few in her life who had always tried to be her friend.

"You've got quite a mouth on you. I'll give you that," Addison said as she sat down in a chair opposite Fran's desk.

"Piss off, Addison. I don't have time for your crap."

Addison considered her next move, but knew she had only one. "Look, I'm sorry. What I just said was...was uncalled for."

In all the years they had known each other, Fran could never remember Addison apologizing for anything. It wasn't in her nature. Apologies meant mistakes and Addison never made a mistake, at least none she had ever apologized for. Fran opened her mouth to speak once and then twice before the words finally came out. "Are you okay?"

Looking up, Addison arched an eyebrow in response. "Don't worry, Fran. Just because I admitted what I said was wrong, doesn't mean I'm still not angry."

"Well, as long as you're not going to continue to take it out on me, then I'll keep working on this," Fran said. "By the way, I was wondering...what about Luce?"

"What about her?"

"She's single, isn't she?"

"Yes, but she's not an option."

"Why not?"

"How long do you think it would take some bloody reporter to dig up her past?"

"Shit, I forgot about that," Fran said with a sigh. "Well, I guess it's back to the Internet then."

"Dating sites, eh? Please tell me they're at least lesbian sites."

"A few are, but depending on what you're going to offer your future spouse, we could also go straight."

"No fucking way!" Addison said, practically coming out of her chair. "If you think I'm going to marry a sodding bloke—"

"I'm not talking about a man, Addison," Fran said, but amused at the thought of Addison having to marry a man, for a few seconds Fran sat with her lips pressed tightly closed. Waiting until the desire to burst out laughing had left her, Fran cleared her throat. "But since this is going to be a marriage of convenience, it doesn't matter if the woman is straight or gay. All we need to do is to trust that she's not going to try to take you for all you're worth after it's over."

"Like that's going to happen," Addison said, getting to her feet. Feeling her annoyance returning, she marched to the door. "I'd better get out of here before another shouting match begins. I'll be in my office if you find the woman of my nightmares."

"Oh, before you go. Take this with you. Read it when you get a chance," Fran said, offering Addison a manila folder.

"What's this?"

"I took the liberty of writing down my thoughts on what we can offer this woman when we find her," Fran said. Seeing that Addison was about to open the folder, Fran reached over and pinched it closed. "I have a feeling you're not going to like what's in there, and since *I* don't want to get into another shouting match, read it over the weekend, and we can talk about it on Monday. Okay?"

"Sure," Addison said, tucking it under her arm. "I'll read it in my wine cellar. That way, I'll have plenty of alcohol to numb the pain."

***

Sighing at the sight of her disorganized kitchen, Joanna Sheppard pushed aside a pile of junk mail and opened the pizza box. About to grab some plates, she stopped when she heard a knock at the door. Trotting over, she pulled it open.

"Millie!" Joanna said, stepping back so the woman could enter. "What are you doing here?"

"My market had a sale on chicken, so I made that casserole your father likes so much. I hope you don't mind," Millie said, walking to the kitchen.

Following in quick pursuit, Joanna said, "You know I don't, but honestly, Millie, you live on the other side of town. You don't need to bring us food. We do okay." Seeing Millie quickly glance around the kitchen, Joanna added, "It's messy, not dirty."

"I never said it was," Millie said, taking off her jacket. "It's just that I know how hard you work, and I do love to cook."

"I used to love to cook. That is, when I had time," Joanna said, opening a cabinet to get some plates.

"Are you working that much?"

"I thought I was going to have a break, but the washer broke yesterday."

"Oh, I see," Millie said as she removed the cover of the casserole. Filling the first plate, she handed it to Joanna. "Why don't you take this up to your father, and I'll get you one, too."

"Thanks," Joanna said, breathing in the aroma of the home-cooked meal. "Dad is going to love this. Be right back."

A short time later Joanna returned to the kitchen to find Millie up to her elbows in soapy water at the sink. "And I suppose you love to clean, too, eh?"

Looking over her shoulder, Millie said, "Actually, I do. It's very gratifying, don't you think? One minute a dish is dirty and the next, it's clean."

"I suppose so, but only when it's your *own* dishes you're washing," Joanna said, folding her arms across her chest. "Please, Millie, you don't have to do that. I'm not working tonight, so I have plenty of time to get this place in order."

"Well, if I do this, and you eat, then you'll be ahead of the game. Now please, dear, sit down and eat it while it's hot. I'm fine, really."

Having had this argument with the woman before, Joanna knew there was no point in going any further. Sitting down at the small kitchen table, she dove into her meal like it was her last.

"This is delicious," Joanna said between forkfuls. "You have to give me the recipe."

"I did already. Several months back, if memory serves."

"Oh...I forgot."

"No worries, dear. I'll write it down again if you'd like?" Millie said, walking to the table to take Joanna's empty plate. "Another helping?"

"Thanks, but I think I'll keep the leftovers for Dad's supper tomorrow. Two nights in a row without takeaway, he'll think he's in heaven," Joanna said with a giggle. "Now, how about you sit, and I'll make us some tea?"

"That would be lovely," Millie said, placing the last dish in the drainer to dry. "It will give us time to talk."

Chapter Three

Joanna returned to the table with a fresh pot of tea, and sitting down, she refilled their cups. She looked around the kitchen, appreciating the sight of the counters now empty of clutter and old pizza boxes. "I can't thank you enough for everything you've done tonight," she said. "You really didn't have to help me clean up."

"My pleasure, I assure you," Millie replied, taking a sip of tea. Stealing a quick look at her watch, Millie sighed. She had been there nearly two hours and had yet to bring up the true reason for her visit. Deciding it was now or never, she said, "You know, the other night in church, you said something that I found quite interesting."

"I did?" Joanna said, looking up from her cup.

"Would you really marry someone just for money?"

Confused, Joanna thought back to their conversation. "It all depends on the day," she said with a shrug.

"What do you mean?"

"Well, when all the bills are paid, Dad's behaving himself, and the visiting caregivers show up on time, then no. But when he spills soup on their shoes or the washer breaks, or I drop the takeaway as soon as I walk in the door, then yes, I think I would."

"Have I ever told you who I work for?"

"No. I mean, I know you work at Kane Holdings, but I don't know for whom exactly. Why?"

"I'm Addison Kane's personal assistant."

"Really?" Joanna said, her smile growing wide. "Wow, talk about a cushy job!"

"Yes, at times it can be, but at others, it can be quite, shall we say, stressful."

"Oh, I'm sorry, Millie. I didn't mean to make light of what you do, but working for someone who's that rich must have its perks."

"It does, but like I said, it also has its problems, and that's what I wanted to talk to you about tonight."

"Huh?"

"How much do you know about her?"

"Who?"

"Addison Kane."

Joanna's brow furrowed as she tried to recall anything she knew about one of the country's richest women. "Sorry, Millie, but I really don't have time to follow the news. I just know she's wealthy, and that's about it."

"That's quite all right, dear," Millie said, taking another sip of tea. "Actually, Addison tries to stay out of the newspapers as much as she can. She hates the intrusion."

"Yeah, I have the same problem," Joanna said, her eyes crinkling at the corners.

Millie's enjoyment of the woman's lightheartedness showed on her face. "Speaking of problems, Addison's having one right now, and it's one you may be able to help her with."

"Me?" Joanna said, jerking back her head. "What in the world could I possibly do to help Addison Kane?"

Seeing no reason to beat around the bush, Millie calmly said, "She needs a wife."

The words took only a second to sink in, but it felt like hours to Millie. Watching as Joanna's expression went from jovial to confused and then to stunned, she waited for her to catch up.

Joanna tilted her head to the side. "Did you just say...did you just say she needs a *wife*?"

"Yes, I did."

"You want me to...you want me to *marry* her?" Joanna said, the pitch of her voice rising just a tad.

"It's perfectly legal. I assure you."

"That much I know, Millie, but why in the world would you think that I was a...a lesbian?"

"You don't have to be."

"Sorry?"

"Joanna, it doesn't matter if you're gay or straight. The marriage would be for convenience only."

"Whose?"

"I would assume both of yours. I'm not privy to the details, but I can't imagine they wouldn't be lucrative."

Joanna narrowed her eyes as she studied the woman across the table. Millie seemed in control of her faculties. She was neatly dressed with not a strand of hair out of place. Her posture was perfect. Her eyes appeared clear, and since they had just spent the last few hours together Joanna knew the woman was sober, but the fact she was answering Joanna's questions as if the subject matter was somehow commonplace was beyond bizarre.

"Um...Millie...I-I don't know how to ask this—"

"Feel free to ask whatever you'd like, dear. I'll answer if I can."

Joanna nibbled on her bottom lip for a moment. "Well, not to sound rude, but...but are you on any kind of medication?"

Millie's face split into a grin. "No, Joanna. I don't take medication."

"And this isn't a joke?"

"No, it's not."

Joanna leaned back and eyed the woman again. She knew Millie well enough to know she didn't lie, and that was enough to get Joanna to her feet. Going into the kitchen, she opened a cabinet above the stove and pulled out a dusty bottle of whiskey. Grabbing two glasses, she returned to the table and offered one to Millie.

"No, thank you," Millie said, holding up her hand. "But feel free. I don't mind."

"Good," Joanna said, pouring a splash of the blended malt into a glass. Taking a quick swig, she hissed at the burn and sat back down. "Now, what's this all about?"

"When Addison's father, Oliver, died, she inherited Kane Holdings, but there was quite a rift between father and daughter, so Oliver attached some conditions to his will. Unless his stipulations are met, Addison has to give up her right to her family's company. Since it's privately held, her stock will be divided up among the minority stockholders, and rumor has it, most of them want to sell. Basically, they're going to take the money and run, and the company will cease to exist."

"And she'll be broke?"

"No, not at all," Millie said, shaking her head. "This doesn't have anything to do with money. She could very easily start another business and be quite successful, but this company is the only connection she has to her family and to her name, and to lose it would be devastating for her."

"And her father's conditions?"

"They're actually based on the bylaws of the original Kane Holdings when it was started in the early seventeen hundreds. The founders believed that those who inherited the company needed to be solid, upstanding citizens, and in their minds, it meant that the men had to be married by the age of thirty-six."

"The *men*?"

"Well, yes, back then women didn't have any rights."

"Of course. Silly me," Joanna said, rolling her eyes.

Tickled by what seemed to be Joanna's never-ending playful spirit, Millie cleared her throat before continuing. "Anyway, because of his will and the way it was written, Addison can't lose the company because she's not a man, but she can lose it...and *will* lose it, if she's not married by her thirty-sixth birthday."

"And apparently she's gay?"

"Why yes, I thought everyone knew that."

"Millie, I don't know what the woman looks like, let alone her sexual preference," Joanna said, before taking another gulp of whiskey. "And why me?"

"For this to work and keep Addison's privacy intact, we need to find someone we can trust. Someone who won't take advantage of the situation or want to dance in the spotlight just because her last name is now Kane."

"And because of some glib remark I made at church last week, you think that's me?"

"No, I think it's you because I've known you for nearly four years, and during that time, you've never struck me as the type of person who takes anything for granted, or anyone for that matter. You go about your days with a smile on your face simply because you know that when you get home, your father is here. It takes a very special person to do the things you do and not have any animosity."

"Thanks for the compliment," Joanna said with a grin. "I guess I should be flattered that you thought of me, but honestly, I...I couldn't do what you're asking, Millie, convenience or not. It would just be too...too weird."

Millie's shoulders slumped. "I understand. Well, it was worth a shot as they say."

"I'm sorry," Joanna said softly, seeing a frown appear on her friend's face.

"Oh, please, you have nothing to be sorry about. It was just my attempt at trying to help Addison. *I'm* sorry if I offended you."

"You didn't."

"Well, I think I've taken up enough of your time for one evening," Millie said, getting to her feet.

"Can I ask you a question?" Joanna said, following Millie to the door.

"Of course."

"I would think someone in Addison Kane's position wouldn't have a problem finding a partner for herself. Why does she have you beating the pavement for one?"

"She doesn't. She has no idea that I'm here."

"No?"

"No. Addison is having a tremendously hard time accepting the fact that this is the only way to keep her company, so until we find a viable candidate, there's really no point in getting her involved."

"We?"

"Oh, yes, I'm sorry. Addison's lawyer, Francesca Neary, is really the one doing the search. This was just my attempt to help. Speaking of that, this sort of thing has to be kept entirely confidential, so I have to ask that you not repeat what I've said here tonight."

"I won't, Millie. No worries."

Millie took Joanna's hand and gave it a squeeze. "I didn't think you would, but I had to make sure. I hope you understand."

"I do," Joanna said, watching as Millie put on her jacket. "So where do you go from here? I mean, surely you have other irons in the fire beside me."

"I'm afraid you were my only iron, but Fran has been working day and night trying to find someone, so I think I'll let her be the matchmaker from now on. I don't really have a lot of friends your age, and whoever we find has to at least *appear* compatible with Addison. I doubt she would appreciate me soliciting gray-haired old ladies for her partner."

"Yeah, probably not," Joanna said with a titter as she opened the front door. "I'm really sorry I couldn't help you."

"Don't give it another thought, Joanna. I'm sure by Monday, Fran will have a long list of possibilities."

***

On Monday morning, as she finished the remainder of her third cup of coffee, Fran sighed as she read through the e-mails she had received over the weekend. After opening up an anonymous e-mail account, she had advertised on several dating websites, and the responses had left a lot to be desired. Contemplating whether her stomach could handle another cup of French Roast, she was saved by someone tapping on her door frame.

"You have a minute?"

Looking up, Fran smiled. "Of course. What do you need?"

Walking in, Millie sat down and crossed her legs at the ankles. Folding her hands in her lap, she pursed her lips as she thought about the words she wanted to say. "I know a young woman who's having a hard time making ends meet."

"Okay?" Fran said, staring back at Millie.

"She's always struck me to be quite an honest person. She attends church regularly and loves her father, and works morning and night to make sure he's taken care of. He's been ill for quite some time, so she's their only source of income."

Clueless as to why Millie felt that she needed to know this information, Fran said again, "Okay?"

"I ran into her on Friday night, and it seems she's working three jobs now. She looks awfully tired for someone so young, and I thought...well, I thought perhaps—"

"Say no more," Fran interrupted, opening the bottom drawer of her desk. Pulling out her purse, she asked, "How much did you need?"

"What?"

"I'm assuming you're taking up a collection for this woman. Yes?"

"No, of course not, and Joanna wouldn't accept if I did. She's *much* too proud for that."

Fran's eyebrows knitted. "Millie, excuse me for being blunt, but I'm up to my eyeballs reading messages from women looking for their soul mate. If you don't want a donation for this...this overworked friend of yours, then I really need to get back to work."

"What about Joanna?"

"You *just* said she wouldn't take a handout!"

Millie looked toward the heavens, let out a slow breath, and very clearly enunciated the next five words she spoke. "What about Joanna for *Addison*?"

It took a moment for Millie's words to sink in, and when they did, Fran's backbone straightened. "What did you just say?"

"You heard me."

"Did you ask her?"

"I mentioned it on Saturday night when I went for a visit."

Fran leaned forward in her chair. "And?"

"Well, as you can imagine, she was quite stunned at the idea, and initially, she told me she wasn't interested."

"Initially?"

"Yes, initially."

Fran began to smile when she saw the tiniest of grins appear on the diminutive woman's face. "Millie, what exactly are you saying?"

"Joanna called me this morning. It seems she's decided to change her last name to Kane."

***

After Millie had left on Saturday night, Joanna sat at the kitchen table sipping her whiskey and laughing to herself about the preposterous offer. Shaking her head at the crazy idea, she climbed the stairs with a smile on her face. She couldn't marry for money, and she couldn't marry a woman. It was sheer lunacy.

She went about her nightly routine as she always did. Exchanging her father's food-stained pajamas for a clean pair, Joanna listened as he talked about the sports he had watched that day. She nodded at all the right times while she tidied the room, gathering the dirty dishes and the discarded newspapers left by the caregivers. Joanna liked football, but she had heard the stories an hour before. He had forgotten he had told her, but she didn't mind. Joanna loved listening to him grumble about blind referees and players who needed to be traded. It made her happy. He had gone through so much, yet he was still her dad, feisty as always.

She wanted to spend the night chatting with him. It was rare they ever had more than just a few minutes in the morning to talk before she went to work, but when he yawned, and his eyes closed, she quietly kissed him good night. She was as tired as he, but there were still things left to be done.

Joanna went to her room and searched her laundry basket for essentials before returning to the kitchen with dirty dishes in one hand and dirty laundry in the other. With the washing machine broken and no money to have it repaired, she had only one option. Filling the sink with water, she turned on the radio to keep her company, and humming along with the music, she spent the evening washing their clothes.

A few hours later, with laundry draped around the house to dry, Joanna returned to her bedroom still wearing the smile put there by Millie's ludicrous proposition. Changing into her pajamas, Joanna crawled into bed and shut off the light. She believed sleep would come easily, but in the dark and quiet of her room, Joanna's thoughts began to wander. Was it really that crazy?

Sometime after midnight, with her mind still reeling with questions, Joanna crept to the kitchen to fix herself a cup of tea. Grabbing some paper, she sat at the table believing if she could write down the answers to her questions, she would finally get some rest. Looking at the blank page, she realized she had only three questions. What could she lose? What could she gain, and would this give her father a better quality of life? Joanna's decision was made before a single word was written.

***

Joanna Sheppard hadn't missed a day of work in nearly twelve years. Colds and the flu had never stopped her, and a root canal had only prevented her from arriving on time. A sprained ankle slowed her down a bit, and two broken fingers taught her to write with her left hand, but she had never missed an entire day...until now.

Sitting cross-legged in the middle of her bed Tuesday morning, she stared at a photograph of her and her father taken before the first stroke took his balance, the next left him weak on the right side, and the last damaged his memory. A few months after the photograph was snapped, they had sat at their kitchen table discussing which courses she wanted to take when she went off to college, and the next day, she sat alone in a hospital praying that he'd be okay. It didn't matter her plans had changed. It didn't matter that she wouldn't continue her education, or visit far and exotic places during spring and winter breaks. The only thing that mattered was she loved him. He had always provided for her, and now she would provide for him. The sound of the doorbell jarred Joanna from her thoughts, and taking a deep breath, she went downstairs.

Grateful for the small overhang keeping her out of the morning drizzle, Francesca Neary stood in front of the bright blue door, trying to decide if it was too soon to ring the bell again. After spending most of Monday morning interrogating Millie, extracting every bit of information the woman knew about Joanna Sheppard, Fran got to work. Deciding until she had all the facts, getting Addison involved would only start another argument, Fran spent the rest of Monday calling in some favors. She found out Joanna Sheppard had never been married, had no criminal record, and had turned twenty-eight earlier that month. After the responses Fran had received from the Internet dating sites, Joanna Sheppard instantly moved to the top of Fran's very short list of candidates. As far as Fran was concerned, there was only one thing left to know. Could this woman *look* the part of Addison Kane's wife? That answer came as soon as the blue door swung open.

Time stood still as both women sized up the other. Joanna had imagined the lawyer for Addison Kane would be an older woman with a pinched face, dressed in an overly-tight tweed suit, carrying a briefcase and looking slightly miffed because Joanna had insisted they meet at her house in Burnt Oak. Francesca Neary definitely did not meet Joanna's expectations. Appearing to be in her early thirties, her blonde hair was styled in an attractive bob, her features were flawless, and her dark blue eyes creased at the corners as she displayed a dazzling smile. Before a word was spoken, Joanna had a feeling she was going to like this woman.

The day before, Fran had deleted over two dozen e-mails from single women wanting no longer to be single, and most had been moved to the recycle bin simply because of the way they looked. She was not a snob, nor did she generally judge a person by their appearance, but she wasn't looking for just anyone. She needed a woman who could become the wife of Addison Kane, and because the marriage would happen so quickly, its haste needed to be answered. Love at first sight seemed to be the simplest explanation, but the only women ever seen on Addison's arm all had one thing in common. They were beautiful.

Fran was not a person who assumed anything. She dealt with facts, precedents, and laws. The woman standing in the doorway appeared to be wearing no makeup, and her hair was pulled back in a casual ponytail definitely not meant to impress, but she was nonetheless, striking. Fran told herself not to presume the woman was Joanna Sheppard, but she prayed to God she was.

Extending her hand, she said, "Hello, I'm Francesca Neary. I'm here to see Joanna Sheppard."

"That's me," Joanna chirped as she shook Fran's hand. "Please come in."

"Thanks," Fran said, walking into the house. "I hope I'm not late."

"No, not at all," Joanna said quickly. "I was just about to make some coffee. Would you like some? Or if you prefer, I can make some tea. I'm not quite sure what I have, but there's a market a few streets over. I'd be happy to go and get whatever you'd like." Seeing the smile on Fran's face grow even larger, Joanna chuckled. "I'm sorry. I'm a bit nervous. I've never been interviewed to be a wife before."

"That's okay," Fran said with a laugh. "Trust me, they never taught this at Oxford."

Chapter Four

As Joanna busied herself in the kitchen fixing some coffee, Fran sat at the table and perused her surroundings. It was a home lived in by those who couldn't afford much. With no wall separating the living area from the kitchen, she could see that the furnishings in the lounge were old and stained. The love seat and upholstered chair showed their age in the faded fabrics covering their cushions, and the rectangular coffee table carried the scars of misplaced glasses, feet, and no doubt a dozen moves over the years. In the corner of the room, a cable wire slithered out of the wall and ran to nowhere, and with a few hooks missing, the drapes covering the front window drooped in despair. There were no magazines or newspapers in sight and as Fran looked around, she realized there wasn't even a light in the lounge to read by. It was just a space forgotten by those who lived there, for they were too busy to notice.

"Here you go," Joanna said, returning to the table carrying two cups of coffee.

"Thanks," Fran said. "So, have you lived here for long?"

"Um…about eight years, I guess. It's a lease."

"One you can get out of?"

"You tell me," Joanna said through a grin.

"Good point," Fran said, smiling.

"So how does this work?"

"Well, I thought today I'd just come over and meet you. See what you were like—"

"Check me out, in other words? See what I look like."

"I'm sorry," Fran said as her shoulders dropped. "I know that probably sounds coarse, but we're talking about a wife for Addison Kane. If you don't look the part, the press will have a field day with it, and the last thing Addison wants is publicity."

"So, should I assume since you're still here talking to me, I at least *look* the part?"

Fran had made it a point of not trying to stare blatantly at the woman, but by asking the question Joanna had just given her permission. Fran sat in silence as she sized up Joanna, and she came to the same conclusion she had when Joanna opened the door to greet her. While the woman looked worn down and her clothes were out of style and somewhat faded, she was nonetheless, attractive. As far as Fran was concerned, with some proper rest and a visit to Bond Street, she was looking at the future Mrs. Addison Kane. With her perusal completed, Fran raised her eyes to meet Joanna's. "You most *definitely* look the part."

Joanna relaxed back in her chair and tucked an errant strand of hair behind her ear. "I wasn't really fishing for a compliment, but thanks."

"You're welcome," Fran said as she reached into her attaché and pulled out a folder. Opening it, she scanned her notes. "I do have some questions I need to ask though."

"Sure, that's fine. I'll answer anything you'd like."

"Good," Fran said, looking up from her notes. "Millie tells me you're working three jobs. Is that right?"

"Yes, I work at Doyle Books during the week, and I have a couple of cleaning jobs I do on nights and weekends."

"What do you do at Doyle?"

"I'm a cashier."

"How long have you worked there?"

"Um…nine years."

"Nine years and still a cashier?" Fran said, cocking her head to the side.

"I've been offered management positions, but their schedules are too erratic. It's hard enough finding caregivers for my dad when I have fixed hours, let alone trying to do it with a rotating schedule, so I always turn them down."

"Wouldn't it have meant more money?"

"Yeah, but it didn't seem worth disrupting my father's weekly routine just for a few more pounds a week."

"So you clean offices instead."

"It helps pay the bills."

"But doesn't that still disrupt his...um...his schedule?"

"Sometimes, but not often. My dad loves sports, and luckily a few of our neighbors are as fanatical as he is. They come over at night or on the weekends and watch football with him, so I take the Tube back to the city and make a few extra quid."

"It must be exhausting. I mean, working all day and then continuing at night."

"I don't mind."

"That's admirable."

Joanna shrugged. "I do what I need to get by. That's all."

Between the chat she had with Millie and a phone call to the manager of Doyle Books, Fran had already known the answers to the questions she had asked, and she was pleased Joanna hadn't lied about anything...yet. Studying the woman for a moment, Fran said, "Can I ask why you changed your mind?"

"What do you mean?" Joanna asked, shaking her head ever so slightly.

"Millie said that when she initially talked to you about this...this idea of ours, you told her no, but then you called her yesterday morning and said you had changed your mind. I was wondering why."

"Will this help my father?"

"Sorry?"

"If this...if this happens, will my father be taken care of?" Joanna said quietly. "I mean, I don't want him to be put in some sort of home or extended care facility. He stays with me, but he gets better food, and nurses to help him bathe and change his clothes. He hates when I have to help him do that."

It was all Fran could do to keep her mouth from dropping open. Knowing that friends were sometimes blind to the imperfections of friends, Fran had graded everything Millie had told her on a curve. She now knew it hadn't been necessary. Millie had described Joanna Sheppard perfectly. She was a kind, compassionate woman who loved her father. End of subject.

"You're doing this for him, aren't you?" Fran asked quietly, suddenly feeling quite humble in Joanna's presence.

"I love him, and if this gives him a better life, then why not do it?"

"I can think of several reasons, the first being that you'll be giving up your freedom. Obviously, if you're Mrs. Addison Kane, you won't be able to date or see anyone until it's all over. You do understand that, don't you?"

"I haven't had a date in years, so what's a few more," Joanna said with a shrug.

Fran had not traveled to Burnt Oak in search of a friend, but as each minute passed, she found herself liking Joanna Sheppard even more. She seemed perfect. She seemed *too* perfect.

"What's wrong with you?" Fran blurted, the words in her mind escaping her lips before she could stop them.

"Excuse me?"

"Oh, Christ, I'm sorry," Fran said as her cheeks flamed. "I didn't intend to say that."

"Well, now that you did, what do you mean?"

"I came here believing I would find a tremendously long list of reasons why you can't possibly become Addison's wife, and so far I haven't found one. So, I have to ask you to be honest with me."

"I have been. I have nothing to hide. Trust me. My life is fairly boring and simple."

"Then why hasn't someone swept you off your feet?"

Joanna let out a throaty chuckle, and after taking a second to get herself under control, she said, "Because I spend my time at work or at home taking care of my father. I don't have time to date, and even if I did, who would want a live-in father-in-law."

"Speaking of men, Millie told me you're straight. Are you sure you won't have a problem playing the part of a lesbian?"

"I don't know. Exactly how does a lesbian act?" Joanna said as she pointed to the ring on Fran's finger, proudly displaying two interlocking female symbols. "You don't seem any different to me."

It was Fran's turn to chuckle. "You're observant. I'll give you that."

A wee bit of Joanna's temper surged. Believing Fran had just insinuated she was dumb, Joanna's jaw tightened. "I am *not* stupid."

Fran's eyes flew open wide. "Oh, shit. I'm sorry. That's not what I meant."

"No?" Joanna said, crossing her arms. "It sounded like it to me."

Fran had just found the chink in Joanna's armor of perfection, and a smile spread across her face.

"You think this is funny?" Joanna asked, glaring at the woman.

"No, not at all," Fran said with a snicker. "And I apologize if you took what I said the wrong way. I never once thought you were stupid, and I'm sorry if that's how it sounded."

"So why are you smiling?"

"For a minute there you reminded me of Addison, only on a much smaller scale."

"What do you mean?"

"She can have quite a temper when she wants to," Fran said, running her finger along the edge of her coffee cup. Taking a deep breath, she said, "Look, you've been honest with me, so I'm going to be honest with you. Okay?"

"Sure."

"Addison's my employer, and even though she makes it difficult at times, she's also my friend. I like her a lot, that is when I don't want to throttle her, but if this is to work, then you need to know exactly what you're getting yourself into where she's concerned."

"All right."

"Joanna, she's not happy, and that's putting it mildly. She's enraged she has to go through this farce to keep a company which is rightfully hers, and you have to know she won't pull any punches when this happens. Addison values her privacy almost as much as she values her work, and this marriage will be an intrusion on that. One, I'm sure, she'll have a tremendous problem dealing with."

"You sure know how to propose to a girl, don't you?" Joanna said with a twinkle in her eye.

"I'm not finished," Fran said, leaning forward. "Addison also has no clue on how the other half lives. She grew up in the world of limousines, servants, and private schools, and had a grandfather who made sure she never wanted for anything."

"In other words, she's spoiled."

Fran snorted. "Not like a sniveling, whiny child, but yes, she does have her moments."

"She sounds absolutely lovely. I'm starting to understand why she couldn't find a wife for herself."

"Oh, Addison can be quite charming when she puts her mind to it, but only when it serves a purpose."

Joanna's left eyebrow arched upward. "Such as?"

"There's no one better at talking someone into selling their business or their property than Addison, and if there's a new piece of technology out there, she'll be downright enchanting in order to get her foot in the door to obtain it. Basically, if Addison sees something she wants, she gets it, so if she fancies a pretty woman, straight or gay, married or single, she'll turn on the charm and win them over. Unfortunately, those poor women have no idea that by the next morning, Addison won't even remember their names."

While somewhat surprised by Fran's less than glowing description of her employer, Joanna was also quite tickled by Addison Kane's apparent haughtiness and overblown ego, and it showed on her face. "Perhaps you should attend Miss Kane's charm school because you're definitely not making this arrangement sound appealing."

Fran leaned back and let out a sigh. "Look, I need to be upfront with you. I don't want you to walk into this believing it will be all cocktail parties and evening gowns, because it won't. Addison lives a solitary life, and there's no room in it for anyone else. You'll be a lodger in her home until the marriage is over, and you shouldn't expect anything more."

"And when would that be? I mean, we haven't talked about *when* this will all happen and when it would end."

"Well, you'll have to visit the registry office within the next five days."

"Five days!" Joanna said, almost coming out of her seat.

"Yes, I'm afraid so. That's why after Millie had told me about you yesterday, I called and set up this meeting. Addison's birthday is in less than five weeks away, and since we have to wait at least twenty-eight days after you register before the marriage can take place, that doesn't leave us a lot of time. As far as how long it's going to last, I can't give you an answer until I talk to Addison. Last Friday, I gave her a list of my suggestions, including the financial details and the length of...well...let's just call it *service*, but she had meetings this morning. I won't be able to talk to her until I get back to the office. Once I do, I can arrange a time when we can all meet, and if possible, finalize the details."

"Are you saying I have the... I have the job?"

"Do you still want it?"

Taking her time, Joanna thought about everything Fran had told her. The fact Addison Kane was apparently a coldhearted bitch didn't sit well with Joanna, but neither did the pile of bills stacked on her kitchen counter. Locking eyes with Fran, Joanna said, "Yes, I do."

A pearl diver couldn't have held their breath as long as Fran felt she had held hers since posing the question, so when she heard Joanna's answer, her exhalation of relief was audible and long. "Well, then after we finish our chat, I'll head back to the office and let Addison know I've found her a wife. She's in no position to argue, so as far as I'm concerned, you'd best start packing."

"Really?"

"It's either this or she loses her company. She doesn't have a choice."

***

No longer burdened by the oppressive weight of finding a spouse for her employer, when Francesca Neary entered Addison's outer office later that morning, she didn't walk in. She practically skipped. Having already called Millie from Joanna's to set up an appointment, Fran wasted no time. After smiling at the two junior secretaries and sending Millie a quick wink, she sashayed over and knocked lightly on Addison's door before walking inside.

Looking up from her desk, Addison didn't waste a second as she grabbed a nearby folder and threw it in Fran's direction. "You have *got* to be fucking *kidding* me" she bellowed, mindless of the paperwork now covering the floor. "Have you *completely* lost the plot?"

With a sigh, Fran knelt and gathered the documents she had given to Addison a few days earlier. After taking the time to straighten them, she stood back up. "No, I haven't, and it's a good deal, although I'll have to amend it a bit."

"You bloody well will!" Addison snarled. "Do you have any clue as to how much money you're talking about?"

"Yes," Fran said as she sat down. "Adding in all the possibilities, as it stands right now roughly nine million pounds, but like I said, I need to make a few changes."

"You sure as hell better believe you're going to make a few changes because there's no *fucking* way I'm going to agree to that!" Addison said, pointing at the papers in Fran's hand.

"Yes, you will, and the sooner you come to terms with this the better!" Fran said as she jumped to her feet. "You're between a rock and a hard place, and all your shouting and bravado are not going to save you. It's time to pay the piper, Addison. If you want to keep your company, then you'll agree to whatever terms I come up with because there's not a woman on the face of this planet who's going to do this for free. You're asking someone to change their name, give up five years of their life at a minimum, *and* live a lie while they're doing it. Trust me, that's worth a shit load, whether you believe it or not."

Addison straightened the stacks of papers on her desk. "I don't even know why we're arguing about this right now. Until you find the sodding tart, there's no point in talking about it." Spinning her chair around, she looked out the window. "Now, if you don't mind, I have things to do."

Others, having been dismissed so curtly by Addison Kane, would have crept from the room, quietly shutting the door behind them, but Fran wasn't so easily rattled. Constantly amused by Addison's spoiled ways, Fran straightened a few of the papers in her hand that were still upside down. She strolled over to where Addison was sitting, and grabbing the arm of her chair, she whipped her around as if she was on a carnival ride. Promptly slamming the papers down on the desk, Fran leaned over and looked Addison in the eye. "The only thing *you're* going to do right now is to go over this deal," she said, pointing to the papers. "We need to come to an agreement, and we need to do it now."

"Why?" Addison said, glaring at the woman.

"Because I found someone," Fran said, straightening so she was no longer hovering over Addison "That's why."

"What? Who?"

"A friend of Millie's. I spoke to her earlier today."

Addison's eyes turned as cold as the color they held. "Why didn't you tell me about this before now?"

"You had meetings this morning, and I didn't see any point in getting you involved until I was sure she'd be able to play the part."

"And you're saying she can?"

"I believe so," Fran said. "She's smart, pleasant, attractive, and as far as I can tell, she's honest. I think we can trust her."

"What makes you so sure?"

"Just a feeling I have," Fran said as she walked back around the desk.

"The same one you get once a month when you bleed?"

Fran winced and sank into a chair. "Okay. So, there's no way I can be one hundred percent sure, but we don't have that luxury. We're going to have to make some assumptions, and we're going to have to trust. I've met Joanna, and I've talked to her, and she doesn't seem like the type of person who wants something for nothing. As a matter of fact, the only thing she seems to want is to make sure her father is cared for."

"I never said anything about taking care of a family."

"You should be thanking your lucky stars she doesn't have a hoard of brothers and sisters, too. All she has is a father whom she loves and wants to take care of. I don't think that's too much to ask."

Addison rocked forward in her chair, her features hardening as she glared at Fran. "Well...I...*do*!"

"Oh, fuck this and fuck you!" Fran yelled as she jumped to her feet and snatched the papers off the desk. "I'm done with this, and I'm done with you! I used to like you, Addison. I used to like your quick wit and your bloody headstrong attitude, but you've turned into an egotistical, haughty cow, and I can't work with you any longer. You'll have my resignation on your desk tomorrow morning!"

Before Addison could say a word, Francesca stormed out of her office and slammed the door, causing more than one painting on the wall to tilt from the aftershock.

***

A few hours later, Fran sat at her desk staring at the blank page on her computer screen. She wanted to type her resignation, but she just couldn't. She couldn't abandon Addison no matter how self-centered the woman had become. Fran pulled a drawer open and rummaged around until she found the emergency cigarettes she had put there a year before. Pausing for a moment, she tapped out a cigarette and lit it, immediately regretting her actions when her lungs began to burn from the stale, acrid smoke.

"You're not allowed to smoke in the building. You know that."

Fran raised her eyes and glared at the woman standing in the doorway. "Like you haven't done it a hundred times yourself."

"True," Addison said, sauntering over and sitting down. "But then again, I *own* the building, so I make my own rules."

Having had enough of the sour-tasting tobacco, Fran scanned her desk. Spying her coffee cup, she dropped the cigarette into the dregs it contained. "You won't hear an argument from me on that one."

Their eyes met, and Fran stared back without saying a word. Addison wasn't the only one who had a stubborn streak.

"It seems I owe you another apology," Addison said quietly.

Fran stiffened, and slowly a grin began to form. "Best be careful. This could become a habit."

"I doubt it."

"Me, too."

"I don't like to lose."

"Tell me something I don't know, Addison."

"I'll agree to whatever you'd like."

Fran rocked forward so quickly that the arm of the executive chair banged into the desk. "What?"

"You heard. I have a business to run, and this has taken up far too much of my time, so the sooner we get this resolved, the better."

"Are you serious?"

Addison locked eyes with Fran. "When have you known me not to be?"

"Good point," Fran said as she grabbed her notes. "Well, the first thing we need to discuss is the living arrangements."

Addison Kane never went into a meeting without being prepared. Having spent the better part of her afternoon thinking about what her future would now hold, she was more than ready for Fran's questions. "She can have the east wing. I'll talk to Evelyn, and she'll have a room ready for this tart when she moves in."

"She's not a tart. Her name is Joanna, and she'll need two rooms. You forgot about her father."

"No, I didn't. You said he was ill, so put him in a home," Addison said, mindlessly picking a piece of lint off her trousers.

"That won't work. Joanna has made it clear that where she goes, he goes."

"Quite demanding for someone in her position, isn't she?"

"The only position she's in is the one that's saving your arse, and I don't believe what she's asking for is demanding at all. I think it shows the type of person she is."

"Stupid?"

"Compassionate."

"You say to*may*to and I say to*mah*to."

Fran grinned. A glimmer of the woman she once knew had just slipped through the barrier. "This isn't something negotiable, Addison, so unless you—"

"Whatever," Addison said, waving her hand in the air to dismiss the topic. "What's next?"

"You'll need to meet her."

"Why in the *hell* would I want to do that?"

"This isn't just about you, Addison. Remember, Joanna is involved too, and I'm sure she'll want to meet you before putting her signature on the registry papers. Call it...curiosity."

"Fine. Talk to Millie, and she can let you know when I'm available."

"Good," Fran said. "And speaking of the registry office, that's something I can't do for you. You'll need to show up in person with the proper identification, and both of you will have to sign the papers. After that, it gets posted for twenty-eight days, and then you'll be married. I'm assuming you'll want it held at your house, and that's doable, but I'm going to have to pull some strings."

"I don't care if you have to pull some strings or grease some palms, but it's sure as hell not going to be at a church or in some fucking registry office," Addison said with a huff. "And as far as what happens at the house, the less, the better. No guests, no reporters, no pictures, no nothing. We do the deed, sign the papers, and that's it. Understood?"

"Yes."

"Anything else?"

Fran looked at her watch. "Well, there's still a lot of time left in the day. How about I call Joanna right now, and we can arrange a meeting together?"

"In your dreams, Fran," Addison said, getting to her feet. "I have more important things to do than listen while my name is being given away." Stomping to the door, she yanked it open and stormed out.

Fran rolled her eyes as she picked up the phone and dialed an extension, but when it rang busy, she got up and headed back to the Addison's office. Acknowledging the other secretaries with a quick grin, she approached Millie's desk just as the woman hung up her phone.

"Well, I know she went to see you, and she was not at all happy when she returned, but by that smile you're wearing, should I assume things went well?" Millie said, keeping her voice low so the junior secretaries couldn't hear her.

"That all depends on your definition of *well*," Fran said, letting out a laugh. "Could you do me a favor and see if she has any time open in the next few days so we can set up a meeting with Joanna."

"Hmm, let me see," Millie said as she brought up Addison's calendar on her computer. "Yes, actually, she's free after three tomorrow, or is that too early?"

"No, that's perfect, but do us both a favor and don't tell Addison until tomorrow morning. The less time she has to stew about it, the better it will be for all of us."

Chapter Five

Addison exited the building with Millie by her side and Fran following closely behind. She slipped on her sunglasses and then looked up and down the street.

"Where's George?"

"I sent him home," Fran said. "We're taking my car."

"Why?"

"Because a limousine on the streets of Burnt Oak will definitely turn some heads, and I'm fairly certain you don't want to do that," Fran said, aiming her remote at the Mercedes parked by the curb.

"And you don't think anyone will notice this classy sedan," Addison said, opening the passenger door.

"At least it doesn't take up two parking spaces," Fran said. "Now get in the car Addison, or we're going to be late. Millie, I hope you don't mind the back seat."

If it had been up to Millie, she would have preferred to stay in the office. Having worked for Addison long enough to know all about her moods, Millie had noticed that since Addison had found out about the meeting with Joanna Sheppard that morning, she had gone quiet. That was *not* a good sign. Addison was holding back, letting her temper fester and grow, and when it was finally unleashed, Millie preferred not to be anywhere near ground zero. Unfortunately, being the administrative assistant to a woman who didn't even carry a pen, when Addison had a meeting, Millie had a meeting.

"Not at all, Fran," Millie said, hastily climbing into the back of the automobile.

Settling into their seats, Fran turned down the radio and pulled out into traffic, and for a short while, the car was quiet.

"So, what's her name?" Addison asked, breaking the silence.

In the back seat, Millie blanched. She could hear the slightest hint of annoyance in Addison's voice, and it was enough to convince Millie she should remain silent. Thankfully, Fran took the lead.

"Joanna. I told you that," Fran said, glancing at her passenger.

"No, her last name, before, of course, it gets changed to Kane."

"Oh. Sheppard…Joanna Sheppard."

"What does she look like?"

When Fran didn't answer, Addison looked over and saw Fran simpering like a fool. "Wipe that smirk off your face. I just don't want to show up at her door and scream in fright."

"You'll hardly do that," Fran said with a laugh. "She's cute, in a bedraggled kind of way."

"What's that supposed to mean?"

"She works three jobs to pay the bills, so she looks a bit tired, but she's attractive."

Addison narrowed her eyes. "What *kind* of jobs?"

"During the day she works at Doyle Books, and on the weekend, she cleans some offices and a few churches."

"She's a *cleaner*?"

Fran flinched at Addison's outburst as the volume of her voice equaled that of a crazed football fan in a stadium, but refusing to get into a verbal sparring match, Fran kept her tone low and calm. "She just does it part-time to make ends meet."

"Turn the car around!"

"What?" Fran said, casting a quick look in Addison's direction. "Why?"

"Jesus Christ, Fran, what the hell are you thinking? The press will have a field day with this!"

"Not necessarily."

"Really? Kindly explain to me how one of this country's richest women would travel in the same circles as a cleaner, let alone marry one?"

"She only does it part-time, Addison. Her full-time job is at Doyle's, and when the press asks, we'll just say you bumped into one another outside the store. She spilled her coffee. You got to talking, and the rest, as they say, is history."

Addison cocked her head to the side. "Correct me if I'm wrong, but wasn't that in a movie?"

"Yes, it was, but it'll work. Besides, you've always been very private about the women you date, so this being a secret shouldn't surprise anyone. It's the way you live your life. Yes, the press might come up with a few amusing headlines, but after a week or two, it'll be old news. You've never allowed them to intrude on your life, so this won't be any different. We keep Joanna away from them until the novelty wears off, and then life goes back to normal."

"Define normal," Addison groused, fumbling for her cigarettes.

"Sorry, Addison, but there's no smoking in my car."

Casting an evil look in Fran's direction, Addison pulled a gold-plated lighter from her pocket. "Get it cleaned and send me the bill," she said as she lit her fag.

***

Joanna had arranged to leave work early, believing she had given herself enough time to get home, grab a quick shower and make herself presentable before she met with one of the wealthiest women in the UK. Unfortunately, her stars were *not* in alignment.

There were delays on the Tube, and when she finally walked into her house, an hour behind schedule, the visiting caregiver suddenly announced she felt a migraine coming on. Before Joanna could say a word, the woman scooted out the front door to enjoy her early reprieve. Shaking her head, Joanna took a deep breath and trotted up the stairs. She poked her head into her father's room, intending to give him a quick hello before going to grab a shower, but startling him, he promptly spilled his juice all over himself and the bed. In an instant, Joanna's plans had changed, but she didn't care. He needed her, and that was all that mattered.

Forty-five minutes later, after the last hospital corner had been tucked and her father was dressed in a clean pair of pajamas, Joanna helped him back into bed. Running downstairs to fetch him more juice, once she returned and made sure he was comfortable, she headed to her bedroom. Glancing at her watch, Joanna looked down at her clothes and shrugged. She didn't really own anything better anyway. Deciding she could at least brush her hair before her guests arrived, she was about to pull the band from her ponytail when the doorbell rang. Chuckling that her plans had gone so awry, she looked in the mirror, tucked a few strands of hair behind her ears and then went to meet her future wife. There was no point in putting on airs. Joanna didn't own any of those either.

***

Fran parked her Mercedes in front of Joanna Sheppard's house and pointed out the window. "It's the one on the end."

"Charming," Addison said, furrows appearing on her brow at the sight of the disheveled row of joined homes.

"Behave. Not everyone has a bank account with eight figures," Fran said, getting out of the car.

Climbing out of the passenger side, Addison slammed the door and flicked her cigarette to the ground. "It's nine, but who's counting."

Fran marched over to Addison, and stopping only a few inches from the woman, Fran looked her in the eye. "I'm going to go knock on the door and say hello to Joanna. You can stay out here and sulk, or you can join me and listen as I tell her what we've decided to offer her, but if you choose to come inside, leave your attitude out here. Don't forget, we're running out of time."

As Fran turned to walk away, Addison grabbed her sleeve. "Fine, but you do all the talking. I don't have anything to say to this woman."

"Works for me," Fran said, flashing a grin. "Now come on, I'm sure she's waiting."

The three women carefully traversed the sections of the sidewalk buckled by the roots of nearby trees. Reaching the last blue door in the row, Fran rung the bell, and within seconds, the door swung open.

"Hiya, Fran. Hi, Millie," Joanna said through the widest of smiles. "Thanks for making the trip again."

"No problem, Joanna," Fran replied, turning to make introductions. "Joanna, this is Addison Kane. Addison...Joanna Sheppard."

Joanna was human, and when she went to work that morning, she did it with her curiosity in tow. Taking an earlier train to give herself more time, once she arrived at work, Joanna had every intention of using the open computers in the employee lounge to run an Internet search on Addison Kane. Even though Millie and Fran had given her a few details about the woman, Joanna wanted more, but before one keystroke was entered, she had changed her mind.

There was no need to delve into the personal and financial details of the woman. Fran had already assured Joanna both she and her father would be taken care of in a manner fitting the wife and father-in-law of

Addison Kane, so finding out the woman's estimated net worth seemed meddlesome and crude. It didn't matter where Addison Kane lived, because Joanna knew the woman's wealth afforded better than Burnt Oak, and tabloid excerpts about affairs of the past may have warranted a read if Joanna was marrying for love, but she wasn't. She was entering into a marriage of convenience to give her father a better life. A life that would give him more than two pairs of pajamas, and dinners that would no doubt be cooked rather than reheated; however, there was one problem. Joanna was still human, and she *really* wanted to know what Addison Kane looked like.

Over the years, she had seen glimpses of the woman on the covers of a few periodicals and newspapers, but there hadn't been any reason to gawk. At the time, Joanna had absolutely nothing in common with Addison Kane, but if Fran's prophecy came true, that was no longer going to be the case. So, Joanna did what any red-blooded woman of the twenty-first century would do…she searched the Internet for photographs.

Before Joanna opened the door to greet her guests, she had already put a face to the name of Addison Kane. Courtesy of the rather limited amount of pictures she had found on the World Wide Web, all of which having once graced the covers of business magazines, Joanna knew the woman wore her dark brown hair short, and if the pictures were any indication, not a strand would be out of place. She also seemed to have a penchant for black three-piece suits and darkly tinted sunglasses, and since Addison Kane hadn't smiled in any of the photos, Joanna wasn't expecting to see one…and she didn't.

For a fraction of a second, Joanna thought the figure standing behind Francesca was a man, but only for a second. Taller than Fran by a few inches, Joanna guessed that Addison Kane was five foot seven or better, and while she was indeed wearing a black three-piece suit, the slim-fitted worsted wool could not hide her femininity. It announced it. With the suit jacket gaping at the chest and the tailored trousers flaring a tad too much at the hips, there was no doubt in Joanna's mind she was looking at her future wife. And while it was easy to see that Addison Kane was displaying a totally menacing scowl, the intensity of her expression was trumped by her beauty.

Although unimpressed by the way the woman's hair seemed to be plastered to her head with something tantamount to coal tar, Joanna *was* impressed with just about everything else. Kane's complexion was darker than most, appearing almost bronze in the late afternoon sun and her cheekbones were high and prominent. Her nose was classically Greek, narrow and straight, but when Addison removed her Tom Ford aviators, Joanna's breath caught in her throat. Behind the darkly tinted lenses were possibly the palest blue eyes Joanna had ever seen.

They seemed almost arctic in their color, made even more striking by the faint black edges that surrounded them, and it was all Joanna could do not to stare. Temporarily mesmerized by the woman's eyes, it took a few rapid heartbeats for Joanna to regroup, and that's when she noticed something else. By the way Addison Kane's jaw was set, Joanna knew in an instant the woman was angry...or perhaps livid was a better word.

Joanna displayed a friendly smile as she held out her hand. "Nice to meet you."

Addison moved back slightly, her posture stiffening as she glared at Joanna's gesture of friendship. "That makes one of us," Addison said, storming past Fran. "Now, let's get this over with."

Stomping into the house, Addison quickly surveyed her surroundings, instantly rolling her eyes when the run-down lounge came into view. She stopped for a split-second to grimace at the sight of the threadbare sofa before striding into the kitchen and throwing herself into a chair.

Even though Fran had used the term attractive when describing Joanna Sheppard, Addison was much too smart for that. Believing Fran would have told her anything to get her to this point, Addison had come to her own conclusions about Joanna Sheppard before the woman had opened the door. Addison had painted a picture in her mind, *painted* being the operative word, and had fully expected to meet an average-looking woman trying her best *not* to look average. She imagined Joanna Sheppard would have run out to buy new clothes, something slimming to hide her otherwise frumpy and overweight appearance, but also something flashy enough to catch Addison's eye. With unskilled hands, she would have applied makeup thick and garish hoping to hide her plain features, and after a quick visit to the neighborhood beauty salon, her hair would no doubt be a new color and most likely styled with the help of a can of hairspray.

One tiny splinter of the tremendously large chip on Addison's shoulder fell away when Joanna Sheppard had opened the door. Unfortunately, with her annoyance distorting her judgment, while the woman wasn't ugly, as far as Addison was concerned, she wasn't beautiful either.

In Addison's eyes, Joanna's hair was the color of rusty water, and the dark circles under her eyes could have been easily hidden behind makeup if she had cared to try, but apparently she hadn't. Her eyes couldn't seem to make up their mind as to whether they were brown or hazel and the slight dimples appearing when Joanna had flashed her smile only added to Addison's foul mood. As far as Addison was concerned, cherub cheeks and pert noses belonged on baby dolls, not on grown women. And then there were her clothes.

The fabrics of the pale green twinset and wrinkled brown skirt the woman wore displayed pilled threads, and more than one faded stain, and her low-heeled shoes were scuffed and in dire need of replacement. In Addison's mind, Joanna Sheppard had either no idea how to dress to impress, or she didn't feel the need, both of which grated on Addison's last nerve.

After talking with Fran and Millie, Joanna was prepared for Addison Kane's snobbish demeanor, so when she closed the front door and turned to the women, her expression remained jovial. "I wasn't expecting to see you today, Millie," she said, giving the woman a quick hug. "Are you here for moral support, and if so…whose?" Joanna said quietly, adding a wink.

"I'm here to take notes for Addison, and as for moral support, I'll give you all I can," Millie whispered through a smile.

"Thanks," Joanna said, squeezing the woman's hand. "I think I'm going to need it."

Fran leaned closer so her voice wouldn't carry farther than the entry. "Sorry about that, but I did warn you about her. This is the last place she wants to be."

"Don't worry about it," Joanna said, whispering as well. "You told me what to expect, and so far you're spot-on."

"*I have better things to do than sit here all bleeding day while you three gossip!*" Addison shouted from the kitchen. "*Let's get this the fuck started!*"

Joanna's mouth twisted into a frown. "Millie, I made some coffee. Would you mind getting out some cups? I want to go up and check on Dad."

"Of course not, dear. Go right ahead."

Flashing an apologetic grin to Fran, Joanna jogged up the stairs. Seeing her father was still asleep, she quietly pulled the door shut until it latched and returned to the kitchen. With Millie and Fran already seated at the table, Joanna took the chair across from Addison Kane and when she spoke her focus was only on Addison. "Before we start, I think I should make it clear to everyone that even though this place isn't much, it is my home, and I have to ask you to respect that. My father is upstairs, and he's asleep, and since he has no idea any of this is happening—"

"Fran, you might want to add liar to this woman's résumé," Addison said, finishing her sentence with a snort. "It seems you forgot to tell me about that part."

Joanna had anticipated iciness from the woman whom she had agreed to marry. She had assumed Addison Kane would be nothing more than curt, but she hadn't expected to be called a liar. Over the years, the edge of Joanna's temper had been dulled by her life situation, but it had yet to be ground down to a nub...and Addison Kane was about to find that out.

"She *also* apparently forgot to tell you that my father has suffered three strokes, one of which damaged his memory," Joanna said, glaring at the woman who was wearing an annoyingly haughty expression. "If I *had* told him about this, he would have forbidden me to do it because he would know that I was doing it for him. With his health, the last thing he needs to be is upset, and since he easily forgets things, we would have had the same conversation *and* the same argument, day after day after day. If you want to call what I'm doing lying, then so be it, but I will *not* have my father put through any unnecessary stress, and you sure as *hell* better remember *that!*" Well aware by Addison Kane's steely stare that she had the woman's undivided attention, Joanna added, "Now, the way I see it, you don't want to be here. Fine, I get that, but continuing to make that crystal clear to me by your boorish behavior is wasting time, and unless I'm mistaken, that's something your money *can't* buy."

"But apparently it can buy you," Addison growled back. "You know. They have names for women like you."

"Addison, that's enough," Fran said.

"She started it," Addison said, pointing to Joanna.

Snickering, Joanna shook her head. "What are you, twelve? Just because you're the famous Addison Kane—"

"That's right. I am," Addison said, leaning forward in her chair. "And you sure as *hell* better remember *that!*"

"Enough!" Fran said, raising her hands in the air. "Addison, Joanna's right. We don't have time for this. Now, I suggest that we all just take a breath, calm down, and let me tell Joanna what we've decided to offer her. Okay?"

Addison rested back in her seat, pausing as she stroked her chin. "Fine. The sooner we get this done, the sooner I can get out of here and take a shower. This place makes me feel dirty."

Inwardly groaning, Fran quickly looked in Joanna's direction, fully expecting to see the woman gearing up for the next battle. Surprised that Joanna appeared calm and under control, Fran let out the breath she'd been holding and opened her attaché. Putting some folders off to the side, she opened her portfolio, but before she could say a word, Addison took center stage again.

"This isn't really my blend," Addison said, pushing her coffee cup toward Joanna. "I don't suppose you have any scotch in the house, do you?"

Joanna had a decision to make. Should she be a proper hostess or let the pompous woman do without? She looked over at Millie, and seeing the amusement twinkling in the woman's eyes, Joanna turned her attention back to Addison Kane. "No, I don't. Sorry."

"Why am I not surprised?" Addison said, retrieving her cup.

Chapter Six

"Right, well, let's get on with this, shall we?" Fran said, and looking up from her notes, her eyes met Joanna's. "The first thing we need to discuss is the time limit on this...on this arrangement. I still plan to challenge some of the details of Oliver's will in court, but you need to go into this knowing the longest possible time frame rather than the shortest. That way, there are no surprises, and we're all on the same page."

"That makes sense," Joanna said.

"Good, I'm glad you agree," Fran said. Inhaling slowly, Fran held her breath as she dropped the bombshell. "We're talking about five years, Joanna."

Without having to look around the table, Joanna knew all eyes were on her. Millie, who had been busily scribbling in a day planner, had stopped writing, and Addison Kane, who had been aimlessly paging through the contents of one of the folders Fran had set aside, had suddenly closed it and placed it on the table. The room was silent, and everyone was waiting for Joanna to back out of the deal.

Five years may have sounded like an eternity to some, but for Joanna Sheppard, it sounded like a gift. It would give her five years of quality time to spend with her father, rather than just a few minutes here and there before she rushed off to work morning, noon, and night. It would give her five years of not having to worry if he was getting the right care, and five years of not having to stress over the ever-growing pile of bills that were delivered almost daily. Time wasn't important to Joanna Sheppard. Her father was.

"Well, that's longer than I expected—"

"But if I manage to win a few of the court battles, your time could be reduced," Fran said quickly, fearing she was about to lose Addison's only hope.

"You make it sound like a prison sentence," Joanna said with a small grin.

"It'll hardly be that I assure you," Fran said, flashing a stern look in Addison's direction. "And I know it sounds like an awfully long time, which is why I wanted to talk about it first. If you don't think you can commit to five years, then we end the discussion right now. It's your choice."

"No, it's fine, Fran," Joanna said. "Five years won't be a problem, as long as I know that my father and I will be taken care of."

"You will be," Fran said, smiling as she glanced back at the papers in front of her.

"So, what's next on your list?" Joanna asked, seeing Fran place a large check mark alongside to the first line on her notepad.

Looking up, Fran said, "Well, what we propose is this. After you and Addison visit the registry office and give notice of your intention to enter into marriage, you and your father will be moved into Addison's home the same day. Since the list is made public, her name will undoubtedly garner attention, and we'd prefer that you aren't in the limelight at this particular time. The press can be quite brutal and unbelievably annoying when they want to be, and any questions that need to be answered, we'll take care of. Is that all right with you?"

"That's fine. I wouldn't know how to handle something like that anyway."

"Good," Fran said, putting a check next to the next line on the paper. "Addison has requested the marriage ceremony occur at her home, in private. Other than those there to witness, no others will attend, so I'm afraid if you have any other family—"

"I don't. It's just my dad and me, so that's not a problem," Joanna said.

"Well, while we're on the subject, once you and he have moved into Addison's home, we'll take over your father's care."

"Excuse me?" Joanna said, sitting up straight. "If you think—"

"Wait. Sorry, that was poor wording on my part," Fran said quickly. "What I meant to say was that all of his medical expenses will be taken care of, and we'll have nurses on duty around the clock to help your father with whatever else he might need."

"There's no need for that. I can take care of him."

"I know you can, but there's no reason why you need to do it twenty-four hours a day. Besides, if I'm not mistaken, when we spoke yesterday you said your father didn't like you helping him bathe or change his clothes. This way, you don't have to."

Impressed that Fran had remembered that particular detail, Joanna nodded. "Actually, you're right, but...but I'd like to help pick out the nursing staff if that's okay."

"Oh, I was hoping you were going to say that," Fran said, her smile spreading across her face. "In all honesty, I don't know the first bloody thing about interviewing nurses, or what kind of care your father actually needs, so that would be great. I have an appointment with the agency tomorrow afternoon so we can go together. I'll take care of the contractual part, and you can handle the nurses. How's that?"

Joanna frowned. "I have to work tomorrow."

"No, you don't," Fran said softly.

"Huh?"

"Joanna, from here on out, things are going to move rather quickly. I've made an appointment at the registry office for this coming Friday—"

"*You did what*?" Addison said, slapping her hand against the table. "When the hell were you planning to tell me about this?"

"Addison, you of all people know we don't have time to waste. We have to move quickly if we're going to meet the deadline, and I, for one, am not going to drag my feet," Fran said. "I've already had Millie clear your schedule, so please let's not argue about this. Don't forget, if we wait one day too long, this is all for naught."

There wasn't a muscle in Addison's body that didn't tighten when she realized her days were now being planned by others. She wasn't a woman who answered to anyone, and even though she knew she had no choice, she was not yet prepared to give in to the inevitable. Opening a folder on the table, Addison shoved it toward Fran. "Aren't *you* forgetting something?" she said in a voice low and void of all emotion.

"What's that?" Fran said.

"There's no medical report in there," Addison said, pointing to the file.

Fran flinched back her head. "Medical report? What in the world are you talking about?"

"What are those?" Joanna asked, pointing to the papers.

"Oh," Fran said as her shoulders drooped. "I'm sorry, Joanna, but I had to run a background check on you. That's the report."

"What's it say?"

"It says you're in debt, but you're definitely not a criminal in any way, shape, or form," Fran said, and closing the folder, she looked at Addison. "But I wasn't told I needed to get a doctor's release, too."

"Did you *actually* think I'd just allow some stranger into my home without first knowing if she's carrying some sort of disease? Marriage of convenience or not, one sneeze and she could infect us all with the plague," Addison said with a sneer. "Before we go to the registry office, she goes to a doctor and gets checked out."

"Addison, we don't have time for this," Fran said.

"*Make* time," Addison said, slamming her hand on the table.

"I'll go," Joanna said, directing her response to Fran. "I don't have a problem getting a physical, as long as she does the same thing."

"*What!*" Addison barked.

"You heard," Joanna said. "If you want a medical report on me, then I want one on you."

"There's nothing wrong with me."

"Then it shouldn't be a problem, now should it?" Joanna said, folding her arms across her chest.

Addison's eyes turned murderous as she glared back at the woman sitting across from her. "Fine! Millie, call my doctor and tell her I'll be over later for an exam."

"Addison, it's nearly five. The office will be closed," Millie said.

"I don't give a damn what time it is!" Addison said, reaching into her jacket pocket. Pulling out her mobile, she tossed it in front of Millie. "Her private number is in there. Call her and tell her I'll be there at six."

Knowing there was no point in arguing, Millie let out a sigh as she picked up the phone. Excusing herself, she left the table and walked to the front hall to make the call.

Once again, Addison's eyes found Joanna's, and raising her chin, she stretched out her legs and crossed them at the ankles. "Satisfied?"

Joanna was bored with the woman's narcissistic attitude. Although successful in suppressing the urge to laugh in the tycoon's face, the corners of her mouth did turn up ever so slightly as she met Addison's stare with one of her own. "Not until I see the results."

Joanna wasn't the only one tickled by the exchange. Concealing her smile as best she could, Fran drew yet another checkmark on the paper in front of her. "Okay, now that we're past that, the next thing on the list is the financial part of this deal," Fran said, raising her eyes to meet Joanna's. "It goes without saying that once you become Addison's wife, money will be the least of your worries. You'll be given a credit card tied to Addison's account so you'll never be without funds, and you'll also receive five thousand pounds per month to do with what you'd like. Your father will only get half that amount each month since we'll be covering all his medical care, and paying off his debt."

"All of it?" Joanna said. "I mean...I mean his care and *all* of his debt?"

"That's right."

"And this monthly allowance, it's...it's ours to keep?"

"Of course, or spend it – your choice," Fran said with a shrug.

"Coming from where I am right now, I think saving it is a much better idea. Don't you?"

Under the table, Addison's boot connected with Fran's shin, but Fran refused to acknowledge the pain shooting up her leg or the woman who had just kicked her. She knew instantly what Addison was thinking, but Fran wanted no part of it. Re-crossing her legs, so she was out of Addison's range, Fran said, "Joanna, as I said a minute ago, as Addison's wife, you won't have to worry about anything, and in five years, after the divorce is final, you still won't."

"What do you mean?"

"After this is all over, you're going to walk away with ten million pounds."

Joanna opened her mouth as if to speak, but then just as quickly it snapped shut. She stared blankly back at Fran for a few moments before finding her voice. "I'm...I'm sorry. Could you...could you repeat that?"

Warmed by the woman's naiveté, Fran said, "You'll be given ten million pounds, free and clear, as part of the divorce settlement."

Fran's words slowly settled into Joanna's brain. "Ten million?"

"That's right."

"Ten...*million*...pounds?"

Fran smiled and nodded in reply.

"Wait...you said as *part* of the divorce settlement," Joanna said, quickly looking in Addison's direction. "What's the catch?"

"What do you mean?" Fran asked.

"There has to be some sort of catch. I mean, you're telling me that for the next five years, my father and I won't have to worry about anything, and after she and I are divorced, I'll walk away with ten million pounds as *part* of the settlement. So, what's the other part?"

"We're going to buy you a home."

Joanna shifted in her chair, uncrossing and re-crossing her legs as she stared at Fran. "And why would you want to do that?"

"Since you'll have been Mrs. Addison Kane for five years, we'll need to make sure you keep up appearances, so instead of you spending your money on a house, we'll buy one for you."

"Where?" Joanna said, narrowing her eyes.

"Anywhere you'd like, within reason of course."

"And why would you do that?"

"We want to make sure you're taken care of?"

"Why?"

"It's just part of the settlement. That's all."

Joanna's suspicions continued to grow. Even hitting the lottery came with consequences. Looking back and forth between the two women sitting at the table, Joanna asked, "What aren't you telling me?"

"Absolutely nothing, I assure you," Fran said.

"Then let me see the contract," Joanna said, pointing at the folders Fran had put on the table.

"What contract?" Fran asked.

"The one you're going to ask me to sign. I'm sure you brought it with you, time being of the essence and all that."

"There isn't going to *be* any contract," Addison grumbled, pushing the folders in front of her into the center of the table.

"Wait. What?" Joanna blurted.

"I said there isn't going to be any contract," Addison said, and leaning back, she crossed her arms.

With a laugh, Joanna shook her head. "You're a piece of work. I'll give you that."

Addison looked around the table, believing she had missed something, but when Millie's and Fran's expressions equaled her own, she looked at Joanna. "Sorry?"

"Just because I've asked a few questions, which apparently your supercilious ego can't take, you're going to call the whole thing off?" Joanna said, rising to her feet. "Fine, if that's what you want, then get the hell out of my house. I've already missed enough time at work, and as those background reports clearly show, I can't afford to do that. So, if you don't mind, I need to go upstairs and get changed. I have offices to clean."

Fran began gathering the papers and folders, but when Joanna looked in Addison Kane's direction, the woman hadn't moved. Her expression was as still as stone, but her eyes betrayed her. They were now glittering slits blazing with the rage that comes from fury. The quiet of the kitchen was interrupted by the click of the latches on Fran's attaché, and Joanna flinched. She looked at Fran and noticed her briefcase was now sitting on the floor, but the lawyer had yet to get to her feet.

"What are you waiting for?" Joanna said, placing her hands on her hips. "Another cup of coffee?"

"I'd love one. Thanks," Millie said, returning to her place at the table. "And then I think you should sit down and let Fran finish what she was saying."

"Millie—"

"Joanna, please. Just refill my cup and sit back down. I promise, when you hear what Fran has to say, you'll know why I thought you were the perfect candidate for this."

Resigned to the fact that no one was leaving her house just yet, Joanna did as Millie asked and then sat down, focusing her attention solely on Fran Neary. "Right, here I am. Explain."

Of all the things Addison Kane had to agree to, the next point had been the most difficult and Fran knew it, so taking a moment, she looked over at Addison. Their eyes met, and Fran silently asked permission to go on.

Knowing she had absolutely no choice, Addison let out a quick breath and bowed her head ever so slightly. It was the only way.

Relieved, Fran returned her eyes to Joanna. "What Addison said was correct, Joanna. There won't be any contract."

"What?" Joanna said, slouching in her chair. "I...I don't understand."

"When Addison's ancestors began the company, they built it on the values of family, love, and trust. Back in the day, when so many marriages were arranged in order to build an empire or fatten the coffers, they believed that marriage was sacred, and it should only happen when two people love one another. Where there's love, there's trust."

"That makes sense," Joanna said with a bob of her head.

"Yes, it does," Fran said. "So, to guarantee their family values would continue, and the company would never fall into the hands of someone just trying to get rich quick, they sculpted the doctrine of Kane Holdings very cleverly."

"How so?"

"Other than the necessary marriage forms, there can be no contract, prenuptial agreement or any other written document when a Kane gets married. There can be no words put on paper, no stipulations, no settlement details in case of divorce...nothing."

Joanna's eyes narrowed, and after stealing a quick glimpse of both Millie and Addison Kane, she focused on Fran. "What *exactly* are you saying?"

"I'll show you." Retrieving her briefcase, Fran removed all the paperwork and files, and methodically began to rip them into pieces. Sliding a small stack in Millie's direction, the personal assistant followed suit, and in no time at all, the table was covered in tiny scraps of paper.

Returning her briefcase to the floor, Fran said, "If this is to happen, Joanna, it must happen on a handshake."

"What?" Joanna said, her eyes growing wide.

"You have to trust us that we won't go back on our word, and we have to trust you that you'll do the same."

"On a...on a handshake?"

"That's right."

"I don't understand. Why can't there just be a contract that no one except us knows about? I mean, it's not like it has to be published or anything."

"That's true, it wouldn't have to be, but unfortunately, there are some people out there who have wanted to get their hands on Kane Holdings since Oliver's death. When this marriage is announced, they are not going to be happy. They'll do everything in their power to try to prove your marriage is in name only, and their first step will be to try to buy off some of our employees for information. Kane Holdings is a huge company, and there's no way we can guarantee all the employees are loyal, but if nothing's written down, then there is no proof. If we did write up a contract, it would have to be signed *and* witnessed, but if we do this on a handshake, Addison keeps her company and in five years, you walk away with ten million pounds."

Dumbfounded, Joanna sat silent, mulling over everything she had heard. She knew that *she* would never go back on her word, but trusting Addison Kane to do the same seemed unimaginable.

"You're asking a lot," Joanna said, directing her statement to Addison Kane. "I don't even know you."

"Ditto," Addison replied flatly.

"How can I be sure that you'll follow through with what Fran has said?"

"How can I be sure you won't bring shame to my name?"

"I'm not that type of person," Joanna said, her voice rising ever so slightly.

"I don't know that."

"I don't know anything about you."

"And you aren't going to learn much more, of that I'll guarantee."

"Can you guarantee you won't back out of this?" Joanna said, pointing to the scraps of paper on the table. "That you'll keep up your end of the deal?"

"*I* don't have a choice."

"*You* didn't answer my question."

"That's the only answer you're going to get," Addison snapped.

"Not good enough," Joanna said, getting to her feet.

Addison rolled her eyes. "Fine, I won't back out on anything. I promise. Now, can we get this thing over with? I'm desperate for a shower, and I have a doctor's appointment to keep." Standing, Addison looked around the table, and then returned her eyes to Joanna Sheppard. Taking a deep breath, she held out her hand. "Do we have a deal...or not?"

Swallowing hard, Joanna slowly took the woman's hand. "We have a deal."

Chapter Seven

Glancing at her watch for the umpteenth time, when Evelyn Ward heard the front door open, she jumped to her feet and sprinted from the drawing room. Watching as George Parker took Addison's attaché from her hand a nanosecond before she allowed it to slip from her fingers, Evelyn frowned. "Do you have any idea what time it is?"

"Close to nine, I think," Addison said, shooing away the butler's intrusion of her personal space with a wave of her hand. "Why?"

"Why? *Why!*" Evelyn said, stomping her foot. "Addison, you texted me three hours ago, insisting that I not leave until we had a chance to talk."

"So?"

"I *do* have a life outside of your home, in case you've forgotten."

"Whatever," Addison said as she took a step toward her study. "Tell Noah I'll have dinner in a few minutes."

"Noah left over an hour ago."

"What?" Addison said, stopping her tracks.

"We all assumed you were eating out when you texted to say you'd be late, so I sent him home."

"And what the hell am I supposed to eat?"

"Well, I know there's some leftover roast—"

"I don't *do* scraps, and you know it," Addison said as she disappeared into her study. A minute later, she emerged carrying a glass of scotch, and after taking a sip, she looked over at her house manager. "Care for one?"

"No, thank you," Evelyn said. "I have to drive home, remember?"

"Right," Addison said as she headed to the drawing room.

Aware Addison expected her to follow, Evelyn did just that. Walking in, she found Addison standing by the fireplace at the far corner of the room, staring into the empty hearth.

"I need you to get the east wing ready," Addison said, over her shoulder.

Evelyn's eyebrows drew together. "Um...ready for what exactly?"

"Guests."

"I'm sorry," Evelyn said, taking a step closer. "Did you just say...did you just say *guests*?"

"That's right."

Since coming to work for Oliver Kane, and subsequently for his daughter, Evelyn didn't need a finger or a toe to count the times when anyone had actually stayed overnight at the house. It just wasn't done. Not by father, not by daughter...not ever.

Evelyn fell into the nearest chair and stared back at Addison as if she'd just been struck in the face. "Do you mind if I ask whom we're expecting?" she said, eyeing the woman who had yet to turn around.

Addison curled her lip, pausing before she looked over her shoulder. "My soon-to-be wife and her father."

If Evelyn hadn't been sitting down, she would have fallen down. After taking the time to retrieve her jaw from where it had landed in her lap, she said, "What did you say?"

"You heard."

"Your soon-to-be—" Evelyn's eyes flew open. "Oh my God, this has something to do with the will, doesn't it?"

"You're as astute as always."

"Who is she? Do I know her?"

"*I* don't even know her," Addison said, her voice trailing off as she stared at the glass in her hand.

Evelyn's brow knitted. "What do you mean?"

Taking a gulp of her drink, Addison let out a long breath and turned to look at Evelyn. "I've run out of time. We lost with the mediators, and unless I get married, I lose the company. Millie has a friend, and she's agreed to become my...my *wife*."

"Oh, I see," Evelyn said, taking time to process the information before she spoke again. "May I ask her name?"

"Sure, it's...Sheppard," Addison said, scowling as she tried to remember the woman's name. "Um...Joanna...Joanna Sheppard."

Having known Addison since she was a child, Evelyn was an expert when it came to her moods, so the sadness which seemed to drape over the woman like a shroud, Evelyn had seen before, but it had been years.

It was rare Addison ever held the posture of one defeated. Her shoulders were slumped and her expression pensive, but fortunately and *unfortunately* Evelyn knew this mood wouldn't last long. It would soon morph into a rage, and furniture, glassware, and anything else in Addison's path wouldn't stand a chance. Preferring not to witness the explosion when it occurred, Evelyn decided to ask the questions she needed to ask before Addison's mood swung foul.

"So...um...when exactly will this be happening?"

"We have an appointment at the registry office on Friday. After that, she'll be brought here to keep her away from the press."

"Friday!" Evelyn blurted, rising to her feet. "*This* Friday?"

"That's right," Addison said, taking another healthy swig of her drink.

"Addison, today is Wednesday."

"What's your point?"

"My point?" Evelyn said, placing her hands on her hips. "My point is the east wing hasn't been opened in decades! How can you possibly expect us to get it cleaned and in order in less than two days? The whole place will have to be washed, the carpets steamed, new linens purchased, and...and I'm sure I'll need to order new bedding and mattresses."

"You have a corporate card. Use it. Bring in a crew if you have to. I don't bloody care. Just get it done, Evelyn, and while you're at it, get the lift repaired."

"The lift?"

"Yes, apparently her father's a cripple."

Evelyn winced at Addison's thoughtless choice of words. "What's wrong with him?"

"Like I give a damn," Addison snarled. "Just get the bloody thing fixed, and make sure you give the bastard one of the adjoined rooms. Apparently, he can't take care of himself, so he'll have nurses around the clock, and the less I see of any of them, the better. Am I understood?"

The tone of Addison's voice had changed, and like a bell signaling for the next round to begin, it told Evelyn it was time to leave, and leave now. "I understand perfectly," she said, quickly retrieving her belongings from a chair where they'd been sitting since six o'clock. Flashing a half-hearted grin in Addison's direction, she said, "Well, if that's all. I'll say good night and leave you be."

"That's fine," Addison said, turning back around to stare into the empty fireplace.

"Would you like me to make you something to eat before I go?"

With a snort, Addison emptied what remained in her glass in one swallow. "No, I have what I need. Go home, Evelyn."

"I think I will," Evelyn said, heading out of the room. "And don't worry about the wing. I'll get it sorted."

"You better believe you will," Addison said, giving Evelyn a sideways glance. "After all, I'm fairly sure that's what I pay you for."

Evelyn stopped, pursing her lips as she counted to ten. Slowly exhaling, she didn't even bother to look back as she walked from the room. "Good night, Addison. Do enjoy your scotch."

Knowing no response would be forthcoming, Evelyn exited the house as quickly as possible. Pulling her mobile from her handbag, she got into her car, turned on the dome light, and sent her staff a text.

"Something has come up. Meeting in the kitchen at 7 a.m. sharp! All must attend. No excuses."

***

Being the only offspring of Xavier Kane afforded Oliver Kane a childhood envied by many. Growing up in Surrey, and attending the most prestigious schools, he lived the life of a rich man's son to the hilt, much to the chagrin of his father. A frugal man, although Xavier had chosen an upscale neighborhood in which to raise his son, where Bentleys and Rolls-Royce could be seen leaving and entering the estates, Xavier had never felt the need to wear his bank account on his sleeve. He saw no point in having a staff of twelve or traveling to the Far East for tailored suits made of silk. In his eyes, owning box seats at the various stadiums and arenas just because he could was absurd, and having more than one automobile in his garage was wasteful. Unfortunately, his son thought differently.

Oliver was all about having money and spending it, and with the help of the inheritance left to him by his grandfather, when Oliver turned twenty-one, Xavier could do nothing but sit back and watch as his son spent and spent and spent some more. The young man's wardrobe changed like the tide, and if there were an event, musical or sporting, being held in the United Kingdom, he'd be in attendance, front row center...as long as the family chauffeur was available to take him.

Oliver knew little, if anything, about automobiles, including how to drive them, but while attending university, one of his classmates invited him to an event held at the Royal Automobile Club in Pall Mall. Enamored with the luxury and history of the private club, he applied for membership and was quickly approved if only for one reason. There weren't many on the election committee who didn't know the name of Oliver's father.

Shortly after receiving his club lapel pin, Oliver learned to drive, and then purchased his first of many vintage automobiles. His father soon grew weary of Oliver's frivolousness, and after endless arguments, Oliver left the house in Surrey, leased a garage for his growing collection, and moved into a penthouse apartment in Knightsbridge.

In an ultra-modern flat, with every convenience money could buy, Oliver embraced the life of a well-to-do bachelor. During the day, he took up space at Kane Holdings, bringing home a pay packet based only on his last name, and at night, he enjoyed the grandeur and ambiance of the finest gentlemen's clubs in London. However, during one of the many charity affairs at the Club, Oliver's interest moved from the opulence of his surroundings to one particular member of the staff bringing food to the table.

Statuesque, with eyes the color of Wedgewood and her long black hair held back by rhinestone barrettes, she was positively the most beautiful woman he had ever seen. The Mediterranean tone of her skin against the crisp white of her blouse made her uniform appear brighter than all others in the room, and her narrow nose and determined jaw were more perfect than any ever sculpted in marble. She was a goddess, and six months later, Alena Zacharias, daughter of a Greek fisherman, and Oliver Kane, son of a British tycoon, were married.

Alena hadn't been born into wealth, but it didn't take long before everyone thought she had. The closets of the penthouse soon overflowed with gowns and dresses for every occasion, and many a night she could be found alongside her husband sipping champagne with the members of the Club.

As time went on, Alena began to grow tired of constantly traveling to the opulent homes of their friends. She demanded a stately manor of her own. A mansion that would dwarf the largest home in all of Surrey, and by simply walking over the threshold, it would announce to those who visited the breadth of the Kane fortune. The only problem was Oliver was content in showing his affluence by the amount of collectible automobiles parked in a leased garage. It didn't matter their shiny bonnets only saw the light of day when they were chauffeured to car shows at the Club because the placards displayed *his* name as the owner.

It was the only argument they had ever had, and it went on for days. Oliver balked at leaving the comfort and convenience of the penthouse. Like his precious cars, the flat was paid for. Since his monthly salary barely covered the bills created by their lavish lifestyle, a new home was out of the question, at least until Oliver could get his hands on his trust fund. Started by his father the day he was born, when Oliver reached his thirtieth birthday, it was his to do with as he wanted. Promising Alena a house second to none if she could wait two years, she reluctantly agreed, and their fight ended in a night of passion. Less than two months later, Alena discovered she was pregnant, and not long after that, her doctor told her she was carrying twins.

Oliver was elated. For generations, there had only been one child born to each Kane forefather, but now he would have two to carry on the family name, and he swelled with pride as he watched his wife's belly grow. As each day passed, his priorities began to change. He was going to be a father, and fathers provide for their young. Unbeknownst to Alena, Oliver sold all of his cars. She was going to give him children, and he was going to give her a mansion like no other.

The task of finding a palatial home in his price range was not an easy one. Oliver now had nearly eight million pounds at his disposal, but the estates in that price range were smaller than he had hoped. After months of searching, he was about to give up when he received a frantic call from his estate agent. A manor situated in the middle of over one hundred acres of land had just been placed on the market.

It had been bought and sold countless times since it had been built. Many of the most affluent had slept in its numerous bedrooms, but when their children grew or their fortune shrunk, they had no choice but to sell. Inventors, rich from the proceeds of their creativity had jumped at the chance to own an estate so fine, but eventually the call of their home countries beckoned them. And the last owner, his coffers filled with lottery earnings, had bought the property on a whim, but soon realized that while he had the money to purchase the home, he had nothing left for renovations or taxes. Deciding to cut his losses and salvage what he could, he asked that it be sold as it stood…completely furnished and in need of much repair.

Wanting to give his wife the most massive of homes, when Oliver saw the estate, he ignored its rundown condition and focused on the obvious. It was huge. Knowing the money from the sale of his penthouse would easily pay for renovations and new furnishings, he offered the asking price, and the deal was done. He mulled over telling Alena right away or perhaps waiting for the birth of his children to give his beloved wife her present, but when he realized her birthday was in a month, his decision was made. He had no way of knowing that her high-heels would never click across the slate floor of the entrance hall, nor would she ever ascend the grand staircase leading to the master suite. The day before her twenty-eighth birthday, during a thunderstorm which rocked the walls of a small clinic, Alena Kane died.

***

As Evelyn drove up the long, winding gravel path leading her to her place of employment, she smiled as the gray and black Bentley S1 Sports Saloon passed her on the way out. Addison's weekly staff meeting at Kane Holdings was held promptly at eight every Thursday morning, and just like so many other things in Addison's life, her Thursday morning regime was almost etched in stone. Waking at six, she would leave the house thirty minutes later, and when she arrived at the office, a catered breakfast would be brought to her. She would read reports while she ate her poached eggs and toast and then wait somewhat patiently for her bleary-eyed personnel to shuffle in the door seconds before their meeting would begin.

Walking into the empty house, Evelyn turned on some lights and placed her briefcase on a chair. Removing a clipboard and measuring tape, she slid a pencil behind her ear and climbed the stairs leading to the upper floor.

She stopped when she reached the doors leading to the east wing, and dwarfed by the majesty of the ornately carved slabs of walnut over eight feet in height, she sighed. The intricate moldings and designs were polished weekly, but much of the detail had been masked by varnish now blackened with age, and she frowned at the loss. Taking a deep breath, Evelyn turned the forged, black lever handles, and as she pushed open the doors, the screech of the hinges echoed through the house.

She wrinkled her nose as the stale air enveloped her, and coughing to clear the musty taste from her throat, Evelyn reached over and flipped on a few light switches. One by one the Edwardian chandeliers in the long hallway in front of her flickered to life, and watching as several bulbs blew almost instantly, Evelyn jotted down a note on her clipboard. It would be the first of many.

It had been years since Evelyn had walked this corridor, and she had done it only once. Oliver, inconsolable at the loss of his wife, had refused to ever acknowledge the existence of the master suite or the wings to the right and left. Turning the drawing room into his bedroom and filling the library with armoires to act as his wardrobe, other than one room at the end of the west wing used by the daughter he loathed, everything else had remained untouched and closed off. Those were his orders, and his orders had been followed. When he died, Addison eventually moved from the paltriest of bedrooms into the master suite, but like her father, the rest of the second floor held no interest…until now.

Evelyn took a few steps into the hallway and opened the first door to her right, her expression brightening instantly as she remembered a little girl's giggles as she hid from sight. It had been a morning fraught with worry. The nanny had announced in a panicked scream that four-year-old Addison was missing, but Evelyn, levelheaded and perceptive, had remained calm. Listening to the sounds of the house, a distant creak of a door not used for years was all she needed to hear, and inside a triple-wide armoire, she found the little girl, tee-heeing at the trouble she had caused.

It was in this room where she had found Addison, and looking around, Evelyn saw nothing had changed, except for the depth of the brown-gray dust covering every surface. The previous owner had never cared enough to protect the furnishings with sheets, so everything was coated in three decades of grime. She squatted down and examined the area rug. Its pattern was hidden by dirt, so she wasn't sure if it was a blue tapestry or a green, but finally deciding it was indeed blue, Evelyn stood and walked to the window. She touched the fabric of the drapes and instantly regretted it when dirt coated her fingertips. Shaking her head at the wastefulness of the rich, she quickly measured the bed before she focused on the rest of the room.

If her memory served, the armoire would be empty, and opening the first of the three doors, she found she was right. The flanking units had shelves and drawers, dusty but empty, and behind the middle door, its mirrored surface hazy with age, were only a few lonely hangers, all of which were draped in cobwebs. Walking to the corner of the room, she opened the door to the en suite and held her breath as she turned on the light. The fixtures were old and in dire need of scrubbing, but relieved to see that nothing was blatantly wrong, she made a note to call a plumber and then shut off the light and focused on the sleeping quarters.

Thankful to see that like the main floor, the fireplace in the far corner had been changed to gas, Evelyn made a note to call a heating company to check both the hearths and the radiators, and then stepping nearer a wall, she ran her finger over the wallpaper. In its day, it had probably been beautiful, but the olive background had faded to yellow in some areas, and the vine and branch pattern with the occasional nuthatch scattered throughout the design had long since lost its depth. Sighing that she didn't have time to have it replaced or even covered with paint, she was grateful the lower third of the walls had been left without design. The white plaster wainscoting and its ogee cap, although appearing quite dingy, would hopefully be much brighter after a good washing, so with a shrug, Evelyn moved on.

The next room she visited was directly across the hallway. Like the first, everything inside was covered in dust and cobwebs, but unlike the first, the only furnishings present was a single bed pushed up against a wall. Noticing a door next to the bed, Evelyn stared at it for a moment. To the best of her knowledge, there were only two full baths and two half baths in the wing, and other than in the master suites of homes as old as The Oaks, closets were rare. Intrigued, she opened the door and found herself standing at the far end of the massive walk-in closet in Addison's room. Looking from the wardrobe to the bed and back again, Evelyn solved the puzzle. It had been a child's room, and with the connecting door leading to the master suite, she believed at some point it must have been a nursery as well. Although she was sure none of their guests would be sleeping on the small bed, Evelyn, nonetheless, went about taking all the appropriate measurements. She had been given the task of cleaning the wing, and by God, the *entire* wing would be cleaned.

Realizing the east wing mirrored the west, other than measuring for mattresses in the remaining four bedrooms, there were no surprises to be found. The two bedrooms on each side at the end of the long hallway were adjoined to the next two through connecting doors, enabling the occupants to share the enormous bathroom at the very end of the corridor. With three doors leading into it, guests and family could enter via the hall or either bedroom into the communal en suite. Although in dire need of a good cleaning, as Evelyn inspected the fixtures and tiles, she decided, it could serve the purpose for which it was built. Noticing that the middle bedrooms had only small radiators, and the last two contained fireplaces as well as cast iron convectors, Evelyn decided the father would be more than comfortable in the one closest to the bathroom, while the nursing staff could wear sweaters in the winter if need be.

Now satisfied she had enough information, Evelyn turned off the lights and left the wing, leaving the doors opened to allow some fresh air to enter. As she descended the stairs, she heard the thumping bass of upbeat music coming from the kitchen, and with a smile on her face, Evelyn headed in that direction.

Chapter Eight

Looking at himself in the mirror, Robert Sheppard tried to remember when he had gotten so old. Where did those wrinkles come from? Why was his hair thin and gray, when last it was thick and brown? When did age spots begin to freckle his face, and pajamas hang so loosely from a frame that used to be strong and muscled? He held up his right hand, now curled permanently under, and shook his head at the disfigurement. He had yet to master being left-handed, and he doubted he ever would. With a sigh, he ran his fingers through his hair and hobbled back to bed. Joanna would bring him breakfast soon, and that would be the highlight of his day.

She looked so beautiful in the morning. Well rested, her cheeks would be rosy and her eyes bright. She would chatter away, trying to cram everything she wanted to say into a few short minutes before she had to rush off to work, and her animations would make him smile. From there, Robert's day would go downhill. The caregivers who visited were mere babysitters, put there by the National Health Service to assist in his care. They administered medication, helped him in and out of bed when necessary, and half-heartedly insisted he perform his physical therapy. Some would not take no for an answer when he balked at their orders, and he liked them the most even though he never showed it. It meant they cared.

Late in the evening, Joanna would return. Looking exhausted and disheveled, she'd still listen to every word he had to say. Laugh in all the right places. Roll her eyes at his stubbornness, and try her best not to show him just how tired she really was. He hated that his body had withered. He hated that his memory failed him daily, but most of all he hated what he was doing to his daughter. Joanna had been young and vibrant once, but his health had caused her to become old. To turn worn and faded like the upholstery of the lone chair that sat in his room. He couldn't believe his life had turned out like this.

As a young man growing up in Cardiff, Robert Sheppard was as ambitious as they came. Handsome, strong, and charming, he took a part-time job at an estate agent's office one summer, and it eventually became his career. With charisma that could sway the staunchest buyer, he sold properties deemed unsellable, and determined to make a name for himself, Robert's focus was only on his career until Moira O'Reilly walked into his life a few days after his thirty-fifth birthday.

Looking for a flat to lease, Moira flounced into the estate agent's storefront office one afternoon, and it was love at first sight...well, at least it was for Robert. Enamored with the ivory-skinned young woman with vibrant red hair, lips painted the color of strawberries, and a buxom figure which stretched the seams of her clothing, he fawned over her. She tittered at his attention for weeks until one day she came to his office to tell him she was pregnant.

An aspiring actress, the last thing Moira wanted was a husband, and the second last thing she wanted was a child. Unfortunately, refusing to accept the possibility she was pregnant, she had waited too long to do anything about it, so she married Robert, moved into his paltry flat in Muirhouse, and a few months later Joanna Elizabeth Sheppard was born. Robert thought he was in heaven. Moira thought she was in hell.

Ecstatic over the birth of his daughter, Robert gave his wife anything she wanted. When she whined about their tiny apartment, he found a larger one, and when she insisted she wanted to be closer to the West End of London, commonly referred to as Theatreland, he did just that. Packing up their meager belongings, they headed east, but knowing he couldn't afford the West End of London, Robert chose North London for their home. After quickly finding a job, Robert bought Moira a house, but again when she complained it was too small, Robert found a larger one and rapidly began to go into debt. The bills began to pile up, and Moira began to care less and less about her daughter and her husband, until one day Robert came home to find Joanna in her crib with her nappy soaked, her face streaked with tears...and her mother gone.

Although devastated by his wife's abandonment of their child, Robert would not let his daughter suffer the loss. Pouring his heart and soul into raising Joanna, he became her father, mother, friend, and confidant. Never allowing her to go without, he worked as hard as he could to provide for them, and when some friends suggested Robert join them in a house-flipping venture, he readily agreed. A few months of sweat in return for thousands of pounds of profit when the renovated homes were sold seemed like the ideal answer for Robert's financial situation. Unfortunately, his mates had no idea how to repair a home, and endless arguments ensued when cash was needed for materials. Several months after the venture started, the homes were sold for less than they had been bought.

Robert never let on to Joanna about his dire straits and continued to give her all he could. If she needed clothes or books, he would shuffle through his stack of credit cards and use the one with the lowest balance, and when they discussed universities over coffee one morning, he never once looked at the price. She was his life, and he was prepared to work until his dying day if need be, but the very next day, blinded by a headache, he fell to the floor. Robert Sheppard would never work again.

***

Buttering some toast, Joanna swore under her breath as she dropped the knife again. Flexing her right hand, she winced at the ache put there the day before by a handshake with a very perturbed woman. Chuckling as she remembered the infantile show of power, Joanna wiggled her fingers, picked up the tray, and went upstairs to deliver breakfast to her father.

"There's my girl," Robert said with a twinkle in his eyes. "Eggs Benedict, I presume."

Joanna smiled as she placed the tray on his lap. "Sorry, Dad, we were all out of hollandaise. I hope you don't mind scrambled with toast."

"Of course I don't," he said, scanning the tray. "No jam?"

"Sorry, all out," Joanna said as she pulled over a chair and sat down.

"What are you doing?" Robert asked.

"What? Can't I spend some time with my dad?"

"You usually bounce around in here doing everything you can possibly do in five minutes, and then you're off." Noticing his daughter's stunned look, Robert said, "While I can't always remember what happened yesterday, your morning routine hasn't changed in years. Repetition, it seems, is my friend."

"I'll have to remember that," Joanna said with a nod.

"You'd best because you sure as hell know I won't," Robert said, laughing as he struggled to keep the eggs on his fork.

"You want me to do that?"

Frowning, he managed to gobble up a bit of egg before it fell from his fork. Sighing at the mess he had just created, Robert said, "You would think that after not having the use of my right hand for so long, my left would eventually step forward and make me proud, but the blasted thing has a mind of its own. I tell it to do one thing, and it does another. It's tremendously annoying, not to mention messy."

Joanna gazed at her father. He was still handsome in her eyes, and although the strokes had done their damage to his memory and mobility, they had not yet touched his sense of humor.

"You're staring."

Broken from her thoughts, Joanna said, "We need to talk."

"I thought that's what we were doing, but aren't you going to be late for work?"

"No, I'm...I'm not going to work. That's what we need to talk about."

Putting down his fork, Robert crumpled up his napkin and placed it on the tray. "What's wrong?"

"Nothing," Joanna said with a small grin. "But I've...I've been given an opportunity to better our situation, Dad, and I'm going to take it."

"What are you talking about?"

"Do you know who Addison Kane is?"

A weak smile spread across Robert's face. "Sweetheart, I barely remember my own name these days."

"So you don't know who she is?"

"Haven't a clue."

Joanna avoided her father's eyes until she decided where to begin. "Dad, I need you to promise me something."

"Anything. You know that."

"I need you to promise that you'll let me finish what I have to say, and not get upset about it."

"Joanna, you're starting to worry me," Robert said, the creases on his forehead deepening to their max. "What's going on, and who the hell is Addison Kane?"

Chewing on her bottom lip, Joanna got up and removed the tray from her father's lap. Setting it aside, she sat on the edge of the bed and took his hand. "In a few weeks, she's going to be your daughter-in-law."

***

Standing in the doorway of the kitchen, Evelyn Ward couldn't help but snicker at Noah Hamilton. Dressed in the standard chef's uniform of black-and-white checkered trousers and a white smock, the brunette, curly-haired man was swiveling his hips to the country-western music blaring from his mobile. Prancing around the room, he was oblivious he was being watched.

"*You're early*!" Evelyn shouted over the music.

Nearly jumping out of his clogs, Noah placed his hand over his heart as he reached over and turned off the music. "Crap! Sorry, I didn't know you were here."

"You're lucky Addison isn't home. She hates that type of music."

"She hates all music, but since it's Thursday, and she's at her staff meeting, I'm safe for yet another day," he said, batting eyelashes most women would kill for.

"You know, even though she never says anything, she truly likes the meals you create," Evelyn said, sitting on a stool by the center island.

"It would be nice to hear it from her sometime."

"Not her style."

"You mean she actually has one?" Noah said, jerking back his head.

"Be nice. She's your employer and the last time I checked, she pays you rather well."

"She pays all of us rather well. Why else would we put up with her bullshit?" Noah said, plopping down on a stool. Rubbing his chin, he stared off into space.

Of all the members of her staff, Noah Hamilton was by far the friendliest and the most pleasant to be around. Always cheerful, almost to the point of being comical, Evelyn adored his quick wit, his boyish charm, and his endearing smile, all of which she had first seen when friends had taken her to an upscale eatery for her birthday a few years prior. After enjoying the most marvelous of meals, they had asked to speak to the chef to thank him for the food he had created, and when the Texas native sauntered over to the table, Evelyn and her friends were as surprised as they were captivated by the young man's charismatic nature. So, when she was given the job of hiring new staff, she sought out the American and made him an offer he couldn't refuse.

Noticing Noah's pensive look, Evelyn asked, "What's going on? I know the others grumble about Addison from time to time, but I've never heard you say one cross word about her. Haven't you had your morning coffee yet?"

"I've had two cups," he said, looking over at the coffeemaker on the counter. "And if that high-end piece of crap would ever stop belching one drop at a time, I'd be having my third."

"Oh, you *are* in a mood," Evelyn said, leaning back on her stool.

"No, I'm not, Evie. I'm bored."

"Bored?"

"Yeah," he said. "Don't get me wrong. I love my job, but I have three degrees from culinary institutes under my fashionable belt, and I'm stuck poaching eggs for breakfast and trying to come up with new and exciting meals for one. Christ, the highlight of my day is making lunch for the staff, and that's hardly taxing, I assure you."

Tickled to hear the American slip into a proper British accent, laugh lines appeared at the corner of Evelyn's eyes. "So you're looking for more of a challenge, are you?"

Rolling his eyes, Noah got up and filled two mugs with coffee. Sliding one toward Evelyn, he spooned some sugar in his and sat back down. "Evelyn, the woman doesn't even eat dessert."

"Yes, she does."

"Oh, okay, my bad," Noah said, holding up his hands. "She grabs herself a pint of ice cream out of the freezer every night. Lord help us if she'd actually allow me to make her some from scratch."

"Yes, but at least you pick the flavors so that should count for something," Evelyn said with a snigger.

"Evelyn, I'm serious!"

Laughing at the man's exasperation, Evelyn said, "Relax, Noah. I, of all people, know how boring it can be around here, but that's about to change in a very big way."

Having been staring into his coffee cup, Noah raised his eyes. "Let me guess. She's decided she wants scrambled eggs instead? Or better yet," he said, placing his hand on his chest. "Be still my heart, tell me she wants Eggs Benedict, and I'll marry you."

"Since when have you been interested in women?"

"I'm not, but I'm desperate here," he said, leaning forward on his stool. "Come on, Evie, tell me she's changing the menu, and I'll make an honest woman out of you."

"I'm as honest as I want to be, thank you very much," Evelyn said, taking a sip of her coffee. "But this *does* have something to do with marriage."

Noah squinted. "Okay, I give. What's this all about?"

"It seems Addison is getting married."

In the middle of taking a sip of coffee, Noah's lips stayed pressed against the porcelain as he slowly raised his eyes to meet Evelyn's. He could tell in an instant that she wasn't joking. Slowly placing his cup on the counter, he said, "One more time."

"Addison is getting married."

"*Addison* is getting married?"

"That's right."

"Addison Kane, wealthy businesswoman and a bitch for all seasons, is getting married?"

"Yes."

Noah stared back at Evelyn for almost a minute until his thoughts finally found their way from his mind to his mouth. "Tell me you're shitting me."

"No, I'm afraid I'm not," Evelyn said, her amusement at the man's colorful vocabulary showing on her face. "That's why I asked everyone to get to work early today. We have a lot of things to do, and I need your help if we're going to get everything done in time."

Noah got to his feet, and after topping off his coffee cup again, he turned to Evelyn. "You're serious, aren't you?"

"Yes, I am."

"Well, I'll be damned. The abominable snow queen has fallen in love," he said, returning to his seat.

"Unfortunately, that couldn't be further from the truth."

"What do you mean?"

"This is about the will, Noah."

Noah's mouth dropped open. Having worked for Addison for almost four years, through no fault of his own, he had overheard enough arguments between his employer and her lawyer to know what Evelyn was saying.

"Shit!" he said. "So, she either does this or—"

"Loses the company."

"The bastard! What kind of fucked-up father does this to his own daughter?"

"Well, if you had ever met Oliver, you wouldn't be asking that question, but we can't concern ourselves with that anymore. We have more important things to talk about."

"Such as?"

"Such as the fact that tomorrow afternoon Addison will be visiting the registry office, and then her fiancée and the woman's father will be moving into the east wing."

"Oh," Noah said, before taking a gulp of coffee. Just as he managed to swallow it, Evelyn's words sunk in, and when they did, Noah scrambled to stop from dropping his mug. "*What!*"

"You heard."

"But I thought it hadn't been opened in years."

Evelyn grimaced. "It hasn't."

"Eww," Noah said, faking a shiver. "Please tell me it's not all covered in cobwebs. I don't do spiders, Evie. I scream like a girl if I see one."

"Well, I did see a few strands here and there, but you won't have to worry about that. You'll be busy elsewhere."

"Doing what?"

"Be right back," Evelyn said as she hopped off her stool. Leaving the room, she returned seconds later carrying a clipboard. "Do you have your company card with you today?" she asked as she sat back down.

"Never leave home without it," Noah said, smiling. "Why?"

"Because I need to get everyone working on the wing, and then arrange for a plumber, a heating technician, cleaners, and someone to fix the lift, so there's no way I can leave the house today."

"Okay, so what do you want me to do?"

"I need you to go shopping?"

"For what?"

Evelyn tore off a sheet of paper filled with notes and slid it to Noah. "Mattresses, box springs, towels, linens, and anything else you think might help brighten up the wing."

Reading down the list, Noah said, "Evelyn, this is a massive list. What the fuck? Six beds!"

"Yes, six. The frames all seem sound, but nothing up there was ever covered, so everything else has to go. Oh, and we'll need pillows, too. Just get an assortment, and they can choose the ones they like. Do the same thing with the mattresses, and we can always swap them around if we need to."

"What about colors and patterns?"

Glancing at her watch, she said, "We have some time before everyone else gets here. Let's go up, and I'll show you the rooms. Most are wallpapered, and since we don't have time to replace the drapes, you'll just have to try to stay as neutral as possible. Oh, and it all has to be delivered today."

Noah looked at the list and then to Evelyn and then to the list again. "That isn't going to be easy, Evie."

"You have carte blanche, Noah. Whatever it takes, no matter how much it costs, just get it done. I'm depending on you, and I know you can do this."

"Why me? Why not one of the women?"

"Because they aren't entrusted with corporate cards and yesterday, Sally had on two different shoes."

Giggling, Noah said, "I was wondering if you had noticed that."

"Yes, but luckily she was gone before Addison got home."

Noah read down the list again. "This is a shit load of stuff, Evie."

"Yes, I know. Are you up for it?"

"Are you kidding? Carte blanche to spend *her* money? Sign me up!"

"Good!" Evelyn said, clapping her hands. "Now, grab the list, and I'll show you what we're dealing with. That is if you can handle a few cobwebs."

"Just don't make fun of me when I let out a girly scream," he said, hooking his arm in Evelyn's.

"I wouldn't think of it, Noah. Now let's go and make sure I didn't forget anything."

Chapter Nine

His breakfast had long been forgotten, and the tea in their cups had grown cold. Methodically, Joanna had told her father everything, from her chat with Millie to the meeting the day before with her future bride. She didn't hide her worries or her reasons, and sitting on the edge of the bed, Joanna waited patiently for him to say something. Like her, he had a temper, and at times it could blaze, and Joanna knew she had just lit a bonfire. If there was one subject never discussed in the Sheppard household, it was homosexuality.

He had sat and listened to his daughter, not saying a word as she spoke the truth she felt she needed to speak, and by the time she was done, his one good hand was fisted, and the veins in his temples strained against his liver-spotted skin. Having spent the entire time staring blankly at his breakfast tray, he finally raised his eyes, and with his teeth clenched and his voice low, he said, "I forbid it."

"Dad—"

"I said I *forbid* it!" Robert bellowed, his face instantly turning scarlet.

"Dad, please just—"

"This conversation is over, Joanna! There is no way in hell anyone is ever going to think that my daughter is one of those...one of those...*deviants*."

"They aren't deviant, Dad."

"They are *disgusting*!" Robert shouted, pounding his curled right hand on the bed.

"No, they aren't!" Joanna said, jumping to her feet. "Look, I know how you feel about homosexuals, but times are changing, and this is a way out for us, Dad. This gives us a new start."

"By my daughter pretending to be a *dyke*? Over my dead sodding body!"

"Dad, please..."

"Joanna, I will *not* allow you to *do* this!"

"You don't have a choice!" Joanna said, waving her hands in the air. "Dad, look around. Look what we have, or better yet, look what we *don't*."

"We have enough. There's nothing else we need."

Up until that moment, Joanna had never realized just how tired she was. She had always gone through her days with him in mind, so she had shrugged off the weariness, wore false smiles to ease his mind, and plodded from one year to the next never having any expectations that her life would ever change. She had never complained. She had never even hinted, but exhaustion has a way of loosening one's lips.

"How about more than five hours of sleep a night, Dad, because that's all I get. Or how about not having to worry about the bills as they keep piling up, or the nurses who won't come back because you argue with them day in and day out? And how about the fact that I'm twenty-eight...and I look *forty*," Joanna said as she crumpled on the edge of the bed. "Dad, I'm sorry. I've tried to be strong. I've tried to get us caught up, but I can't. There's always something. The bloody washer breaks or food never stretches as far as I think it should. I work three jobs, Dad, and I... and I can't work another. I just *can't*." Bowing her head, Joanna's shoulders shook as the emotions she had kept in check for so long finally escaped. Gasping for air, she wept...and wept.

The redness of his anger drained from Robert's face as Joanna's words acted like a bayonet and pierced his heart. Due to his health, for the most part, he lived the years unaware, free of stress and worry. Tomorrow when he awoke, he'd return to that blissful state of oblivion, only remembering bits and pieces about the day before, but for now, he was cognizant, and he was devastated.

He searched his mind, trying to find the flashbacks that would hold the truth and when a few appeared, he paled even more. Yes, he had noticed she was tired at times and her smile sometimes seemed forced, but he couldn't remember asking why. Had he, or lost in the monotony of his day, had he only thought about himself? Staring blankly at Joanna, Robert's jaw began to quiver.

Twice he tried to speak, but like a noose around his neck, his tears choked off his words. How could he have been so stupid? How could he have done this to his daughter? Slowly shaking his head, Robert drew a ragged breath. "Christ, I've ruined your life."

Joanna looked up and quickly wiped away the tears staining her face. "No! No, you haven't. You're the most important thing in my life, but I just can't catch up, Dad. I need a break. *We* need a break."

"Not like this, though. Not like this," Robert said, sniffling back some tears. "Not by putting yourself in the gutter with them and making everyone believe you're a...you're a pervert or a...or a freak."

"They aren't freaks!"

In an instant, Robert's prejudice rose to the surface like lava from a volcano, his contempt for the gay community far overshadowing his love for his daughter. "Yes, they are! Those people are sick, and I'd rather die than see you pretend to be something so vile and repugnant."

"What about me, Dad? Do you want me to die, too? Because that's what I'm slowly doing to myself."

"Stop being so dramatic. You just need a bit of rest."

"A bit of *rest*?" Joanna said, leaping off the bed. "*A bit of rest!*"

Bolting from the room, Joanna returned a minute later holding a wad of envelopes in her hand. Tossing them on the bed, she said, "These are bills from just last week. How the hell am I supposed to get rest and pay these things off—huh? I've opened and closed so many credit cards that I've lost track, just trying to buy us some time, but I'll never be able to pay off the interest, let alone the principal. Do you have any idea how much you owed before you got sick? Well, double it, Dad, or maybe even triple it because that's what we owe now."

"What?" Robert said, fumbling through the bills. "That can't be right. How can that be right?"

"It's called interest compounded daily on over a dozen credit cards that you stretched to their limits, Dad. It's called food and rent, and visiting nurses and medications and clothes. It's called Tube fares and bus tickets and utility bills that just seem to keep going up and up and up."

Robert ran his hand over the envelopes scattered across the bedspread. "I just tried to give you the best life I could. I never thought...I never thought this would happen."

"Well it has, Dad. We're in a pickle, and unless I do this, things are only going to get worse."

"Then file for bankruptcy," Robert blurted.

"What?"

"You heard. File for bankruptcy. That will take care of the bills, and we can get on with our lives without you having to pretend to be something you're not."

Joanna plopped down on the bed and let out a sigh. "So we just tell all those creditors sorry about your luck? Thanks for the money, but we won't be paying you back. Have a nice day? Is that really the way you raised me because I can't seem to remember that particular lesson."

"It's the only way."

"No, it's not! I have a way out, and it's a good one. Everyone gets paid, and we get a better life. Why can't you just put your bloody prejudice aside for a sodding minute and see that?"

"I do *not* want people to think my daughter is a *queer*."

Joanna tilted her head to the side. "So, it's your pride then. Is that it? You're worried about what people will think."

"Call it pride if you want."

"Well, your *pride* is going to put us out on the *bloody street!*"

Robert flinched, the tone of Joanna's voice getting his full attention. As a child she had screamed at him, tantrums of a little girl not wanting to go to bed or to eat her peas, but those paled in comparison to what was happening now. This wasn't a prepubescent girl testing the waters or finding that line she shouldn't cross, this was a woman willing to sacrifice her reputation and give up five years of her life...for him. For a man who would never walk down a street unassisted again, or help around the house or even cook a meal. His world had shrunk to a bedroom and a television and one wash a day, and that was all he needed, but what about her? Robert hung his head, his mind aflame with a battle between prejudice and love, but when he lifted his eyes and saw his daughter, he didn't see the woman she had become. He saw the child he had held in his arms so many times. A child he swore he would keep out of harm's way.

Robert drew in a shuddering breath. "You know, most of what you've told me, I'll forget by tomorrow."

Raising her eyes to meet his, Joanna said, "I know, but I had to tell you the truth. I needed to know what you thought."

"I think five years is a long time."

"It's just time, Dad. I don't mind."

"And marrying a woman?"

"It's not against the law."

"Blast the law. It's against God."

Joanna let out an audible sigh. "I know you don't want me to do this, and I know how you feel about gays, but this isn't about them or God or right or wrong. This is about you and I having a better life and in five years, in five *short* years, we will have everything we'll ever need."

Robert appreciated his daughter's optimism, but what he needed, money couldn't buy. He had a time bomb in his head. Weakened walls of blood vessels just waiting to break open and spill blood where it didn't belong. He had survived three strokes, but he knew the odds of living through another were against him. It was a subject they didn't talk about often. He hated to see the sadness in her eyes; the tears fighting to stay hidden as she tried to remain upbeat about their future together. He loved that about her. All he had ever wanted was to give her a future...and now he would.

His opinion about homosexuality would never change. His stomach churned just thinking about his daughter married to a woman, but Joanna was willing to give up five years of her life for him, so he would quiet his opinions for her. He would ask questions and be the father he always was because he knew in his heart this marriage would give Joanna what he could not. A future filled with promise instead of debt.

Relaxing back onto the pillows propped behind his back, Robert took a deep breath. "Well, it seems our future is going to be much brighter than we expected."

"Yeah?" Joanna asked quietly. "So...you're okay with this?"

"No, I'm not, but I won't stand in your way either. If this is what you want to do, I'll support your decision and not say another word about it. It just would be a lot easier if you were marrying a man for convenience, instead of a...a woman."

"I'm sorry, Dad, but this is the only offer on the table, and it's a good one. You've got to see that."

"Yes, well it is a lot of money," Robert said as he eyed his daughter. "Can she really afford it?"

"And then some," Joanna said, bobbing her head.

Rubbing his hand over the two-day-old whiskers covering his chin, he said, "I suppose if she owned a sports team, I'd know more about her."

"Yes, you probably would," Joanna said with a chuckle.

"Well, I'm not sure I'm going to remember all of this tomorrow, but how about you tell me a little more about Miss...um...Miss—"

"Kane. Addison Kane."

"Yes, that's right," Robert said, his voice fading to a whisper. "What's she like?"

Joanna's brow furrowed as she thought about Addison Kane. "Well, she's my age or maybe a few years older. Tall, thin...um...she has dark brown hair and...and she has these really odd eyes."

"Odd?" Robert said. "What do you mean like...like glazed over or something?"

"No, silly," Joanna said, playfully slapping her father's leg. "They're just...they're just really light blue, like one of those Alaskan dogs."

"I see," Robert said, studying his daughter. "What kind of person is she? You said she was here last night. How'd she strike you?"

Joanna's dimples appeared as she tried to find the appropriate words. Quickly giving up, she began to snicker. "Dad, she's filthy rich, and she knows it. She's more than a bit full of herself, and it seemed to me that she's quite used to getting her own way."

"Oh, a haughty cow – eh?"

"She's definitely that," Joanna said, snickering again. "But I can handle her."

Robert Sheppard laughed louder than he had in a very long time. He couldn't remember what he had for dinner the night before, but the pluckiness of his daughter was etched into his brain. Addison Kane was undoubtedly rich and apparently arrogant, but when it came to tenaciousness, Robert knew she was about to meet her match.

"What's so funny?" Joanna asked, smiling at her father's guffaw.

"The woman's going to have no idea what hit her," he said as he threw back his head and laughed again.

"I haven't a clue what you're talking about," Joanna said, holding her head up high.

"The hell you don't. A rabid pit bull doesn't stand a chance against you if you've set your mind on something."

"If you haven't noticed, I've mellowed over the years."

"I'll give you that, but underneath that calm exterior still lurks my feisty lass, of that I'm sure."

Beaming from the exchange, Joanna checked her watch. The last thing she wanted to do was leave, but time was not yet on her side. "I've got some errands to run, and Pearl will be here any minute. Is there anything you need while I'm out?"

"You wouldn't consider getting your dear old dad some ice cream, would you?"

Joanna got up and leaning over, gave her father a kiss on the cheek. "I'll see what I can do," she said, giving him a wink as she picked up the breakfast tray. Noticing all the food that remained, she said, "You know, you didn't eat much of this, and now it's cold. Would you like me to fix you something else?"

"No, I'm not that hungry, and Pearl will make me some tea when she gets here. You run along. I'll be fine."

"Okay, Dad," Joanna said, heading out the door. "See you later."

Robert watched as his daughter exited the room, and looking at the bills still on his bed, he picked up an envelope and peeked inside. Blanching at the balance, he set aside the statement, and opening the drawer on his nightstand, he pulled out a pen.

***

With purpose in her step, Fran Neary entered the outer office of Addison Kane. Acknowledging the junior secretaries with her usual quick smile, she walked over to Millie's desk.

"How's her schedule today?" Fran asked.

"Well, good morning to you, too."

"Sorry, lots of things on my mind. Good morning, Millie."

"Hello, Fran," Millie said as she tapped away at her keyboard. Pulling up Addison's calendar, she scanned the entries. "She's got from eleven to one free, and then busy the rest of the day. Why?"

"Hold on," Fran said, pulling her mobile from her pocket. Walking away from the desk, she made a call and then returned.

"Do me a favor and pencil in Herbert Fitzsimmons, will you?"

"Who?"

Looking over her shoulder at the two junior admins, Fran moved closer to Millie's desk. "He's one of the managers at Garrard. I've made arrangements for him to bring over some rings for Addison to look at."

"Oh, I see," Millie said as she returned to the calendar and quickly blocked out the time. "Does she know?"

"Not yet. That's why I'm here. Is she in a meeting?"

"No, she's alone. She just finished a conference call. Go on in."

"Thanks."

Fran made her way across the expansive outer office, and after lightly tapping on Addison's door, she sashayed in wearing the best smile she owned.

"What the hell do you have on?" Addison said, tossing her pen on the desk.

Fran looked down at her vest, jeans, and trainers. "Relax, I'm not working in the office today."

"And why not?"

"Because I'm taking your fiancée for the physical you demanded she have, and then I'm going to help get her affairs in order."

"Who made you her BFF?"

"No one, but since she doesn't have a car, and we all agreed last night that I'd handle her creditors, this will give Joanna and I some time to go through everything. That is unless you want her to get her own lawyer?"

"Of course not, the fewer people involved in this, the better."

"Good, then you won't mind if I'm not in the office today."

Exhaling slowly, Addison said, "No, I suppose not. Do what you have to."

"Thanks," Fran said, walking over and taking a seat. "And speaking of things that need to be done, I've filled up your diary for today."

Addison's entire body went rigid, and she slowly raised her eyes to meet Fran's. "Sorry?"

"I've arranged for one of the managers of Garrard to stop by. Millie penciled him in at eleven."

"What the hell do I need a jeweler for?"

"Because you're getting married and that normally means an engagement ring and wedding bands, neither of which you have."

"If you think—"

"What I think is that once Joanna is out and about again, the press will be extremely interested if the wife of one of the richest women in this country isn't wearing an engagement ring, let alone a wedding band. Now, can you please do us all a favor and stop arguing every bloody point of this marriage. It may be in name only, but you need to make sure it doesn't look that way. You and I both know people are watching."

"I don't know her ring size," Addison said, rocking back in her chair.

"Oh, Jesus Christ!" Fran said, getting to her feet. "Just pick something out, and we'll get it sized later, but when she walks into the registry office tomorrow, she's walking in as the fiancée of Addison Kane. Remember that."

"You could have picked a cheaper jeweler."

"I know, but where's the fun in that?" Fran said as she walked to the door. "Look, I have to head out, but I can be reached by mobile if you need me. All right?"

"Hold on. You may as well take this with you," Addison said, holding out a manila folder.

Fran went over and took the file. "What's this?"

"My doctor's report."

"I'm impressed," Fran said, hiding her amusement as she tucked the folder under her arm. "I didn't think you'd follow through with it."

"I didn't think I had a choice," Addison growled as she turned her attention back to the papers in front of her. "And I will expect hers on my desk tomorrow morning."

"It'll be there."

"It sure as hell better be."

**

Prior to Oliver Kane's death, Evelyn Ward's position was that of the housekeeper. In charge of all the female staff members, she oversaw the cleaning and upkeep of the interior of the home, while the rest of the servants, along with the budget, scheduling, and payroll were handled by Oliver's butler, Hugo Marwick. A portly man with bushy, gray mutton chops, Mr. Marwick had never hidden his dislike for Addison over the years, but when Oliver Kane died, Hugo became the master of the bootlickers. Much to his dismay, it didn't work. Seeing no need to fill her home with those who had scorned her, a few days after her father's funeral, Addison marched into the house and fired everyone *except* for Evelyn Ward.

Evelyn was the only constant in Addison's life. She was the only face that had never changed, the only smile that had never been false, and the only person who had ever spoken only the truth, no matter how hard, and Addison respected that. While she didn't always appreciate Evelyn's stern looks and scolding tones during her adolescence, Addison knew in her heart the woman did it because she cared. So, that afternoon after dismissing all those whom she couldn't trust, she turned to the only one she could and allowed her defenses to weaken. Her staunch exterior faded for only a few moments, but it was enough time for Evelyn to see an old friend. The little girl who liked to hide appeared when Addison flashed a quick smile as she began to speak, and seconds later, racking her brain for just the right words, her expression reminded Evelyn of a teenager, desperate to understand her lessons.

Finally, trying her best to keep the conversation on a professional level, Addison returned to the posture of an employer. Explaining she had neither the time nor the patience to hire new staff, she offered Evelyn twice her salary to stay on and assume the role of house manager. Evelyn would hire and fire when needed, make up the schedules, manage the household budget and payroll, and basically be in charge of everything and everyone under Addison's roof.

Addison made it clear she wanted only the most necessary of personnel on her property. She required a cook, two chauffeurs, and as many maids as it would take to keep the living areas clean and orderly. She didn't want a gardener. She didn't want a butler. She didn't want intrusion. She wanted a staff that would blend into the background, stay out of her way, and be there only when she called for them.

It was a good speech. It was professional. It was effective, and it was Addison Kane at her best, but her best crumbled when she saw the hurt in Evelyn's eyes. Evelyn hadn't worked for the Kanes because of money. She hadn't spent years answering to the supercilious Hugo Marwick because there weren't other opportunities elsewhere. She had done it for Addison. She had remained in a house of darkness and doom because she would not walk away from the little girl she had once held in her arms. A little girl who Evelyn had tried to save so many times, in so many ways, only to be defeated by the child's hateful father and his underlings.

Undone by the sadness etched on Evelyn's face, in a voice cracking with emotion, Addison spoke words she hadn't spoken in years, and it was those words that turned the tide. She admitted how much she cared for Evelyn. While their lineage differed, Evelyn had been the closest thing to a mother in Addison's life. She knew all Addison's secrets, and she had even known Addison was gay before she could admit it to herself. Evelyn knew Addison's faults, and like any parent, she had looked past them. In her heart, Evelyn was sure the child she loved still existed, but the walls Addison had erected as an adult were formidable. Luckily, on that day the bricks had loosened enough for Evelyn to see that leaving was impossible. Addison needed someone on her side. Someone who would protect her privacy, accept her quirks and understand her need for peace and quiet.

Standing at the foot of the stairs, Evelyn silently thanked God that Addison *never* came home during the day. By shortly after nine that morning, a cleaning crew of over a dozen people, complete with steam machines for the drapes and rugs, had shown up, followed by a plumber, a chimney sweep and finally, a crew of men to fix the lift. Chauffeurs carried out mattresses and rearranged furniture, and maids scrubbed bathrooms like they had never been scrubbed before. The janitorial service washed every wall, ceiling, and floor until the last remnant of grime had been eliminated, and the men hired to fix the lift worked feverishly to remove the broken, grease-covered parts of the antique vertical transport. Replacing everything with new, they tested and retested until the lift earned their seal of approval. The fireplaces were cleaned and the gas lines checked, and every fixture in the bathrooms, although still quite antiquated, was guaranteed to be leak-free.

Expecting casualties, Evelyn took each in stride. When one set of drapes and two area rugs basically disintegrated during the cleaning process, she merely had her staff swap them for the best that remained. Flaps of wallpaper that had drooped when water was applied to their design, were glued and taped back into place as discreetly as possible, and stains which refused to disappear from walls were hidden behind carefully placed furniture.

It had been a long, hard day, but not one member of Evelyn's staff had complained. When given the position of house manager, she had taken her time in choosing her personnel, making sure each knew their place and understood that Addison Kane's privacy came first. At seven that morning, standing in the kitchen, she had told them what was about to happen, and while all of their jaws had dropped in unison, not one had asked a question. It wasn't their place. Theirs was to do as asked and do it, they did. They had remained cheerful throughout the day, enjoying the fact a part of the house that had been hidden for so long would finally see life. While Evelyn knew Addison was dreading what was about to happen, she could tell that her staff was not. They were looking forward to finally earning the hefty pay packets they took home every week. Yes, she had chosen them wisely.

Hearing the sound of a car horn, Evelyn walked over and opened the front door, immediately smiling at the sight of Noah's red Vauxhall Corsa coming up the driveway, followed by three taxis in close pursuit. As he came to a stop directly in front of the stairs leading to the house, Noah scrambled to get out of his car. "Can I tell you how much fun I had today!"

"By that look on your face, I'd say quite a bit," Evelyn said, walking across the massive front stoop. Waving her arm in the direction of the taxis, she asked, "But what's all this?"

"Well, you didn't think I'd be able to fit all of it in my car, did you?" he said as he came to stand by her side. "Were the mattresses delivered?"

"About two hours ago," Evelyn said with a nod. "Dare I ask how you managed it?"

Noah's face creased into a smile. "Let's just say that money *definitely* talks."

"Yes, it does," Evelyn said, looking past Noah as the staff helped the drivers unload their taxis. Thinking back to what they had accomplished in only one day, her face turned rosy. "Yes, my dear, Noah, it most certainly does."

***

Addison did nothing to hide yet another yawn. Her desk was filled with trays lined in black velvet, each holding rings of gold, silver, and platinum. Clasped in prongs were diamonds of every shape and size, and while some were classically elegant, others were frighteningly obscene. She was tempted to buy the most garish. Thick and speckled with a legion of faceted chips, they were the style seen on the wrinkled fingers of dowagers craving to regain the attention they lost when their beauty abandoned them. Toying with the idea, Addison pulled the ugliest from the tray.

Seven rows of channel set diamonds made up the monstrosity. Set in white gold, it was nearly blinding as she held it up to the light streaming through the window behind her, and heavy between her fingers, she wondered if her soon-to-be wife were ever to go swimming, would she sink because of it? The thought brought the tiniest of grins to Addison's face.

Herbert Fitzsimmons stood silently with his hands clasped behind his back. His pencil-thin mustache twitched in anticipation as he saw Addison Kane choose the most expensive ring in his entire collection. Noticing the smile on her face, he was about to rattle off all the pertinent details about carat weight and clarity, but the words died in his throat as she returned the ring to the tray.

Addison was not stupid. While forcing Joanna Sheppard to wear something tasteless and gaudy for five years had its appeal, whichever ring Addison chose would reflect more on her than on her future bride. Putting the atrocity back into the slot, she curbed her desire to be spiteful. Scanning over the selection again, she stopped when one caught her eye. Seemingly out of place in a row filled with rings of yellow gold, the Princess cut solitaire diamond perched atop a sturdy band of platinum was elegant and timeless. By the size of the stone, Addison was sure it was well over a carat, but the square-edged band balanced the setting perfectly. Slipping it on her pinkie, she studied it for a while before setting it on the desk and turning her attention to the tray filled with wedding bands.

***

After placing two cups of tea on the table, Joanna sunk into a chair. She had visited Fran's doctor to get her physical first thing that morning, after which it was off to the bookstore and then to the churches where she had once spent her nights and weekends cleaning. Profusely apologizing to all for the lack of notice, before the clock struck noon, Joanna was unemployed for the first time since she was seventeen. Returning home with empty boxes from a nearby market, she and Fran spent the rest of the afternoon packing up the personal belongings of Joanna and her father. Framed photographs and keepsakes were carefully wrapped in towels before being packed away alongside a small collection of books Joanna had gathered over the years, and other than toiletries and clothing, everything else was to be left behind.

"You okay?" Fran asked, spooning some sugar into her cup.

"Yeah," Joanna said, looking over at the stack of boxes and bin liners near the door. "Just tired and I have no idea why. Up until a few days ago, I worked three jobs without a problem, but now I feel like I could sleep for a week."

"I think that's called stress."

"You think I'm stressed?"

"I would be if I just quit my jobs, packed up my life, and was about to marry someone who positively loathes the idea."

"There you go again, making this sound *so* attractive," Joanna said with a snigger.

Fran smiled. "Sorry, but with all of that going on, you've got to feel a little on edge, but it's totally understandable given the circumstances."

"I suppose," Joanna said with a sigh. "Can I be honest with you?"

"Of course."

"I don't know the first thing about living the kind of life Miss Kane lives."

"What do you mean?"

"She's…she's rich."

"I believe the term is *filthy* rich," Fran said, grinning. "But as they say, she still puts her trousers on one leg at a time, just like you and I."

"Except that hers are tailored, and mine are off the rack."

"Not for long."

"You see. That's what I mean," Joanna said, slumping in her seat. "I don't have a clue as to how to act or...or what's to be expected of me. I've never had tailored clothes or...or—"

"Maids, chauffeurs, and a personal cook?"

"Really?" Joanna said, wincing.

"Yes, plus a house manager who I know you'll adore," Fran said, but when she noticed Joanna's frown, Fran reached over and touched her on the hand. "Relax, Joanna. You'll be fine. Nothing is going to be expected from you at first, and when the time comes for you to appear in public with Addison, you'll have had plenty of opportunities to brush up on your haughty skills. Trust me."

"I don't ever intend to be haughty," Joanna said quietly.

"Good."

"Thanks for everything you did today."

"I hardly think you need to thank me for forcing you to get a physical."

"I didn't mind. I hadn't had one in years, so it's good to know I'm okay."

"Oh, speaking of that...hold on," Fran said, pulling her briefcase from a nearby chair. Opening it, she pulled out a folder and slid it across the table to Joanna.

"What's this?" Joanna asked.

"Addison's medical report."

Joanna snickered as she pushed the file back toward Fran. "Not interested."

"What?"

Joanna shrugged. "I just figured since she was forcing me to get one, I'd do the same. I don't need to see what it says."

"Nicely done," Fran said, chuckling as she returned the file to her attaché.

"Thanks."

"And speaking of nice, I like your father. He's quite a character."

"Well, he definitely likes you," Joanna said with a laugh. "I always forget how charming he can be when he puts his mind to it. I apologize for all those winks he was sending your way earlier, but he insisted on meeting you."

"He's adorable. I didn't mind at all," Fran said, taking a sip of tea. "Can I ask what made you decide to tell him the truth?"

"Because he's my dad. Yeah, he's going to forget most of what I told him today, and I'll have to repeat it again and again, but making up a story, basically telling him a lie, well that would have made him look stupid, and my dad's not stupid."

Gazing at the woman across the table, Fran said softly, "From where I'm sitting...neither is his daughter."

Chapter Ten

In the back seat of a Rolls-Royce parked outside the registry office, Robert Sheppard sat silently as he waited for his daughter to return. Although a bit tired from the activities of the morning, he was alert and knew exactly where he was and why he was there.

When he awoke that morning, he had been surprised to find two crumpled envelopes stuffed in his slippers. The first caused his blood pressure to rise to the top of the chart, but the other gave him pause. There was no doubt the words scrawled across the paper were written by his hand, and reading a dozen times what he had written, he took a deep breath and accepted the reality of Joanna's decision. Knowing he would need a constant reminder about the deal his daughter had made with the devil, he folded the envelopes and placed them in his Bible on the nightstand just before Joanna walked into his room.

Joanna had been fully prepared to refresh her father's memory about what the day would bring, so she was surprised to find he had beaten her to the punch. Quickly explaining about the notes he had written to himself, he promptly shooed her out the door, informing Joanna he was going to bathe, shave, and dress himself that morning. Although he saw a flicker of doubt in his daughter's eyes, Joanna, nevertheless, left him on his own, giving him the time he needed to rein in what remained of his disgust.

Robert wasn't the only one who had a surprise, and after being ejected from her father's room, Joanna skipped down the stairs with a smile on her face. She had decided the day before to treat her father to a full English breakfast, so gathering her purchases from the refrigerator, she began frying up tomatoes and cooking the bacon and sausage. It had been over a decade since last she had spent so much money on so little food, but as the aroma filled the house, Joanna breathed it in. It felt good to do something without worrying about where she'd find the money to buy food for tomorrow, or how many offices she would need to clean in order to pay the bills for the week.

Nearly an hour had passed before Joanna heard her father's bedroom door open. Walking over to the stairs, she looked up, and tears sprang to her eyes. Robert Sheppard looked better than he had in almost a decade. Owning only two pairs of trousers, he had chosen the dark brown, and while they were now baggy in the seat and a bit worn at the cuffs, with his pale blue Oxford shirt and royal blue tie, he looked positively dashing. Not a strand of his gray hair was out of place and his face, lacking the stubble that had become his norm, looked years younger. His eyes were as bright as his smile, and Joanna had never felt so proud.

Father and daughter enjoyed their morning together, laughing and chatting in between sips of coffee and bites of their breakfast, but as noon approached, Joanna grew quiet. When he asked, she spoke honestly of being nervous about the future, and Robert almost voiced his opinion, but then he remembered this wasn't about *his* future. It was about *hers*.

***

Looking around the car, Robert noticed two knobs tucked into an opening near his shoulder, and examining both, he turned one and watched as the glass divider between the front seat and the back slid downward.

Startled by the sound of the window opening, David Turner turned quickly in his seat. "Is there something you need, sir?"

"I'm sorry," Robert said as the corners of his mouth turned downward. "I've forgotten your name."

"It's David, sir."

"Oh, of course, David. That's right," Robert said, looking at the young man smiling back at him. "Tell me, David, what year Rolls is this?"

David's teeth gleamed in his grin. "It's a 1961 Phantom V, sir."

"It's quite impressive," Robert said, running his hand over the gray leather upholstery.

"Yes, sir, that it is."

Studying the rear partition covered in polished burled veneer, Robert counted no less than five integrated hatches. Thinking for a moment, he said, "David...I don't suppose behind one of these little doors, I'd find some liquid refreshment, would I?"

Briefed by Evelyn Ward, before David Turner got behind the wheel of the Rolls that morning, he was fully aware who he was picking up and why. After stopping at Kane Holdings to get Francesca Neary, he drove to Burnt Oak and parked on a narrow street where a Rolls-Royce had never been seen. Accustomed to Addison Kane's abruptness, meeting Joanna and Robert Sheppard had put a smile on David's face that had yet to disappear. Even though it was his job to open and close doors, and assist his passengers in and out of the limousine, each time he had, the father and daughter had displayed the sincerest of smiles as they thanked him. They were polite. They were pleasant, and they didn't treat David like he was invisible. He liked that.

Pointing over the partition, a twinkle appeared in David's eyes. "I believe if you pull open that door in the middle, sir, you may find what you're looking for."

"Oh, do you mean this one?" Robert asked as he reached over and tugged at the polished chrome handle.

The compartment swung open to display a small storage area with a mirrored back, the courtesy light inside casting brightness over two crystal decanters nestled into openings made specifically to fit their size.

David had been watching Robert, so when he saw the glint in the old man's eyes, he said, "The one on the right contains scotch, and the other has gin, sir."

"Oh, how thoughtful," Robert said, eyeing the bottles. "But I don't see any glasses."

David reached over the seat and pulled open the picnic tray to the left of the liquor cubby. "They should be right underneath, sir."

Robert's face lit up as he peered under the open shelf. "Well, now isn't that convenient," he said, spying the four Cumbria crystal tumblers in the velvet-lined niche.

"Yes, sir," David said with a nod. "Would you like me to pour?"

**

Just after he had finished his third splash of scotch, Robert was surprised when David quickly exited the car. Seconds later, the back door opened, and Joanna and Fran climbed inside. Offering her father a weak smile,

Joanna let out a long breath as she looked down at the engagement ring she was now wearing.

Earlier that morning, Fran had handed Joanna a small box containing the ring Addison had chosen, explaining that even though the marriage was in name only, appearances had to be kept. Joanna was taken aback by the sentiment, but as she opened the box, she fully expected to see a band of inconsequential size with an equally deficient chip of rhinestone. She couldn't have been more wrong, and she couldn't have been more shocked. It was positively the most beautiful ring she had ever seen, and as Joanna slipped it on her finger, somewhat impressed it fit so perfectly, reality hit home. Her life *would* never be the same.

Startled from her thoughts by the clink of glass against glass, Joanna looked up just in time to see her father fumbling with one of the etched decanters housed in the compartment directly in front of her. "Dad, what do you think you're doing?" she said, pushing his hand away. "That's not for you."

"Sure it is," he said, straightening his spine. "I'm the father of the bride, aren't I?"

Fran couldn't stop a laugh from escaping. "He's right, you know?"

"You're not helping," Joanna said, all the while finding it hard not to show her own amusement. "Besides, it's not even two o'clock."

"Well, you know what they say. It's five o'clock somewhere," Fran said.

Joanna turned to look at the woman sitting next to her. "Whose side are you on anyway?"

"I'm on the side of having a drink," Fran said, leaning forward to reach a decanter. "Robert, how about you?"

"That would be lovely, but make it a short one. I don't want to be a sloppy arse when I meet Miss Kane," he said, looking through the rear window. "By the way, where is she?"

"She went back to the office," Fran said, pouring a splash of scotch into Robert's glass. "You probably won't see her until later tonight, if at all."

"If at all?" Joanna asked, raising her eyebrows. "What's she planning to do, hide from us?"

"No, but she does own a suite at the Langham," Fran said, returning the decanter to the compartment. "And I wouldn't put it past her to stay there tonight."

"She *owns* a suite at the Langham?"

"Well, technically she doesn't own it, but she does pay for it by the year."

"Christ, she must be loaded," Robert said somewhat louder than intended.

"Dad!" Joanna said, playfully slapping her father on the arm.

Fran's enjoyment of the exchange showed on her face, and after taking a sip of her scotch, she leaned forward. "David, take us home please."

"Yes, Miss Neary," the chauffeur replied, raising the glass privacy panel as he started the car.

"Exactly where is home?" Joanna said as she eyeballed the empty glasses under the open picnic tray.

Fran jerked back her head. "You don't know?"

Like separation, anxiety comes in varying degrees. Waking up to a grumbling stomach, Joanna attributed it to the light dinner she had had the night before. When the Rolls-Royce parked in front of her house that morning and butterflies began to flutter in her belly, she had convinced herself it was because of the prestigious automobile. And walking into the registry office, when she tripped on a small carpet, Joanna had blamed it on being unnerved by the unbelievably fake smile Addison Kane flashed her as she met her at the door. However, sitting in the back of a vintage automobile with the smell of wealth wafting from the wool carpeting, leather upholstery, and highly polished details, wearing a ring worth thousands of pounds, Joanna knew she was either about to have a heart attack...or she was nervous.

Joanna reached for a glass and filled it with scotch, and after taking a sip, she relaxed back against the seat. "I have no idea where we're going. I just figured it was going to be nicer than where we lived before."

Fran took a sip of her drink and shrugged. "I guess that all depends on your definition of *nice*."

***

They hadn't yet made it out of the city before Robert Sheppard rested his head on the seat and fell asleep. With Fran on her mobile, chattering away about contracts and deadlines, Joanna was left to sip her drink as they left the noise of London behind them. One town blended into the next as they drove down streets lined with homes and businesses, but it wasn't until they turned onto a two-lane country road when Joanna began paying attention. It had been years since she had been in the country and with her vision no longer filled with tall buildings, double-decker buses, or billboards, a smile grew on her face. She had forgotten how much she loved the changing seasons.

A spring and summer lacking in moisture, but plentiful in heat, had caused autumn to come early, and leaves of orange, red, yellow, and brown filled the maples and oaks within view. On both sides of the road, meadows were covered in golden barley ready for harvesting, and the breeze, although slight, made it appear as if the fields were undulating toward the conifers dotting the hills in the distance.

The scenery changed like the fencing lining the road. As the wire mesh protecting the crops was replaced by wooden pickets, homes could be seen just off the lane. Tucked behind trees and shrubs, if it weren't for their white façades and the cobblestone driveways leading to their front doors, they would have been swallowed up by the landscape surrounding them.

It seemed to Joanna as they casually followed the twists and turns of the road, the further they went, the narrower the asphalt was becoming. With no more fencing to block their path, shrubs littered with dead leaves and twigs encroached as much as they dared, and old, crooked trees near the edge of the road were losing their lives to the ivy encasing their trunks in green, leafy cocoons.

Joanna felt the car slow, and as David smoothly guided it around a sharp turn, the overgrown foliage and scrub ended and pastures of grass, green and thick, appeared on the right. Intuition told her they were nearing their destination, and holding her breath, Joanna watched as another fence came into view. Unlike the ones before it, this one was intimidating. Columns of stone sprang from the earth, rising at least seven feet in the air before they were capped with pyramids made of concrete. Between each was lengths of vertical wrought-iron fence, and the Fleur de Lis finials that topped the spires came to sharpened points waiting to pierce.

Just inside the fence line, pine and firs holding their emerald firmly in their needles blocked Joanna's view of the estate until an opening appeared. Through the stands of white-barked birch the expanse of the property could be seen, but unable to see a house, disappointment showed on Joanna's face.

"Christ, I'm sorry," Fran said, slipping her mobile into her handbag. "I didn't think I'd be on the phone that long."

"No worries. I'm just enjoying the scenery," Joanna said, glancing at Fran.

"Well, I was hoping to tell you something about the house before we got there."

"We're there?" Joanna said, sitting up straight.

"Close," Fran said, pointing out the window. "Just up ahead is the drive."

Turning her attention to the road, Joanna squinted. Straining to see through the shadows of the oaks near the road, she felt the car slow again as David maneuvered the car down a rutted dirt path before coming to a stop in front of a pair of bow-topped iron gates.

Joanna moved to the edge of her seat and peered through the windscreen, her eyes settling on a plaque embedded in one of the stone columns supporting the gates. Even though its surface was dulled and green with age, Joanna could still read the raised letters on the thick plate of copper. Confused, she looked over at Fran. "Egerton Oaks?"

"That's what the estate used to be called back in the day," Fran said. "It was built by one of the first families in this area almost three centuries ago. The sign is embedded in the mortar, so no one ever bothered to take it down, but most of us just call this place The Oaks."

"Wow," Joanna said, looking back at the gates. Having paid more attention to the sign, than to what existed beyond the barred entry, her eyes grew large as the iron bars swung open.

The gravel driveway was entirely bordered in majestic English oaks. Stately and thick, with ragged crowns of branches filled with orange-brown leaves, tiny streams of sunlight struggled to reach the car as it drove under the density of the numerous branches covering the path. In the blink of an eye, they drove from shadow to sunlight, and blinking at the brightness, it took Joanna a few seconds before she saw the mansion. It was massive...and it was almost entirely entombed in ivy.

Once used as a ground cover in the gardens surrounding the base of the home, the English ivy had gone unchecked since Oliver Kane had bought the estate over three decades before. Appearing as if it had been poured from the heavens, the green, woody vines draped over the parapets of the roof, cascading down the walls until they puddled over the gardens and across the strip of lawn between the drive and the house. The windows, entryway, and front terrace had been kept clear of the invasive plant, but everything else...*everything* else was completely covered in ivy.

"Jesus," Joanna said as all the air left her body.

"I hope you like green," Fran said with a chuckle.

"Apparently, Miss Kane does. I've never seen so much ivy," Joanna said leaning even closer to the window.

Before Fran could respond, the car door swung open. She took David's outstretched hand and climbed out of the car, and then leaned down and smiled at Joanna. "You'd better wake up your father because...you're home."

"I'm awake," Robert Sheppard murmured as he looked out the window. "But I think I had too much to drink. The sky is green."

Joanna giggled as she gave her father's hand a squeeze. "That's the house, Dad. Stay here, and I'll come around and help you."

David offered his hand as Joanna exited the car, and after graciously thanking him, she stood straight and filled her lungs with the clean country air.

"David, how about you help Mr. Sheppard while I introduce Joanna to Evelyn," Fran said.

"Right away, Miss Neary," he said, trotting around the car.

Fran, seeing Joanna's forehead fill with creases, reached out and touched her on the arm. "Don't worry, he'll be all right," she said, motioning toward the stairs leading to the massive terrace that spread across the middle of the mansion. "Come on. Let me introduce you to the woman who runs this place."

When the gates were opened, the security panel in the kitchen had chimed, alerting Evelyn that the new woman of the house had arrived. Gathering the staff, she led them outside and waited patiently as the Rolls crept up the driveway. Evelyn had no idea what to expect, but she knew Addison would never have agreed to anything unless the woman could at least *look* the part of her wife. Evelyn shielded her eyes from the sun, her expression remaining neutral as she watched Fran get out of the car, but when another woman emerged, Evelyn instantly beamed. She looked over her shoulder at her staff and wasn't surprised in the least to see their expressions mirroring her own.

Having only a few seconds to scan the people standing on the slate porch as she followed Fran up the stairs, Joanna guessed the older woman standing at the front was Addison's house manager. Appearing to be in her mid-fifties, her sandy-blonde hair was neatly styled, and the dark-blue trouser suit she wore was pressed and crisp. She was also displaying a sincere smile. The first of many Joanna would see that afternoon.

Climbing the six steps leading to the terrace, Fran stopped and waited until Joanna was by her side. "Evelyn, I'd like you to meet Joanna Sheppard. Joanna, this is Evelyn Ward, Addison's house manager."

"It's a pleasure to meet you, Miss Sheppard," Evelyn said as she extended her hand. "Welcome to The Oaks."

"Thank you," Joanna said, her dimples emerging instantly. "And please, call me Joanna."

"As you wish," Evelyn said with a nod.

For a moment, there was silence, and sensing Joanna Sheppard's awkwardness, Evelyn took the lead. "I asked the staff to gather so you can meet them," she said, motioning toward the people standing in a row behind her.

Before Joanna could answer, a shadow crossed the step, and as she turned, her father came to her side. Stunned by his ashen appearance, she grabbed his arm as he began to wobble. "Dad, are you okay?"

Robert offered Evelyn a weak grin of acknowledgment as he tried to catch his breath. "I'm fine, lass," he said, turning to his daughter. "Just a bit tired."

Without missing a beat, Evelyn raised her hand as if to block the sun, even though it was no longer directly in her eyes. "You know, I didn't expect today to be so bright. Perhaps we should get out of the sun. There's plenty of time for introductions later."

"Thank you," Robert said, leaning heavily on his cane. "It is rather warm for this time of the year."

"I totally agree," Evelyn said, motioning with a sweep of her arm toward the doors several yards behind her. "Let's go inside where it's cooler. Shall we?"

Joanna took her father's arm, and slowly they walked across the expansive terrace and into the house that would be their home for the next five years.

Chapter Eleven

Commissioned to design and build a home like no other, the architect for the Egertons had done exactly what he had been hired to do. However, his forte had always been churches, cavernous and chambered, with high ceilings and panels of wood to absorb the sound, and his proclivity could be seen as soon as Joanna walked in the door.

Like many of the oldest houses of worship, the floor was slate, and the darkness of the variegated shades of gray, blue, and green rock was lightened only slightly by the aged, stained mortar between the joints. Panels of wood covered the lower third of the walls, and while the pattern was interrupted by the doors dotted down both sides of the entry, the color of all the woodwork remained the same. Oil stains and varnishes applied years before had deteriorated to the color of motor oil, and while the upper sections of plaster were free of wood, they had not escaped the ravages of time. Hairline cracks could be seen, and the once vibrant rose-colored paint had faded to the shade of weak tea, easily seen in the light streaming down from above.

The foyer was in the shape of an octagon, and the geometric pattern repeated in an opening cut into the ceiling, allowing the sunlight streaming through the second-floor windows to find its way downstairs. From where she stood, Joanna could easily see the iron handrails on the second floor surrounding the opening, as well as an obscure design painted on an octagonal inset of plaster at the highest point of the dome, nearly fifty feet above her head.

At first, Joanna believed the ceiling was the key feature of the space, but when she lowered her eyes, she was no longer sure. The grand staircase was situated near the back of the foyer, with its first step directly centered under the aperture in the ceiling. Although the wood was as dark as pitch, the tapestry carpet runner covering the center of the stairs was not. Against a background of burgundy, a design of gold, cream, and copper wove its way through the woolen fibers, and with the runner held in place by long, slim bars of bronze, it was absolutely regal.

The entrance hall alone was larger than her entire house in Burnt Oak, and trying her best not to allow her jaw to drop, Joanna stood in awe...and in shock. Its size was impressive, as well as a few of the architectural details, but overall the entire space seemed forgotten. There were no touches of modern and no attempts to hide age. The minimal furnishings scattered about held no photographs, and the paintings on the walls were of ancestors long since gone. It wasn't lived in. It was merely there.

Wednesday night, Evelyn had spent hours at her kitchen table, writing out a long list of things that needed to be done. Thursday, the entire day was spent completing the tasks with the help of her staff, and a horde of workers paid three times their normal rate, but when Evelyn awoke on Friday, she realized there was one more thing she wanted to do...find out something about Joanna Sheppard besides her name. With Addison refusing to say another word about the woman, Evelyn called her friend, Millie Barnswell. Having both worked for the Kane family for years, their paths crossed almost weekly, so the conversation was easy. By the time Evelyn had hung up the phone, she knew Joanna Sheppard and her father did not come from money, so the look of astonishment on the young woman's face was to be expected.

Noticing Robert Sheppard's color had yet to return, after giving Joanna only a minute to take in her surroundings, Evelyn quickly rattled off the names of her staff and then sent them on their way. Taking a step toward the stairs, she said, "Addison doesn't normally get home until six, so I've asked Noah to make us an early dinner. You've had a busy day, and I'm sure you'll want to relax. Why don't I show you where you'll be staying and then, if you'd like, I'll give you a tour of the house while we're waiting for dinner to be served?"

Joanna smiled at the invitation, but when she glanced at her father and saw his deeply furrowed brow, her smile faded. "What's wrong, Dad?"

"Those stairs look daunting. Perhaps there's somewhere down here where I can catch my breath."

"That won't be necessary, Mr. Sheppard. We have a lift," Evelyn said.

"You have a lift?" Joanna blurted.

Amused by the woman's bug-eyed stare, Evelyn walked just past the stairs and opened the door to Joanna's right. Sliding the gate aside, she said, "It was added years ago, but it's been checked quite recently, and I can assure you it's quite safe."

Robert limped over and let out a hearty guffaw at the sight of the wood-paneled lift. "Well, I'll be damned."

"David, why don't you accompany Mr. Sheppard, and Joanna and I will meet you upstairs," Evelyn said, stepping aside.

"It would be my pleasure," the young man said, patiently guiding a very weary Robert Sheppard into the lift.

"Ladies, shall we?" Evelyn said, gesturing toward the stairs.

Joanna took a deep breath. "Lead the way."

"If you two don't mind, I'm going to sneak into the drawing room and return a few phone calls," Fran said. "I'll catch up with you later."

"Okay. See you in a bit," Joanna said before following Evelyn up the stairs.

Stopping when she reached the top, Evelyn said, "I must apologize. Addison gave me very little notice of your...well, of your arrival. We only had a day to get the wing ready, so if there's anything you don't like or anything I've forgotten, please let me know, and I'll take care of it immediately."

"I'm sorry, did...did you say the *wing*?"

"That's right," Evelyn said, with a grin. "This house has an east and a west, and Addison asked that the east wing be prepared for you and your father. Unfortunately, it's been closed up for years, so I fear that it still needs some work, but it's clean, and all the bedding is fresh."

"I'm sure it'll be fine," Joanna said in a whisper.

"Are you all right?"

"Yeah," Joanna said, letting out a little snort. "It's just going to take some time to get used to all of this."

"Well, from what I hear, you'll have plenty of that," Evelyn said as she noticed the lift door open. "And there's your father, safe and sound."

Joanna followed Evelyn's line of sight down the walkway surrounding the railed off octagonal opening in the floor, and at the far end on the left stood her father who was doing an excellent impression of a Cheshire cat. Even though he had his cane, Joanna knew the walk was a long one for her dad, but before she could offer her assistance, she saw David hook his arm through her father's and slowly walk him up the carpeted passageway.

"How was your ride?" Joanna chirped.

"Totally delightful," Robert said, coming to a stop. "So, where to now?"

"This way," Evelyn said, opening the double doors leading to the wing.

Cautiously, Joanna and her father walked through the doorway, their eyes darting back and forth as they tried to absorb all they could see. Well lit by four chandeliers, the corridor was long and wide. Slender tables sat against the walls, and atop each were vases holding fresh flowers, many of which were varieties Joanna had never seen before. The hall runner wasn't as ornate as the one on the stairs, but the blues, greens, and tans in the threads, while appearing slightly faded, still added color to the space.

The group came to a stop when Evelyn opened the first door on the right. "Joanna, this is your bedroom, and your father's is the farthest down on the left."

At the very least, Evelyn had expected Joanna to look inside, but seeing the woman grimace as she looked down the long hallway, Evelyn said, "I put you in here because there's an en suite, plus a rather large wardrobe. Your father's room is adjoined to the next, so the nursing staff will have a place to stay without hovering over him, but still be close enough in case they're needed."

"Oh," Joanna said quietly.

Evelyn motioned down the hall. "Why don't we go and take a look, and if you still think this is better for your father, we'll switch?"

"Thanks. I'd appreciate that," Joanna said as she turned to her father. "Can you make it, Dad?"

"I got a bit of my wind back in the lift. I'll be fine. Lead the way, Miss Ward."

"Call me, Evelyn, please."

"Only if you call me Robert."

"Consider it done, Robert," Evelyn said with a smile. "Now, let's go show you the room."

***

A short time later, it was decided the bedroom at the far end of the hall was perfect for Robert Sheppard. The sleigh bed was higher than most, allowing for easy entry or exit by someone not in the best of health, and with a fireplace and a radiator, he would never get a chill. After her chat with Millie, Evelyn also knew Robert had developed a shuffling gait due to his partial paralysis. Preempting any trips or falls, she had the staff use the largest area rug in their possession to cover the cold wooden floor, and small tables and non-essentials were removed so the nurses could move about freely. Two upholstered chairs were arranged in the far corner for the comfort of visitors, and the bathroom, while old in fixture, had been updated with grab rails around the tub and toilet.

After making sure her father was safe and comfortable in his room, Joanna made her way back down the long corridor to her own. She had hardly given it a second glance when Evelyn had opened the door earlier, but as Joanna walked into her bedroom, she found herself enthralled.

Larger than the entire first floor of her home in Burnt Oak, it was furnished with everything a bedroom needed and then some. Along the wall closest to the door stood an eighteenth-century mahogany tallboy, its surface shiny and its hardware polished, and to her left was a triple-wide armoire to match. Unlike the sleigh bed in her father's room, the one Joanna was now admiring sat high off the ground. Surrounded by four massive posts reaching toward the ceiling, they were connected at the top by a thick wooden rail, framing the queen size bed below. On either side of the bed were nightstands with marble tops, and sitting on each were tall lamps with brass-beaded chains dangling just below the ivory fabric shades. In the far corner was a cast iron Victorian fireplace as tall as it was wide, and to its right were two towering windows looking out over the front of the estate.

Joanna moved slowly through the room, and running her fingers along the edge of one of the tallboy drawers, she pulled it open. Joanna did a double take when she saw some of her clothes neatly folded inside, and looking over her shoulder, she realized the rubbish bags containing her clothing were nowhere in sight. "That's interesting," she mumbled, pushing the drawer closed. The next surprise came when Joanna opened the door in the right corner of the room. Flicking on the switch, she smiled. She had never had her own bathroom before.

With the claw-foot tub, pedestal sink, and tile covering the floor and walls all white, it was easy to see the room had been designed decades before, but someone had taken the time to soften the starkness by adding accents of color. Pink bars of English rose scented soaps were in dishes near the sink and tub, and while the towels on the bars were as white as the rest of the room, facecloths of mauve, to be used as hand towels, had been rolled tightly and placed in a pyramid by the sink.

"Wow," Joanna said under her breath. She stood in the doorway feeling more than a little out of her element, but she was also fairly certain that rolled hand towels were the tip of the iceberg when it came to being a Kane. Shutting off the light, she headed to the door in the far corner of the room, and opening it, she flicked on the switch.

She blinked at the brightness, and for a split-second, she believed it to be another bedroom until she noticed the pole running under the shelf on three of the walls. "Oh my God," she muttered. "It's a bloody wardrobe." Shaking her head at the overkill that comes with wealth, she returned to her room and with a giggle, she ran over and flopped onto the bed.

Joanna stared at the ceiling, trying to decide what tickled her fancy more. Was it the fact in a few weeks she'd be marrying a woman, or was it because, at the ripe old age of twenty-eight, she had absolutely no idea what the word wealthy really meant?

Lost in her thoughts, Joanna continued to titter to herself until she heard a tap on the door frame. Looking over, she saw Evelyn smiling back at her.

"All settled in?" Evelyn asked.

"There wasn't much for me to do," Joanna said, sitting up. "It seems someone already unpacked for me."

"That would have been Sally. I hope she got everything in order."

"Everything's fine, but I could have done it myself."

"It's part of her job, and trust me, she enjoyed doing it," Evelyn said. "I wanted to let you know that dinner will be ready shortly. I wasn't sure if your father had any special dietary needs, and since we didn't know your likes or dislikes, we'll be having something simple."

"That's fine, but honestly, I'm not sure Dad will be ready to go back downstairs again."

"Yes, he did look worn out."

"Well, between you and me, I think it has something to do with the scotch he was drinking in the car, but he doesn't get out much. I'm sure between the ride and the walking, he overdid it a bit."

"I have an idea," Evelyn said, stepping into the room. "How about I have dinner brought up here instead? And if you don't mind, I'll join you, and we can all get to know one another a little better while we eat."

"I don't want you to go to any trouble."

"It's no trouble at all, I assure you," Evelyn said. "So, are you still interested in touring the house?"

"Yes, I am," Joanna said, springing from the bed. "I want to see everything there is."

"Well, I can't guarantee that, but you'll see most of it," Evelyn said, walking from the room. "Follow me."

Exiting the wing, Evelyn stopped and pointed to a set of doors nearly fifty feet from where they were standing. "Those lead to the west wing. It's almost identical in size and shape to yours, but I'm afraid it hasn't been lived in for years. I thought we'd just skip the mess if that's okay with you."

"That's fine."

Gesturing to another set of doors directly opposite the stairs, Evelyn said, "Those lead to the master suite. As I'm sure you're aware, Addison isn't taking any of this very well, so I think it best we not trample on her privacy."

"Good plan," Joanna said, her eyes creasing at the corner. "So, I guess that means we're heading downstairs," she said, taking a step in that direction.

"Not quite yet," Evelyn said, touching her on the arm. "Follow me."

Earlier, when her father had stepped out of the lift, Joanna had noticed the three large windows centered behind the railed opening. It was impossible not to. Running from floor to ceiling, they were massive, but their size wasn't what had caught her attention. Damask fabric in the hues of tobacco and beige surrounded each and held open by gold drapery cords with puffed-up tassels dangling from their ends, the combination was positively ghastly. However, what Joanna hadn't noticed came into view as she followed Evelyn past the lift. In front of the gargantuan windows was a sitting area, complete with a Victorian double end settee, the pattern of its upholstery a fine stripe of light and dark olive, while the two button-backed chairs bordering it were covered in sage and cream floral toile.

"Oh, this is beautiful," Joanna said, her entire face spreading into a smile.

"It's actually my favorite place in the entire house, as long as I don't have to look at the draperies," Evelyn said, wrinkling her nose as she looked over at the window coverings. "It's always quiet up here, and the morning sun is absolutely wonderful. It's a great place to relax, read a book, and have a cup of tea."

"I bet," Joanna said quietly, running her fingers over the walnut trim on one of the chairs.

"Is something wrong?"

"No, but I just realized I haven't read a book in years, and I'm not sure I know *how* to relax anymore."

"Well, our library definitely needs work, but I'm confident we can remedy that, and as for relaxing, I think that'll come back to you," Evelyn said, gesturing toward the stairs. "Now, how about we head down?"

"All right."

As they descended the grand staircase, Evelyn said, "Oh, the nurses you hired stopped by this morning to get their bearings. They've been given entrance codes and know where everything is. The first will arrive tonight and work through until tomorrow morning."

"That's a long shift."

"I agree. Apparently, there was some confusion as to who was working when, but the agency promised me by tomorrow morning, it will all be sorted. We'll have nurses on eight-hour shifts around the clock, so I think that between you, me, the nurses, and the staff, your father shouldn't want for much."

Stopping at the foot of the stairs, Joanna blushed as she cast her eyes downward. "Actually, there is one thing I noticed..."

"Yes?"

Raising her eyes, Joanna said, "I hate to ask, but Dad really likes to watch sports on the telly and—"

"Blast!" Evelyn said, stomping her foot. "I *knew* I forgot something."

"It's not really a problem—"

"Of course it is," Evelyn said, glancing at her watch. "I don't know what I was thinking, but let me make a quick phone call, and we'll get this sorted out immediately."

"You don't have to rush."

"Yes, I do," Evelyn said, tickled by the woman's naiveté. "So, why don't you take a look around, and I'll catch up with you in a few minutes? There's nothing off limits down here, so feel free to open any door you'd like. Oh, except those two over there."

Joanna looked over to where Evelyn was pointing and saw a set of arched-top double doors toward the front of the house. "O-*kayyy*?" Joanna said, squinting back at Evelyn.

"Nothing maniacal, I assure you," Evelyn said with a little laugh. "They lead to a formal living area which hasn't been used in decades."

"Why not?"

"No need," Evelyn said with a shrug. "Addison's father never cared to open it up, and Addison cared even less, so it remains empty and well...rather dusty. You get the idea." Not waiting for a response, Evelyn said, "And now I need to make a phone call."

"Okay," Joanna said, watching as Evelyn hurried off to make the call.

Taking a deep breath, Joanna stood in the middle of the entrance hall, having no idea which way to go. Pondering all the doors she could see, she walked over and opened the first one to her left. Flicking on the light, she found herself standing in a cloakroom larger than her kitchen at Burnt Oak. With only a half-dozen coats hanging from a wooden rod wrapping the room, there was nothing else to be seen, so shutting off the light, she proceeded to the next door in line. Opening it, she peered inside.

With walls covered in wood panels, and a massive desk and high-backed leather chair filling the space in front of an enormous triple window, it was obvious the room was Addison Kane's study. Taking another step, Joanna could see a laptop situated perfectly in the middle of the desk, as well as three pens neatly lined up in a row atop a leather-edged desk pad. A small green-shaded lamp hovered at the ready, and below it, two newspapers were expertly folded, waiting to be read. Across from the desk were a pair of wing-back chairs and behind them, partially filling the wall, was a marble-topped credenza situated between two stately bookcases. Square crystal decanters filled with assorted liquors stood at the ready atop the variegated rock, and a highly-polished silver tray off to the side held six sparkling Royal Brierley tumblers.

Although tempted to pull out one of the glass stoppers from the array of bottles and take a sniff, Joanna suppressed her urge and instead walked nearer the bookshelves to scan the titles. She promptly sighed. Economics, industry, and commerce had never held her interest, but by the amount of volumes standing neatly at attention, it was apparent Addison Kane felt differently.

In the far corner of the room was a fireplace similar in size and shape to the one in her room; however, instead of being constructed of cast iron, the surround was rock and the mantle, barren of even the smallest keepsake, consisted of a thick slab of wood. Frowning at the lack of any personal touches, Joanna decided to continue her self-guided tour. Noticing a door to the left of the hearth, she didn't think twice about opening it. Finding herself in shadows, she felt around for the switch, and when the light came on, Joanna's eyes grew wide.

Except for a fireplace in the corner and the windows hidden behind heavy curtains across the front wall, the rest of the spacious room was covered from floor to ceiling in bookcases. Complete with rolling ladders so the highest volume could be reached, the wooden cases were impressive, but Joanna's smile faded when she realized only five shelves held any books. With a sigh, she pulled one from its resting place and instantly chuckled. "Why do I have the feeling this is somehow appropriate?" she muttered to herself, placing the copy of Mary Shelley's *Frankenstein* back on the shelf.

Kneeling, she tilted her head to read the rest of the titles and was surprised by the variety. While they were all classics, the writers went from one extreme to the other. Dickens and D. H. Lawrence stood in line with Sheridan Le Fanu and Bram Stoker. Robert Louis Stevenson, H. G. Wells, and the complete works of Sir Arthur Conan Doyle filled another shelf, and stories by the Bronte sisters, Jane Austen, Oscar Wilde, and Virginia Woolf were crammed into the next. It was virtually the who's who of British writers, and as she debated which would be the first she'd read again, her eyes wandered. Seeing a few other books on a bottom shelf a few feet away, Joanna crawled over and pulled one out, practically dropping it when the cover came into view. Displayed in all their glossy glory were two nude women passionately embracing. Quickly placing the book back from where it came, Joanna squeezed her eyes closed and tried to force the image from her mind.

"I'm afraid the classics are all we have right now," Evelyn said as she came into the room and then she realized where Joanna was kneeling. "I'm not sure those books will interest you."

Joanna immediately blushed. "I'm sorry. I didn't mean to pry."

"Don't worry, you didn't. I honestly forgot they were there. I hope you weren't offended."

"No, I'm fine."

"Well, now that you've discovered Addison's erotica collection, why don't I show you the games room?" Evelyn said with a cheeky grin.

Visions of leather and straps instantly came to mind, but dismissing them with a shake of her head, Joanna got to her feet and caught up with Evelyn just as she was opening the door in the far back corner of the room.

"After you," Evelyn said, waving her arm.

Joanna crept through the opening and immediately smiled to herself. Appropriately named, the games room was exactly that. A card table covered in green felt was just inside the doorway, but what grabbed Joanna's attention was the billiard table in the middle of the room. Massive and ornate, the rosewood aprons were intricately carved with a repeating design of egg-and-dart, and the pattern repeated around the center of the bulbous tulip legs holding up the regulation-size table.

Walking over, Joanna couldn't resist running her hand over the blue-dyed worsted wool covering the slate. "This is beautiful."

"Do you play?"

"No. Do you?"

Evelyn nodded. "Yes, Noah and I have been known to play a few games. It can get a bit boring around here at times."

"Yeah?"

"Well, up until you and your father showed up today our only concern has been Addison. Her needs are hardly demanding."

"Funny. She strikes me as someone who could be quite difficult at times," Joanna said, keeping her smirk to a minimum.

"Maybe I should rephrase," Evelyn said with a snicker. "Addison can be quite demanding when she puts her mind to it. She likes things a certain way, but since we've all worked for her long enough to know that, it no longer fills up the hours like it used to."

"Oh, I see."

"Shall we continue the tour?" Evelyn asked, walking to a door to Joanna's left.

"What's through there?"

"The drawing room."

Joanna shook her head. "Exactly how many rooms does this place have anyway?"

"You know, I've never actually counted them," Evelyn said, and pausing, she mentally tallied the totals. "Let's see…we have twelve bedrooms, not including the master suite or servants' quarters. Then there are eight full baths, seven powder rooms, the study, library, games room, living room, drawing room, and what I call the parlor, and of course, the dining area and kitchen. How many is that?"

"I have no bloody idea," Joanna said with a laugh. "Just tell me you sell maps."

"It's really not that confusing. If you get lost, just start calling out. We'll eventually find you," Evelyn said with a humorous glint in her eyes. Opening the next door, she said, "Shall we?"

"Sure," Joanna said.

Two steps into the drawing room, both Joanna and Evelyn stopped in their tracks when they saw Fran throw her mobile on the sofa. "*Fucking unbelievable!*"

"Are we interrupting?" Evelyn asked.

"Oh, crap. Sorry," Fran said, grabbing her phone. "I didn't know you were there."

"Is there a problem?"

"Depends on how you look at it, I guess," Fran said, slumping on the couch. "I just got off the phone with Millie. It seems that Addison had her rearrange her schedule."

"In what way?" Evelyn asked.

Rolling her eyes, Fran said, "Addison's on a flight to France. She won't be back for four weeks."

Chapter Twelve

Joanna had never slept on silk sheets. For that matter, Joanna had never owned *anything* silk, so waking up with a smile on her face was a foregone conclusion. Under a duvet the color of champagne, she rolled onto her stomach and buried her face in a pillow of down. Sighing into the cool, smoothness of the fabric, she breathed deeply, filling her nostrils with the faintest scent of roses that had somehow magically appeared on the sheets. She could hear rain patter against the windows, and errant strands of ivy scratching on the glass, but the weather no longer concerned her. She didn't need to run through puddles to get to the Tube or fight an uncooperative umbrella against the wind. She was a woman of leisure now, and as the thought crossed her mind, Joanna broke into giggles.

After another minute, she rolled over and opened one eye. Surprised to see the grayness of rainy-day sunlight coming through the panes, she blinked and then blinked again. She hadn't slept in for years. Sitting up, Joanna let out a yawn, eyeing the pillow as it tempted her to return, but as she filled her lungs to capacity, she heard a scream.

Joanna scrambled out of bed and bolted from her room. She raced down the corridor, and reaching her father's room, she burst inside and found him sitting up in bed, looking harried and wild as he clutched the bedcovers to his chest.

"Who the hell are you?" he yelled at the shocked nurse standing in the adjoining doorway. "Where the hell am I? Joanna...Joanna...what's going on? Christ, what am I doing in a home? Why did you put me in a home? I can take care of myself. You didn't have to do this!"

"Dad, relax," Joanna said, sitting on the bed as she took his hand. "Please, calm down. You're not in a home. I wouldn't do that. You know I wouldn't do that."

"Then where are we? What is this place, and who the hell is that? That's not Pearl. That's not someone I know."

"I'm sorry," Joanna said, glancing over her shoulder at the wide-eyed nurse. "Could you please give us a minute?"

"Yes, miss," the frazzled woman said, quickly disappearing into the other room.

Joanna turned back to her father and squeezed his hand. "Dad, she's just a nurse, hired to help out. That's all."

"She's not Pearl. She's no one I remember."

"That's because she's new. Her name's Irene, and she's been here all night."

"Here? Where the hell is *here*? I don't recognize anything. I don't know this place," Robert said, grasping the bedcovers even tighter to his chest.

Seeing his Bible on the nightstand, Joanna picked it up and pulled out a folded piece of paper. "Here, read this."

"What is it?"

"It's something you wrote."

"What?" he said as he opened the paper. Recognizing his own scrawl, his eyes narrowed. "Joanna—"

"Just read it, Dad. I'll wait."

***

Evelyn stood at the entrance to the east wing, waiting in silence with the nurse. Hearing the bedroom door open, they both watched in anticipation as Joanna walked toward them.

"Is everything all right?" Evelyn said.

"Yes. Dad was confused, but he's okay now," Joanna said. Looking at Irene, she said, "He'd like to take a bath and may need some help. Do you mind?"

"Of course not," she said cautiously. "Is there anything I should know?"

"No, he's fine," Joanna said with a wave of her hand. "He knows where he is, and he won't shout at you anymore. I promise."

"Well, that's good. I'm not sure who was more scared, him or me," the woman said before plodding down the hall.

"Sorry about that," Joanna said, looking at Evelyn. "I hope he didn't wake anyone."

"Addison's not here, and the only reason I heard him is that I was just coming up to see if you were awake," Evelyn said.

"I am now," Joanna said, laughing as she looked down at her disheveled pajamas. "But I'm a mess."

"You're fine, but if you'd like to get cleaned up, I'll meet you downstairs. Noah is waiting to find out what you and your father would like for breakfast."

"You mean we have a choice?"

Once again forgetting that the world of wealth wasn't one Joanna Sheppard was accustomed to, Evelyn grinned as she headed to the stairs. "Take your time, and come down whenever you're ready."

Joanna smiled as she returned to her bedroom. If breakfast was anything like the dinner she had had the night before, taking her time was *not* an option.

***

Joanna knew simple. She had lived it for years. Clothes were purchased without print or pattern, making it easier to mix and match without fear of clashing stripes with checks, and shoes in black, brown, and cream were all that were needed to cover the seasonal change. One pair of boots, warm and knee-high, when properly cared for, could last for years, and a raincoat used in the spring, when equipped with a liner, provided the warmth necessary on wet, winter days. Shopping at the market never took place without coupons or vouchers, and the food purchased was for meals requiring little extra than what her pantry contained. Joanna was all about simple, but when dinner was served the night before, she realized her simple and the Kane simple had two *entirely* different meanings.

Having eaten many a meal on a tray table in her father's bedroom in Burnt Oak, Joanna assumed she would be doing the same thing on her first night in the Kane mansion. When Evelyn offered to have dinner brought upstairs, although Joanna hadn't seen any stacked or racked tables in her travels through the house, she assumed they existed. They did not...at least not in the home of Addison Kane.

While Evelyn and Joanna were saying goodbye to Fran, the staff had turned the bedroom across the hall from Robert Sheppard's into a makeshift dining room, complete with a small table and three Queen Anne upholstered chairs. Upon a cloth of linen and lace, place settings had been arranged, and each held plates of china edged in gold, silver flatware, and Waterford crystal goblets in varying sizes. By the time Joanna walked into the room, her father was already sitting at the table, positively beaming as he admired the finery of wealth.

Their meal began with what could have been an unpretentious starter. However, by adding a touch of cream, fresh basil, and croutons, Noah had turned the tomato soup into something beyond the norm. After their empty bowls had been cleared, all breathed in the scent of the braised lamb shank in red wine sauce as their dinners were placed in front of them. Accompanied by buttered carrots and new potatoes swirled with roasted onions, the entrée was completed with glasses filled with a ten-year-old Cabernet, its bouquet rich in black currant and its finish, smooth and graceful.

No one had noticed Noah's stealth in preparing their food. After peppering David with endless questions about their infirmed guest Noah had taken Robert's impairments into consideration with every course. With several sets of dinnerware at his disposal, Noah asked that the table be set with the one having the largest and deepest soup spoon, thus enabling the less than ambidextrous man the ability to ladle his soup comfortably. The carrots and potatoes were small, easily speared with a fork, and the lamb, although typically served on the bone, had been neatly carved into bite-sized pieces, again allowing Robert to keep his pride intact.

Savoring every bite, they enjoyed their dinner, all easily conversing until over an hour had passed, and the staff returned to remove the empty plates. The last course brought smiles as well as groans, but no one could refuse the steaming coffee or the martini glasses filled with raspberry sorbet drizzled in chocolate.

Last-minute details coupled with the day's anxiety and a scrumptious dinner had caused more than one person at the table to yawn before the last course was cleared. Evelyn had been up since before five, ensuring everything was in order for the Sheppards' arrival, and Joanna had awoken at six after a less than restful night. It had been a long day, but for Evelyn and Joanna, it was not yet over. Knowing they needed to wait until the arrival of the nurse, after Joanna helped her father to bed, she rejoined Evelyn, and they spent the rest of the evening touring the house.

***

Wrapped in a towel large enough to cover a yeti, Joanna emerged from the bathroom, but her forward progress stopped instantly when she realized she wasn't alone.

"Good morning, miss."

Joanna racked her brain, trying to remember the maid's name. The day before she had met the staff, and while their duties and names had been rattled off rather quickly by Evelyn, Joanna always prided herself on having a good memory.

David Turner was the young man who had acted as their chauffeur. Well over six feet tall, with broad shoulders, a barrel chest and a narrow waist, it was obvious to Joanna he had spent some time in a gym. With chiseled features, wavy brown hair, and dark eyes, although he appeared to be in his late twenties, his charm belonged to that of a boy.

Equally as charming was the cook, Noah Hamilton. Enthusiastic, with a hint of naughtiness lurking in his light blue eyes, he had shaken Joanna's hand as if he had been trying to produce water, and as he was chattering away, Joanna learned two things. He was an American, and he was adorable.

Although Joanna had yet to be formally introduced to the other chauffeur, George Parker, the first of the maids she met was his wife, Fiona. A buxom woman with graying hair, her standard black uniform stretched at the seams as it tried to hold in her plumpness. With chubby cheeks and a warm smile, she reminded Joanna of a German barmaid, easily able to fist a half-dozen beer steins in one hand if the need arose.

Appearing to be Fiona's polar opposite, the next maid, Sally Dixon, was a wisp of a woman. An inch shorter than Joanna and a stone lighter, it was evident the brown-haired woman was shy and somewhat nervous. Unable to maintain eye contact with Joanna for more than a second before looking away, she had actually attempted a curtsey when they were introduced, and the ice was broken very easily when Joanna curtsied back with a wink.

All of a sudden, Joanna's face brightened as she finally remembered the last maid's name. Gaunt and lanky, with loopy arms, bulging eyes, and frizzy bleached blonde hair, she was a caricature of her own handle.

"Good morning, Iris," Joanna said, tugging up the towel. "You startled me."

"Oh, I'm sorry, miss. Evelyn said you were awake, so I thought I'd bring you a spot of tea and tidy up your room while you bathed."

Noticing the woman had already made the bed, Joanna said, "I could have done that."

"Oh, no, miss. It's my job," Iris replied, plumping a pillow. "And if there's anything you'd like done a certain way, please let me know, and I'll be sure to follow your instructions to the letter."

"I'll remember that, but I'm fairly easygoing."

"Yes, miss," Iris said as she walked to the door. "If there's nothing else, miss, I'll leave you to dress."

"Thank you, Iris, and please call me Joanna."

"Oh no, miss. I don't think that's allowed."

"No?"

"I doubt Miss Kane would approve," Iris said, closing the door behind her as she left the room.

***

Evelyn sat at the island counter, sipping her tea and watching as Noah idly paged through a cookbook. Like Noah, she generally didn't work weekends, but she felt it her duty to show up on Saturday morning to make sure Joanna and her father had had a comfortable night. She didn't expect to see Noah that morning, but then again, she wasn't all that surprised when she had walked into the kitchen and saw him looking like a canary-fed cat.

The night before, Joanna had made it a point of thanking him for the fabulous dinner again and again. Heaping on accolades about the flavors, the aromas, and especially the dessert, Evelyn couldn't help but notice the young man's chest swelling with pride. For Joanna, it was simply common courtesy, but for Noah, it was not. It was all the reason he needed to get up early on a Saturday and go to work...even when he didn't have to.

The door to the kitchen swung open, and Joanna wandered in. "Good morning," she said, holding her empty tea cup. "Where does a girl get a refill around this place?"

Evelyn and Noah briefly glanced at one another, and then in unison, they smiled.

"At your service," Noah said, taking the cup from Joanna's hand. "What kind would you like?"

"Huh?"

"We have black, white, green, oolong, and herbal, in English, Irish, Scottish, and Chinese blends."

"Wow."

"We aim to please," Noah said, batting his eyelashes. "Now, what's your pleasure?"

"Seriously?" Joanna said, looking back and forth between Noah and Evelyn.

"Of course."

"You wouldn't have any coffee, would you?"

"Coming right up," he said, turning to get a new mug. Filling it to the brim, he placed it on the counter. "It's Kona, and it's hot, so please be careful."

"I will," Joanna said, but as she reached to pull out the stool next to Evelyn, she stopped. "Do you mind if I sit?"

Once again, Evelyn glanced at Noah, and once again, his expression mirrored her own. "Joanna," Evelyn said, turning to the young woman. "You don't have to ask. I work for you, not the other way around."

Joanna had awoken feeling relaxed, but the awkwardness caused by her surroundings had returned by the time Iris had left her room. Joanna wasn't used to being waited on, and Evelyn's statement, while not exactly false, instantly rubbed her the wrong way.

"I think we need to get something straight," she stated. "I may be marrying Addison Kane, but I am *not* like her. I don't need to be coddled or called miss. I don't need maids to make my bed or...or bring me tea in the morning, and I was raised to be polite and to ask before assuming. I have no intention of changing who I am just because my last name is going to be Kane, and the sooner everyone understands that, the better off we're all going to be. Fran told me that everyone here can be trusted, and they know what this marriage is all about, so there's no need to put on airs. Okay?"

"I'm not sure that'll be as easy as you think," Evelyn said, enjoying the pluckiness of the future Mrs. Kane.

"Why not?"

"Because while it's true my staff knows why this marriage is taking place, you're still going to be Addison's wife, and that position demands respect. To not give it would go against everything they've been taught. It took me weeks to interview and choose this staff, and the result is a group of people who are proud of what they do, where they work, *and* who they work for. They were hired for their aptitude, their decorum, *and* for their diplomacy. They know not to tell tales outside these walls and to give respect to those who live under this roof. Of course, eventually a few of them may call you by your first name, but that's not going to happen overnight. They're much too professional for that."

Mulling over what Evelyn had said, Joanna sighed. "It sounds like I have a lot to learn, but I don't want them to think I come from money and expect all the pomp."

With a snigger, Evelyn said, "I'm fairly sure that they don't."

"No?"

"Most of the upper class I've met don't use bin liners for suitcases."

Having not yet heard that particular detail, Noah burst out laughing, and his loud, unexpected guffaw caused both women to jump. Covering his mouth to prevent any more shrieks from escaping, he turned around and buried his head in his hands as he tried to get himself in check.

For a split-second, Joanna got angry, believing the man thought her stupid, but the more he fought to rein in his funny bone, the more his mirth became contagious. After all, she *was* about to marry one of the richest women in the country, and she *did* use rubbish bags as her suitcases.

Joanna looked over at Evelyn to see if she was equally as tickled, and when she saw tears of laughter forming in the woman's eyes, Joanna decided to fan the flames. "It's not that funny," she said with the straightest face possible. "It wasn't like they were used."

As soon as her words reached their ears, there was nothing they could do to restrain their merriment as it erupted from within. Noah crumpled to the floor, and Evelyn bowed her head as her shoulders quaked, and less than no time, Joanna had joined in. It was nice to laugh again.

***

A breakfast of Eggs Benedict was delivered to Robert Sheppard's room a short time later, and with Joanna at his side, eating scones and sipping coffee, father and daughter enjoyed yet another meal together.

A staff of cable experts arrived shortly after nine and spent the next few hours trying to figure out ways to run wires through walls of plaster and stone over a century old. By noon, flat-screen televisions were delivered and promptly set up in both of their rooms, and when Joanna handed her father the remote, explaining there were over four hundred channels at his fingertips, it was as if he had won the lottery. She left the room with a smile on her face, but it paled in comparison to the one he was displaying.

With nothing but time on her hands, Joanna aimlessly wandered the house, admiring the architecture, but for the most part, grimacing at the décor. The rooms in the east wing, courtesy of Evelyn and Noah, had been lightened by bedcovers in muted tones and modern designs, but all the rooms on the main floor seemed dark and old. The colors and patterns of upholstery and draperies reflected hues in the deepest tones or the most repulsive combinations, and the furnishings seemed to be a mixture of expensive antiques and clunky knockoffs. Accent tables of mahogany, oak, and rosewood were displayed throughout the house. Standing proudly on turned or tapered legs, the swirls of their grain were visible through the layers of polish that made them shine, but the chairs and sofas they bordered, were hefty and annoyingly masculine.

With the dense clouds blocking out the sun, the staff had been forced to turn on the interior lighting, but it only added to the gloom of the house. Bulbs trapped behind frosted globes and silk shades stained by the passage of time cast only minimal light, creating eerie shadows in the corners of the rooms and down the long hallways.

Joanna made her way to the library, and grabbing a book, she backtracked to what she decided was her favorite room in the house. It wasn't because it was cheery and colorful, and it wasn't because it was modern and well lit. It was simply because she thought it was amazing.

The parlor, as Evelyn had labeled it, was situated behind the grand staircase between the drawing room to its right and the kitchen to its left. Massive round columns, assisting in supporting the upper floor, flanked the openings on either side of the stairs, creating quite an impressive entrance feature, but the room itself created the awe. Larger than the foyer, the area could have easily been a small theater if it hadn't been for a wall of stone dividing the room in half. A large hearth, accessible from either side of the wall, was centered in the rock and on the back side, reachable through two archways cut into the stone, was a modest sitting area.

Like the front entry, the back wall of the room was angled on two sides, and both sections held windows draped in burgundy velvet. Double doors leading out onto the veranda filled the center wall, but with the rain starting the night before, Joanna had yet to set foot outside the house.

Settling into an armchair, Joanna propped her feet on a small ottoman and opened the book. She had never read it before, but after chuckling over its discovery, she couldn't resist losing herself in the pages of *Frankenstein*.

Chapter Thirteen

The next week moved slowly along as both Joanna and Robert adapted to their surroundings. For Robert, he was content with his television and occasional strolls up the hallway, but for Joanna, other than spending time with her father, her only outlets were to read or catch up on sleep, both of which she was becoming an expert at.

"How come I knew I'd find you here," Evelyn said, walking into the parlor.

"Probably because this is my favorite room," Joanna said as she closed her book.

Evelyn scowled as she scanned her surroundings. "It's a bit draconian, don't you think?"

"I suppose, but it could be so much more," Joanna said, looking around.

"I'd have to agree."

"Evelyn, can I ask you a question?"

"Of course."

"Why is everything so dark and dreary around here? It's like nothing's been changed in decades."

"That's because it hasn't," Evelyn said, taking a seat in the chair next to Joanna.

"But why not? Does Miss Kane like living in the early eighteen hundreds?"

"It's not that she likes living amongst antiquities and disrepair," Evelyn said with a slight shake of her head. "It's more the fact it just doesn't matter to her."

"I don't understand."

"She simply doesn't care, Joanna. She doesn't see the cracks in the plaster or the outdated lighting because she grew up with it. It's normal to her. Of course, if something does break, we get it repaired, but as for replacing furnishings or painting the walls, as far as she's concerned, there's no need. She has a bedroom in which to sleep, a dining room in which to eat, a study where she spends her nights and weekends working, and a gym in which to exercise. Everything else is inconsequential."

"Wait," Joanna said, sitting up in her chair. "This house has a gym?"

"Oh, my," Evelyn said, letting out a gasp as her fingers flew to her lips. "It seems I forgot to tell you about that."

"I've spent an entire week locked up inside this place because of the rain, putting on God knows how much weight due to Noah's culinary wizardry, and *now* you tell me there's a gym," Joanna said, rolling her eyes.

"I'm so sorry," Evelyn said as her cheeks grew rosy. "But the rain has finally let up, so how about you and I take a walk around the grounds, and then I'll show you the exercise room?"

"As long as she doesn't go out the front door," Fran said, coming into the room.

"I didn't know you were here," Joanna said, smiling as she got to her feet. "And why can't I go out front?"

"Because there's a horde of reporters by the gate and down the fence line, most of which, I may add, have cameras with lenses longer than my arm."

"Huh?" Joanna said, quickly looking back and forth between Fran and Evelyn.

"Haven't you been watching the news?" Fran asked.

"Actually, no. I've been catching up on my reading. Why?"

"Because you and Addison are the talk of the town," Fran said, placing her briefcase on the floor. "The nightly news is filled with special reports about your upcoming marriage, and the tabloids are doing their best to uncover every photograph and bit of information they can find on you."

"Really?"

"I told you once the banns were announced, all hell was going to break loose, and it has. I spoke to her this morning, and she's positively livid. It seems she can't even leave our office in Paris without the paparazzi chasing her down the street, so she's made it clear you aren't to go anywhere near the front of the estate."

Crossing her arms, Joanna eyed the lawyer. "Why? If she thinks I'm that repulsive, why are we doing this? I'm not planning to spend five years locked in this bloody house, and if that's what she—"

"Joanna, calm down," Fran said, holding her hands up. "That's not what she wants."

"Really?" Joanna said, changing her stance. "It sure as hell sounds like it to me."

"Look, all we want to do is control the photos that are released," Fran said, taking a step in Joanna's direction. "So, until we can arrange to have some taken, we thought it best to keep you away from the paparazzi. That way, another grainy, misrepresentation of you doesn't show up on the front pages of the newspapers."

Joanna opened her mouth to speak, but shut it just as quickly. Pausing, she stared at Fran. "Um...what do you mean *another*?"

Fran tried her best to hide her grin. "Well, it seems that someone got hold of the photo you used on your badge at the bookstore."

"What?" Joanna shouted. "Oh, crap! I looked like a bloody squirrel in that picture. I had my wisdom teeth taken out that morning. Shit!"

"Yes, well I was going to ask you why you looked like you were storing nuts for the winter," Fran said with a chuckle.

Joanna threw herself into a chair and buried her head in her hands. "Oh, this is just great!"

"Relax, Joanna. You aren't the first to be intruded upon by the press, and you won't be the last. Trust me, when we do release photos, there'll be a lot of reporters wearing egg on their faces."

Joanna looked up. She appreciated the compliment, but it didn't show in her expression. "So, I guess going shopping is out of the question, too?"

"Shopping?" Evelyn said. "Don't tell me I've forgotten something else."

"No, but I thought I'd get a couple of new books, and Dad needs some pajamas."

"Crap!" Fran blurted. "Crap. Crap. Crap. Crap. *Crap!*"

Joanna cocked back her head and then began to giggle. "What is *wrong* with you?"

"Oh, it's been bloody crazy at work and somewhere on my desk is a list of things I still needed to do concerning the deal you and Addison made. I'm sure in there somewhere was a requisition for a mobile, and possibly even a computer."

"Don't worry about a mobile, Fran. I don't have anyone to call, and as far as a computer, it's not so much about shopping as it is about just getting out of the house."

"Unfortunately, I'm afraid you can't do that right now. Until things calm down, you have to stay here."

"I know," Joanna said with a sigh.

"I've got an idea," Evelyn said. "Why don't you use my laptop to at least order a few books and some pajamas for your father? Then, once the coast is clear, you'll be able to get to the shops for whatever else you'd like."

"That'll work," Joanna said, smiling.

"Good! Then it's settled."

"Speaking of settling, how's your father adjusting? Everything okay?" Fran asked.

"He's doing all right. At first, when he woke up in the morning it was a bit hectic, but he's been writing down a few notes to help jog his memory and putting them in places where he'll see them when he wakes up, so he's doing much better. The nurses are wonderful, and he absolutely adores his television."

"So the decision to become Mrs. Kane was a good one?"

"I don't know. I'm not Mrs. Kane yet," Joanna said with a twinkle in her eye.

"Actually, that's the reason I'm here," Fran said. "I've arranged for the registrar to come to the house on the thirtieth to perform the ceremony. He'll be here at nine, and Evelyn and I can act as witnesses."

"Wow! No moss grows on you," Joanna said with a laugh. "What is that? Exactly twenty-eight days?"

"Actually, it's twenty-nine, but you knew we had a deadline to meet and Addison's birthday is on the fourth."

"I know. I'm just kidding."

Studying Joanna for a moment, Fran quietly said, "You're still okay with this, aren't you?"

"Yes, actually I'm fine. I know this is going to sound weird, but I think I was more worried about moving house than getting married. This past week has given me the chance to get to know the staff and my way around. I figure by the time Miss Kane gets back, I'll be more than comfortable here, so putting my name on a piece of paper isn't really that big of a deal."

Fran arched an eyebrow. "You don't think?"

Joanna shrugged. "It's just a name."

***

"Did you mean what you said?" Evelyn asked as she put on a light jacket.

"About what?" Joanna said, slipping into her tattered raincoat.

"That marrying Addison isn't any big deal."

"It isn't. I mean, we all know she's not happy about this, so I doubt she and I will spend much time together. At least, I don't think we will. I'm imagining the next few years of my life are going to be spent reading, entertaining my father, and working out in the gym, that is if you ever show me where it is."

Evelyn smiled as she opened the doors leading to the patio. "I promise, you'll see it soon enough, but first, how about we take a walk and get some fresh air."

They stepped out onto the back terrace, both blinking at the brightness of the late summer sun. Dampness hung in the air from the rain which had fallen all week, and the temperature had dipped enough that the coat Evelyn suggested Joanna put on was definitely needed. It was a day with just a hint of a breeze, and the first thing Joanna did was fill her lungs with the cool, moist air.

"It feels great to be outside," Joanna said as she closed her eyes and turned her face to the sun. She soaked in the warmth, allowing its comfort to regenerate her spirit before she opened her eyes and took in the view. More than once during the week of non-stop storms, she had stood at a window peering through the blurry glass. Although unable to make out any details, Joanna knew the patio was huge and the grounds beyond it appeared unkempt. Joanna quickly discovered she was right on both counts.

The veranda was gargantuan. As deep and as wide as the house, its enormity caused the small iron table and chairs sitting off to one side to seem almost Lilliputian in size.

"Wow!" Joanna said, laughing at the extravagance. "Anybody for a game of football?"

"I'm afraid I wouldn't recommend that."

"No? I'm sure we could move the table," Joanna said, her eyes crinkling at the corners.

"Yes, we could, but falling might be an issue," Evelyn said, tapping her foot on the slate.

Stunned by the massive patio, Joanna hadn't noticed its surface was entirely covered in the same slate that appeared in the foyer as well as in many rooms of the house. "What? Was somebody having a sale on this stuff?"

"I'm not sure, but whoever it was had no idea what they were doing," Evelyn said through a frown.

"What do you mean?"

"Inside isn't bad, but out here the mortar has deteriorated due to the weather. Between how slippery it gets when it rains and the crumbling grout, you need to be careful. Some of the sections seemed to have taken on a life of their own."

"So...no jogging allowed?"

With a laugh, Evelyn motioned toward the stairs. "If you want to jog, I'd suggest doing it around the grounds. Up here is far too dangerous."

Joanna only doubted Evelyn's warning for a second because as soon as she took a step, she heard the mortar crunch as the slate under her feet shifted ever so slightly. Glancing at Evelyn, Joanna grinned. "Um...point taken."

"Good. I knew you'd agree," Evelyn said as she slowly walked to the railing.

Joanna cautiously followed until they reached the iron balustrade surrounding the perimeter of the patio. "Is it safe to lean on this or am I going to plunge to my death?"

Evelyn smiled. "The railing is quite safe, and we're on a hill, so if you fall over the side, the most you'll do is roll to the bottom and land with a thud."

Joanna looked down over the railing and drew in a quick breath. The slope of the grassy hill on which the veranda was built was the steepest she had ever seen. Grabbing the railing, she gave it a quick shake, and feeling its sturdiness, she looked out over the property and immediately glowered.

The gardens, like everything else she had seen, were massive, but all were overgrown with weeds, brambles, and vines. Amidst the tall stalks of field grass swaying in the breeze, Joanna could make out a few low walls of rock, but like the house, the vines were doing their best to strangle everything in their path.

"Not what you expected is it?" Evelyn said.

"To tell you the truth, I've looked out the windows a few times, but I kept thinking the rain was distorting the view."

Evelyn sighed. "I'm afraid not."

Stunned by the appearance of the neglected property, Joanna shook her head. "Let me guess, she doesn't like flowers?"

"As a matter of fact, I think the first flowers ever brought into the house were the ones I put in your wing the day you arrived."

Joanna smiled as she remembered the splendid fragrances that had filled the east wing that day from bouquets in vases of every shape and size. "I never thanked you for those. They were wonderful."

"You're quite welcome, and that reminds me, I need to order more," Evelyn said as she pulled her mobile from her pocket and quickly typed in a note.

Turning her attention back to the gardens, Joanna said, "So, why not just knock it all down and turn it into lawns? Why leave it like this?"

"Because Addison doesn't care. She hasn't come out here in years, and since we have no visitors, there's no point in maintaining something that won't be appreciated," Evelyn said and then she pointed to a mulch-covered track that wrapped the back of the house. "The only thing maintained is that footpath."

Joanna looked down and saw a swath of mulch at the bottom of the hill. "It almost looks like a driveway."

"It used to be one, but we don't use carriages any longer."

"Sorry?"

"Come on. I'll show you, " Evelyn said, gesturing for Joanna to follow her to the stairs. "Just make sure you hold onto the handrail. If you fall here, you won't bounce."

Joanna's first thought as she approached the stairway was it seemed as if it was an afterthought in the design of the patio. Unlike everything else she had seen so far, the staircase simply didn't fit. It was void of even the simplest of decorations, and while slate had been applied to the surface of the treads, the balustrade system was the most basic of black wrought iron.

Taking Evelyn's warning to heart, Joanna gripped the iron rail firmly as she descended the stairs. Reaching the bottom, she turned to look up at the patio now nearly thirty feet above her head. "You weren't kidding about this being a hill, were you?"

"Not at all, and now I'll show you just how creative the Egerton's architect was. Follow me."

Intrigued, Joanna kept pace with Evelyn on the path as it curved around the house, the slope of the hill slowly becoming less steep as they walked. Her attention held by a long brick building off in the distance, it wasn't until Evelyn stopped when Joanna saw the tunnel running under the patio.

"What the fu—" Blushing instantly as the expletive almost escaped her lips, Joanna said, "Um...sorry, Evelyn."

"That's quite all right. I've heard the word before."

Joann peered into the ominous shaft. "What is this?"

"I believe it's called a tunnel," Evelyn said with a snicker.

Joanna playfully glared at Evelyn as she took a step into the dark passageway. The smell of earth was thick in the air, and as a leaf crackled under her foot, the sound echoed off the arched ceiling high above her head. Turning to look at Evelyn, she said, "Okay, so I get it's a tunnel, and by the light over there, it goes completely under the patio. Right?"

"You are correct."

"But why is it here?"

"I asked myself the same question over thirty years ago, so I did some investigation and discovered that when the Egertons bought the land, they chose this particular spot for their house because of the hill. It overlooks the rear of the property, and they wanted to be able to look out over their land and their gardens."

"All right, you're making sense so far."

"The story goes that when they commissioned the architect to design their home, they gave him quite a challenge. They demanded nothing blocked the view of their land, meaning no barns or carriage houses on the property, at least not where they could see them."

Joanna sighed. "I'm sorry, Evelyn. I'm not following."

"That's okay, dear. I'll show you," Evelyn said as she pulled a small flashlight from her pocket. Flicking it on, she motioned for Joanna to follow. Halfway down the tunnel, Evelyn stopped. Directing the light at the wall, she slowly moved it across the stone until a section of brick came into view. "Notice anything?"

"Sorry, Evelyn, but I still don't understand. So they ran out of rock. It's not like anyone could ever see it down here."

"No, unfortunately, the idiot responsible for putting slate on the patio did this about eighty years ago, but before that, there were doors here...leading to the carriage house."

"What! It was *under* the house?"

"Yes, quite ingenious when you think about it. I mean, lots of homes have basements, but very few are large enough to hold horses and carriages, along with sleeping quarters for the stable master, the grooms, and the footmen, I might add."

"And that bloody idiot walled it in! My God, what was he thinking?"

"He apparently wanted to use the space for something else. Let's go back inside, and I'll show you."

***

A short time later, Joanna followed Evelyn into a section of the house she had not yet visited. Situated off the kitchen, Evelyn explained that it was originally used as servants' quarters, but since Addison refused to have any of the staff living under her roof, changes were made. The first of the three bedrooms had been turned into an office for Evelyn, and the second remained as a bedroom, but it was only used by Evelyn on the rare occasion when she had to spend the night. The third and largest room had been converted to hold not only the laundry facilities, but also a small lounge for the staff.

After giving Joanna a short tour of the area, Evelyn led her back the way they came, and after closing the door leading to the kitchen, Evelyn opened yet another one hidden behind the first. Turning on the light, she motioned toward the stairway leading down. "After you."

"Okay," Joanna said, cautiously walking down the steps. As she reached the bottom, she noticed the walls of the spacious room were lined with shelves, a few of which held paper goods and household supplies. "Let me guess...the pantry?"

"Very good," Evelyn said, walking past her to open a narrow door. "And through here is the wine cellar."

"Now you're talking," Joanna said, happily following Evelyn into the ante-chamber.

Like the pantry, the floor of the sizable room was dirt and the walls stone, but in place of shelving holding supplies, two rickety wooden racks with crisscrossed partitions stood against a wall. Bottles poked out of almost every opening Joanna could see, and while some were rather dusty, others were not.

"I'm still not seeing it," Joanna said, turning to Evelyn. "I'll give you these rooms are big, but how could they possibly hold carriages, let alone horses?"

"They couldn't," Evelyn said as she pointed to the far corner of the wine cellar. "But through that door is what takes up most of the space."

Joanna looked past Evelyn at the battered door and then back at Evelyn. "You're not setting me up for some sort of joke, are you?"

"Hardly," Evelyn said with a laugh. "Go on, open it. I'm not sure impressed is the right word, but I do believe you'll find it ...um...interesting."

"Okay, but I swear if something jumps out at me, you are no longer my friend," Joanna said as she walked over and slid the iron latch from its keeper. The door instantly popped open and just as quickly Joanna was awash in warm air smelling of bleach. Running her hand down the wall, Joanna found the light switch and flipped it on.

"Oh my God," she said, quickly looking back at Evelyn. "It's a pool!"

Without waiting for a response, Joanna took another step and stared slack-jawed at the rectangular swimming pool, the surface of the water gently rippling as the filter did its job.

"This is why he walled it off," Evelyn said, coming to a stop next to Joanna. "I'm assuming the barn doors didn't keep out the cold, so after they concreted the floor and put in the pool, they bricked up the openings. And in case you're wondering, the exercise area is down there on the right."

Still unable to form a sentence, Joanna headed toward the light streaming from the far corner of the room, but when she reached the alcove, her mouth dropped open. The area was filled with an array of high-end fitness aids, but it was impossible not to notice something else. Every piece of equipment was dotted with spots of rust. Taking a deep breath of the moist air, she glanced toward the ceiling and saw that the acoustical tiles had fared no better. Each was showing stains caused by the humidity.

"I'm afraid the rust is a constant problem down here. We have to replace the equipment every few years because of it," Evelyn said, walking into the room. "There's an exhaust system, but it's fairly antiquated, and it's not like she doesn't have the money to buy new when it's needed."

Noticing that there were two more doors on opposite walls of the area, Joanna asked, "And what's behind those?"

"Well, the one on the right leads to a stairway and a lot of rock."

"Rock?"

"Yes, when they were digging the foundation for the home, they discovered a great deal of bedrock just below the surface, but the Egertons didn't want to move the house, so they built around it."

"And the stairway?"

"It leads to Addison's study."

"Oh, so that's how she gets down here."

"Exactly."

"And what about the other door?"

"Behind it is all that remains of the original stables, plus a small section that holds all the heating and water systems for the house, plus the pool filter, of course, and the rest is just a lot of support columns and dirt floors," Evelyn said, wiping her brow. "I don't know about you, but this humidity is getting to me. Do you mind if we go back upstairs?"

"No, not at all, but are you sure she won't care if I use this equipment when she's not here?"

"I can't imagine it would be a problem."

Chapter Fourteen

Yanking open the door, Addison glared at her visitor. "You're late."

"We don't usually meet on Sundays," Luce said as she walked into the suite. "I had to find someone to watch the kids."

Addison locked the door and then turned to eye the lanky woman dressed in painted-on jeans and a fitted black crepe top. Giving Luce an indifferent glance, Addison stomped past. "Whatever."

Luce rolled her eyes and tossed her handbag on a nearby chair. Keeping her smile to a minimum, she strolled into the lounge. "I'm actually surprised you rang me up."

Addison stopped midway through the room and turned around. "Why?"

"Well, from what I've read in the papers, you're getting married tomorrow."

"*That* doesn't change *anything*."

"No?"

"*No.*"

It was a one syllable, two-letter word, but the disinterest in Addison's tone told Luce Gainsford the conversation was over. Unfortunately, Luce had never let a little thing like Addison's attitude get in the way of her curiosity.

"So, you're marrying to keep your company. Aren't you?"

"I've told you before not to ask questions I won't answer," Addison said, heading toward the bedroom. "That's not what I pay you for."

"It wasn't a question," Luce said, following Addison into the room. "It was a statement."

Standing near the bed, Addison bowed her head, rubbing the back of her neck as she turned to face Luce. "I should never have told you as much as I did, and I'm not in the mood for semantics."

"Apparently not," Luce said as she pointed at the vibrator on the nightstand. "Did you start without me?"

Following Luce's line of sight, Addison shrugged. "I need to relax, Luce. If I don't, I can't sleep. You know that."

It was rare Addison's tone wasn't authoritative and demanding, so when her voice dropped almost to a whisper, Luce narrowed her eyes. "Are you okay?"

As if someone had flipped a switch, Addison set her shoulders straight. Reaching into the nightstand drawer, she pulled out an amber-colored medicine container, twisted off the lid and tapped a pill into her hand. Taking a glass of scotch from the nightstand, she downed the tablet with the alcohol that remained.

"I wish you wouldn't do that," Luce said, her brow creasing with worry.

"We've had this conversation before. I know what I'm doing."

"Mixing sleeping pills with alcohol isn't a good idea."

"Like I said, we've had this conversation before!" Addison said as she tossed the pill bottle back into the nightstand and slammed the drawer shut. "A half glass of scotch, a pill, and an orgasm and I'll sleep until morning. Now, I've had the pill, and I've had the drink, so it's time for you to do your bloody job."

It was indeed a conversation that had been repeated over the years, so knowing there was no point in continuing it, Luce sighed. Walking into the bathroom, she turned on the tap to wash her hands. "So, what would you like tonight?" she called out. "Toys, oral, or just feel you up until you come?"

Not at all surprised that Addison hadn't felt the need to respond, she grabbed a towel, and returning to the bedroom as she dried her hands, Luce came to a stop in the doorway and grinned. Addison was already lying on the bed, wearing only a white fitted shirt unbuttoned at the collar, and her suit jacket and trousers, along with her knickers and socks, were in a puddle on the floor.

"You know, you should really take better care of your things," Luce said, picking up the discarded clothes and draping them on a chair.

"When I want your opinion, I'll ask for it."

Addison's gruffness did nothing to erase the grin from Luce's face. She was used to the woman's bravado and attitude. Without the occasional rudeness and caustic responses, Addison Kane just wouldn't be Addison Kane.

"So, what'll it be?" Luce asked, sitting on the edge of the bed.

Bending her left leg at the knee, Addison said, "Just use your hands. If I need your tongue, I'll let you know."

"So I'm assuming that tonight isn't mutual then," Luce said, placing her hand on Addison's thigh.

"That's right. It's not," Addison said, shifting slightly as Luce's finger dipped between her legs. "And I don't want you here when I wake up."

Slipping her fingers through Addison's folds, Luce said, "When am I ever?"

***

"When am I going to get it through my thick head Addison follows her own bloody schedule," Fran said, pacing the foyer like a caged lion.

"I thought *I* was the one who was supposed to be nervous."

Fran stopped mid-stride and looked at the woman sitting on the stairs. "No, *you* should be terrified."

"She'll be here," Joanna said with a chuckle. "She can't afford not to be."

"You're awfully calm about all of this. I'll give you that."

"What's there to worry about? We both know she can't back out now, so she's just posturing for the sake of posturing."

Fran's smile filled her face. "Christ, a month in this house, and you're as cocksure as she is."

"No, I'm not. I'm just content. This has been like a holiday for me. I've eaten every meal with my father. I've played cards with him, watched football with him, and even managed to get him to take walks around the house. You have no idea how long it's been since we've been able to do any of that. I'm not cocky. I'm just happy, and there's nothing Miss Kane can do to change that."

"Well, we're about to find out," Fran said, looking out the window. "The Bentley is pulling up the drive now."

Joanna took a deep breath and letting it out slowly, she got to her feet. After straightening her skirt, she descended the stairs just as Evelyn came from the parlor to open the front door. Seconds later, Addison Kane marched in.

"Welcome home," Joanna chirped, doing her best to hide her amusement at the shocked look instantly appearing on Addison's face. Adding a little more syrup to her tone, Joanna said, "Fran was beginning to worry."

Addison glared first at Joanna Sheppard and then at Fran, who unlike Joanna, could not hide her mirth.

Fran's funny bone was tickled even more when she saw the dirty look Addison was giving her, and taking the time to rein in her gaiety, she finally managed to say, "You're late."

"You said nine. I still have five minutes," Addison said, glancing at her watch. "Where's this happening?"

As usual, Addison was all business and Fran wasn't the least surprised. "In the drawing room. The registrar is already in there."

"Then let's get this over with."

Hearing the chime of the lift, Joanna took a quick step, blocking Addison's path. "Not yet."

"You do *not* give me orders," Addison said, looking down her nose at her soon-to-be wife.

"Maybe not, but my father is about to come out of that lift, and he wants to meet you," Joanna said, eyeing the woman up and down. "But for the life of me, I don't know why."

Meeting Joanna's gaze squarely, Addison said, "The feeling is mutual, I assure you."

Before the discussion could continue, the lift door opened, and with cane in hand, Robert Sheppard hobbled out. His face lit up when he saw his daughter, but the intense expression she wore caused him to look at the only person in the foyer he didn't know, the woman who was returning Joanna's glare with one of her own.

Joanna was not afraid of Addison Kane. She wasn't impressed by her money, by her cars, or by her attitude...quite the opposite. She viewed the woman as a spoiled child. Accustomed to getting her way, she'd growl, snap, and bark, and if the woman had hair on her back, there was no doubt in Joanna's mind it would be standing on end right now, but Joanna didn't care. Joanna liked dogs.

Tickled by her own thoughts, Joanna flashed an easy grin at her father as she stepped forward. "Dad, I'd like you to meet Addison Kane. Miss—" Cutting herself off, Joanna looked at the woman she was about to marry and made up her mind formalities needed to change. With a smirk smearing its way across her face, Joanna said, "*Addison*, this is my father, Robert Sheppard."

Addison's first thought was to smack the smug look off Joanna's face, but she had never hit a woman before, and no matter how tempting the idea she wasn't going to start now. In order to keep her temper in check, she turned to the man leaning heavily on a cane. Addison had expected he would be frail, and he was. She had assumed a man his age would have gray hair, and he did, but what she didn't expect was the strength in his eyes. His piercing stare met hers, and in the black-brown, she saw a silent demand for respect and decorum. He was weak, and he was old, but he was Joanna Sheppard's father, and he was telling her she had better remember it. In spite of herself *and* her mood, Addison was impressed.

Holding out her hand, she said, "Pleasure to meet you, Mr. Sheppard."

"The pleasure is all mine, Addison," he said, placing his twisted right hand in hers. "At least, I hope it is."

Addison raised an eyebrow, and with a nod, she shook Robert's hand with a grip neither warm nor firm. Returning her focus to Joanna, she gestured toward the drawing room. "I don't think we should keep the registrar waiting any longer. Do you?"

Disinterested in any response that might be forthcoming, Addison continued down the hallway, pausing when she reached the door to the drawing room to wait for the others to catch up. Flashing a wink in Fran's direction, Addison faked a smile and led them into the room.

If Joanna hadn't seen it for herself, she would never have believed it. Charm didn't come close to describing what Addison Kane exuded as she strode across the room to the registrar. Enthusiastically shaking his hand, she thanked him profusely for taking time out of his busy day to travel to The Oaks. Explaining that her fiancée was shy and reserved, even though Addison had wanted to celebrate their nuptials in a grand manner, she had bowed to Joanna's wish to keep them private.

The ruddy-faced man's eyes immediately darted to the woman whose picture he had seen in the paper. He was impressed. She wasn't at all the thimble-faced woman he had expected to meet, and by the blush on her cheeks, he assumed Addison Kane's words were true. He had no idea Joanna was doing her best not to laugh out loud at Addison's display, and her blush was simply due to her amusement.

Introductions were quickly made, and they gathered near a small table where the registrar had set out the papers, atop which sat two pens at the ready. Addison had come prepared. Pulling a small box from her pocket, she flipped open the lid to reveal their wedding bands wedged into slots of velvet. The moment of truth had arrived, and after only a few short words from the registrar spouting luck, life, and love, Addison reached over and took Joanna's hand.

No love-filled promises were spoken as bands of platinum were slipped onto fingers, and with the registrar's polished, black lacquered fountain pen, filled with the most permanent of blue-black inks, they signed their names...and the deed was done.

***

Fran came from the kitchen carrying a bottle of champagne in one hand and three glasses in the other, but she stopped when she saw Joanna sitting on the stairs, Noticing how the woman was aimlessly spinning the wedding band around her finger, Fran went over and sat down next to her.

"Does it fit?" Fran asked.

"Perfectly," Joanna said without looking up.

"You're not regretting this already, are you?"

"No, it's just...it's just weird," Joanna said, turning to look at Fran. "This morning I woke up as Joanna Sheppard, and now I'm Joanna Kane."

"Speaking of that, do you have a passport or driver's license?"

"Yes, both. I got a passport just before Dad got sick. It's never been used. Why?"

"We'll need to get copies of the marriage license to the Passport Office and the DVLA to reflect the name change."

"Do I have to?"

"What? Change your name?"

"Yeah."

"Honestly, it would look better if you did," Fran said softly. "There are some people out there who would just love to challenge the validity of this marriage in order to get their hands on Kane Holdings. Even though they don't have any proof, we can't be too cavalier. After the divorce, you can always change it back."

Joanna sighed and leaned back, resting her elbows on the step behind her. "Okay. I guess that'll work."

"I'll help you with it. I promise."

"Thanks."

Trying to lighten the mood, Fran held up the bottle of champagne. "So, where's your father? I thought he'd enjoy a bit of the bubbly."

Joanna grinned. "He would, except he wasn't feeling well. He went to lie down."

"Is he all right?"

"Yeah, he's okay. I just think he's getting a cold," Joanna said, taking the glass Fran was offering. Joanna took a sip, and her grin grew even larger, tasting the swirling, earthy essence of pear and pineapple. "This is *really* good."

Fran nodded as she watched Joanna take another taste. "It should be at two-hundred and fifty pounds a bottle."

Joanna gasped, instantly sending the champagne in her throat in the wrong direction. Coughing and sputtering until her lungs were clear, she eyeballed Fran. "*What!*"

Fran broke out in giggles at Joanna's reaction. After quickly looking around the foyer to make sure no one had come running because of Joanna's scream, Fran said, "Addison may not give a shit about furniture or paint, but when it comes to food and drink, she demands only the best."

"Yeah, but two hundred and fifty *pounds* a bottle?" Joanna said, looking at the sparkling beverage in her glass.

"You'll get used to it," Fran said, smiling. "And by the way, you did well today."

"What do you mean?"

"With the registrar," Fran said, pouring another splash of champagne into Joanna's glass. "You smiled in all the right places and didn't try to steal the show. You played the shy fiancée, just like Addison described you to be."

"That's because I was shocked at how charming she became all of a sudden."

"She can pour it on thick when she wants to," Fran said as she stood up. "And speaking of Addison, if I were you, I'd disappear for a while."

"Why?"

"Let's just say, in a few minutes there's going to be an explosion, and unless you want to get hit by shrapnel in the form of books and lamps flying from the study, I'd find another place to sit."

Fran tiptoed across the foyer to Addison's study, and after peeking inside, she turned back to Joanna. Keeping her voice as low as she possibly could, she said, "And I would definitely suggest somewhere out of the line of sight."

***

"Where the fuck is it?" Addison grumbled as she got down on her hands and knees and looked for the ring she had just thrown across the study.

Spying it under a table, she snatched it up, returned to her desk, and sank into the executive high-back leather chair.

Holding the platinum band between her fingers, she glared at it, setting her jaw at what it represented. For most, it was a symbol of love and fidelity, holding promises of forever within its circumference, but for Addison, it didn't spout love. It screamed hate. With her pulse rapidly increasing as her anger grew, she opened a drawer and dropped the ring inside, slamming the drawer closed with so much force that the tiny chain hanging from the switch of the green-shaded lamp atop her desk clinked against the glass.

Addison heard a rap on the door and looked up to see Fran ambling into the study carrying a bottle of champagne and two glasses. "Exactly where the fuck have you been?"

"I was helping Joanna sort out some details so we can get her name legally changed to Kane," Fran said, placing the champagne and glasses on the desk. "And then I raided your wine cellar. Care for some?"

Turning the bottle so she could read the label, Addison said, "Do you have any idea how much that Dom Perignon is worth?"

"You can well afford it," Fran said as she sat down and filled the glasses. "Besides – celebrations call for champagne."

"And what exactly do you think I have to celebrate?"

"How about the fact you get to keep your company?"

"By living a fucking charade," Addison grumbled.

"You agreed to it."

"I didn't have a bloody choice!" she shouted, slamming her hand on the desk.

"We've been over this, Addison. It's done, and the papers are signed," Fran said, sliding a crystal flute in Addison's direction. "And speaking of that, you put on quite a show. Really turned on the charm for the registrar."

With a sigh, Addison grabbed her champagne and emptied it in one gulp. "After being hounded by reporters for the last two bloody weeks, did you really think I'd want to add more rumors to the mill? I'm not stupid, Fran."

"Stupid is not a word I would ever use to describe you. Stubborn, yes. Stupid, no."

"Speaking of stupid, where is she?"

Fran winced. "Her name is *Joanna*, and you know it. She's a nice woman, Addison, and once you get to know her—"

"I don't *want* to know her! I don't give a shit if she's nice or if she's not, so stop being her fucking press agent. Your job is to get me out of this as soon as possible and don't you forget it."

"That's going to take time. Until I can find a precedent or a chink in the armor of your father's will, I'm afraid you're just going to have to make the best of this situation."

"That's easy for you to say. Your home's not been invaded by strangers."

"I honestly doubt they're going to be in your way, Addison. Because of his health, Robert will most likely spend most of his time upstairs, and by what I've been told, Joanna stays with him. If anything, you'll most likely only see them at meals."

"Great," Addison said, pinching the bridge of her nose. "There goes my appetite."

"They aren't bad people," Fran said, leaning forward in her chair. "They really aren't."

"I don't care if they're bad, good, or somewhere in between. I don't want them here!"

"Well, that's too bloody bad because as of this morning, you're married to one of them!" Fran said, getting to her feet. "Joanna's your wife now, Addison, and she'll remain your wife until we can break the will, so please stop bitching. It's getting boring."

For a moment, Addison stared back at Fran, before finally letting out a sigh. "Fine, but your priority is to get me out of this."

"Tell me something I don't know."

"Where do I start?" Addison said, her expression showing not one ounce of humor.

"You can start by telling me where your ring is."

Meeting Fran's stern look with one of her own, Addison said, "It *was* under a chair, but now it's in my desk."

"You need to put it on."

"In your dreams."

"Addison, it's all about appearances, so please don't argue."

"I don't like it."

"You picked it out."

"It doesn't feel right."

"Well then get it sized!" Fran snapped as she walked around the desk. Yanking open the drawer, she grabbed the ring and slammed it on the desk blotter. "Now put the bloody thing on and stop pouting."

Incensed, Addison shot Fran a murderous look. "Do you have any idea how much I hate it when you tell me what to do?"

"Well, then you're about to get really, *really* angry."

"What *exactly* is that supposed to mean?" Addison said as she jammed the ring back on her finger.

"You're not going to work today. Actually, you won't be there all week."

"Are you off your trolley? Of course, I'm going to work."

"Afraid not," Fran said, her eyes creasing at the corners. "Did I forget to mention you're on your honeymoon?"

Seconds later, Francesca Neary was running for her life.

Chapter Fifteen

The first few days, weeks, or even months of marriage are referred to as the honeymoon. It's a blissful time when two newly married people are in harmony. They are one. There is goodwill. There is laughter, and there is love...usually.

Joanna had taken Fran's advice about getting out of Addison's line of sight, but just because she couldn't see Addison's anger, didn't mean she couldn't hear it. Expletives were bellowed from the study and more than one vase met its demise as Addison's fury erupted Monday afternoon, but then the house grew eerily quiet. The type of quiet that gives a person pause, tells them to proceed with caution or perhaps not proceed at all, and Joanna decided to do just that. For the next four days, like a ninja, Joanna Kane became stealth.

Joanna continued to enjoy her meals with her father upstairs, but she refused to remain hidden in the east wing all day long. So, once Robert became engrossed in whatever sports program caught his fancy, she would listen for the sound of doors opening and closing throughout the house. The first was when Addison left her bedroom in the morning, the second and third were her entering and exiting the dining room, and the last was when she went into the study and slammed the door behind her. That one would make Joanna chuckle, the infantile show of force fitting of a woman, spoiled and arrogant, but it also signaled Joanna's freedom.

Up until their wedding day, Joanna's normal morning routine had included a workout in the exercise room, but with Addison home, there was a problem. Joanna knew the shape of the equipment, or rather the squeaks and squeals emanating from the rapidly rusting treadmill and elliptical, so she decided against visiting the room directly below Addison's office for fear she'd awaken the beast. So, when she crept down the stairs, she headed to the kitchen to enjoy a cup of coffee with Noah and Evelyn and then went outside for some fresh air and sunshine.

On Wednesday and Thursday, Joanna's trip to the great outdoors was cut short by the weather. Storms rolled in by late morning, dampening not only the property, but Joanna's spirit as well. However, on Friday the sun shone brightly as she stepped out onto the patio with travel mug in hand.

The air was cool, as autumn had just begun, but her denim jacket provided enough warmth, so after carefully making her way across the ever-shifting slate on the patio, she descended the stairs and looked out at the gardens.

"What a shame," she said, surveying the travesty caused by disinterest. Weeds and scrub, along with untamed grass and ivy had taken over what looked to be gardens that had once covered acres. From where she stood, Joanna could make out the tops of a few statues buried in the mess, and topiary having gone unchecked had morphed into shrubs slowly being strangled by ivy. Dotted throughout the jungle of green and tan were flickers of color, perennials planted years before that had yet to meet their demise, and deep in the center of the tangle, Joanna could make out what appeared to be a fountain long since forgotten.

Shaking her head, she let out a long breath and then began to pace the footpath along the back of the house. After her fourth trip from end to end, she stopped and peered around the side of the mansion, hoping not to see what she did.

As they had been since Monday, dozens of reporters still lined the fence, their cameras propped on their tripods or slung around their necks, waiting and hoping the new Mrs. Kane would make an appearance. Although tempted to step out from behind the house and wave a quick hello, dressed in faded jeans and a tattered denim jacket, Joanna decided she didn't *quite* look the part of Mrs. Addison Kane...yet. So, she made another lap across the mulch, but stopped on her return trip when she noticed David disappear into a lengthy brick building a good distance away. Two weeks earlier, when she had toured the grounds with Evelyn, Joanna assumed the building to be an abandoned guest house. Over a story in height, with a steeply pitched roof, and set off from the mansion far enough for total privacy, it seemed the obvious choice, but Joanna was wrong. Evelyn explained that while George and Fiona did indeed live on the upper floor of the building, the lower housed Oliver Kane's extensive automobile collection.

Again, hiding at the corner of the house, Joanna considered making a quick dash across the lawn to quench her curiosity as to what exactly *extensive* meant, but chewing on her lip for a moment, she changed her mind. It wasn't worth having her picture again plastered across the tabloids looking less than her best.

Returning to her constitutional, she paced back and forth for a few more laps, eventually coming to a stop in front of a break in the thick entanglement of the weeds and grasses around the garden acreage. Most likely trampled by the workers who kept the mulched path free of ivy, the clearing enabled her to see what appeared to be a raised garden bed only a few steps away. Looking down at her clothes and the old trainers she was wearing, Joanna shrugged, and then traveled where no one had traveled in over three decades.

***

"So, how do you think it's going?" Noah asked as he set the coffeemaker to brew for the third time that morning.

"What do you mean?" Evelyn asked, looking up from her day planner.

"Between the *two* Mrs. Kanes."

Letting out a snort, Evelyn put down her pen. "I think they're doing a stand-up job living in the same house without ever having to set eyes on one another."

"I suppose," Noah said, letting out a sigh as he sat down.

"What's wrong?"

Noah puffed out his cheeks as he thought about his answer. "I guess I just miss seeing them. Before the wedding, Joanna would bring her dad down here for their meals whenever he felt up to it. Hell, she even took him on walks around the house a couple of times, but now they're locked away in the east wing for fear the great Addison Kane might get a bug up her ass. It's not fair. They aren't lepers."

"It *is* Addison's home."

"Yeah, but it's also Joanna's. Isn't it?"

"Well, technically it is. Yes," Evelyn said with a nod. "And I'm not arguing with you, Noah. I don't like it either, but you have to remember how proud of a man Robert appears to be."

"What's that supposed to mean?"

"Do you honestly think I haven't noticed how you prepare his meals?" Evelyn said with a gleam in her eye. "Bite-sized pieces easily speared with a fork, the largest napkins we own, silverware of gargantuan proportions—"

"They aren't that big!"

Letting out a laugh, Evelyn reached across the island and placed her hand over Noah's. "I know they aren't, and I know you're doing a bang-up job making sure Robert is comfortable, but the man has his pride. I'm not saying he's the only reason they don't come downstairs any longer, but Joanna asked us on Monday to have all their meals brought upstairs, so I have to think that's probably got something to do with it."

"It still sucks," Noah said with a pout.

"Yes it does," Evelyn said with a sigh. "Isn't it funny how quickly you can become accustomed to life."

Raising his eyes to meet hers, Noah said, "What do you mean?"

"Life," Evelyn said, motioning with her head toward the kitchen door. "Having someone around who, when she laughs, manages to brighten everyone's day. When she skips down the stairs in the morning, you can't help but smile, and on the rare occasion when Robert shuffles by, we simply can't stop ourselves from wanting to chat with him."

"That's because they're nice people."

"Yes, they are..." Evelyn said, her voice trailing off as she thought about the last three weeks. Straightening her backbone, she jumped off her stool. "You know what? You're right."

"About what?"

"It *is* Joanna's home and Robert's, too, for that matter. There's no need for them to feel as if they have to hide. I mean, seriously, it's not like this arrangement is going to last for only a few weeks, so I think the sooner we start making some changes, the better," Evelyn said as she marched toward the door.

"What are you going to do?" Noah said, getting to his feet.

"I'm going to ask Joanna to dinner."

***

Joanna had never believed herself to be an explorer. The deepest and darkest parts of Africa held no interest, nor did brushing away layers of earth to find fossils buried deep, but as she pushed aside dead leaves and branches, and sat down on a granite shelf atop a raised bed, her interest was piqued. What lay beneath the overgrowth? What secrets were hidden under the layers of composting stalks and weeds? Was this garden really once as prestigious as she believed it to be?

"There's only one way to find out," she muttered to herself, grabbing a fistful of weeds and freeing their roots from the black soil below. "It's not like I have anything else to do."

With no gloves to protect her hands, Joanna carefully pulled out tufts of grass with roots not strong enough to withstand her tug, but flora too stubborn was left to stand for yet another day as she worked methodically on the bed. She had no idea how large it was, but it really didn't matter, and as each small bit was cleared to show the soil underneath, she smiled at her accomplishment. The sun was at her back, giving her the heat she needed against the chill in the air, and as the breeze blew, she inhaled the smell of earth uncovered. The rain which had fallen for two days previous had nestled its way deep into the thatch, so it didn't take long before Joanna's hands were wet and stained with shades of green and brown. She wiped her brow to push aside some strands of hair. Grinning at the few square feet of soil she had just uncovered, she got up, stretched, and then took another step. Once again clearing off leaves and debris from the top of the raised bed wall, Joanna sat back down and began attacking the overgrown vegetation within reach.

"Well, here you are. I've been looking all over for you."

Joanna flinched at the unexpected interruption and swiveled around. Shielding her eyes from the sun, she said, "Hiya, Evelyn."

"Hi yourself," Evelyn said, stopping just short of the pile of dead weeds near Joanna's feet. "I'd ask you what you're doing, but it's fairly obvious, although I'm not sure *why* you're doing it."

Joanna shrugged. "It gives me something to do."

"Oh, I see," Evelyn said, watching as Joanna turned back around to pull out more stalks and stems. "So, you like gardening then?"

"I don't know. I've never had one, but I do like being outside, so I figured why not do something productive. You know?"

When Evelyn didn't answer, Joanna looked over her shoulder and found Evelyn frowning back at her. "What's wrong? Is there a problem with me doing this?"

"Honestly?"

"Of course."

Pursing her lips, Evelyn took a step closer to where Joanna was seated. "My first thought was Addison won't like it."

"Oh," Joanna said, the brightness seeming to drain from her face as she looked down at the ground.

"And my second was...too bad."

Looking up, Joanna said, "Huh?"

"Too bad," Evelyn said as she squatted down by Joanna. "Too bad if Addison doesn't like it, because, quite frankly, this arrangement you two have isn't exactly temporary, and Addison needs to understand that. She can't expect you to just wile away your hours with books or the telly or long walks around the estate, nor can she expect you and your father to hide out in the east wing whenever she's home."

"We're not hiding."

"No?"

"Okay, maybe a little," Joanna said as her shoulders drooped. "I'm just trying to keep the peace, and Dad doesn't care where he eats his meals, as long as he gets them."

"I know that, Joanna, but is this *really* the way *you* want to live for the next five years?"

"No, of course not."

"Then stop hiding. Come to meals and take your proper place at the table. It's where you belong, and it's where your father belongs, too. And if you want to read in the parlor or use the gym, then by all means, do it."

"Evelyn, you're asking me to poke a stick at a sleeping bear. You know that – right?"

"Well, as long as you don't draw blood, I'm sure Addison will survive the jab."

"Yes, but will I?"

Evelyn laughed as she got to her feet. "I have no doubt you'll come up smelling like a rose."

"Speaking of roses, do you have any idea what this place looked like before the ivy and weeds took over?" Joanna said as she got to her feet.

"No, I'm afraid not," Evelyn said, looking out over the mess. "It was already in disrepair when Oliver bought it, and when Alena died, he lost all interest in improving anything."

"Alena?"

"My God, you don't know anything about the family, do you?"

"Very little. Who's Alena?"

"Addison's mother. She died in childbirth, as did Addison's twin."

Joanna's eyes flew open. "Addison had a twin?"

"Yes, a brother."

"Oh my God, how sad. What happened?"

Before Evelyn could speak, her mobile chimed, and pulling it out of her pocket, she turned it off. "I'd really like to continue this conversation, but that was my reminder that I have an appointment. Perhaps another day?"

"I'll look forward to it."

"Good," Evelyn said, flashing a smile as she began to walk away.

"Wait," Joanna said, taking four quick steps to catch up. "Do you know if there are any photographs around?"

"Photographs?"

"Yes, of the gardens," Joanna said, quickly scanning the weedy acreage behind her. "I'd like to know at least the layout of the raised beds, so I don't go killing myself by tripping over one of them."

Evelyn's mouth fell open. "You can't...you can't possibly be considering clearing it all."

"Why not?"

"Joanna, look behind you," Evelyn said, her voice raising an octave. "It's massive!"

"So," Joanna said, slipping her hands into the pockets of her jacket. "It's not like I'm a stranger to hard work."

"That may be true, but it's one thing to come out here and do a bit of weeding. It's quite another to clear an entire hillside."

"It's not like I don't have—"

"Lots of time on your hands. Yes, I know," Evelyn said, furrowing her brow.

"What's wrong?

Looking beyond Joanna to the thickets of earthly nastiness, Evelyn let out a sigh. "You know, I could ask Addison about getting the groundskeeper we use for the front to clear out this mess."

"Absolutely not."

"What? Why?"

"Because I think we both know she'd say no, and then *I* wouldn't even be allowed to do it. This way, she has no say in the matter, and I get to keep myself busy."

"But it's a tremendous undertaking for just one person. Don't you think?"

"I suppose it could be," Joanna said as her eyes began to sparkle. "Except when that person is me."

***

"I heard your father is ill. Shall I call a doctor?" Evelyn said, watching as Joanna descended the stairs.

"No, he's fine," Joanna said with a wave of her hand. "He's got a cold, so he's cranky and miserable and taking it out on everyone else. He's asleep now, so I thought I'd come down and take you up on that suggestion of yours."

Evelyn's face split into a grin. "Oh, I was hoping you were going to say that," she said, clapping her hands together. "I took the liberty of having places set for both you and your father...just in case."

"I'm sure the other Mrs. Kane must have *loved* seeing that."

"I think it's safe to say you can call her Addison now."

"I've done that once. She didn't look too happy about it."

"You'll soon find out Addison never looks too happy about anything unless it has something to do with business."

"Lovely," Joanna said before looking toward the study. "So, is she still in there?"

"No, Addison insists dinner is served promptly at half six," Evelyn said, checking her watch. "Which means you have two minutes to spare." Sweeping her arm in the direction of the dining room, she said, "Why don't you go in and sit down, and I'll let Noah and the girls know you'll be dining down here tonight."

"Okay, thanks."

With pep in her step, Joanna approached the pocket doors. She was not afraid of Addison Kane, and filled with that confidence, when Joanna pulled the doors apart, she did so with the energy that comes from determination. The heavy slabs slid effortlessly into the walls, building speed as they went and when they finally reached the end of their tracks, the bang that followed echoed in the dining room, causing Addison to jump.

"Oops," Joanna said with a little titter. "Sorry about that."

Joanna wasn't surprised when Addison didn't even acknowledge her existence by looking up, so spying the place setting awaiting her arrival at the opposite end of the table she strolled over and plopped down into the chair. Admiring the finery in front of her, Joanna looked up to comment only to have the words die in her throat. Staring back at her was the most hideous thing she had ever seen.

Blocking her view of Addison was a gargantuan bronze candelabra, the base of which displayed four Gorgon heads, each facing a side of the table. In true Medusa fashion, erupting from the top of the heads were spirals of twisting snakes making their way toward the ceiling. Weaving in and out of each other, the bronze tentacles hindered most of Joanna's view, and the rest was thwarted by pumpkin-colored pillar candles scattered throughout the monstrosity.

Joanna's first instinct was to curl her lip at the ugliness, but the more she stared open-mouthed at the serpent-headed candelabra, the more amusing it became. It seemed poetic to Joanna that a centerpiece displaying a woman famous for turning people into stone with just one look blocked her view of Addison.

Tickled by the thought, when the swinging door from the kitchen opened, and Fiona and Sally paraded out with the first course, Joanna was wearing a wide smile which grew even wider when a starter of seared scallops was placed in front of her.

"Thank you, Sally," Joanna said.

Sally's eyes bulged at the mention of her name. Not to respond would be rude, but to speak in the presence of Addison Kane was not allowed. The staff was to be seen, but never to be heard. Seeking out Fiona, Sally silently pleaded for direction.

"That will be all, Sally," Evelyn said, standing in the doorway leading to the foyer.

Sally turned back around long enough to give Joanna a hasty bob of her head, and then she scurried back to the kitchen as fast as her little feet could carry her.

Over the past three weeks, Joanna had come to know all the members of the staff, and while Sally was by far the shyest, she had never once rebuffed Joanna. Looking over at Evelyn, Joanna opened her mouth to speak, but was quickly silenced when Evelyn placed a finger to her lips, her eyes darting toward Addison and then back at Joanna. With an infinitesimal nod, Evelyn stepped into the foyer and slid the doors closed.

It took a moment for Joanna to understand and when she did, she almost burst out laughing. In an instant, she decided that if Addison believed silence was golden, then Joanna would stick to silver.

"This smells delicious," she announced, picking up her fork. "Don't you think so?"

Not surprised by Addison's lack of response, Joanna consumed her appetizer with glee, more than once adding a rather loud pleasure-filled purr of delight at the sweet, rich flavor of the scallops and herbs.

A short time later, Fiona and Sally appeared again, followed by Noah. While he filled the wine glasses with a South African Chenin Blanc, the women cleared the plates, and then returned with the main course of pork chops, roasted potatoes, and plum chutney.

Joanna decided not to bring the staff into the battle she had chosen to start, so smiling graciously at each, she said not a word. Waiting until they had returned to the kitchen, Joanna picked up her wine, took a sip and then professed loudly, "*Blimey*, this is good!"

Truthfully, the wine was indeed delicious. Its aroma reminded Joanna of spring flowers, and it left a pleasing hint of apple and pear on her palate, but her overzealous proclamation had nothing to do with her enjoying the flavor of the drink. Joanna was enjoying poking a stick. The only problem was Addison didn't seem to want to poke back.

Listening intently for even the smallest grunt of disapproval, when not a sound came from the opposite end of the table, Joanna resigned herself to having no more fun at Addison's expense.

While it was true, Joanna and her father had eaten several meals downstairs, both still refused to accept the formality that came with Joanna having the name Kane, so every attempt to have them sup in the dining room had been rebuffed. Instead, at a small table tucked into the corner of the kitchen, on plates of china and with silverware plated in gold, they had eaten their meals...until now.

As Joanna ate her food in silence, allowing only the occasional sigh of pleasure to escape her lips at the tasty entree, she spent time looking around the expansive dining room. Having only seen it once before, on her tour with Evelyn the day she arrived, as she sat at the end of a table meant for sixteen, Joanna felt dwarfed by her surroundings.

The table and chairs were bulky and old, and the species of wood was unidentifiable due to the stain now aged to the color of espresso. The area rug hiding much of the worn wooden floorboards seemed almost as ancient. Its edges were frayed, and its colors faded, and there was no way of knowing whether the russet in its threads was once a vibrant red or perhaps maroon.

The wainscoting covering the lower third of all the walls was most likely once the focal point in the room. The stiles and rails of the panels were thick and stately, and under the layers of paint now covering its surface, Joanna could still make out faint scrolled carvings in the wooden slabs, but time, as it had throughout the house, had done its damage. Over the years, the wood had expanded and contracted, and the paint had not, so splits and cracks were visible everywhere. The shade of the enamel chosen was a deep burgundy, and the color swept not only over the panels, but up the walls and across the ceiling like a plague.

Except for the wainscoting and the three doorways leading into the room, almost every other square inch of the walls was hidden behind massive gilded-framed paintings. Hunting scenes of red-coated men on white steeds filled the canvases, and with their trusty hounds at their side, the hunters traversed the countryside in search of the lowly fox. As Joanna studied each painting, she was pleased to see the fox had apparently gotten away.

Bored with the artwork, Joanna returned to her meal. After finishing the last bite, she reached for her wine, but stopped when she heard the pocket doors latch. Confused, she looked around to see if someone had entered, but coming up empty, she slowly stood up and peered over the monstrous candelabra.

"What the hell?" she said, seeing Addison's chair was now vacant. Joanna walked to the far end of the table and did a double-take when she saw the empty plate. How could anyone eat an entire meal without making a sound?

***

The next morning, after visiting her father to make sure he was comfortable and aware of his surroundings, Joanna returned to her room. She opened the armoire and browsed her limited collection of clothes, and slowly a smile spread across her face. Quickly donning her sweatpants and hoodie, Joanna trotted downstairs.

"Good morning!" she said as she walked into the kitchen. "Beautiful day, isn't it?"

Noah glanced over at the bank of windows above the sink. The skies were dark, and the rain was coming down in buckets, and in the distance, he could see lightning split the sky. He cocked his head to the side and looked in Evelyn's direction. Her head was tilted as well.

"Um...it's raining," Noah said.

"Yes, I know," Joanna said as she took her place at the island. "But I have other things I can do to fill my time. Right, Evelyn?"

Evelyn's expression was blank only for a moment before her eyes began to twinkle. "You're absolutely correct," she said, sitting taller on her stool. "So, what are your plans for today?"

Acknowledging Noah with a smile as he handed her a glass of orange juice, Joanna said, "Well, first I think I'll get back to my routine and hit the gym. After that, a shower, a good book, and if it ever stops raining, maybe a bit of gardening."

"Gardening?" Noah said, looking back and forth between the two women.

"Yes, Joanna has decided to spend some of her time working in the gardens," Evelyn said. "Speaking of which, if you make me a list of any hand tools you may need, I'll check with David and George and see if we have any in the garage. If not, I'll send someone out to buy them."

"Wait!" Noah said, holding up his hands as he looked at Joanna. "Are you serious?"

"Yep," Joanna said, hopping off her stool. Gulping down the rest of her juice, she winked at Evelyn. "Time for the gym," she said, quickly disappearing through the swinging door before either Evelyn or Noah had a chance to say a word.

Reaching for the coffee pot, Noah refilled Evelyn's cup. "Why do I think that someone's about to poke a bear?"

"Nonsense," Evelyn said, bringing her coffee cup to her lips. "Whatever gave you that idea?"

***

Appreciation is the ability to understand worth or the importance of something or someone, and it was an ability that had escaped Addison until today. Sitting behind her desk in the study, thinking about the work she had accomplished the previous week, she finally found herself appreciating something. Technology.

With the help of smartphones, computers, and two junior secretaries who had shuttled documents back and forth between the offices of Kane Holdings and The Oaks, no hiccup had occurred in the daily goings-on of the company that was now solely hers. Millie had become her eyes and ears, and via texts, e-mails, and phone calls with Fran, deals were made, and every slot in her daily planner for the next two weeks had been filled. Addison hadn't let anything get in the way of her business, but then again, she never did.

Rocking back in her chair, she picked up the synopsis of a company she'd had her eye on for years and began to read the report again. With pen in hand, she jotted down notes as she went, but before Addison reached the third page, she scowled at a repetitive beat that kept forcing its way into her head.

Da-dum. Da-dum. Da-dum.

Addison's head snapped up. "What the hell is that?" she said, looking around the room. She sat stock-still, listening for even the slightest blip of noise, but when all she heard was her own breathing, she frowned and returned to the papers in her hand.

Da-dum. Da-dum. Da-dum. Da-dum.

"Bloody hell!" Addison said, tossing her pen and papers on the desk. "Whoever the fuck is making that racket is going to be unemployed!" Jumping to her feet, she strode to the door and pulled it open. As it slammed against the wall, Addison marched into the foyer.

Busy dusting the banister at the top of the stairs, the shock wave caused by Addison's fury caused Iris to jump. Losing her balance, she grabbed the railing, and promptly sitting down on a step, she placed her hand over her heart. Sally, in the midst of exiting the drawing room, didn't fare any better. Letting out a shriek of fright, she dropped the cleaning supplies she was carrying, and bottles and aerosol cans bounced and rolled their way toward Addison. Not daring to raise their eyes to meet their employer's, Iris and Sally became statues, but thankfully the only Gorgon in the house was in the shape of a candelabra.

Addison ignored the women she had just traumatized while she strained to hear the noise again, but the room was deathly silent. She shot the two maids a look, silently damning them for their intrusion, and convinced they wouldn't do it again, she stomped back into her study. Retrieving the papers she had tossed on her desk, Addison sat down and began to read again.

Da-Dum. Da-dum. Da-dum. Da-dum. Da-dum.

In an instant, Addison launched out of the chair, but this time the papers and pen weren't treated so nicely. The report flew in one direction, and the Montblanc rollerball spiraled out of control in the other. She strode back to the foyer, intent on beheading her staff, only to find herself alone. "What the fuck?" she said, jamming her hands in her pockets. Addison stood there, squinting and listening and waiting for something or someone to make a noise, but when not a sound reached her eardrums, she turned on her heel and returned to the study. She made it halfway to her desk before she abruptly came to a stop and looked down at the floor.

Da-dum. Da-dum. Da-dum. Da-dum. Da-dum. Da-dum.

The house had been designed around the passions of Burgess and Winifred Egerton. For Winnie, gardens vast and ever-flowering had been her dream and Burgess had given them to her, but his obsession was born from his love of steeds and mares. It was soon after Burgess began to walk that he began to ride, and his adoration for the stateliness of one of God's greatest creatures continued to grow through the years. So, the stables being under the house served two purposes. The view from the back of the mansion was unobstructed, and at any time during the day or night, Burgess Egerton could visit his beloved animals.

Addison walked to a small door tucked into the corner of the room behind her desk, and sliding the latch, pulled it open. The smell of earth and rock filled her senses, and flipping on a light switch, she descended a narrow spiral staircase leading to the gym. Careful to keep her hand off the wooden railing, its grain now opened and raised by the moisture in the subterranean passage, Addison circled downward, the oak treads under her feet creaking every step of the way. Reaching the bottom, she slowly opened the door.

She made not a sound as she stared at the intruder, trying to discern which unfortunate employee was about to lose their job, but then Addison noticed the ponytail. Lifeless rusty-brown hair tied with a band and flip-flopping in time with the woman's strides, reality all but slapped Addison in the face, and her blood pressure began to climb. "What the *hell* do you think you're *doing*?" she roared.

As she always did, Joanna had slowly increased the speed of the treadmill over the past several minutes, so when Addison screamed, Joanna was almost at a full run. Startled by Addison's voice booming over the equipment's squeaks and squeals, Joanna broke stride for only a moment, but it was enough to send her scrambling for the safety cord to shut off the machine, hoping to stop the inevitable. She didn't. As the treadmill jerked to a halt, Joanna fell to the floor.

"Fuck," she said under her breath, pushing herself off the concrete. When she saw the red scratches on the palms of her hands, for a split-second Joanna's temper surged, but then she remembered about a bear...and a stick.

Joanna looked over at Addison, and when she saw her wearing yet another three-piece black suit, even though there was no one around to impress with her professionalism, Joanna's sense of the ridiculous turned her mood chipper. "I'm exercising. You?"

"I *was* trying to work," Addison said, placing her hands on her hips.

"Well, don't let me stop you," Joanna said, stepping back onto the treadmill. "Carry on, as they say."

Addison's eyes turned hard, and taking three long steps, she snatched the safety cord from the machine.

"Hey, what are you doing?" Joanna asked. "It won't run without that."

"Then *neither* will you," Addison said, stuffing the cord in her pocket.

"Oh, come on, Addison. All I want to do is get some exercise. It's not my fault all this stuff makes noise," Joanna said, holding out her hand. "What do you say? Please?"

Common courtesy was *almost* an oxymoron when it came to Addison Kane. True, if it was necessary when she conducted business, she could be as well-mannered and diplomatic as the staunchest of candidates running for office, but in her day-to-day dealings with society in general, she neither used it nor was impressed by it.

"You can say please, thank you, or have a nice day, but it's not going to work," Addison said with a sneer. "Until my business is done, if you can't be quiet down here, this place is off limits."

"Really? What about the bike?" Joanna said, taking a step in its direction. "I'll peddle slowly. Promise."

Addison's hands turned to fists. "You are *seriously* trying my patience."

"I don't mean to," Joanna said, fighting the urge to bat her eyelashes to complement her tone. "All I want to do is work out."

Addison knew there wasn't a piece of equipment in the gym that didn't squeak, squawk, or clatter due to its age or condition, but bored with the conversation, as she turned and walked toward the stairs, she said, "Then go for a bloody swim. It's great exercise, and it's quiet."

"Sorry, that doesn't work for me. I'm not a very good swimmer."

Addison turned to face Joanna, her sneer spreading across her face like jam on toast. "Then by all means...go for a swim."

Chapter Sixteen

Her arms slipped through the water as if it didn't exist, silently entering and exiting in a freestyle honed from years of practice. Her feet, perfectly synchronized with her stroke, kicked in faultless rhythm, and when the need for air arose, she turned her head, filled her lungs, and then continued on her way.

In an Olympic-sized pool or the twenty-five-meter models found in some upscale hotels, she would have stopped at five or ten lengths, but as her fingertips brushed the wall, she turned, pushed off and began her fifteenth lap of the twelve-meter pool.

It had been two weeks since Addison had been freed from her exile and her return to work had been fast and furious. Although she hadn't missed a beat working from her study, to be amidst the chaos that only she could create at the offices of Kane Holdings was where Addison was in her element. Barking orders, shouting directives, and demanding nothing less than excellence, she had effortlessly conquered the two opponents who had been on her docket for far too long with a fervor born from anger.

The first was a small chain of hotels which had been on her radar for almost five years. Although strategically placed throughout the busiest cities in the UK, dwarfed by their competitors and unable to update their antiquated facilities with the newest of technologies, she had watched as their income diminished and their buildings lost their luster. Having spent much of her honeymoon studying the reports again, less than one week after returning to the office, she made the Denholm Hotel Group an offer so lucrative, refusal was not an option. It wasn't the first hotel chain she had turned around, and it wouldn't be the last.

Before the end of the next week, she had done the same with a company whose primary source of income had been the manufacturing of models and toys. Tiny trains on plastic tracks and sailing ships built with glue and string were no longer on anyone's gift lists, and although once a leader in the industry of children's entertainment, Addison had spent the last three years watching Tattersall Toys slowly fade away. Technology was again on Addison's side, but this time in more ways than one.

A family-owned business and on the verge of bankruptcy, Hubert Tattersall signed the contracts to sell his company the day after Kane Holdings made him the offer. Hardly one who could be called an entrepreneur, Hubert had no way of knowing that with a bit of re-tooling, and some new presses and molds, his sizable factory could once again produce something in high demand.

With its sapphire glass and constructed out of titanium, Addison's mobile needed no other adornment and certainly not a bulky, plastic cover, but most couldn't afford titanium. They could, however, bear the expense of the newest in polyurethane or silicone-enhanced smartphone covers, a product easily mass-produced in a factory the size of the one that *used* to house Tattersall Toys.

Always one to plan far beyond the takeover or purchase, Addison's strategy for turning massive profits on both the hotels and the toy company were already in the works, but it wouldn't be until she returned to work the following week when the deals and bartering with possible buyers would begin. That was her favorite part. The end game. The time when those who saw themselves as savvy industrialists would posture and boast, spouting numbers, trends, and distributing hastily-assembled prospectuses in hopes they could persuade Addison to lower her asking price. She would listen intently and incline her head at all the right times, but Addison knew the numbers too, and they were all in her favor. So, when she left the office late Friday afternoon, she had more energy than she knew what to do with.

With facts and figures swirling in her head like a hurricane, Addison was riding an adrenaline high when she climbed into the 1952 Rolls-Royce Silver Wraith to go home. If it had been up to her, she would have told George to take her to the Langham where, at the hands of Luce Gainsford, she would have had her energy pleasantly depleted, but knowing the woman was on holiday in Spain left Addison with only one option. It was an option she knew all too well.

As soon as she was old enough to reach the pedals on the stationary bike, she had begun spending a few hours every night in the exercise room one floor below her father's office. Waiting until liquor took him to his own dreamless sleep, when his snoring could be heard from the games room, she would creep into his office, descend the spiral stairs and exercise until her young body gleamed with sweat. Like everything in her life, she would push herself, forcing a few more minutes on the bike or a few more laps in the pool until she barely had the strength to make it back to her room. Collapsing on her bed, sleep would come, and if she were lucky, for a few hours, her mind would quiet. She wasn't lucky often, but upon losing her virginity at the age of fifteen, obtaining a prescription for sleeping pills at the age of eighteen, and developing a taste for scotch before she reached twenty, Addison had hit the trifecta...at least when it came to sleeping.

Coming to the end of her twentieth lap, Addison slowed her stroke and glided to the wall, pulling off her goggles and tossing them on the deck before resting one hand on the side of the pool. She took a moment to catch her breath, and after running her fingers through her hair, she slowly scissor-kicked her way to the ladder in the corner.

When Addison climbed out of the pool, she glanced at the door leading to the wine cellar and then silently admonished herself for her inability to break a habit born in her youth. More than once the staff had reported to her father that while he was at work, she had been found in an area forbidden. They had always come through *that* door. Pushing it open so hard it would bang against the wall, they'd order her out of the water, and when her father eventually came home, punishments would follow. But she was no longer a child cowering in the shadows, and servants no longer entered any room without her permission. So, ridding herself of the memories with a shake of her head, Addison hooked her fingers in the straps of her one-piece black Speedo and stripped it from her body. It slipped from her fingers and landed with a splat against the damp concrete floor, where it would remain until someone else picked it up. When next she returned to the pool, she knew the Speedo would be back in its place, cleaned, dried, and folded neatly atop a fluffy white towel in the bath area.

Like so many other parts of the house, the gym's bath had fared no better. Once separated from the pool by a wall, the moisture had done its damage. The plaster and lath had long since rotted away, and by the time her father had purchased The Oaks, the only thing allowing any privacy was a vinyl curtain hung from a long drapery pole, behind which was a sink, toilet, bench, and shower. Every year Evelyn would have the rusty rod and plastic curtain replaced, but Addison had never noticed. For her, the area was only a means to an end.

Pushing aside the curtain, Addison turned on the taps in the shower and then stepped under the warm spray. For the most part, the calisthenics performed for the past two hours had slowed her adrenaline, and she breathed easily, her mind more on ridding herself of the offensive chlorine than on the business dealings which would occur the following week. A short while later, she emerged feeling refreshed and then continued a routine that was a carbon copy of one she had repeated dozens of times.

After toweling herself off, Addison pulled the tracksuit from the padded hanger dangling from a hook on the wall, and after donning the pants and tank top, she sat down long enough to pull on her socks before heading back upstairs. She was mindless of the lights she had left on and didn't give a second thought about stepping around the clothes she had worn to the office that day, now littering the floor near the treadmill, for Addison had a staff to keep things tidy. It was not *her* job. It was theirs.

Ascending the spiral stairs, she entered her study, walked to the credenza and poured herself a healthy dose of scotch. Taking a sip, she welcomed the warmth in her throat from the single malt and then exited the office with glass in hand.

Those employed had long since gone, and those encroaching on her life were asleep in their beds, so as Addison made her way through the dimly lit foyer, the only sound heard was the faint ticking of the mantle clock in the drawing room. Unlike those who may have been bothered by being alone in a mansion the size of The Oaks, filled with gloom and shadows, Addison relished the stillness around her. As a child, there had been many nights when she had trembled in her room listening to the drunken tirades of a man mourning a wife long since gone, so she now embraced the solitude surrounding her because with it came freedom. It was the only time she would allow her hardened façade to fall away and reveal the woman underneath.

Although not gregarious by any stretch of the imagination, just the fact she was walking across the foyer in socked feet made her feel normal. She was free of her name and of her wealth, free of the empire she had built, and free of those who tried to grovel and impress in hopes of an audience with the president of Kane Holdings. In the darkness of the evening, with her mind now void of business, Addison was at peace.

Addison headed to the kitchen, and opening the door of the commercial refrigerator, she perused the collection of frosty containers filling one shelf. Grabbing a pint of chocolate-raspberry ripple ice cream, she walked over to the center island to retrieve a spoon lying atop a linen napkin before she leaned against the corner. She crossed her legs at the ankles, and like she had done for most of her life, alone and in silence, Addison enjoyed her dessert.

A short time later, bored with the flavor, she dropped the tub and spoon on the counter, picked up her glass of scotch and left the room, slowly climbing the stairs as exhaustion finally began to set in. Entering her bedroom, Addison flicked on the second of four switches on the wall and with only the light of the bedside lamp illuminating the room, she placed her glass on the nightstand and then made her way to the master bath for her final shower of the night. The first had only eliminated the chlorine, but with the help of luxury soaps smelling of almond and honey and hair care products scented with coconut, when she emerged from this shower she smelled almost as much as she was worth.

Addison slipped on her black silk pajamas and then looked at herself in the mirror. She ran her fingers through her hair several times, enjoying the fact there was no gel locking it into place. She had debated numerous times about using it, but she believed anything feminine would show weakness, including the natural waves of her dark brown hair. So, the ambiguity of her gender remained hidden behind suits and hair product. After finger-combing her hair one last time, Addison brushed her teeth and headed to bed.

Sitting on the edge of the king size mattress, she opened the nightstand drawer and pulled out a bottle of pills. Tapping one out, she popped it into her mouth and washed it down with the rest of her scotch, thus ending her nightly routine. Flicking off the light, she waited for the alcohol and barbiturate to take effect.

***

Since moving to The Oaks, Joanna's morning regimen was much like Addison's nightly one, unwavering and predictable, except on the weekends. On Saturdays and Sundays, Joanna became the reincarnation of the young Addison Kane, banished from most areas of the home simply because she existed.

Joanna spent Saturday afternoon and Sunday morning continuing her safari through the jungle of gardens, but when the rains began, she sloshed back inside. After taking a quick shower, she made her way to her father's room.

Expecting to find him either snoozing or intent on the latest football match, when she saw him standing by the window staring out the rain-spattered glass, her momentum stopped. One glimpse at the television proved it to be on and in working order, and Joanna knew enough about sports to recognize, by the colors of the jerseys, the teams playing were two of her father's favorites. She scratched her head as she looked around, and noticing a few tabloids at the foot of the bed, she went over and picked one up.

"Not like you to read this rubbish," she said, tossing the newspaper back on the bed.

Slowly, Robert turned to face his daughter. "And I wish I hadn't."

"What?"

"So, you're a gardener now?" he said, gesturing toward the window with his head. "The hired help?"

"What are you talking about?" Joanna said, grinning as she walked toward him. "You know I'm just doing it to keep busy. We chat about this every morning. Did you forget?"

"No, I didn't," Robert said, limping by his daughter to get to the bed. Sitting on the edge, he picked up one of the tabloids. "The nurses leave these around. I don't usually pay them any mind, but this morning I did." Raising his eyes to meet his daughter's, he said, "They're filled with articles about you."

"Me?" Joanna said, her voice raising an octave.

"Column after column of ugliness and lies," Robert said, tossing the paper aside. "Calling you a cleaner, a janitor...an ugly illiterate who most likely blackmailed Kane into marrying her. Do you know that photo of you they keep using? They're saying your cheeks aren't filled with nuts...they're filled with *gold*."

Hearing a blip of a laugh escape Joanna's lips, Robert's eyes turned dark. "Do you think this is funny?" he growled. "That the whole bloody world is calling my daughter a *thief*! It's bad enough they believe that you're a sodding dyke, but now they're calling you a common grifter!"

"Dad, relax," Joanna said, sitting on the bed. "You and I both know it's not true."

"Oh, so that makes it okay?" Robert said. "I know we don't have any family, but what about the friends we made in Burnt Oak, or those people you worked with at the bookstore? What about those churches you cleaned? Do you really want those priests and pastors to think you're a bloody thief?"

"Of course not, Dad, but what do you want me to do?"

Grasping the handle of his cane, Robert pushed himself to his feet. "I want you to stop hiding! I want you to stop spending your days bored out of your mind, and your meals holed up with me in the kitchen or up here for fear of upsetting that woman. This is as much your house as it is hers, and since this is the life *you* chose...start bloody *living* it!"

"I am living it, Dad. When she's not around..."

"That's exactly my point!" Robert said, pounding his cane on the floor. "That woman..." Robert stopped, running his fingers through his hair, "Oh hell, what's her name."

"Who?"

"Older one. Seems to run the place."

"Oh, you mean Evelyn."

"Yeah, that's right," Robert said, nodding. "She told me you ate dinner with Kane one night. Is that true?"

"Yes. It was when you had the cold."

"Why did you stop?"

"Sorry?"

"Why was it only one meal?"

"Look, Dad, I only did it because Evelyn thought I should start taking my place around here given the fact I'm Addison's wife, but it fell flat. Addison acted like I didn't even exist. She didn't say one word. Hell, she didn't even make a sound. Besides, I'm not going to have you eating supper up here alone."

Robert's expression hardened, his eyes turning to slits as he looked at his daughter. "Well, from now on you *are*. I agree with Evelyn, and you're going to take your proper place in this house, and you *are* going to stop hiding. You're going to prove to the world you're not a thief. You're not ugly, and you're not stupid. And you're going to prove to that woman you *married* she will *not* walk all over you! I didn't raise my daughter to be a doormat for anyone, and right now I couldn't be more ashamed of you if I tried. Not only do I have to live with the fact people think you're perverted, but now I know they also think you're a swindler!"

If it hadn't been for the scarlet of Robert's face, Joanna would have tried to continue the conversation, but two things stopped her. Her father's health, and the fact he was right.

Finding it easier to appease than provoke, Joanna had done exactly what Addison Kane had wanted her to do. True, she had agreed to the marriage only to provide a better life for her father, but along the way she had forgotten something. She deserved one, too.

***

"I take the afternoon off, and I come back to find some changes have been made," Evelyn said, smiling at Joanna as she walked down the stairs.

"Hi, Evelyn," Joanna said as she reached the bottom step. "What did you hear?"

"I heard you'll be eating dinner in the dining room from now on, but I was expecting your father to join you," Evelyn said, looking toward the lift. "He's not?"

"No, he basically told me I made my bed, so now I have to lie in it."

"Oh, my."

"It's okay," Joanna said, snickering. "He's just a bit cantankerous at the moment. He saw some articles in the tabloids and now thinks the world believes I'm some unscrupulous woman. He told me to stop being a doormat and take my place in this house."

"I can't say I disagree."

"Don't remind me," Joanna said, grinning.

Evelyn returned Joanna's grin with one of her own. "Well, I've been told the table's already set for two," she said, motioning toward the dining room. "Would it help if I wished you luck?"

Joanna considered Evelyn's question and then let out a laugh. "Just tell Noah I'd like red wine tonight, and lots of it."

Chapter Seventeen

Addison had spent the last hour listening to the noise that was Joanna. Between her vocal enjoyment of her meal and her silverware occasionally clanking against the china, it was all Addison could do not to get up and pummel the woman. So, as soon as her appetite was sated, Addison's only thought was escape. Get away from the annoyance, the noise, and the woman who was now her wife, but as she headed for the door, she glanced in Joanna's direction and immediately stopped. Joanna was wearing jeans and a loose-fitting blouse, and on her feet were a pair of loafers, shabby and scuffed. She looked like she belonged in a food line, and Addison's blood pressure skyrocketed.

Hearing the faintest of sounds, Joanna looked up and saw Addison staring back at her from across the room. Her stare was colder than the color of her eyes.

For a few seconds, they had a silent duel of wills as they stared at each other until Addison's patience ran out. "You're not dressed."

Joanna raised an eyebrow and looked down. Just as she suspected, she was definitely *not* naked. "Yes, I am," she said as she popped up her head.

"You are not *properly* dressed," Addison said, enunciating every syllable spoken.

"Define proper," Joanna said, getting up from her chair.

Addison shook her head as she let out a grunt of disgust. "How come I'm not surprised you don't know the word?"

"I know lots of words," Joanna said, taking a step in Addison's direction. "I know arrogant and autocratic. I know pretentious and abrasive, and I know haughty and...*cow*." Noticing that the veins in Addison's temples had swelled instantly, Joanna folded her arms across her chest. "What, you don't like my words?"

"What I don't like is for you to come to my table dressed like a common cleaner. In my house, proper attire is worn during meals. So, the next time you plan to sit at *my* table, you're to be dressed accordingly. Do I make myself clear?"

"What's clear is that you're used to getting your own way, but I have news for you. You don't own me. The staff may tremble at your glowering, but I don't. If I had known there was a dress code, I would have done my best to follow it, but seeing there are no guests in this house and there's no one here to comment on my clothes other than you, why does it really matter what I wear?"

"It matters to me!"

"Really?" Joanna said as she placed her hands on her hips. "Why, sweetheart, I didn't think you cared."

Addison's nostrils flared as she took a step toward Joanna. "I don't like your mouth."

"Well, add it to the list," Joanna said, waving her hands in the air. "Look, I'm sorry I'm not dressed to the nines, but I don't own nines. Hell, I don't even own eights!"

"Then get some new clothes. God knows I'm paying you enough to afford them."

Joanna's smile brightened the room. "Are you saying I can go shopping? Leave the house?"

"In your dreams."

"Well, then how in the hell am I supposed to get new clothes so I can be *properly* dressed for dinner?"

The tiniest of laugh lines appeared on Addison's face as she opened the pocket doors. Turning around, she eyed Joanna from head to toe. "I guess you can't. Pity, I'll so miss your company."

***

With the weeds still covered in morning dew, Joanna paced up and down the footpath waiting until the sun had done its job. As she reached the end of the path, she peeked around the corner of the mansion like she had done so many times before, immediately sighing at the stubbornness of the three photographers still camped outside the fence line. About to turn around and go back the way she came, Joanna noticed David, once again, entering the garage she had yet to visit, and all of a sudden she remembered the conversation she had had with her father the day before. She wasn't a thief, and she wasn't a grifter. She was *Mrs.* Addison Kane.

"Screw this," Joanna said, and setting her jaw, she took off running.

It wasn't until she reached the brick walkway around the garage when the paparazzi began calling out her name in hopes she'd turn toward their cameras to capture her for posterity, but the photos they managed to take would only show a blur in blue jeans. Giggling at the craziness, Joanna reached the wooden paneled door at the end of the building. Thankful that it was unlocked, she slipped inside, practically bumping into David when she did.

Startled, David whipped around to view his assailant, and when he saw Joanna standing behind him, he took a quick half-step backward. "Miss Sheppard? Oh...um...I mean, Mrs. Kane. Is there something wrong?" he asked, looking past her to the door. "Are you being chased? Is there a problem?"

"No, I just needed to move fast or get caught on camera," Joanna said, motioning toward the door. "I didn't mean to run into you. Sorry."

"It's quite all right. As long as you're okay."

"I am," Joanna said, smiling up at the man.

David Turner knew his place. A chauffeur for nearly eight years and a member of the Kane staff for almost three, he well versed on the etiquette of his profession as well as what was required by Addison Kane, so he had just run out of conversation. It wasn't his place to question Joanna's presence in the garage, so he returned Joanna's smile with one of his own and waited for her to speak.

Joanna hadn't been in many garages in her life. The last was years before when she had been told her father's car wasn't worth repairing, yet it seemed to her that all garages looked the same. Tools were scattered about. The floor was stained with spots of oil and grease, and the air smelled of tire rubber and petrol, so as Joanna looked past David to what was before her, she was confused.

A single row of fluorescent lights running the length of the ceiling lit up a broad walkway down the center of the building, and the black-and-white tile floor it illuminated was shiny and clean. Although there was a hint of automobile polish and petrol in the air, from where she stood Joanna couldn't see a car or even a tool cabinet.

"David?" she said, looking up at the man.

"Yes, miss."

"I thought this was the garage."

"It is, miss."

"Then where are the cars?"

David seemed to grow an inch or two taller, and reaching over he flicked on the remaining seven switches. As he flipped each toggle, arrays of LED downlights on each side of the building sprang to life, and as they did, Joanna's eyes bulged. No longer in the shadows, before her was twenty-four collectible automobiles lovingly polished to brilliance, and behind each, was a tall, red tool chest assigned to that particular car.

"Oh, my God," Joanna said, taking in the view. "I had no idea there were so many."

"There's actually two more. George is driving the '58 Bentley today, and the '84 Daimler is in the paint room."

"The paint room?"

"It's a small garage just through that door," David said, pointing toward the far corner of the building. "It's where we touch up dents and scratches when they happen."

"I'd hate to be you having to explain to Addison how one of these cars got dented."

A glint of humor appeared in David's eyes. "Yes, well...um...she takes it in stride, as they say," he said, trying hard not to grin. "So, should I tell you about the cars?"

"Yes, please," Joanna said with a nod.

David's face lit up the garage, and motioning for Joanna to follow him, he moved nearer the line of cars on the right. "These are all the limos and touring sedans. The first nine are Rolls-Royces, and the last three are Bentleys."

"Nice."

"Yes, they are. Especially this one," David said, going over to the third car in the row. "It's a 1951 Rolls-Royce Phantom IV."

Joanna studied the car. Vibrant red in color, with wide whitewall tires and polished chrome trim, it was indeed vintage and pristine, but she couldn't see anything distinctive about it. "What makes this one so special?"

"It was only ever sold to royalty or heads of state. Only eighteen were ever made."

"Wow," Joanna said, looking at the car again. "So how'd it get here?"

"One was sold to a chap in India. There was an agreement stating he could never sell the car, but when he died, his wife did just that. To a hotel in the States."

"A hotel?"

"Yes, apparently they used it to chauffeur their guests, but the story goes that the boot was so small it wasn't practical to use the car for the purpose for which it was bought, so it was sold to someone else. Mr. Kane was trying to collect every Phantom model there was, and when he found out there was a Phantom IV available, he tracked it down and bought it sight unseen. When it was delivered, it was in horrible condition—"

"How do you know all of this?"

"Oh, when George and I were hired, we made a point of ringing up the previous chauffeurs and mechanics to get all the information on the cars. Between what they told us, the repair records, and our own research, we know almost everything there is to know about these babies."

"Babies?"

"Sorry," David said, dipping his chin slightly as his face began to redden. "I'm a bit of a car fanatic."

"I'd think you'd have to be to work on these," Joanna said, looking around the garage.

"Shall I continue?"

"Yes, please."

Slowly sauntering down the row, Joanna peeked in windows and carefully opened doors to peer inside, while David rattled off all the pertinent information on the Rolls and Bentleys lined up side-by-side. The oldest was a 1920 Rolls-Royce Silver Ghost, and the newest, a 1972 Phantom VI, but out of all the cars she had seen so far, Joanna's favorite was the 1936 Brooklands Bentley. Classically gangster in style, the two-toned paint in beige and chocolate brown seemed to add to the automobile's vintage. The spare tire sat at the ready, mounted on the running board, and when she opened the suicide doors, she breathed in the scent of leather and wood polish.

"This is incredible," she said, looking back at David. "Does it come with a Tommy Gun?"

"You like old movies, too. I see," David said with a grin.

"Actually, my dad does," Joanna said as she stood straight and closed the doors. "He'd love to see this."

"Then we'll have to arrange a way to bring him down here. I'm sure George and I can figure out something. We love talking about the cars."

"Well, how about talking about those?" Joanna asked, pointing at the row on the other side.

"You've shown great restraint," David said, chuckling as he headed to the row of roadsters, sports cars, and vintage racers lining the opposite wall. "When Mr. Kane began this collection, he was only interested in limousines and touring saloons, but as new members began joining his club, showing off their high-end speedsters, he soon joined their ranks."

"I can see that," Joanna said, eyeing a royal blue racer with "Marmon Missile" painted down the side. "Marmon Missile?"

"It's a 1929 Racer, and believe it or not it can go over a hundred miles an hour."

"You're kidding," Joanna said, eyeballing the open-air driver's compartment of the eighty-five-year-old car. "I'm not sure I'd like to try to do that in something that old."

"It's more for show than driving now, but it still runs like a champ," David said as he continued down the line.

The next he stopped beside was a 1929 Pierce Arrow Golfer's Convertible, and when Joanna questioned the name, David quickly pointed out a small rectangular door in the rear quarter. Opening the hatch, he explained its sole purpose was to hold the owner's golf clubs. After that was a 1930 Talbot or as David explained, what most would refer to as a Woodie, followed by a 1952 Lagonda Coupe, but then the style of the cars began to change.

The first sports model was a 1953 Jaguar XK120, and while the car's exterior was black, the interior was blood red and racy. Parked next to it was a silver 1964 Aston Martin DB5. Made famous in the cinema, David opened the driver's door to point out the corded phone concealed behind a small compartment just like it had been in the movies. Seeing Joanna's smile, he said, "Don't worry. No machine guns or ejector seat. We checked."

Occupying the next space was a car that captured Joanna's attention and held it for more than just a little while. Lamborghinis have a tendency to do that.

Like several of the cars in the garage, it was also black, but when David opened the doors, lifting them toward the ceiling, Joanna's eyes grew wide. Other than the dashboard and the carpeting, which were charcoal gray, everything else was covered in white leather. Joanna chewed on her lip for only a moment before carefully lowering herself into the driver's seat.

"Oh, my God," she said, running her hand over the steering wheel. "This is amazing."

"I'd have to agree, and you *don't* want to know how fast this one can go."

"No," Joanna said, quickly climbing out of the car. "No, I don't think I do."

Waiting until David lowered the doors of the 1983 Countach 5000S, Joanna meandered around the next two cars in line. David explained the highlights of both the cherry red 1988 Ferrari 328 GTS and the royal blue 1994 Porsche Turbo Cabriolet, but when he began to talk about the last, a two-toned, blue and white 2004 Morgan Aero Roadster, Joanna quickly interrupted.

"What do you mean it's made out of wood?"

"Not the entire car," David said with a laugh. "Just the framework for the aluminum body."

"Seriously?"

"Yes. It's part of what makes Morgan – Morgan."

"Well, color me surprised," Joanna said, admiring the car. "So, tell me, which is her favorite?"

"Who?"

Joanna turned around. "Addison, of course."

"Oh, Miss Kane—" David stopped and grimaced. "I mean, *Mrs.* Kane, doesn't drive any of the cars."

"Why not?"

"She doesn't know how."

"*What*?" Joanna blurted. "Why have so many cars if you don't know how to drive?"

"Well, it was her father's collection, and they do increase in value every year. I guess she just keeps them as an investment."

"I suppose," Joanna said, running her hand lightly over the front fender of the Morgan. Tilting her head to the side, Joanna shifted her focus to the line of cars to her right. "David?"

"Yes, miss."

"Where do you keep the keys for these?"

Chapter Eighteen

Intent on the task at hand, Kenneth Richards didn't look up from his computer until the person who had entered the office was standing in front of his desk. Raising his eyes, he knew in an instant she didn't work for the company. Attire at Kane Holdings was professional at all times. Suit and ties were worn by the men, and women dressed to the same high standards; however, the woman in front of Kenneth wasn't dressed to any standard he had ever come across.

"Can I help you?"

"Yes, I'd like to see Francesca Neary please."

Kenneth swiveled to his keyboard and tapped away at the keys. "I'm sorry," he said, crossing his arms as he spun back around. "I don't seem to find any appointments at this time. Do you have one?"

"No, but if she isn't too busy, I'd really like to see her."

"That's not possible," he said, pointing at the door the woman had just come through. "Without an appointment, you don't get past this desk, so please leave."

Joanna was a very resourceful woman. She had to be to keep her father and herself afloat for so many years, so after traveling the distance to reach Kane Holdings, she wasn't about to be turned away.

After convincing David to hand over the keys to an automobile worth nearly fifty thousand pounds, she hadn't even changed her clothes when she climbed into the Ferrari. Wearing jeans, trainers, a loose-fitting vest, and a faded blue cloth jacket, Joanna had gotten behind the wheel, and after David quickly installed a portable GPS unit, she left The Oaks in search of the only friend she thought could help her out of the predicament she found herself in. Now, the only person who stood between her and Fran was a needle-nosed man who apparently liked to judge books by their covers. The only problem was Joanna's cover had a name on it...and it was engraved in gold.

"I think I'm about to prove you wrong," Joanna said with a grin.

Kenneth rocked back in his chair. "Is that so?"

"Yes," Joanna said, placing her hands on the desk. "That is unless you want to tell Fran why you kept Joanna *Kane* waiting."

It had only taken a second for the name to register, but it was the longest second of Kenneth's life. Unable to bring himself to look Joanna in the eye, he cleared his throat and picked up the phone. "Yes, sorry to disturb you, Miss Neary, but there's a...a Joanna *Kane* out here to see you."

A moment later, the door leading to Fran's office flew open. "Joanna!" Fran said, striding across the room. "What in the world are you doing here?"

Before Joanna could answer, Fran took her by the elbow and guided her into her office, closing the door before saying another word. "Now, what's this all about?"

"I need your help."

"My help? With what?"

"I need some new clothes."

Fran leaned her head to the side as she stared at Joanna. "You need some new clothes?"

"Yes, but I have two problems, and I was hoping you could help me out with them."

"Okay, I'll certainly try. What are they?"

Joanna lowered her eyes, shifting her weight from one foot to the other. "Well, I know you're a busy woman and maybe...um...well, maybe you're not the person I should be speaking to, but trying to talk to Addison is like trying to talk to a wall, and I doubt Evelyn would know anything about—"

"Joanna, you're rambling," Fran said. "Now please, just say it. I'm sure whatever it is won't be a problem."

"Well, like I said, I need some new clothes, but I'm not sure how I'm supposed to pay for them."

"How to pay—" Fran's mouth snapped shut. Stomping over to her desk, she picked up the phone. "You know that woman *really* gets on my nerves at times," she said, punching in a number.

"What?" Joanna asked.

Fran held up her finger hearing the call go through. "Hi Millie, it's Fran."

"Good morning, Fran," Millie said. "How are you this lovely Monday?"

"Doing well, and you?"

"As they say, can't complain. Busy as always."

"Well, then I won't keep you," Fran said as she sat down. "Several weeks ago, I sent you over some documents for Addison to sign concerning the bank accounts for Joanna and her father. Have you seen them?"

"Oh yes. I put them on Addison's desk right away, but the last time I saw them, she had them pushed off to the side."

Pinching the bridge of her nose, Fran let out a sigh. "Well, could you do me a favor and put them under her bloody nose, and while you're at it, order Joanna a corporate card so if Addison decides to try to delay this any longer, at least her *wife* has something to use for cash."

"Consider it done," Millie said, smiling through the phone. "Anything else?"

"No, the rest I can handle. Thanks, Millie!"

"You're quite welcome, Fran. Enjoy your day."

Fran hung up the phone and frowned. "I am so sorry. I promise you I set those accounts up weeks ago, but apparently, Addison hasn't signed the automatic transfer approvals."

"Why am I not surprised?" Joanna said, chuckling to herself. "Wait, isn't that going to be a problem? I mean, nothing was supposed to be written down. Right?"

"No, in this case, it's fine. She's a rich woman and there's nothing saying she can't give her wife some money of her own to spend. We're covered."

"Oh, okay."

"So," Fran said as she leaned a little closer. "You said you had two problems. What's the other one?"

"Well, I'm fairly sure I shouldn't be visiting thrift shops any longer, and I'm assuming that being her wife demands a certain style, but I don't really know what that is? I thought maybe you could point me in the right direction."

Fran pursed her lips as she thought about the question. "The problem isn't where you need to go, it's the fact you're going to draw a crowd."

"What do you mean?"

"Who brought you?"

"What?"

"David or George, and what car did they drive today?"

"Um...I brought myself."

Fran's mouth went slack. "What did you say?"

"I brought myself. I took the Ferrari."

"You took...you *took* the *Ferrari*?"

Joanna lowered her chin and raised her eyes, which were twinkling like fairy lights. "It was either that or the Aston Martin."

Fran burst out laughing, and leaning back, she pulled herself together while she collected her thoughts. "Where's it parked?"

"I took Addison's space. There was a sign."

Fran continued to titter as she pondered the situation, and then suddenly she rocked forward and held out her hand. "Give me the keys."

"What? Why?"

"Don't worry, just give me the keys," Fran said as she picked up her phone and dialed her assistant. "Kenneth, come in here please."

Before Fran hung up the phone, Kenneth walked into the room. "Yes, Miss Neary."

Holding out the keys, she said, "There's a Ferrari parked in Addison's reserved spot. I want you to move it into the garage under the building, then call Millie and ask her to have one of Addison's chauffeurs pick it up."

"Right away, Miss Neary," Kenneth said. Snatching the keys from her hand, he quickly left the room, shutting the door behind him.

Returning her focus to Joanna, Fran said, "Now that we have that taken care of, we can talk about the rest of our day."

"*Our* day?"

"Yes," Fran said as she reached into the bottom drawer of her desk and pulled out her handbag. "Since this fiasco about your bank accounts is Addison's fault, the least she can do is pay for everything."

"What?"

"I happen to have a hair appointment this morning, so why don't you come with me and...um...and get a trim, and afterward we can go shopping. I *do* have a corporate card, and I'm more than willing to use it."

"I can't ask you to do that."

"You're not. I insist," Fran said, looking at her watch as she got to her feet. "And we really need to go. My appointment's at ten."

"Fran, I really appreciate what you're trying to do, but I doubt that wherever you go to get your hair cut takes walk-ins."

Rolling her eyes, Fran led Joanna out of the office without saying a word.

***

There are a lot of words in the English language to describe velocity. Torrents of rain, stampedes of animals, squalls of snow, and gusts of wind all embellish the act, but when it comes to Joanna's outing with Fran, one word said it all. Spree.

Their first stop was Fran's favorite upscale hair and beauty salon, and although Joanna had insisted on no special treatment, and apologized profusely for not having an appointment, but when you're the wife of Addison Kane, you need no appointment. The owner of the salon waved off her concerns with a flick of his wrist and within minutes, clientele having appointments made months in advance were shuffled about as the most educated of stylists, colorists, manicurists, makeup, and skin care experts were led to the private room containing Mrs. Addison Kane. Even though her clothes were still dowdy, when Joanna and Fran left three hours later, heads turned...and it wasn't because of Francesca Neary.

From the salon on Kensington High Street, they traveled to Knightsbridge and Joanna was introduced to the first of many stores she had read about, but had never visited. With seven floors, if those below street level were included, Harrods was prestigious, opulent, and had all the glitter that came with gold.

Joanna came to an abrupt stop a few feet inside the entrance. She had never seen so much glitz and elegance in one place. "Wow," she said under her breath.

"You okay?" Fran asked.

Joanna thought for a moment. "Is this really who I am now?"

"Yes, it is."

"Can I tell you a secret?"

Taking a step closer, Fran touched Joanna's sleeve. "Of course. Anything."

"A long time ago I convinced myself that nice things...*pretty* things didn't matter."

"Okay?"

Chewing on her lip, Joanna turned to face Fran. "I really like pretty things. I just never could afford them."

A dazzling smile spread across Fran's face, and hooking her arm in Joanna's, she said, "Well, you can now."

***

Climbing out of the taxi, Joanna stopped and looked up at the house. It was the first time she had seen it at night, and it didn't look any better. Insignificant lighting cast weak streams of illumination across the massive slate front porch, and if it wasn't for the moonlight, Joanna doubted she would have been able to make out the stairs. As the cab pulled away, she carefully made her way up the steps.

As Joanna came into the light streaming out the opened door, Evelyn beamed. While Joanna's clothes hadn't changed, her appearance most definitely had.

Although minimalistic, it was clear to Evelyn that Joanna was now wearing makeup, and the result was subtle, yet stunning. Mascara and eyeliner now defined her eyes, enhancing their shape and size, and with the help of a hint of blush, her cheekbones had become prominent, making the dimples that appeared when she smiled even more pronounced.

While the length of Joanna's hair had remained the same, the once lackluster reddish-brown hue had not. Being the masters of all things hair, the experts at the salon had used color intensifiers to return Joanna's hair to its true dark cinnamon shade, and when they added volume, the natural waves she believed had disappeared years before, returned in force. The final touch was the addition of understated highlights one shade lighter, and the result belonged on the cover of a magazine.

"Well, I must say, you look absolutely lovely," Evelyn said, standing in the doorway "I see the visit to the salon went well."

"Yes, it did," Joanna said with a grin. "Sorry, I'm so late."

"No worries," Evelyn said as they walked into the house. "Fran called to say you were going to be late, and by the number of deliveries we had today, I can see why."

"What do you mean?" Joanna said as she took off her jacket.

"Let's just say, Sally and Iris were scrambling to keep up."

"Huh?"

"We didn't have enough hangers, and every time they went out and bought some more, another delivery would show up, and they'd have to run out again. It was actually quite amusing."

Joanna stopped and thought back over her day. If it had been up to her, she could have easily purchased enough clothes at Harrods to suit her needs, but Fran wouldn't hear of it. After buying a few odds and ends at Harrods, she insisted they go to Harvey Nichols, so jumping in Fran's sedan they traveled to 181 Piccadilly, home to the prestigious Fortnum & Mason. While well known for their selection of gift baskets and teas, Fran explained their beauty department was one of the finest in the area. An hour after they arrived, a rather large package of skin and hair care products, along with perfumes and make-up, was scheduled to be delivered to The Oaks later that day.

Forgoing the larger department stores in the area, after leaving Fortnum & Mason, Fran decided the personal touch was more in line with Joanna's new lifestyle, so it was off to London's famous Bond Street. Home to some of the most illustrious designers, for the rest of the afternoon and early evening, Joanna found herself immersed in the worlds of Prada, Louis Vuitton, Saint Laurent, Armani, and Jimmy Choo...to name a few.

"That can't be right," Joanna said, shaking her head. "I didn't get that much. Just some lingerie, jeans, and some clothes I thought would be proper to wear at dinner."

Evelyn pressed her lips together, and crooking her finger, she silently motioned for Joanna to follow her upstairs. When they reached Joanna's bedroom and walked inside, instead of Evelyn heading toward the armoire, she continued across the room to the door in the far corner. "Take a look," she said as she opened it.

Joanna's forehead furrowed, and walking over, she peeked inside. The rod running the length of the closet was now filled with clothes and below them was a row of shoes and boots. "What the hell is this?" she said, taking a step into the wardrobe. "Evelyn, we have to call the stores. I didn't buy these things."

"I know. Fran did."

"What?"

"When she called to say you'd be late, she also mentioned you were having a bit of sticker shock and were being quite frugal with your decisions about what to buy and what not to, so she stepped in and bought what you wouldn't."

Joanna walked further into the wardrobe, admiring the garments suspended from padded hangers. "I can't believe she did this, she said, turning around to face Evelyn. "But that doesn't mean I can't still send them back."

"I'm afraid Fran thought of that. All the tags were removed before they got here. We have no receipts either."

"Shit," Joanna said, placing her hands on her hips.

"Pardon me for saying this, but most women I know would be ecstatic to have an entirely new wardrobe. I must say, from what I've seen, these clothes are beautiful."

Joanna reached out to finger the fabric of a silk blouse. "It's not that," she said, her voice sinking to a whisper.

"Then what is it?"

"Honestly? Who's going to notice?"

Chapter Nineteen

Standing in front of the mirrored armoire, Joanna fastened the last tiny gold button on her cream-colored silk blouse. "Not bad," she said to herself, turning around to look over her shoulder. "Not bad at all." With the first part of her ensemble chosen, Joanna headed to the wardrobe to retrieve a skirt, but she only made it a few steps before she practically jumped out of her skin when the door to her room swung open and banged against the wall.

"What the hell do you think you're doing?"

Spinning around to face Addison, Joanna held her chin high. "I'm trying to get dressed. Do you mind?"

With her mindset one of murder, or at the very least a form of maiming, it took Addison a moment to realize the woman she wanted to kill was wearing only a blouse, the tails of which came to a stop just a hint above a pair of ivory lace knickers. Distracted for a moment by the sight of Joanna's naked legs, when Addison finally did raise her eyes, it took yet another moment before she found her voice.

"What...what I mind is this," Addison said, tossing a newspaper on the bed. "Who the hell told you that you could leave this house?"

Joanna's eyebrows squished together. Assuming the newspaper held the clue she was looking for, she went over, picked it up, and immediately tried to suppress a grin. On the cover was a photo of herself apparently taken during her shopping trip with Fran the day before. "Well, I guess we weren't as covert as we thought."

"We?"

"Yeah, I went with Fran."

"You went with *Fran*?"

"Yes," Joanna said, turning around. "I drove to the office—"

"You drove?"

"Yes, I drove the Ferrari actually."

"*You* know how to drive?" Addison said, crossing her arms.

Joanna's eyes creased at the corners. "Of course, doesn't everyone?"

The cords in Addison's neck became visible, her thoughts returning to carnage as she glared at Joanna.

Glancing at the paper again, Joanna shrugged and tossed it back on the bed. "Oh well, shit happens."

"Shit happens? Is that all you have to say?" Addison said, taking a step into the room.

As a child, there had been numerous times when Joanna had been reprimanded by her father for doing the wrong thing or acting not as he had expected, but that's part of parenting. To teach, to guide, to nurture, and to correct, but as Joanna stood there, she decided *she* wasn't the child. *She* was the parent.

"No, I have *plenty* more," Joanna said. Mindless she was only partially dressed, Joanna walked toward Addison. "First, this is my room, and if you care to enter it, you *will* knock first. Second, I never agreed to be your bloody prisoner, so I don't need *anyone's* permission to leave this house. And third, you made it crystal clear I wasn't allowed at dinner unless I was properly dressed, and since I don't have access to the Internet to get anything online, the only way to buy clothes is to go *out* into the big bad *paparazzi-filled* world and buy some!"

Infringing on Addison's space, Joanna said, "Now, if you don't mind, dinner in this house is served promptly at half six, and I don't want to be late." Placing her hand on Addison's chest, Joanna gave the woman a small shove, forcing her to take a step backward.

A second later, Addison had the door slammed in her face.

***

Addison had become an expert in *not* acknowledging Joanna's existence, but seeing a woman partially dressed has a way of changing one's mind. When Addison heard the doors to the dining room slide open, she couldn't stop herself from looking in Joanna's direction and when she did...the temperature in the room seemed to increase.

To go with the billowing-sleeved silk blouse, Joanna had decided on a peasant style skirt. In the color of caramel, the faux suede fabric ended just below her knees, and to complement the ensemble, she had chosen a braided belt and a pair of dark brown slouch boots. The result was trendy and sexy, and Addison swallowed the saliva building in her mouth.

Joanna went over and took her place at the table, paying no attention to the woman who had never paid any to her. She had no idea that up until she disappeared behind the Gorgon candelabra, she had become Addison's sole focus.

As always, Noah had prepared a marvelous dinner starting with an appetizer of artichoke soup with truffles and chives, and even though she was no longer trying to poke any bears, Joanna couldn't contain her murmurs of pleasure as she consumed the scrumptious appetizer. After cleansing her palate with a sip of Pinot Gris, her bowl and glass were removed and replaced with new. The main course placed before her was roasted chicken with Cornish potatoes and the beverage to complement was a Sauvignon Blanc with a slightly fruity, yet dry finish. Again, everything was delicious, and Joanna couldn't help but announce it. "God, this is good."

Stopping mid-chew, Addison grew rigid even though she knew Joanna was speaking the truth. There had never been a meal prepared by Noah that hadn't been excellent, but staring at the food remaining on her plate, Addison was surprised to see it almost gone. Visions far less than pure, brought on by the memory of a half-naked Joanna, had whirled about Addison's mind throughout the entire meal, and the flavors of her food had been lost to the possibility of another flavor...a flavor far more pleasurable.

That thought, in and of itself, wasn't a problem. Addison was a lesbian, after all, but the fact her fantasies for the past half hour had revolved solely around Joanna, irked the hell out of Addison. Picking up her wine, she emptied the glass in one swallow, and curbing her desire to smash the crystal against the wall, she safely returned her goblet to the table before getting to her feet. She felt the urge to run, to dash from the room and distance herself from Joanna, but fighting the impulse, Addison walked casually to the door. Escape was within her grasp.

"Aren't you going to say anything about my new clothes?" Joanna said, standing up.

Addison stopped just short of the doors, and hanging her head, she closed her eyes as she struggled to gather her composure. Her mind and body were in a sparring match, pummeling her with indecision, and as each second passed, Addison's indignation grew. Turning around, she gave Joanna a quick once over. "What would you like me to say?"

"I just wanted to make sure they were *proper* enough for you, or if you prefer, I could go shopping for some evening gowns?"

Slowly, Addison studied Joanna's outfit again. "They call that a peasant skirt. Don't they?"

"Yes, I think they do," Joanna said, looking down at her clothes. "Why?"

"It suits you," Addison said with a snort before she walked from the room.

***

September and October crept along, and due to Addison's numerous business trips, Joanna ate with her father upstairs as much as she did with Addison in the dining room.

With a wardrobe filled with outfits to choose from, whenever Addison was home, Joanna dressed accordingly even though she really didn't think it mattered. As far as Joanna was concerned, Addison's demand to have her dress for dinner was yet just another way for the woman to swing her mighty snobbish sword of power; however, unbeknownst to Joanna, Addison had noticed every single outfit. So, when Joanna walked into the dining room one night in early November, Addison again raised her eyes. It was a newly acquired habit and one she was unable to resist.

November brought with it more rain and much cooler weather, and the mansion's heating system left a lot to be desired. Fireplaces and radiators kept the bedrooms warm, but the rest of the house was drafty and cool. Dressing for both the temperature outside as well as in, Joanna was wearing a speckled gray wool wrap-around skirt and a cashmere rolled-edge sweater in the same shade. Fashioned for comfort, the lining of the top was silk and the last layer hung a few inches below the hem of the cardigan, adding a soft and stylish finish to the ensemble.

Joanna had always chosen her shoes based on comfort rather than style, but when one can afford the likes of Jimmy Choo or Giuseppe Zanotti, comfort and style go hand-in-hand. Not a stranger to high heels, although she hadn't worn any since attending a few dances in her teens, tonight's choice of footwear had the highest heels Joanna had ever owned.

Pushing her height almost four inches past its norm, the smoky-gray brushed suede ankle boots complemented her outfit perfectly while stretching her calves to their extreme.

Addison had done her best to find fault with Joanna's choice in clothing each time she had walked into the dining room, but sneaking a peek at the woman as she appeared in the doorway, Addison inwardly sighed. Again, the outfit was perfect, and while sedate, there was nothing boring about it. The skirt ended just above Joanna's knee, and the sweater hugged her curves a little tighter than others she had worn, but nevertheless, the outfit was classy without being pretentious.

Addison hadn't intended to gawk, but between the shape-hugging clothes and Joanna's calves so nicely defined by muscles pulled taut, it was impossible to look away. Drinking in the view, Addison felt her body respond to the salacious thoughts running through her mind, and that's when she made a mistake. She raised her eyes, and they instantly met those belonging to Joanna.

Joanna was only two steps into the dining room when she unconsciously looked in Addison's direction and found the woman ogling her. Before her father's second stroke, Joanna had managed to get out of the house on the occasional Friday night to meet up with friends at local pubs. Over a pint or two, and amidst the smoke, the smell of ale, and bargain-basement cologne, she had received her fair share of leers from young men, but she had long since forgotten the look, but not any longer.

Taken aback by the way Addison's eyes were roaming over her figure, Joanna forgot about the worn area rug covering the floor. Threadbare in some areas and tattered in others, in its heyday it may have welcomed stiletto heels, but that was then...and this was now.

Like a bull in a rodeo, the heel of Joanna's left boot was lassoed by a loose thread, and in a blink of an eye, with arms flailing and appearing as if she was dancing to a song by Chubby Checker, Joanna twisted herself to the floor.

When Joanna landed with a loud thud, Addison forgot for a moment that she was supposed to hate the woman. Jumping to her feet, in two quick strides, she was standing over Joanna, who was still a crumpled mess on the floor. "Christ, are you all right?"

Embarrassed and already aware tomorrow would bring more than one bruise, Joanna winced as she pushed herself into a sitting position. Looking up at Addison, she said, "Bet you were hoping I'd break my neck."

While not quite having the same velocity as a sucker punch or a backhand, Joanna's retort, nonetheless, caused all the air to escape Addison's lungs. She had strayed outside what was expected and offered assistance, only to have it rebuffed simply because it had come from her. The pain of that rebuke made its way to her face, drooping the corners of her mouth and clouding her stare until nothing remained but a sad, empty shell.

It was just another barb, and they had exchanged many, but when Joanna saw Addison's expression, she was rattled. The woman's stern intensity had disappeared and in its place was something Joanna thought she would never see. Her flippant response had done the unimaginable. She had hurt the unhurtable.

Regretting her sarcastic remark, Joanna held out her hand. "Help me up?" she said softly.

Addison stared at Joanna's outstretched hand. It was an olive branch, and to take it would mean at least for the night, there would be peace between them. Refuse, and the hostility would continue. After spending the last ten days traveling all over Europe, the only thing Addison wanted to do was eat her dinner, have a scotch, swim some laps, and get some sleep, so drawing in a breath, she let it out slowly as she slipped her hand into Joanna's.

Joanna gasped at the display of strength. Addison's grip was firm, but not so crushing to cause her hand to ache the next day like it had not so long ago. In seconds, Joanna was on her feet and just as quickly, Addison released her hand.

"Are you sure you're all right?" Addison said, watching as Joanna straightened her clothes.

"Yes, I'm fine," Joanna said through a grin. "More embarrassed than anything else."

"Well, embarrassment never killed anybody," Addison said, motioning toward the chair at the end of the table. "Shall we?"

"Yes, of course."

As if preparing for a duel, they both turned and headed to their respective seats, but as Joanna saw Addison sit down, disappearing behind the candelabra that blocked their views, Joanna said, "Addison?"

Addison let out a sigh. "Yes?"

"Thanks...thanks for helping me."

The door to the kitchen swung open, and Iris shuffled out carrying their first course, distracting Joanna just enough that she never heard Addison quietly reply, "You're welcome."

***

Addison let out a huff as she looked at her watch, and getting to her feet, she strode from the room only to come to a stop when she reached the foyer. Out of the corner of her eye, she saw Sally disappear into the east wing carrying a large silver tray, and Addison's anger began to simmer. Shoving her hands into her trouser pockets, she stood her ground and waited. A few minutes later, Joanna appeared and made her way down the staircase.

After her fall the week before it seemed to Joanna that Addison had placed a moratorium on her attitude, at least when it came to acknowledging Joanna's presence at dinner. Though no words were exchanged during the meal, when she walked into the room, Addison had begun to offer a quiet "Good evening" before Joanna took her place at the other end of the table, and she eagerly replied in kind.

It wasn't much. It was hardly anything actually, but after over three months of almost total disdain, it seemed to Joanna that one chip in the bedrock of Addison's granite façade had finally broken loose. So, when she came to the last step, Joanna's dimples appeared. "Good evening."

Narrowing her eyes, Addison said, "You're late."

Joanna's shoulders fell when she heard Addison's stern tone. "Sorry, it couldn't be helped."

"It's the third time this week."

"I know, and I *am* sorry, but my father's been a bit cranky of late, so it's taking a little longer to get him settled for dinner."

"I *thought* he was ambulatory."

"He is…well, for the most part."

"Then care to explain to me why my staff is taking him his meals on time, yet I have to wait for mine?"

Before Joanna could answer, Addison turned and marched into the dining room. Dropping her chin to her chest for a moment, Joanna let out a sigh and followed.

"This is *not* a hotel," Addison said as she yanked out her chair and sat down.

"I know that," Joanna said, coming to a stop just inside the door.

"Then I suggest you tell your father just because *your* last name is Kane, that doesn't mean he deserves any special privileges. He's only here because you refused to put him in a home."

Everyone has buttons that when pushed trigger responses. It's human nature. Push a happy button and a good memory puts a smile on your face, but push a sad one and tears can flow. However, of all the buttons that could be pushed, the one that most prefer not to, Addison just did, and Joanna's temper fired.

"That's because *he doesn't belong in a home!*" she yelled. "The strokes muddled his memory, and he gets disoriented at times, but that doesn't mean he belongs in a bloody home. All it means is he *deserves* a little consideration, and by God, he's going to get it!" Taking three quick steps, Joanna stood an arms-length from Addison. "Look, from what I hear your father was a piece of work, and I'm sorry you didn't have a dad like mine, but not all men are bastards. Yeah, he may have some issues, and his views may be contrary to the most popular, but he's the man who raised me. He's the man who loves me, and he's the man who *will* get special privileges in this house as long as *I'm* living here!"

Hearing the door to the kitchen open, Joanna swung around and saw Iris staring bug-eyed back at her holding the small plates containing their appetizers. Giving Addison a cursory glance, Joanna shook her head. "I've lost my appetite," she said, walking out of the room. "Enjoy your dinner, Addison. Good night."

Chapter Twenty

A few hours after he dozed off watching a football game, Robert woke up, but unlike the mornings when eight hours of slumber had erased most recollections, the two hours lost to the nap only caused his past and present to become jumbled. Like dice in a cup, his memories were shaken and then scattered, and what was left was a puzzle with several of the pieces now missing.

He knew the woman snoring in the chair by the door was his nurse, hired by his daughter to watch over him, but how could Joanna afford that? He recognized the room as his own, but when did they leave Burnt Oak, and why?

His stomach announced itself with a hungry grumble, and rubbing his belly, he paused for a moment before tossing back the bedcovers. Glancing at the nurse to make sure she was still asleep, he slipped out of bed and stood on wobbly legs. Taking his cane from its place against the nightstand, he hobbled from the room without making a sound.

Robert looked up the hallway and rubbed his stubbly chin. Dimly lit and lengthy, the corridor was formidable, but when his stomach growled again, he grasped his cane firmly in his hand and limped up the hall. As he exited the east wing, Robert stopped and perused his surroundings before taking a few more steps, but when he came to the top of the stairs, he paled.

***

Addison went to the credenza to pour herself a scotch, but instead of leaving the room in search of ice cream to complete her evening routine, she flopped down in a wing-back chair and stared at the amber liquid in her glass.

In a silence seemingly more deafening than it had ever been before, a few hours earlier she had sat alone in the dining room to eat her dinner. There were no clinks of silverware against gold-rimmed china or sounds of culinary pleasure coming from the other end of the table, and when Addison got up to leave she found herself missing the obligatory farewell. She should have been happy, but she wasn't. Why?

When did noise once obtrusive become expected, almost to the point of appreciation? Why had she allowed Joanna to chastise her with no rebuttal? And what was this connection between Joanna and her father that made it so unwavering?

Dismissing her concerns with a large swallow of scotch, Addison got to her feet and walked from the room. It was late, and she expected to be alone, so when she saw the old man sitting on the stairs, her forward momentum stopped with a jerk, sending the alcohol in her glass over the sides. "Shit!" she said, flicking the liquid off her hand.

Robert was as surprised as Addison, but disoriented and nervous, he did the only thing he could think of. Pretend he wasn't afraid. "Who the hell are you!" he barked. "And what the hell are you doing in my house?"

The only time she had ever seen him was on the day of the wedding, and since it had only been a few months before, Addison knew her memory was sound. While elderly and weakened by illness, he had still been well-kempt, alert, and as she recalled, quite formidable; however, the man sitting before her seemed to be none of those things. Now, he reminded her of a gnarled old tree, bent and broken by the ravages of time. White stubble covered his cheeks and chin, and the thin strands of his gray hair were going in every direction imaginable. His pajama top was misbuttoned, and the bottoms were hiked up to his knees, displaying scrawny legs and bare leathery feet. But what struck Addison most were his eyes. She remembered them to be bright and challenging, but now they were dull and darting back and forth as if looking for a way to escape. As a businesswoman, one of Addison's most valuable assets had always been the ability to read someone's body language, and right now it was clear Joanna's father was terrified.

Robert stole a quick look at Addison, trying to place her in his memory. Surely a beautiful woman with eyes the color of the sky could not easily be forgotten, but try as he might there was no flicker of recollection. He didn't know her. He didn't have any idea where he was, and quickly staring at the floor, Robert's hands began to shake.

If it hadn't been for the fact she saw his hands trembling, Addison would have taken the steps two at a time, found the nurse supposedly on duty and demanded she retrieve her charge, but as Addison stared at Robert, a memory of her own came flooding back.

A few days before her grandfather's death, Addison had been summoned to his house. Sitting by his bed, she remembered wanting to reach out to him, to take his quivering hand and offer some sort of comfort, some assurance he would be okay, but she didn't know how. Compassion was foreign to her, so Addison had left his room without so much as a kiss to his wrinkled brow, and three days later she was told he had died. It was the only regret she had ever had.

Addison took a slow, steady breath, her expression softening as she knelt in front of Robert. "Are you all right?"

Robert raised his eyes, but strangled by his fear, he could not find his voice.

When she saw his eyes glassy with tears, Addison lowered her tone to a whisper. "Are you okay, Mr. Sheppard?"

"Do...do you know me?"

"Um...yes," Addison said, eyeing the man. "We've met before."

"I'm...I'm sorry," Robert said, running his fingers through his hair. "I...I don't remember you. Do...do you work here?"

Addison arched an eyebrow, hesitating before she spoke again. "No, Mr. Sheppard, this is...this is my house."

"*Your* house?" he said, tilting his head to the side. "But I thought...I thought...then what am I doing here? Why is my daughter here? This doesn't make sense. None of this makes any sense!"

Addison could be as ruthless and shrewd as any businesswoman, but when it came to lying she had always drawn the line; however, sensing Robert's fear was getting the better of him, Addison decided honesty, perhaps, wasn't the best policy. The truth could make matters worse, and since the man was obviously confused and scared, Addison decided to err on the side of caution.

"Mr. Sheppard, you *do* live here. Your daughter...your daughter works for me, and as part of her stipend, I agreed to...to allow you and her to live in the east wing."

"Joanna *works* for you?"

"Yes. She's...she's my house manager."

"House manager?"

"That's right. She keeps the place in order while I'm at work."

Robert looked around the massive entrance hall and then at the grand staircase behind him. Straightening his posture, he said, "Sounds like a very important job."

"Yes sir, it is," Addison said as tiny lines formed at the corners of her eyes.

"I wish...I wish I could remember," Robert said, scratching his head.

"Well, it's late. You're probably just tired. Where's your nurse? I'll have her take you back to your room so you can get some sleep."

"She's sawing logs."

Addison flinched back her head. "Sorry?"

"That's what woke me up. She's sawing logs."

"I see," Addison said, her eyes turning cold as she looked toward the upper floor. "Wait," she blurted as her focus jumped from the steps to the man and back again. "If she's asleep, how did you get down here? I didn't hear the lift."

"There's a...there's a *lift*?"

"Yes, but if you didn't take it, how the hell did you get down here?"

"Came down on my arse," Robert said, motioning with his head to the stairs behind him.

"You fell!" Addison said, jumping to her feet.

Robert screwed up his face as he looked at Addison. "Bloody hell, woman. Are you daft? I'm a twig. I'd have ended up as kindling."

"But you just said —"

"I said I came down on my arse," Robert said, and quickly demonstrating, he scooted his bottom from one step to the next. Landing with a faint thump, he grimaced. "But don't have as much meat back there as I used to."

Letting out the breath she'd been holding, Addison said, "You about gave me a heart attack."

"Better than a stroke," Robert mumbled, reaching for his cane.

Robert didn't think he had said it loud enough for Addison to hear, but he had, and she did, and her reaction was instinctual. She couldn't help but look at his twisted hand and then lowering her eyes, she noticed that like his hand, his right foot was curled slightly inward. Addison quickly decided Robert Sheppard was a contradiction in terms. He appeared weak, yet he *was* strong, and even though his intrusion had interrupted her nightly routine, Addison found herself intrigued by the old man.

"Why did you come down here?" she asked, offering her arm for support as Robert got to his feet.

Now knowing he was a mere boarder in the house, Robert said, "No reason."

For a split-second, Addison believed him, but when she heard the man's stomach growl rather loudly, she said, "Did you have dinner?"

"Don't remember," Robert said, unable to look the woman in the eye. "Now...where's that lift?"

Sensing a bit of duplicity, Addison grinned. "Mr. Sheppard, are you hungry?"

Before he could answer, Robert's stomach grumbled again.

"I'll take that as a yes," Addison said, watching as the tips of the man's ears began to redden.

Robert let out a sigh. "It's all right, lass. I can wait until morning. Now, where's that lift hiding?"

"The lift is over there," Addison said, motioning with her head. "But the kitchen is that way," she said, pointing in the opposite direction. "I was actually about to raid the freezer when I...when I bumped into you. Tell me, Mr. Sheppard, do you like ice cream?"

**

"This is bloody *marvelous*!" Robert announced, diving his spoon into the container of coconut and lime ice cream. Taking another taste, he spun the container in his hand. "I never had this brand before. Quite creamy, isn't it?"

For the last half hour, Addison had stood there casually eating her black currant ice cream while Robert had devoured one small container of mint chocolate chip, before starting on the coconut and lime. She could never remember anyone taking so much joy in eating something as simple as ice cream and her appreciation showed on her face. "Yes, it is."

"Good color, too."

Addison lifted her head. "What's that?"

"The color," he said, tipping the container in her direction. "It's my favorite."

"Green?"

"Yeah, it reminds me of life."

"Life?"

"Yep," Robert said before spooning more of the creamy sweetness into his mouth.

Addison cocked her head to the side. "How's that?"

"It's like the grass and the trees. The greener they are, the more alive they are. Don't you think?"

"I never thought of it that way, but I suppose you're right," Addison said with a nod. She placed another spoonful of ice cream in her mouth, and staring at what was left in the container, she debated on whether to finish it or toss it out.

"Is my daughter a good worker?"

"Sorry?" Addison said, quickly looking up.

"Joanna...does she do a good job?"

"Yes. She's very...um...strong-willed," Addison said, but when Robert scowled back at her, she rethought her words. "Meaning...meaning when she wants something done, it gets done."

"I taught her that," Robert said, puffing up his chest. "Can't get anywhere in this world if you let people walk all over you."

"No...no, I suppose you can't."

"And she's smart. Have you noticed?" Robert said, putting down his midnight snack. "She was at the top of her class at school. Could have been anything she wanted to be. That is...that is until I got sick. She gave it all up. Do you know that? Gave up her dream for me."

Curious as to what fantasies a woman like Joanna could possibly have beyond paying the bills and sales at second-hand stores, Addison said, "What dream?"

"To get an education..." Robert's voice trailed off as he thought about his daughter. "I remember one morning we were talking about her studies. She had no idea what she wanted to be yet, but she said something would eventually click. The important thing was she was going back to school. Higher learning, she called it, and because of me...she never got the chance." Letting out a sigh, he pushed the ice cream container away. "I think I'd like to go back to my room now."

***

By the time the kitchen door was swinging behind them, Addison could see Robert leaning heavily on his cane, so offering him her arm, they moved like snails toward the lift. When they exited one floor up, Addison stopped briefly, and again at the entrance to the wing, giving the man time to catch his breath. Fifteen minutes after leaving the kitchen, they finally made it to Robert's bedroom.

Mindful not to awaken the snoring lump of a nurse snoozing in the chair, Addison carefully stepped over the woman's outstretched legs and got Robert to the bed. Waiting until he climbed under the covers, Addison turned to walk away, but was stopped when Robert grabbed her hand.

After glimpsing at the nurse to make sure she hadn't awoken, Addison returned to the edge of the bed and leaned in close. "What's wrong? Do you need something?"

"No, lass," Robert said quietly. "I just wanted to thank you for the ice cream and...and the company. Now that I know this is *your* house, I'll try my best not to go wandering about again. Please accept my apology for intruding upon your evening."

Addison stood straight and gazed at the ashen old man. She had called him an intrusion more times than she could remember, but he hadn't interfered with her evening, he had added to it. His delight in his dessert, his pride when it came to his daughter, and now his acceptance of what he believed was *his* place was as enchanting as much as it was sobering.

Running her fingers through her hair, Addison bent over so she could whisper her words. "You're quite welcome, Mr. Shep—"

"Please call me Robert. After all, we've eaten ice cream together, and I'm not one to eat around."

If it hadn't been for the sleeping nurse, Addison would have laughed out loud, but clamping her hand over her mouth, she smothered all but one little gurgle from escaping. Shaking her head at the mischievous look in the man's eyes, she said, "All right. I'll call you Robert, but in turn, I have a favor to ask."

Robert's smile faded as he rested his head on his pillow. "Anything, lass. This is your house, and I'll abide by your rules."

Casting a quick look at the snoozing nurse, Addison returned her attention to Robert. "Next time, take the lift."

Addison mirrored Robert's grin as she watched his eyes flutter closed, and after waiting for a little while to make sure he was asleep, she turned to the nurse and tapped her on the shoulder.

Awakening with a jolt, the woman's eyes became the size of saucers when she saw Addison Kane towering over her, but before she could speak, Addison pointed to the door and walked from the room.

Seconds later, bleary-eyed and puffy-faced, the nurse appeared in the hallway. "Mrs. Kane—"

"Don't say a word," Addison said, looking down her nose at the woman. "Just get your things and get out of my house."

"But—"

"Perhaps I didn't make myself clear," Addison said, moving close enough to invade the woman's personal space. "You're to gather your things and get out of my house or tomorrow morning when I talk to your supervisor, and I assure you I *will* talk to your supervisor, you won't just find yourself unemployed. You'll find yourself *unemployable*. Now...does that unmuddy the waters?"

***

Irene Rumsey walked as fast as she dared across the wet slate, her large purple brolly protecting her from the onslaught of rain falling from the heavens. Thankful for the small overhang above the front door, Irene took the time to close her umbrella and fasten it before entering the house. Flicking on a switch, the entrance hall emerged from the darkness, and after placing her umbrella in the stand to dry, she hung her coat in the cloakroom. She didn't need to look at her watch. She knew she was an hour early, but well aware Prudence Craddick had covered the night shift, *early* seemed to be the lesser of two evils.

Irene was not a woman to judge others, but when it came to Prudence, it was hard not to find fault. Having worked with the woman on and off for almost fifteen years, Irene had had her fill of Prudence's constant complaints and her holier-than-thou attitude. As far as Prudence was concerned, she knew everything. She spoke for everyone, and even though there was no hierarchy in place, pity the nurse who didn't stand her ground when she replaced Prudence on a shift. More than once Irene went to their employer to complain about Prudence's peevish and sometimes sly work ethic, but the lack of experienced private nurses had always been her downfall.

Letting out a sigh, Irene headed to the stairs. The sooner this was over, the sooner she could enjoy the rest of her day conversing with Robert and taking care of his needs. She was accustomed to the stillness of the house at this hour, and with carpets on the stairs and down the corridors, she made not a sound as she headed to Robert's room, but when she walked inside, the silence of the house was *almost* broken.

"Mrs. Kane!" she said, trying her best to keep her tone hushed. "What are you doing here?"

Holding back the groan that came from sitting in the same chair for nearly four hours, Addison got to her feet. Grabbing her mobile and iPad from a nearby table, she motioned to the door. "Drop the *Mrs.* Kane and follow me."

In less than no time, both women were in the hallway, and being a woman of very little pretense, Irene thought nothing about standing toe-to-toe with the Addison. Her job was to take care of Robert Sheppard, and that was the only thing on her mind. "What's wrong? Has something happened? Where's Pru—"

"I sacked her last night," Addison said in a whisper.

It took all the self-control Irene had not to smile, but she still couldn't stop the corners of her mouth from turning up just a tad. "You fired her? Whatever for?"

"I don't pay people to sleep, especially ones who are supposed to be caring for someone who is ill."

"Oh, my," Irene said, peeking through the open door for a moment. Assured Robert was still asleep, she turned back to Addison. "Is he okay? Were there any problems?"

"No," Addison said, shaking her head. "He slept through the night. Now, if you don't mind, I need to get ready for work."

"Wait?" Irene said, touching Addison on the sleeve as she began to walk away. "Were you here all night?"

Addison turned around, about to scold the nurse for her continual questions, but when she saw the expression on her face, Addison could tell the woman was genuinely concerned. "Yes," she said, letting out a long breath. "But I'd prefer if that stays between you and me. Do you understand?"

"But—"

Addison's expression hardened. "Just say you do and leave it at that."

"Of course, Mrs....um...*Miss* Kane," Irene said softly. "Mum's the word."

Chapter Twenty-One

"Okay, what's Irene's secret?" Joanna said, coming into the kitchen.

Evelyn turned away from the window. "What's that?"

"She never had a problem getting Dad to do anything, but ever since she's been covering the night shift this past week, every time I suggest he gets some exercise just like she did every morning, he says he's tired," Joanna said, plopping down on a stool. "He doesn't look tired to me."

Evelyn laughed. "I think it's got to do with respect."

"Are you saying my dad doesn't respect me?"

"Oh no, not at all," Evelyn said. "But he knows if he complains or pouts, you'll give in. You love him, and he uses it against you, but Irene is being paid to do a job. There's no doubt in my mind she cares for him, but she won't let that get in her way, and he knows it."

Joanna thought about what Evelyn had said, and as she did, she began to squint. She was being played by her father. "Bastard."

Evelyn chuckled and reached for the coffee pot, but by the time she filled their cups, her expression had turned grim.

"What's wrong?" Joanna said, noticing Evelyn's frown.

"It's this bloody weather."

"I saw the forecast. It's awful."

"Yes, and it's only going to get worse," Evelyn said. "After Noah called this morning about the roads, I sent out a text and told everyone else to stay home. And it seems we won't be having nurses for a few days either. Just after I hung up with Noah, the agency called and said it was too dangerous."

"That's not a problem. I can take care of him, even if I can't get him to do his bloody exercises."

"Oh, speaking of your father. How'd he like his omelet?"

"He loved it," Joanna said with a grin. "You're a good cook."

"Addison wasn't too impressed."

Joanna snorted. "Does that come as a surprise?"

"No, I suppose not..." Evelyn said, her voice drifting off as she became lost in her thoughts.

"Evie, what's wrong?"

It's nothing," Evelyn said, waving her hand in the air. "No worries."

"It's something, or you wouldn't look like the Grim Reaper. Now come on, out with it. What's wrong?"

"My neighbor's on holiday," Evelyn said, taking a seat.

"And?"

"She watches my cats when I'm away, and in turn, I watch her dogs. That's the reason I've been leaving early all week, but with this rain, if I don't go soon, I won't be able to get home. And if I do leave, there's no one to take care of Addison since George and Fiona are on holiday."

"There's me," Joanna said, straightening her backbone. "I know how to cook, and with this weather, Addison can't go anywhere anyway, so she won't need a chauffeur."

"Oh, I can't ask you to do that."

"You're not asking. I'm volunteering," Joanna said, hopping off her stool. "Besides, according to what they're saying on the telly, this rain isn't supposed to stop for at least another day. You have responsibilities at home, so go take care of them, and I'll take care of Addison."

"I know, but Addison—"

"Addison will survive. Trust me."

"Yes, but will you?"

***

The intercom buzzed for the umpteenth time, and Joanna stopped reading long enough to smile...again. Over the last hour, as she sat perusing cookbooks at the small table in the kitchen, the electronic signal for assistance had gone unanswered over a dozen times. She had no problem planning and preparing their meals, but she had no intention of being at Addison's beck and call.

Hearing the kitchen door swing open, Joanna refused to raise her eyes, preferring to wait until the intruder announced herself.

"I've rung the bloody intercom a dozen times! Doesn't anyone around here value their jo—" Addison's mouth snapped shut when she realized the only other person in the kitchen was Joanna. "What the hell's going on? Where is everyone?"

Joanna looked up to see Addison standing near the doorway with an insulated coffee jug dangling from her fingertips. "If you mean the staff, they aren't here," Joanna said, glancing back at the recipe she'd been reading.

Addison took a step in Joanna's direction. "What do you mean they aren't here?"

Closing the cookbook, Joanna leaned back and raised her eyes. "I *mean* they aren't here. I don't know if you've noticed the monsoon we've been having the last few days?"

"So?"

"Addison, the roads are starting to flood or worse, wash away. There was no need for the staff to risk life and limb just so they can bring you your bloody coffee. Evelyn told them not to come in, and I sent her home a few hours ago."

"You did what?" Addison said, slamming the jug down on the island.

"Look, can we *not* do this?" Joanna said, getting to her feet. "Let's just meet in the middle."

Addison didn't want to admit it, but arguing with Joanna *was* getting old. Although not yet ready to concede she had met her match, the woman was annoyingly right more than she was wrong.

"Fine," Addison said, crossing her arms. "What did you have in mind?"

A smile slowly spread across Joanna's face. "I'm more than capable of making our meals for a day or two, and I'll even take care of cleaning up the kitchen. All you have to do is make your own coffee or tea, or whatever. I agreed to be your wife in name only, but I didn't sign up to be your servant. Okay?"

It was indeed a fair compromise, and most wouldn't have balked at agreeing to it, but when you're raised with spoons of silver and uniformed staff, even the simplest of tasks can prove to be daunting. Racking her brain, Addison tried to think of a counteroffer as her face began to heat.

Joanna thought the arrangement was fair, but when she saw Addison's face flush scarlet, she prepared herself for the woman's temper to flame. As she waited for the explosion of attitude, Joanna couldn't help but notice that Addison seemed to be staring at the coffee jug on the counter as if it was a bomb.

The silence was broken by Joanna's loud guffaw. "Oh, my God! You don't know *how* to make coffee?"

Addison's expression darkened instantly as her nostrils flared. "I don't like your tone."

"Yeah? Color me surprised," Joanna said, hopping to her feet. Strolling over, she snagged the insulated carafe from the island and then walked past Addison to what was easily the newest appliance in the kitchen. Having watched Noah set up the combination grinder and brew system dozens of times, Joanna deftly began opening compartments and pushing buttons, and in no time at all, the aroma of coffee filled the room.

Joanna turned to face Addison and then pointed to the glass-fronted commercial refrigerator across the room. "The milk's in there. The sugar, if you so desire, is in here," she said, picking up a covered sugar bowl on the counter behind her. "Spoons are in this drawer," Joanna said, opening one in the island and closing it just as quickly. "And cups are in there," she said, gesturing to a cabinet behind her as she headed for the door. "And now that you know your way around *your* kitchen, I'm going to go visit my father. Try not to make a mess."

***

Knowing that Addison's lunch on the weekends was always served at one o'clock sharp, Joanna delivered her father his tray at noon and then went about getting the dining room ready. Deciding silverware wasn't necessary, she filled the water goblets, placed the linen napkins where they belonged and then returned to the kitchen to make one of her favorite meals.

When the clock chimed one, Joanna pushed open the kitchen door with her foot and carried two plates into the dining room. Placing one in front of Addison, Joanna walked the length of the table and took her seat, but before she could open her napkin, a voice boomed from across the room.

"What the *hell* is this?"

Joanna looked toward the heavens and prayed for strength. "It's lunch. Grilled ham and cheese on farmhouse with crisps."

"It's a sandwich."

"Why, yes it is."

"There's crust on it."

Joanna fell back in her chair, and cupping her chin, she rubbed it slowly. Feeling her tension continuing to build, she rose to her feet and went to the kitchen, only to return seconds later carrying the largest, sharpest, weapon of singular destruction in the shape of a knife. She paused when she noticed the blood starting to drain from Addison's face, but refusing to allow her amusement to show, Joanna went over and gingerly placed the knife alongside Addison's plate. "Then cut it off, sweetheart. That is...if you know how to use a knife."

**

Entering her father's bedroom, Joanna placed the tray over his lap. "Hope you don't mind chicken and rice casserole for dinner."

Robert's eyes lit up. "Millie's recipe?"

"It took me a while to find it, but yes, none other," Joanna said as she took two glass jar candles from the tray. "I also found these, just in case we lose power."

Placing the candles on the bureau, she lit the wicks and then slipped the lighter back into her pocket. "Are you going to be okay if I leave you alone with this?" she said, returning to her father's side.

"Of course. Though I can't promise, I won't make a mess."

Joanna leaned down and kissed her father on the forehead. "Make all the mess you want, Dad. I'll be back in a little while to check on you. Okay?"

Robert nodded as he dove his fork into the cheesy rice. "You go along and feed Her Highness. I'll be fine."

"Thanks, Dad," Joanna said, and flashing him a toothy smile, she left the room.

Making her way back to the kitchen, no sooner had the swinging door closed behind her when the lights flickered again, but then they went off...they stayed off.

"Shit!"

Joanna hesitated long enough to get her bearings before fumbling for the lighter in her pocket. Lighting the three candles she had left on the island, she carried one into the dining room and lit every candle erupting from the Gorgon head. Once the room was aglow in candlelight, she returned to the kitchen to check on dinner, totally forgetting there was someone else in the house possibly in need of a candle.

***

Addison sat in the darkness, drumming her fingers on the desk as she tried to will the lights back on. Due to the storm, she had lost her Internet connection earlier that morning, so she had spent her time reading and rereading reports she had already read a dozen times, and as each hour passed, her annoyance grew. Boredom was something entirely new *and* entirely aggravating. "Fine!" she blurted, tossing the papers on the desk. "I need more coffee anyway."

Confidence is a state of mind. When it came to business, Addison had what it took to seal the deal, talk the talk, and walk the walk, but when trying to cross a room in total darkness, her confidence tanked. Addison's first adversary was her desk, and her right hip met not one, but two of the corners as she walked around it. Her next nemesis was one of the wing-back chairs as it met her shin full force, and the last was the door leading out of her study. Believing it to be more than an arm's length away, when she reached for the door knob, she promptly punched her hand into the wood.

"Son of a bitch!"

Addison stood in the dark, cradling her hand until the pain finally went away, and after flexing her fingers a few times, she reached out ever so slowly to open the door. Like her study, the foyer was pitch black, but spotting a sliver of light coming from under the kitchen door, Addison let out a sigh of relief and crept across the entrance hall.

Joanna looked up as Addison walked into the room. "Hiya. I was just going to go find you. Dinner's ready."

Addison opened her mouth to speak, but no words came out. Courtesy of the candles flickering on the island, the glow of their flames had turned Joanna's hair from dark red to a fiery crimson and unbound and free, the long, wavy tresses washed over her shoulders like a brilliant wave. Joanna's smile was the most dazzling Addison had ever seen, and wearing painted-on jeans and a snug green sweater, every curve the woman owned was in view...again.

Addison hadn't intended to ogle, and she certainly hadn't intended to be caught doing it, but when her eyes met Joanna's, Addison quickly cleared her throat and said the first thing that came into her head. "You've...you've done something with your hair."

"Um...yes, several weeks ago, actually."

"Oh."

For a few seconds, Joanna stared back at the statue that was once Addison Kane before her curiosity got the better of her. "Are you all right, Addison?"

Addison wanted to answer yes, to dismiss Joanna's concern with a witty reply or perhaps even a cutting remark, after all, she was an adult with several degrees to her name and a vocabulary to prove it. The problem was, at that particular moment, Addison felt like a schoolgirl...with a crush.

"Addison, are you okay?"

Brought back to now by the sound of Joanna's voice, Addison jerked her head up. "Yes, I'm...I'm fine," she said, running her fingers through her hair. "Um...what...what can I help you with?"

It was Joanna's turn to lose the ability to form a sentence. She knew the woman across the room was Addison, after all, she was wearing her standard black suit, and those eyes couldn't be mistaken for anyone else's, but something was different. Something was *very* different.

A dozen thoughts ran through Joanna's mind, reasons why Addison's disposition had suddenly changed, but deciding to chalk it up to their situation, Joanna returned to the matter at hand. "We need wine," she said, looking back at Addison. "And honestly, I don't know a thing about it."

Addison stood a bit taller. "Well, luckily I do," she said, making a beeline toward the wine cellar. "Consider it done."

"Oh, Addison?"

Stopping at the door, Addison turned around. "Yeah?"

"I think you may need this," Joanna said, picking up one of the candles.

It was simply a gesture of kindness, an assurance Addison wouldn't meet her maker by falling down the stairs, but when Joanna walked over and placed the jar in Addison's hand, their fingers touched.

The body rush Addison felt was undeniable. It coursed through her veins like a train out of control. It had been but a touch, a simple brush of skin meeting skin, but it had taken her breath away in an instant.

Joanna forced a grin, hoping it would somehow lessen the heat in her cheeks. Her fingers had only touched Addison's for an instant, but like a lit fuse, the sizzle of that touch slithered through her body until it reached her core...and detonated. Refusing to make eye contact with Addison, Joanna scurried back to the stove. She prayed her blush had gone unnoticed, and holding her breath, she didn't exhale until she heard Addison descending the pantry stairs.

Joanna stared at the empty plates in front of her, mentally scolding her body for reacting to the impossible. It wasn't who she was, and repeating those words in her brain like a mantra, she snatched a serving spoon from the counter and began heaping spoonfuls of steaming casserole onto the plates.

Lost in her thoughts, Joanna didn't notice that Addison had returned until she placed the candle and two bottles of wine on the counter.

"I wasn't sure what we were having, so I brought up a red and a white."

Joanna was about to reply, but when she looked up, she burst out laughing. "What did you do? *Feel* your way?"

Addison tilted her head to the side, and following Joanna's line of sight, she discovered that her once black trousers were now covered in splotches of gray and brown dust. "Christ," she said, reaching down to brush off the dirt. "I guess I rubbed up against the wall."

"Looks like you became one with the wall if you ask me," Joanna said, picking up the plates. "See you in the dining room."

Joanna walked around Addison as she headed to the door, but when she noticed something on Addison's jacket, she came to a dead stop. "Um...Addison?"

Intent on removing every last speck of soot, Addison didn't look up. "Yeah?"

"How do you feel about...about spiders?"

Liquid nitrogen could not have worked any faster. In an instant, Addison became a hunched over sculpture in the middle of the kitchen. Finding it almost impossible to breathe, it took everything Addison had to raise her eyes.

Joanna wasn't fond of spiders, but more times than not she had ushered them out of her house on scraps of paper, allowing them to live out their days amongst the blades of grass and weeds. It seemed the humane thing to do, but seeing the absolute terror in Addison's eyes, Joanna knew this particular arachnoid wasn't going to be so lucky.

"Where...where is it?" Addison croaked.

"It's on the back of your jacket. Just give me a second, and I'll get it off."

A second seemed like a lifetime, which left Addison with two choices. Wait a lifetime or become the village idiot. Addison chose the latter.

Springing into action, she stood straight and ripped the jacket from her body. Tossing it on the floor, she became an enraged flamenco dancer as she stomped, stamped, and tramped the fabric into oblivion. Seconds later, the spider *and* the Italian worsted wool had met their demise.

Joanna pressed her lips together, trying to keep her giggles to a minimum at the sight of Addison's staunch exterior becoming dislodged. Her hair gel was no match for the dance of death she had just performed and her face was now framed in wisps of dark brown hair, loose and wild. One tail of her crisp white shirt had come out of her trousers and sometime during the frenzy Addison's tie had loosened, and the top button of her shirt had opened. One would have to be blind not to see Addison was attractive and Joanna certainly wasn't blind, but as she stood there staring at the woman, it seemed to Joanna that disheveled added to Addison's beauty. Gone was the stiffness. Gone was the propriety, and in its place, Joanna saw something natural *and* exquisite. Once again, the fuse Joanna thought she had extinguished was lit and she felt her face heat.

Satisfied nothing could have survived her attack, Addison raised her eyes. She noticed Joanna's rosy complexion immediately, but believing it to be caused by her laughter, she didn't give it a second thought. Kicking her suit jacket into the corner of the room, Addison said, "I don't like spiders."

Thankful Addison hadn't mentioned her blush, Joanna relaxed, and remembering what she just saw, her eyes began to sparkle. "Yeah, I kind of figured."

"I must have looked like a bloody fool."

Joanna's face split into a grin. "No, but after that interpretative dance you just performed, I don't think we need to dress for dinner. Do you?"

***

"You really need to stop canceling appointments I make for you."

"And you really need to remember who *owns* this company," Addison said, glaring at Fran as she stood in the doorway. "And besides, it wasn't an appointment. It was a party invitation, and you know how I loathe those."

"It wasn't just any party invitation."

"Oh, that's right. It was a *Christmas* party," Addison said, rolling her eyes. "More the reason why I won't be attending."

Shaking her head, Fran went over and planted herself in one of the chairs opposite Addison's desk. "Did you happen to pay any attention to who was throwing the party?"

"No, but it doesn't matter."

"Yes, it does."

"So says you."

"That little Christmas soiree is being put on by none other than Bradley Easterbrook."

Addison curled her lip hearing the name, but Fran had just piqued her attention. Resting her elbows on the desk, she steepled her fingers. "Go on."

"We've been wooing that son-of-a-bitch for months, and he's been playing us against Firth Enterprises every step of the way."

"Tell me something I don't know."

"What's the one thing that motivates Easterbrook more than anything else?" When Addison's only response was to stare, Fran said, "Ego."

Addison cupped her chin, stroking it slowly as she studied the woman sitting across the way. They may have butted heads on more than one occasion, but she respected Fran. Addison may have been the driving force behind the success of Kane Holdings, but there was another force to be reckoned with, and she was sitting in a wing-back chair with not a strand of her blonde hair out of place.

"I'm still listening," Addison said, reaching across the desk for her cigarette case.

Fran's eyes began to twinkle as she leaned in closer. "Easterbrook lives and breathes attention. From the fancy cars he drives to the beautiful women on his arm—"

"I'm telling you right now, he's paying for those tarts."

"Of course he is," Fran said with a laugh. "But the point is the man likes to dance in the spotlight. He courts attention like it was a mistress, and I have it on good authority that he'll beg, borrow, or steal invitations to the biggest events just to say he was rubbing elbows with the latest and greatest."

"So the man's an ego-maniac. What's your point?"

"When I accepted that invitation for his Christmas bash, I accepted it for both you *and* Joanna."

"And why exactly did you do that?" Addison said, rocking forward in her chair.

"Because when he finds out that the elusive Addison Kane and her never-before-seen-in-public-*wife* will be attending, he's going to make sure everyone knows. Paparazzi will be hanging from the bloody trees trying to get photographs, and if I know Easterbrook, he's going to be in every one of them."

"I still don't get your point. Just because I show up at his party doesn't mean he's going to sign on the dotted line. He could still sell to Firth."

"He won't."

"How can you be so sure?"

"Because we know what Firth is offering, and we know what we're offering, and it's the same bloody thing. Easterbrook has been riding this deal for months just to keep his name in the papers and the speculation up. Once the deal's done, he's going to be just another ex-owner of a company, and he knows it, but if he comes out of this with a story to tell, something to boast about for the rest of his life, he won't dare sell to Firth. You can't very well big yourself up about having convinced Joanna Kane to make her first public appearance at your party if you dissed her wife...now can you?"

By the smirk slowly making its way across Addison's face, Fran knew she had made her point. Getting up, Fran strolled to the door. "Oh, there's one more thing," she said, turning back around.

"What's that?"

"I know how you hate attention, but if this is to work, attention is what we need."

"What's that supposed to mean?"

Fran smiled. "You have nine figures in your bank account. Make sure Easterbrook knows it."

Chapter Twenty-Two

Joanna saw the door to the study cracked open, and deliberating for a moment, she tapped on the wood and walked inside.

Addison looked up. "Yes?"

"I just wanted to thank you for the mobile. It was delivered this afternoon," Joanna said. "I'm not sure why—"

"Fran will be texting you tomorrow to set up a time when you and she can go shopping, and that can't be done if you don't have a mobile."

"Shopping?"

"Yes," Addison said. "There's a party we'll be attending on the tenth of December, and I doubt whatever you have in your wardrobe will be appropriate. Since you and she have apparently become bosom buddies, I've assigned her the task of you not embarrassing me."

"We? As in you and I?"

"Do I need to use smaller words?"

"No," Joanna said, mentally counting to ten before continuing. "I'm just trying to figure out why suddenly you'd want to be seen in public with me. That's all."

"It's for business purposes only. I assure you."

"Business?"

Addison pinched the bridge of her nose and shook her head ever so slightly. "Yes, business, but the details don't involve you. All you have to do is show up, and keep your mouth shut."

Joanna stiffened, and arching an eyebrow, she stared at Addison. "Do you treat all the women you ask out on a date like this?"

"This is *not* a date!" Addison said, getting to her feet.

"Well, it's definitely not if you're going to ask like this," Joanna said, and turning on her heel, she marched from the room.

"Shit," Addison said as she hung her head. After letting out an exaggerated sigh, she hurried to catch up to Joanna. By the time she reached the foyer, Joanna was already at the top of the stairs.

"Joanna," Addison called out.

Stopping mid-stride, Joanna turned around. "What?"

Addison slowly climbed the stairs until she reached Joanna. She had no idea what to say, and it was crystal clear when she tried to speak. "Look...I just need...can't you just—"

"Apologize."

"What?"

Looking Addison directly in the eye, Joanna said, "Apologize...and *mean* it. I know I'm not your wife in the true sense of the word, but *this* isn't about being your wife. *This* is about respect, and I'm tired of being treated as if I don't deserve it. So apologize and then tell me what this is all about, or don't...and find yourself another *date*."

***

They say eyes are the windows to the soul, and while Addison had always scoffed at the notion, as she sat alone in her study, she began to have her doubts. All she could think about were a pair of eyes the color of cognac rimmed in gold. Glassed over and filled with hurt, they had made her do the unthinkable. Standing on the stairs, she had hung her head and apologized...*and* she had meant it.

Being bested by logic or an argument founded on facts was one thing, but being beaten by righteousness, by the hurt in another's eyes was entirely different. To *feel* was entirely different. Nothing and no one had ever pulled at Addison's heart or made her rethink her words, but Joanna just did, and she had done it with only a look. One look that burrowed into Addison's psyche, and undaunted by walls and attitude, it found its way to her heart, and the pang it caused would not soon be forgotten.

Shaken from her thoughts by the sound of something in the foyer, Addison made her way to the entrance hall just in time to see a nurse assisting Robert Sheppard from the lift.

Feeling another presence, Irene looked up. "Oh, Miss Kane," she said. "I'm sorry. We didn't know anyone was still awake."

"Is something wrong?" she asked, looking back and forth between Robert and the nurse.

"No," Irene said, smiling. "Robert just had a bit of a sweet tooth and wanted to raid the kitchen. He insists you have ice cream."

Addison glanced at Robert, and the gleam in his eyes told her all she needed to know. She walked over and offered him her arm. "I'll take it from here," she said.

"Oh no, Miss Kane, you're far too busy—"

"Irene, isn't it?"

Having a sneaking suspicion she was about to be unemployed, Irene sighed. "Why, yes...yes, it is."

"Well, Irene, I have this covered, so why don't you go up and tidy or something. I'll call you if I need you." Noticing a flicker of doubt in the woman's eyes, Addison said, "I promise. If we can't reach the spoons or open the containers, you'll be the first to know."

Irene had heard all the scuttlebutt about Addison Kane from the other nurses, and she wasn't a stranger to reading newspapers. She knew the woman was powerful and had the wherewithal to get what she wanted, but for the second time, Irene found herself impressed by the billionaire. Right then and there, Irene Rumsey decided there was more to Addison Kane than met the eye. Much more.

***

A short time later, while Addison was slowly making her way through her container of ice cream, Robert had finished his first and had just opened another.

"I'm not sure that much ice cream is good for you," she said.

"A little too late for me to worry about that, now isn't it?" Robert said, raising his eyes. "The damage has already been done. Nothing left to do but live life until I don't have one to live."

"That's a bit cynical, don't you think?"

"No, it's just truthful," Robert said, putting down his spoon. "I suppose if I had a clean bill of health it would be different, but I don't. So, why worry about having too much of this or having too much of that? I'd rather die knowing I had the pleasure of tasting the finest scotch or the tastiest ice cream than to die wishing I had."

There were not many who impressed Addison, but standing in her kitchen, she found herself fascinated with Robert, and as she mulled over his point of view, she found herself in agreement. "Makes sense," she said, nodding.

"So," Robert said, stopping long enough to take another taste of his dessert. "What do you do?"

"Sorry?"

"For a living...what do you do?"

"Oh," Addison said, putting aside the container in her hand. "I own a company that buys other companies that are in trouble financially or otherwise, and then I turn around and sell them for a profit. I do the same with real estate and new technology, as long as it's worth my time."

"By the size of this house, I'm thinking it's worth your time."

Addison nodded again. "I do okay."

"So, the chances of you continuing to need a house manager are good then?"

"I don't see any change where that's concerned. Why?"

"Well, you said Joanna was doing a good job, so I know she'll be okay."

Addison frowned. "You think a lot about death. Don't you?"

Robert sat straight on his stool. "I'm not thinking about death. I'm thinking about life...my daughter's life. I'm all she has, and I want to make sure she'll be all right after I'm gone. Nothing wrong with that."

"No, I suppose not," Addison said as she stared at the man. "Can I ask what happened to her mother?"

"Up and left us before Joanna turned two," Robert said matter-of-factly. "Wanted to be an actress more than she wanted to be a mum."

"And she never came back? Never tried to see her daughter?"

"Not once," Robert said, shaking his head. "When I was served with the divorce papers a few years later, Moira handed me over all the rights to Joanna. She wanted nothing to do with her. All she wanted was to be free of both of us."

"I'm sorry. That must have hurt."

"Yeah, well, that's what you get for marrying someone so young. I was blind and stupid. What middle-aged bloke wouldn't want a young thing like Moira pining all over you, but I got Joanna out of the deal, and that's all that matters."

"You love her very much, don't you?"

"Of course I love her. She's my daughter," Robert said, lifting his eyes to meet Addison's. "You know, I tried for years to understand how Moira could do that. How in the hell can any parent walk away from their own flesh and blood, but I eventually came to a conclusion about Moira, and it carried me through."

"A conclusion? Can I ask what it was?"

Robert scraped the rest of the ice cream from his container, and after enjoying the last little bit, he pulled the spoon from his mouth. "Sorry, but I don't use that particular word in front of ladies."

Addison burst out laughing. She wasn't prepared for the man's honesty or his sense of humor, but she liked them both...a lot.

Robert's eyes twinkled. Other than his daughter, he couldn't remember enjoying anyone's company as much as he was Addison's. "You know, I'm glad I remembered you."

"I was going to ask you about that," Addison said, walking toward the island. "Pardon me for saying this, but I didn't think you'd remember me *or* the ice cream."

"Don't forget the lift."

Addison smiled. "Point taken."

"Kind of surprised me, too," Robert said as he slowly stood up. "I woke up hungry, and then I recalled your eyes."

"My eyes?"

"Yeah, and that made me think of the sky and then the grass, and then pistachio ice cream popped into my head. The next thing I knew I was looking for the lift."

Addison smiled again. "Well, I'm pleased you remembered about the lift...and about me."

"So am I," Robert said, taking his cane from the counter. "Not that I want to impose on you every night, but I like talking to you."

"The feeling's mutual."

"Yeah?"

"Yes."

"Why in the world would you like talking to an old man like me? You gotta have better things to do with your time."

Addison paused, trying to find the words. "It's nice to...to talk to someone who doesn't...who doesn't care who I am."

"You that important?"

At times, arrogance was Addison's middle name. She knew it. Others knew it. Others dealt with it, but right now, the taste of arrogance was foul. "Yes," she said with a nod. "In my own circles, I'm...I'm that important."

Robert saw sadness cross Addison's face. Even her eyes seemed to lose their light as she mindlessly fiddled with the spoon in her hand. Unintentionally, he knew he had opened a wound, but why was it there?

In a voice louder than needed, Robert said, "So, do we ever talk during the day?"

Addison looked up. "Um...no. I'm at work."

"Oh, that's right," Robert said. "Busy lady."

"At times I am, but...um...I wouldn't mind doing this again. That is if you'd like to?"

Robert flashed an irresistible grin. "Oh, I would so enjoy that! You really don't mind?"

"No, I don't," Addison said, her eyes creasing at the corners. "I don't mind at all."

***

Standing in front of the Victorian cheval floor mirror in her room, Addison zipped up her trousers. Made of the finest virgin wool and fitted to her frame, they were unlike any pair she had ever worn before.

It had been a conscious decision to dress like a man, made years earlier when her young mind believed emulating her father would somehow get him to accept her as his own, but she had been wrong. Nothing could erase the color of her skin or the shape of her nose. She had her mother's height as well as her beauty and curves, and while their eyes differed in shades of blue, there was no mistaking she was Alena's daughter, no matter what clothes she wore.

At first, it seemed being androgynous suited her. It had tempered her gender identity while adding a tenacity that allowed her to compete and best others in her field. They didn't need to know that under suits of wool was lingerie of silk and lace. What they saw was what she wanted them to see. A force formidable and sexless...but that was going to end tonight.

Tonight was about attention. It was about garnering gawks and whispers of awe, while photographers scrambled for extra film or memory cards. In a frenzy of flashbulbs, their fingers would press the shutter releases of their cameras, and the quiet darkness of the night would be filled with the cacophony and brilliance of a man-made storm only notoriety could provide.

Hearing a familiar tap-tap-tappity-tap on the door, Addison called out, "Come in, Evelyn."

"There's a swarm of people helping Joanna to get ready, so I thought I'd just pop in and see if you needed any help," Evelyn said, closing the door behind her.

"I haven't needed help dressing since I was two."

"You were three and a half before you stopped wearing your clothes inside out," Evelyn said. "And almost five before you got the colors and patterns sorted."

Evelyn knew Addison couldn't argue the statement, so she made no attempt to hide her grin as she walked across the room. Well aware of Addison's penchant for fine lingerie, the black bra edged in lace was no surprise, but the fitted, high-waisted trousers were. Unlike her usual flat-fronted ones with boxy, straight legs, those she wore tonight were pleated in the front, and with the legs narrowing as they got closer to the floor, the design was undeniably feminine.

After giving Addison a very slow once over, Evelyn's grin grew broader. "But it appears you've sorted them quite nicely tonight."

Evelyn's comment had nothing to do with the styled trousers and everything to do with Addison's overall appearance. A woman who normally used makeup sparingly, if at all, tonight she had chosen to highlight her features, and the result was stunning. Now framed in charcoal liner and with a hint of gray and white blended eye shadow, the arctic color of her eyes had been accentuated to the nth degree, and the strength of her jaw and her high cheekbones were now emphasized with a touch of blush, but Addison hadn't stopped with just makeup.

Although she had a standing appointment every five weeks for a haircut, the stylist's talents had been all but wasted by Addison's continual use of the best and strongest gel on the market, but tonight Addison had set her hair free. The layered tresses on the top were now ruffled and sexy, and using a dollop of mousse, she had finger-combed the tapered sides, silhouetting her face perfectly, yet still allowing her natural color of chestnut to show through.

Lost in her admiration as to what stood before her, it took almost a full minute before Evelyn finally raised her eyes. Flinching when she saw Addison's menacing glare, she said, "What?"

"You're staring."

"Am I?"

"Yes!"

"Sorry."

"Are you?"

Evelyn began to snicker. "Not in the least. It's about time you stopped hiding behind men's suits and starched shirts. You and I both know you're a woman, and you and I both know you *enjoy* being a woman. It's about bloody time you show it."

"I don't know what the hell you're talking about," Addison groused, reaching for the padded hanger holding her black dress shirt. "And if all you're going to do is stare, go stare somewhere else. I'm busy."

Watching as Addison slipped the blouse from the hanger, when she saw her fumbling to unbutton the shirt, Evelyn pressed her lips together to silence a laugh. Managing to get herself in check, she said, "If I didn't know any better, I'd say you were nervous."

"I don't *do* nervous," Addison said. Quickly donning the shirt, Addison paid no attention as she slipped the buttons through the holes until she discovered she had one more button and no more holes. "Shit!"

"Apparently, you don't *do* buttons, either," Evelyn said, chuckling under her breath as she walked over and swatted Addison's hands away. "Here, let me do it."

Admiring the silk as she released all the misguided fasteners, Evelyn was about to re-button the shirt when something about the buttons caught her eye. Leaning in close, she fingered the red gems surrounded by silver prongs. "Addison?"

"Yes?"

"Are...are these rubies?"

Addison couldn't help but smile. "Yes, they are."

"*Real* rubies?"

"Are there any other kind?"

Addison stood still so Evelyn could button the shirt, but noticing that the woman now seemed intent on examining every ruby fastener, Addison turned the tables. Slapping Evelyn's hand away, she said, "I'll do it. I don't want to be here all night."

"This is a bit over-the-top for you. Isn't it?" Evelyn said, pointing at the gems.

"It was Fran's idea," Addison said, slipping the last ruby into a buttonhole. "Something about garnering attention."

"You hate attention."

"I know!" Addison yelled, grabbing for a set of cufflinks on the dresser. "But Fran insisted I add something red. I have no bloody idea why."

Evelyn's expression didn't change, at least not on the outside. "I see," she said, turning toward the door. "Well, if you don't need me, I think I'll toddle back to Joanna's room and make sure everything is going as planned."

"That's fine," Addison said, looking in the mirror as she straightened her shirt. "Oh, I arranged with Garrard Jewelers to borrow some jewelry for tonight. It should be here soon. The large box goes to Joanna, and the small one comes to me. Bring it up when it gets here."

"You *borrowed* jewelry?"

"It's a hire, but it was better than spending a few million pounds."

"A few million—"

"Enough!" Addison shouted. "You know what tonight's about, and if I can get this deal signed, it's worth ten times that, so just bring me the bloody jewelry when it gets here. Can you do that?"

"Of course, Addison," Evelyn said, slipping through the open door. "Anything you say."

***

Joanna slowly made her way down the hallway to her father's room, feeling taller than her three-inch heels had made her. As a child, she had never played dress up. She had never wanted to be a princess or wear jewels and fancy gowns, but as an adult, Joanna couldn't deny there was something to be said for dress up.

She had always liked being a woman, but tonight *like* didn't even come close. Joanna knew she wasn't unattractive. She wouldn't have become Addison's wife if she was, but she also knew there was a fine line between conceit and confidence.

Before leaving her room, Joanna had stood in front of the mirror and found herself holding her chin a smidgen higher. For a moment, it had bothered her, but then she remembered she was the wife of Addison Kane. She told herself she needed to look the part and act the part, but in the back of her mind, in the crevices Joanna rarely allowed herself to acknowledge, lurked something else, and as she had stared into the mirror, it bubbled to the surface. She *wanted* Addison to like what she saw. She wanted to beguile and tempt, and have Addison notice her not as a trespasser in her home, but as a desirable woman. Those thoughts had caused Joanna to jerk back her head at such a velocity she startled those assisting with makeup and hair. Fighting to curb her blush, she had quickly left the room, but she could not escape the question she kept asking herself. How in the hell had she fallen for Addison Kane?

Robert looked up from his book, hesitating before it registered that the stunning woman standing in his doorway was his daughter. He had seen her at good times and bad, and as a child and a woman, but he had never seen her like this. "Wow."

"Hi Dad," Joanna said quietly.

"You look...you look positively ravishing."

Robert had never known his daughter not to smile at one of his compliments, so this was a first, and the expression she wore didn't seem to fit the occasion. "Why the frown?"

"Am I frowning?" she said, coming into the room.

"A little."

"Just a few worries, I guess."

"Worries? About what?"

"It's just that tonight is terribly important to Addison. I wouldn't want to do anything that would cause her any embarrassment."

"And you honestly think you would, dressed like that?"

"It's not just about the clothes, Dad. I'd hate to disappoint her. That's all."

Robert set aside his book and studied his daughter. Her face was clouded in sadness, but in her eyes, he saw a sparkle, a vibrant flicker of something he couldn't quite put his finger on. Rubbing his chin, he said, "It seems you've come a long way since you married her."

"What do you mean?"

"I remember a time not too long ago when you didn't give a toss about what she thought of you *or* how you looked, yet now you're all about pleasing her."

"It's not about pleasing her. It's just—" Joanna clamped her mouth shut, blood rushing to her face as she realized she was about to confess something to her father she could never confess. "Don't mind me," she said, dismissing the conversation with a wave of her hand. "I'm just being stupid."

Joanna was far from stupid, and neither was Robert. He cocked his jaw to the side and gazed at his daughter. The weight of worry no longer sagged her shoulders and the lines creasing her face had faded away. Her skin glowed and her hair shone, and suddenly he recognized the glint in her eyes. His, too, had once sparkled like that, and Robert was as elated as he was somber. Joanna had found her place, and he knew it.

"Are you okay?"

Robert looked up. "What?"

"You just looked a million miles away."

"I'm fine, sweetheart, and if you have any doubts about tonight, I suggest you look in the mirror a few more times. You're absolutely stunning."

"It's not about how I look, Dad. It's about...it's about who I am?"

"Joanna, you haven't changed," Robert said, reaching out to take her hand. "Yes, your clothes are better, and your hair is styled, but when I look into your eyes, I still see the same lass I saw when you were one or two or twenty. And just the fact that you're worried about possibly being...um...damn it all to hell, what's the word?"

"Pretentious?"

"Yes, that's right, pretentious," Robert said. "And since it's on your mind, that tells me you haven't changed one bit, and you won't no matter how many parties you attend or jewels you wear. I raised you better than that."

Joanna couldn't hold back her grin as she leaned down and placed a soft kiss on her father's cheek. "Thank you," she whispered. "I needed that."

Robert could feel his emotions beginning to stir, and refusing to blubber in front of his daughter, he said, "Now, get the hell out of here before you're late."

"Okay," Joanna said as she stood straight. "I'll check in when I get home. All right?"

"I'll expect a full report," Robert said as he picked up his book.

"Good night, Dad."

"Good night, lass," Robert said as he watched his daughter head out of the room. "Oh, Joanna?"

"Yeah, Dad?" she said, peeking back in.

"Do me proud tonight. All right?"

A dazzling smile appeared on Joanna's face. "I will, Dad. I promise."

Robert waited a minute before opening his nightstand and pulling out a notebook. Fumbling for a pen, his expression turned stern as he wrote down his thoughts. He had never kept a diary before, but after screaming out in terror more than once when he had awoken in a strange house, only to be calmed down when he read his own scribbles, Robert decided that a diary was a good idea. He wanted to always remember what brought them to this place. He wanted to always remember how his daughter's life was changing for the better since they arrived, and he never wanted to forget the woman who had become much more than just a small part of Joanna's life...whether Joanna cared to admit it or not.

***

Forty minutes later in the entrance hall of The Oaks, Addison had become a Serengeti leopard locked behind invisible bars. Pacing forth and back across the slate, she checked her watch again only to find the sweep hand had moved a mere thirty notches since last she looked. Her blood pressure crept up yet another tick, and it would have continued if she hadn't seen Evelyn coming down the stairs.

"Where in the *hell* is she?" Addison said, placing her hands on her hips.

"She'll be down in a tick. Relax," Evelyn said, coming to a stop when she reached Addison. "She wanted to say good night to her father."

"I don't like being kept waiting."

"*You* do it to people all the time."

"That's *business*."

Evelyn cocked her head to the side. "And you're saying this isn't?"

"I keep *them* waiting. They do *not* keep *me* waiting!"

"Well then, I guess you shouldn't have married a woman," Evelyn said as she reached over and dusted off an infinitesimal piece of lint from Addison's tuxedo.

Without waiting for a response, Evelyn gave Addison a quick wink before gathering her coat and handbag from a chair. "And with that, I think I'll bid you farewell for the night. I do hope you and Joanna have a marvelous evening."

"As long as she blends into the background and doesn't embarrass me, that shouldn't be a problem."

Evelyn's face grew rosy as she opened the front door. Turning around, she said, "Addison?"

Staring at her watch, Addison looked up. "What?"

"I doubt very much Joanna will do anything to embarrass you, but as for blending into the background..." Evelyn stopped and tapped her finger against her chin. "That *may* be a problem."

Before Addison could even process the comment, Evelyn walked out into the night, closing the door quietly behind her.

Glancing at her watch again, Addison was about to fly up the stairs and drag Joanna from her room when she heard a faint swishing sound from the second floor. Looking up, Addison lost the ability to breathe. Evelyn was right. Blending into the background would *not* be an option for Joanna tonight.

Chapter Twenty-Three

For nearly a half hour no words were spoken as Addison and Joanna were driven to their destination. Addison kept telling herself there was no need to be nervous, but then again, everyone has their own comfort zone, and hers didn't include parties, paparazzi, *or* a wife. Addison re-crossed her legs again, but when she saw Joanna do the same, Addison reached over and opened the liquor compartment.

"I'm going to have a scotch. Do you want one?" she said, removing one of the decanters from its holder.

"I'm not sure that's a good idea," Joanna said, shaking her head.

"Why not?"

"I...I don't have any food in my stomach."

"We just had lunch a few hours ago."

Joanna gave Addison a weak grin. "It didn't stay down."

"Oh," Addison said, turning her attention back to the liquor. Pouring some scotch into a glass, she handed it to Joanna. "Just take a few sips. It'll help."

Watching as Addison filled another glass, Joanna smiled when she saw her take a large gulp of the malt. "It seems I'm not the only one who's nervous," she said, taking a sip of her drink. "Either that or you *really* like scotch."

Addison suppressed a laugh, but just barely. "I just want tonight to go well. I have a lot riding on it."

"Yeah, Fran told me you've been working on this deal for a long time, but she also said you don't like these types of things. Parties, I mean."

"I don't," Addison said, taking another swig of scotch. "I don't like being on display, but then again—" Addison stopped and looked at Joanna. "Tonight, I don't think *I'll* be the one they're watching."

Joanna swallowed hard and quickly took several sips of her drink. "I'm not sure if that's a compliment or...or an expectation of disaster."

"It's a compliment," Addison said softly. A lot of adjectives came to mind as she admired the woman sitting next to her, but when push came to shove, there was only one Addison dared to use. "You look...you look *nice*."

Joanna lifted her chin just a tad. "Thank you."

"You're welcome."

In unison, both women stared at the glasses in their hands, until Joanna broke the silence. "Look, I...I just want you to know that I promise I won't do anything to embarrass you," she said, turning to Addison. "Evelyn has been coaching me for weeks, and I know what to expect and what to do. After dinner, I'll just meander around the room and get lost in the crowd. I promise."

Addison had no doubt Joanna believed she was telling the truth, but Addison wasn't blind, and she was reasonably sure neither were the multitude of people most likely attending Bradley Easterbrook's party that night.

A chime sounded, and while its volume was low, the interruption caused both women to jump. Addison pressed a button, and the glass partition between the driver and passengers opened. "What is it, David?"

"I just wanted to let you know we're about five minutes away," David said over his shoulder.

"Thank you," Addison said. Pushing the button again, Addison didn't say a word until the glass panels had closed. "It's almost showtime. You ready for this?" she said, looking at Joanna.

Even though Joanna had yet to utter a sound, the liquor in her glass told Addison all she needed to know as it began sloshing against the crystal as if the car was driving across rumble strips. Leaning closer, Addison placed her hand on Joanna's knee. "Relax," she said softly. "It'll be okay. It's just a party."

Joanna raised her eyes to meet Addison's. "It's *just* a party?" she blurted. "I'm wearing a dress costing thousands of pounds and jewelry worth—" Joanna stopped long enough to glance at the diamond encrusted bracelet encircling her wrist. "Worth I don't know how much, and you say it's *just* a party? *Really?*"

Addison let out a snort, and quickly finishing her drink, she placed the crystal tumbler back into its holder. "Okay, so it's not *just* a party, but I'm out of my element, too, if that helps."

"It doesn't," Joanna said, reaching for the decanter.

"No, you've had enough," Addison said, closing the compartment.

"Addison, I have no idea what the fuck I'm doing!"

"Joanna, relax," Addison said, turning so she could look Joanna in the eye. "In a few minutes, David is going to open this door," Addison said, gesturing to the one on her side of the car. "I'm going to get out and offer you my hand, and you're going to take it. We're going to smile for the photographers for a minute or two, and then we're going to go inside. After that, all you need to do is nibble some appetizers, have a cocktail or two, eat dinner, and make small talk."

"But I don't know how to make small talk, especially not with people wealthier than God!"

"You talk to me, don't you?"

Addison rarely tried to be funny, at least not intentionally, but when she saw Joanna's face split into a grin, she knew her attempt had been successful. Returning Joanna's grin with one of her own, Addison squeezed Joanna's knee. "That's better."

Better didn't quite describe the feelings Joanna was experiencing, but this time it wasn't her worries getting the best of her. This time, it was the warmth of Addison's hand on her knee. It seemed to spread throughout her body, a tingling of awareness and heat, and unlike the scotch, Addison's touch calmed her concerns in an instant. As for the rest of the nerves in her body...not so much.

***

Generally, Addison couldn't care less about her mode of conveyance. Cars were just cars, built to get a person from one place to another, but four weeks earlier her mood had changed.

Keeping in mind Fran's directive that attention needed to be received, Addison had called her chauffeurs into her study and explained that she and her wife would be attending a very important party where appearances were everything. There was only one car in her garage she believed fit the bill, and George and David readily agreed.

It was the only automobile in Oliver Kane's collection he had demanded *not* be returned to its original factory condition. Owning one of only eighteen in existence should have been enough for Oliver Kane, but like Bradley Easterbrook, Oliver's ego had needed more. When the Rolls-Royce Phantom IV had rolled out of the factory a half-century earlier, its interior had been red leather, and its exterior a dark forest green. However, believing its mundane appearance would be lost amid a sea of other collectibles at the car shows where it appeared, Oliver had ordered changes be made. So, instead of returning the car to the authentic factory specifications, he had the red leather replaced with black, and much to the dismay of car collectors around the world, the car's exterior was now metallic carmine.

The smile on David's face hadn't wavered all day. Before Addison had brought an end to the cars appearing in shows across the country, he had driven the Phantom on and off transportation lorries, but guiding the masterpiece down country roads and highways was a dream come true.

He and George had spent every spare minute preparing the car for its journey. Each part of the engine was inspected, and pristine fluids were emptied and replaced with new. Once they were satisfied the engine was in perfect working order, they turned their attention to the car's appearance.

They buffed the clear coat that protected the deep red paint until it gleamed, and the chrome trim had been polished until it sparkled with brilliance. The leather interior and carpeting had been cleaned until not a speck of dust existed, and the burled walnut trim accenting the seats and panels had been made lustrous with the softest cloths known to man. Not one item on the car was overlooked, so when David turned the automobile onto the long, curved driveway leading to the mansion belonging to Bradley Easterbrook, he sat tall in his seat. He may not have been the registered owner of the car, but tonight it belonged to him.

Addison had prepared herself for what she thought was about to happen, but as soon as the tires of the Phantom hit the interlocking brick of the driveway leading to the Easterbrook mansion, her jaw dropped open as what seemed like a thousand flash bulbs went off at the same time. Flash after flash lit up the vehicle, and the metallic paint reflected each back onto the bystanders, creating almost an endless strobe of lights flickering in the night.

The smile on Bradley's face almost reached the back of his head as he stood on the front patio of his palatial mansion. Anticipating the excitement, he had hired a force of security men. Looking quite official in their crisp gray uniforms, they stood outside the ropes of velvet, preventing the photographers and onlookers from approaching the car.

"Jesus," Joanna said, shielding her eyes from the light. "I can't bloody see."

"Yes, a bit more than I was expecting, too," Addison said, giving Joanna a quick look. "Just look down for a minute. It'll clear."

Feeling the car come to a stop, Addison looked through the window. Thankful to see more velvet ropes in place to protect the stairs leading to the house, when David opened the door, Addison took a deep breath and stepped out into the crisp winter night. Her amusement at the hubbub as reporters repeatedly called her name showed on her face, and turning back to the car she held out her hand and waited for Joanna to take it.

The only thing Joanna could think of was to pray. Nervous didn't come close to what she was feeling. Her heart was pounding in her ears, and her palms were wet, and if there had been a compartment in the Rolls in which to hide, she would have gladly climbed inside. She had spent weeks drilling Evelyn on all the pomp and protocol of events like this, but the crowd and the noise had erased all that she had learned. And when she saw Addison hold out her hand, the fluttering feeling in her belly turned into a tsunami. Joanna inhaled as much air as her lungs could hold, and letting it out slowly, she licked her lips, held her breath, and took Addison's hand. Showtime.

The chilly air felt good against Joanna's skin. Her dress wasn't designed to protect her from the elements, but she didn't mind. She welcomed the cold as it extinguished the heat of her nerves, so when she felt Addison squeeze her hand, Joanna squeezed back. Everything was going to be all right.

Instantly, Addison and Joanna found themselves ablaze in bursts of light. Bordering on hysteria, the paparazzi were shouting their names as they snapped their pictures, but matters were made much worse when Joanna smiled.

When she had stepped out of the Rolls, intent on not falling flat on her face, Joanna's expression had remained blank, but as the frenzy of light and attention swept over her, she thought back to a time not too long ago when she was scrubbing floors on her knees. That memory, mixed with the commotion now surrounding her, caused her best smile to appear, and although Joanna had no way of knowing it...she had just captured the world with that smile.

It was infectious, and even the staunchest of reporters felt goosebumps creep over their skin as they smiled in return. It was true. It was honest. It was Joanna.

For a short while, they stood just outside the car allowing photographers to do what they were paid to do until Joanna felt Addison squeeze her hand again. Joanna raised her eyes to meet those gazing back at her, and the world stood still for just a second. Without thinking, Joanna stood on tiptoes and placed a light kiss on Addison's cheek.

When Addison felt lips, soft and warm, against her skin, her heart stopped for a moment, and it was the longest moment of her life. She told herself Joanna's kiss was spontaneous, just part of the act of being who they were or rather who people *thought* they were, but the smile on Addison's face wasn't an act...and neither was the look in her eyes.

***

Bradley Easterbrook was what most would call new money. Like many in his youth, he had spent his time playing endless video games, and as he grew older, he not only played them, he learned how to create them. A genius when it came to computer graphics and game design, before he graduated college he was being wined and dined by the largest gaming companies and studios from around the world, but the establishment was just that, and Bradley wanted no part of it...at least not yet. So, in the basement of his family's home he designed and built a game called War of Avengement. Studying the gaming consoles on the market, he made it available in all the popular formats, and then late one winter night, he released it on his website. One month later, gamers the world over couldn't get enough of War of Avengement, and Bradley was set for life.

He started his own company and quickly released Avengement Two and Avengement Three, and as the money rolled in, his interests began to change. He discovered fast cars and even faster women, and after being stuck in a borough south of London for most of his life, he began to travel. He saw the sights and tasted the foods and fell in love with both, but it was the delectable cuisines of foreign lands that caught his interest and held it. Never one who had ever been labeled lithe, by the night of his Christmas party, Bradley had already begun to work on his third chin.

Like Bradley, Addison had also been around the globe, so when the young entrepreneur strutted down the stairs in his polished black wingtips, silk-lapelled tuxedo, and bright red glittery waistcoat, the image of a male Frigate Bird popped into Addison's head. Inwardly smiling at the resemblance, before Bradley had reached them, Addison already knew Fran was spot-on. When throwing a small party, it's appropriate to meet each guest at the door, but when an event includes invitees numbering over one hundred, those in attendance are greeted inside, far away from the prying eyes of photographers.

Well out of her element, Joanna remained silent while Bradley and Addison exchanged greetings, but when Addison once again took her hand, Joanna knew it was her turn.

"Bradley, I'd like to introduce my wife, Joanna," Addison said, giving Joanna's hand a tug to pull her a step closer.

Like a helium balloon filled to its limit, Bradley took Joanna's small hand in his pudgy one. "It's a great pleasure to meet you, Joanna. I could have bitten off my arm when I was told you were coming."

"Oh how...how *sweet* of you to say," Joanna said, pulling her hand from his sweaty grasp.

"Bloody hell, I'm totally chuffed," Bradley said, and unable to contain his excitement, he stepped far outside the formal line between guest and host and pulled Joanna into a great, big bear hug.

Addison heard Joanna's squeal of surprise and seeing her wrapped in the rotund arms of their boorish host, the thought of actually having the man eat his own arm came to mind instantly. True, the night was about attracting attention and stroking Bradley's ego until he signed on the dotted line, but it wasn't about whoring her wife, and Addison's anger flared. Reaching over, she placed her hand on Bradley's shoulder and squeezed like she had never squeezed before.

Feeling as if his clavicle was about to be crushed, Bradley released Joanna in an instant. Splotches of crimson mottled his face, and it took all he had to look Addison in the eye. "Um...yes. Well, perhaps...perhaps we should go inside so you can meet the other guests," he said, waving the arm that still worked. "Shall we?"

***

Once inside, Bradley brought them to the expansive arched entrance which led to the spacious formal living area six steps below them. Looking out across the room, Addison and Joanna saw before them a sea of white and black evening gowns and tuxedos. While Bradley had colored outside the lines by wearing his glittery waistcoat, all others had followed the rules. Well, *almost* all others.

The color of Addison's tux matched the others in the room, but that's where the similarities ended. Most wearing dinner suits had chosen the classic single-breasted shawl collar jacket, whereas hers was double-breasted with a peaked lapel trimmed in satin. Like her tailored trousers, it was made to fit her curves, not to hide them, and it announced her sex in a way subtle yet undeniable. Addison had also chosen to wear a red waistcoat, but unlike their host, Addison's was the deepest of reds and made of the finest of silks. Forgoing the masculine ties that had become her norm, her black silk shirt was open to where it met her waistcoat, revealing not only more than a hint of cleavage, but also a loose-fitting silver mesh necklace dotted with well over a dozen blood-red Burmese rubies. Between the buttons on her shirt, the cufflinks on her sleeves, and her shimmering waistcoat, it was clear to all that Addison Kane had not quite followed the black-and-white theme of the night...and it would soon be discovered her wife hadn't either.

Slowly, a hush grew over the room as guest after guest turned their attention to those standing next to their host, and when Bradley announced, "Ladies and gentlemen, Mrs. and Mrs. Addison Kane," the room went still.

Addison held her head high, but instead of focusing on the crowd in front of her, she looked at her wife, and unable to stop herself, she gave Joanna a wink. It surprised them both, but it took the edge off the ceremony surrounding them, and carefully they descended the stairs. Although they already had the attention of everyone in the room, Addison knew Joanna would soon own the room...and she did.

Fran knew Addison didn't take disappointment well. So, when she was assigned the daunting task of finding the perfect gown for Joanna, Fran went in search of a dress designer whose excellence bordered on sainthood. Ignoring the cutting edge of the new and bold, and the boredom of the tried and true, Fran set her eyes on the most sought-after dress designer in all of England – Terrance St. John. Without batting an eye, Fran tripled the man's going rate and paid for a gown like no other.

Before he met his actual client, Terrance had spent an afternoon with Fran browsing through his sketches of dresses and gowns, so by the time he met Joanna face-to-face, he already knew what was expected. It was called perfection. Stunning and unequivocal perfection in the form of a black evening gown which would turn *every* head in *every* room it was in. Terrance's ego told him it could be done, but it wasn't until he finally met Joanna when he realized he was already halfway there. Now all he needed to do was to try to turn a black evening gown into something more than *just* a black evening gown...and he did.

Strapless, with a low cut notched neckline, the A-line gown was made of the finest silk duchess satin on the planet. The fabric's sheen alone outdid all others in the room and even those who had dared to wear sequins that night faded into obscurity. But the uniqueness of Joanna's dress wasn't truly appreciated until she took a step, and as she and Addison walked slowly down the stairs, the intake of breath around the room was audible.

It had taken four solid weeks and a staff of twenty seamstresses to carefully stitch a red silk lining inside the black satin, and as the front split opened to allow Joanna freedom of movement, the shimmering, ruby-red lining appeared. Between the shock of the red and the awe of Joanna's shapely legs, before she reached the bottom step, there was not a person in the room who would ever forget her entrance...especially the woman standing to her right.

Chapter Twenty-Four

As Fran had predicted, the attention drawn by Addison's and Joanna's appearance at Bradley's party caused the man to forego his hosting duties toward everyone else in the room. At first, it was merely a photo session. Wrapping his arms around their shoulders, Bradley smiled left and then smiled right to the photographers he had invited inside the house, but eventually the need for drinks and conversation took precedence. Well aware the night was more about business than pleasure, in a feigned search for the ladies' room, Joanna politely excused herself, leaving Bradley and Addison alone for the first time that night. For over an hour, standing far away from the hubbub of the partygoers, Addison and Bradley spoke in hushed tones, and by the time his other guests demanded his attention, the deal was done.

Celebrating with a scotch, Addison found a quiet corner and sipping her drink, she scanned the crowd of tuxes and gowns. With her business all but done, there was no need to stay, and checking her watch, she tried to decide if she should just find Joanna and suggest they leave before dinner began. Addison scanned the room for her wife, but when she saw a familiar figure walking in her direction, her backbone instantly grew rigid.

Addison had been introduced to Maxwell Firth when she was twenty-four years old, or rather *he* had introduced himself when he strode into her office at Kane Holdings without even knocking. Explaining that Oliver had hired him to be the company lawyer, he went on to boast that from that day forward any business dealings or contracts she was involved in would require his seal of approval.

At first glance, most would have found Firth appealing. Tall and slender with jet black hair, his accent was posh and his posture perfect, but looks can be deceiving, and when it came to Maxwell Firth, they downright lied. Underneath the handsome exterior lie a cunning adversary, one who followed no rules except his own, and although his skill as an attorney could not be questioned, his morals as a human being were virtually non-existent.

After making her life a living hell for a few years, and with his friends now sitting on the board, Firth left Kane Holdings to start his own company, so it had been almost eight years since she had last seen him. His picture had been in newspapers and magazines, but she hadn't paid attention until his interest in the law became secondary to becoming an industrialist.

Over the past several years, he had bought up as much low-income housing as he could and then finding false fault in the construction, he had the occupants evicted, the buildings razed, and new ones constructed where the rents were more in line with his greed. Family-owned businesses were his next victims, and buying the leases on neighborhood markets and shops, he raised the rent when agreements came up for renewal. Slowly, stores emptied and doors were boarded, and when new businesses opened, they paid him the rent he demanded. It wasn't long before he began dabbling in company takeovers, snatching up little hotels and small technology firms as they came along. After turning some fairly sizable profits, he set his sight on the big leagues, or rather Addison's league, and that's when she began keeping track of his dealings.

As Maxwell approached, Addison could see the changes caused by time. His once black hair was now grayed at the temples and slightly thinner than she remembered, and the cut of his single-breasted tuxedo did nothing to hide the paunch of a middle-aged man. However, his deep-set eyes were still as inky, and his smirk was still as arrogant.

Preparing herself for what was to come, Addison snagged a fresh drink from a waiter walking by, and taking a sip, she waited for Firth to speak.

"That was quite an entrance you made," Firth said as he ambled up to Addison. "*Very* impressive."

"Well, you know we can't all own SUVs."

"I was actually surprised to hear you'd be here tonight," he said, scanning the room. "A last-ditch effort?"

"I have no idea what you mean, Max," Addison said, taking a sip of her scotch. "I'm just here for the free booze."

Maxwell let out a snort as he raised his chin. "Sure you are, and that's why you spent the last hour monopolizing Bradley's time."

"He didn't seem to complain," Addison said, looking at the man. "So why are *you*? Worried?"

"Hardly," Maxwell said with an over-exaggerated laugh. "I upped the ante earlier today. We're no longer neck and neck with the price, and since I know you don't do bidding wars, I win."

"Is that so?"

"It's time to fold your hand, Addison. You can't win them all."

She wasn't about to fold her hand, but Addison wasn't prepared to show it either. Deciding not to play the verbal chess match, she turned her attention to the room, hoping Firth would get the message. He didn't.

"Although, I'd have to say you did win when it came to her. Didn't you?"

Addison dropped her chin to her chest. She hated riddles, and she hated Firth, but combining the two pushed her over the top, and she shot the man a look that could kill. "What the hell are you going on about now?"

Maxwell shook his head as he leaned in close. "You and I both know your marriage is a sham, but at least you picked a looker. I'll give you that." When Addison's expression didn't waver, Maxwell decided to try again. "But it seems to me she's drawing a crowd, and lo and behold, they're all blokes. Maybe you don't have what it takes, Kane," he said, quickly giving Addison the once over before focusing on something else. "But I'm sure *they* do."

Following Maxwell's filthy leer, Addison spotted Joanna across the room surrounded by men. She shouldn't have cared. After all, Joanna wasn't making a spectacle of herself. She was just sipping champagne and chatting with a few blokes, none of whom impressed Addison in the least. The first was far too tall for Joanna, and the next could have easily been a jockey for all she knew. Another sported a beard that could have been licked off by a cat if it tried hard enough, and the last obviously couldn't afford to buy a new tuxedo, since the one he was wearing was at least one size too small.

Addison shifted in her stance, and emptying what remained in her glass, she set it on a nearby table and walked away from Firth without saying a word.

Addison wasn't blind. When Joanna had descended the stairs at The Oaks, she had indeed admired the woman who was her wife, but Addison had hidden her admiration behind a painted-on scowl. In the Rolls, her own nerves had caused her to waver. Forgetting for a moment about Easterbrook and contracts, she had stolen a few glances and even a touch, but once they walked into Bradley's home, Addison forced herself to keep her mind on business. It wasn't easy. Actually, it took every ounce of concentration she had not to allow her eyes to stray. Somewhere in the crowded room was a woman who made all other women pale in comparison.

Single-minded, Addison sauntered across the room. Sidestepping guest after guest, she remained focused on her goal, drinking in the view every step of the way. Earlier, she had noticed Joanna's upswept hairstyle, but it wasn't until now, in the brilliance cast by crystal chandeliers, she saw how Joanna's hair shimmered in the light. A few loose tendrils were framing her face perfectly, and as Addison's eyes wandered, they found the bare skin of Joanna's shoulders and arms, which seemed to hold a delicious mystery all their own.

Slowly, Addison's gaze slid downward and her breath caught in her throat. As if being strapless wasn't enough, with the help of the gown's deeply cut neckline, Joanna's breasts presented themselves like a banquet above the fabric. Creamy rounds, soft and full, blossomed forth, and in the shadows of her cleavage was nestled the lowest jewel dangling from the necklace Addison had chosen.

It had been a detail Fran had overlooked, but Addison had not. Although she balked at attending parties, some had been necessary, and Addison knew that when an event demanded formal evening gowns and tuxedos, most of the women in attendance would be draped in jewels.

A week before the party, Addison strolled into Garrards. While others may have perused diamond hearts on chains of gold and ruby necklaces on ropes of silver, Addison wasn't looking for ordinary. Calling ahead, Herbert Fitzsimmons met her at the door and escorted her to a private room which housed collections that rarely saw the light of day since very few could afford to lease them let alone buy them. In that small room smelling of leather and polish, Addison found what she sought. Connected to a choker filled with alternating diamonds in round and square were twelve three-stone pendants, each of which held brilliant-cut diamonds in shapes of oval, round, and pear. It was as magnificent as it was opulent, and at first, Addison found it to be pretentious...but that was then.

Addison said not a word to the men surrounding Joanna as she joined the circle. Her eyes darted to each, a silent condemnation for their existence, and with only one look, she quickly caused a shuffling of feet, a clearing of throats, and a mass exodus of rented tuxedos and trendy stubble-faced men.

Joanna smiled as she watched her admirers flee the scene. "You sure know how to clear a room," she said, taking a sip of champagne. "I'm impressed."

Addison moved a step closer so she could keep her voice low. "I didn't say a word."

"I don't think you had to," Joanna whispered. "Well played."

Addison knew her possessive display wasn't an act, so faking a grin she casually looked around the room. Eventually, her attention returned to Joanna, and noticing the empty champagne flute in her hand, Addison said, "Would you like another drink?"

Joanna no sooner opened her mouth to speak when a member of the wait staff appeared out of nowhere. "My apologies for interrupting," the silver-haired man said. "But dinner is being served on the rear veranda. If you follow me, I'll lead you to your seats."

"Shall we?" Addison said, holding out her hand to Joanna.

"Of course," Joanna said, slipping her fingers through Addison's.

Bradley's home, while massive, could not comfortably seat a hundred people within its walls, so other measures had been taken. Addison and Joanna found themselves being escorted through the house, and onto the patio at the rear where marquees had been erected to protect the partygoers from the elements. Complete with flooring, heat, and tables covered in linen, silver, china, and crystal, if it hadn't been for the plastic palladium windows stitched into the walls of fabric, it would have felt as if they were in just another room of the house.

It was customary at large formal events that spouses were separated during dinner in hopes new friendships or business relationships could develop, so Addison wasn't surprised when Joanna was sat at one table for eight, while she was guided to another. They wouldn't see each other again for nearly two hours.

***

Shortly after ten Addison and Joanna finally bid their farewell and left the party, and unlike when they were introduced, this time Bradley refrained from hugging his guests. Still smiling and as puffed up as a man could be, he walked them out to the Rolls. Waiting while unrelenting photographers took even more pictures, he then proceeded to hang in the opened door of the automobile for several more minutes, bubbling over with delight until he finally allowed them to leave.

Neither Joanna nor Addison said a word as David pulled away from the house. The party and the food had taken its toll. Content in staring out their respective windows, a half hour passed before the quiet in the car was finally interrupted when both women let out audible sighs at the same time.

Joanna broke out in giggles at their unintentional duet. "You too – eh?"

"It was a long night," Addison said, running her fingers through her hair.

"But did it go well?" Joanna said, twisting in her seat. "I mean with Bradley."

"Yes, it did," Addison said with a bob of her head. "He'll be stopping by the office next week to finalize details."

"That's great!"

"Thanks."

In the shadows of the limo, Joanna chewed on her lip for a second. "Um...can I ask you something?"

Addison turned, leaning against the door so she could look directly at Joanna. "Sure. What is it?"

"Why would Bradley sell his company? I mean, he looks very successful. So why sell?"

"Because he's young and he's stupid."

"What do you mean?"

"He's a flash in the pan," Addison said as she reached over and opened the liquor cabinet. "He's made a lot of money in a very short amount of time, and it's gone to his head." Pouring some scotch into a glass, she said, "Would you like some?"

"No, thank you," Joanna said, holding up her hand. "But how's that make him stupid?"

"Because he's about to sell me his company for half what it's going to be worth in a few years."

"How do you know what it's going to be worth?"

Addison's face brightened at the question. "Because it's my job to know."

"Oh," Joanna said, staring at the woman. "Um...maybe I will have that drink."

Addison poured a splash into another glass and handed it to Joanna. "So, did you enjoy yourself tonight?"

"Actually, once I figured out how to stop everyone from asking questions, I did."

"Questions?"

"Yes," Joanna said, taking a sip of her drink. "About how you and I met."

"Shit!" Addison said, letting out a sigh. "I forgot all about that."

"That's all right. I handled it."

"May I ask how?"

"I told them the same thing Fran had released to the newspapers. We met accidentally, and it was love at first sight."

"And they believed it?" Addison said, drawing back her head.

"I didn't give them a chance not to," Joanna said with a laugh. "And I quickly became an expert on how to change the subject, so you don't have to worry. I didn't embarrass you or tell any tales. I just drank my champagne and did more listening than talking."

Addison was impressed, and taking a sip of her drink, she gazed at the woman to her left. "Thank you for that."

"You're welcome."

With The Oaks now within sight, both women grew quiet as David crept the Rolls up the gravel drive. A few minutes later, he was opening Addison's door.

Addison stepped out into the evening mist, mindless of the drizzle against her skin. Photographers were no longer present, and the need for the masquerade of spousal duties had long since ended, but nevertheless, she held out her hand and helped Joanna from the car.

Joanna squinted at the feel of the fine spray, but the chill of the water was bested by the warmth of Addison's hand wrapped around hers. In silence they climbed the stairs, their fingers remaining intertwined until the front door swung open, causing both women to jump.

Releasing herself from Addison's grip as if she'd been burned, Joanna quickly walked inside. "Fiona, it's late. You should be in bed."

"Yes, miss," Fiona said, her eyes betraying her as they darted to Addison for a split-second. "But someone always waits up just in case anything is needed."

Forgetting for a moment the demands made by the woman to her right, Joanna sighed. "We're fine, Fiona. That'll be all for the night."

Fiona summoned up a half-hearted smile in reply, and squeaking across the entrance hall in her orthopedic shoes, she disappeared into the kitchen.

"Well," Addison said, looking toward the second floor. "I don't know about you, but I think I'm going to call it a night."

"That makes two of us," Joanna said, and following Addison's lead, she climbed the stairs.

When they reached the landing, there was an awkward pause. Addison was supposed to go left, and Joanna was supposed to go right, but neither could convince their feet to move.

Searching for the words, Joanna said, "I...I just want to thank you for tonight. I had fun."

"You're welcome," Addison said softly. "And thank you for agreeing to do it."

Joanna shrugged. "Anytime," she said as she turned toward the entrance to the east wing. "Good night, Addison."

"Good night, Joanna."

Addison went into her bedroom and closed the door behind her. It had been a long night, and she was exhausted, but her brain was firing on all cylinders, and each spark held a flicker of Joanna in its flash. She let out an audible breath and headed to the wardrobe, but when she reached up to release her necktie, she stopped for a moment, chuckling when she realized she wasn't wearing one. Unclasping her necklace, Addison dropped it on the bureau, but as she began to remove her tuxedo jacket, an ear-splitting scream sliced through every wall in The Oaks.

Addison flinched and whipping around, she bolted from the room. No sooner had her feet hit the carpet outside her door when she came to an abrupt stop as she looked down the corridor. At the far end of the east wing, Irene was standing just outside Robert's door holding onto Joanna as sob after sob spilled from Joanna's lips.

In an instant, Addison knew what had happened, and slumping against the wall, she closed her eyes and hung her head. "Shit."

***

She stood outside, halfway between the house and the hearse, mindless that the thick fog had dampened her hair and clothes. The door opened behind her, but Addison didn't turn around. She remained a statue while four men dressed in black carried out another clothed in pajamas of blue and white, now hidden under a sheet rapidly becoming speckled with rain.

They were respectful as their profession dictated. The gurney's wheels rattled across the slate for only a second before it went quiet as wheels were lifted so those mourning would not forever be haunted by the sound.

Was she mourning, too? She hardly knew the man, yet suddenly she felt as if a black hole had appeared inside of her, devouring her every thought and instinct. She couldn't sense the cold or feel the wetness of the fog as it wrapped its whiteness around her, and it wasn't until Addison heard the hearse door close when she finally lifted her eyes.

A man barely five feet tall was walking toward her. He, too, didn't seem to care about the weather. His black, round-rimmed glasses were spotted with mist and his bald head glistened from the moisture in the air, but he didn't acknowledge it. Tonight wasn't about being inconvenienced or uncomfortable. Tonight was about loss. It was about understanding those who were left behind with holes in their hearts and muddled thoughts twisted by pain.

He stopped a few feet from where Addison stood. "We'll be leaving now," he said in a quiet and dignified tone. "We can discuss arrangements tomorrow or...or whenever you're ready." Receiving an infinitesimal nod in response, the man did the same and then headed back to the hearse. He knew at times like these, solitude often brought the most peace.

Addison watched as the man walked away, his shoulders hunched against the chill and the drizzle, but just as he began to open the car door, a thought crossed her mind. "Wait," she called out. "Please wait."

In no time flat, he was once again standing in front of Addison. "Yes, madam."

Addison frowned. "I've...I've forgotten your name."

"McPherson, madam. Nigel McPherson," he said, reaching into his pocket to pull out a card. Although he had already given her one an hour earlier, he placed another in her hand. "My card."

Addison gave the card a half-glance before slipping it into her pocket. "It...it goes without saying, you're to spare no expense."

"Of course, madam."

Nigel paused, and believing the conversation had ended, he began to walk away.

"McPherson."

"Yes, madam," Nigel said, turning around.

Addison knew if she spoke too soon her voice would crack, so hanging her head, she took the time she needed to collect herself. After a short while, she cleared her throat, raised her eyes, and looked at the little man standing a few feet away. "His...his favorite color is green."

A faint smile crossed Nigel's face. "I'll make a note of it, Mrs. Kane. Don't you worry."

***

When Addison went back inside the house, she saw Evelyn descending the staircase with a man carrying a small black bag. Ignoring them, Addison walked into her study and poured herself a drink. Sipping the liquor, she didn't return to the foyer until she heard the front door close.

Finding Evelyn standing at the bottom of the stairs, Addison asked, "How is she?"

"Not well," Evelyn said, shaking her head. "The doctor gave her something to help her sleep."

"Oh."

Evelyn cocked her head. For the first time in forever, Evelyn couldn't read Addison's expression. There was no flicker of emotion good or bad, and if pain or loss existed it was hidden behind a canvas, smooth and blank.

"Are you all right?" Evelyn asked, touching Addison on the sleeve.

"Yeah," Addison said, taking a sip of her drink. "I'm fine."

"You should go up and get out of those wet clothes."

Addison glanced at her tuxedo jacket, confused to see it glistening with water.

The longer Evelyn waited for a response, the more furrowed her brow became. "Addison," she said, tugging ever so slightly on Addison's sleeve. "Did you hear me?"

"Yes, I heard you," Addison said as she lifted the glass to her lips. Emptying it in one swallow, she handed the tumbler to Evelyn. "I'm going to bed. Good night."

"Before you go, I'd...I'd like to stay the night. Someone should be here if Joanna needs anything. Is that all right?"

Evelyn was only offering the sympathy that comes from compassion and friendship, but her words, however innocent, had pained Addison. Evelyn had just made it very clear she believed Addison wasn't capable of the same.

Addison bowed her head as she started up the stairs. "Stay as long as you'd like, Evelyn," she said without looking back. "Good night."

Chapter Twenty-Five

An unexpected winter squall enveloped the motorcade as they made the slow and dignified drive to Highgate. Robert hadn't had many friends, but Addison's staff, the nurses who had attended him, and a few neighbors from Burnt Oak were there to say good-bye to their friend. Most had never set foot in limousines, stretched and black, but respectfully they held their awe behind eyes filled with sadness.

Prior to the late 1800s, like so many others, Kane ancestors had been buried in family plots on their property, forever in peace with their husbands, wives, and children, but toward the end of the nineteenth century, the head of the family purchased numerous plots in Highgate Cemetery. Believing that he and his descendants deserved more than a grave lost in a field of flowers, he ordered a family mausoleum be erected so he and his descendants would have a resting place equal to their name.

The burial chamber was built into the side of a hill. With walls of granite and angelic statuary adorning the pediment above the entry as well as the columns right and left, it was as imposing as it was solemn. Prayers and poems were intricately carved into marble slabs decorating the walls and floors, and down the center of each section was a long granite bench, allowing those who mourned a place to rest or reflect.

When the question was asked of Addison, the answer came easily. By the time the mausoleum was completed, fifty bearing the last name of Kane had been assured a final resting place fitting their name and position and Robert deserved the same. It didn't matter his surname differed from hers. In her mind, he'd forever be a Kane.

Even though she had a staff at her beck and call, Addison hadn't trusted any with the arrangements. She was the one who had chosen a casket of solid mahogany. With its finish polished and its accents silver, she believed it befitted the man lying inside on the cross-pleated velvet of pale emerald green. She had asked her tailor to create a suit of the finest fabric for Robert to wear, and within two days it was delivered to the funeral director. The shirt chosen was white and crisp, and the tie was silk, with diagonal stripes in shades of green, but the last touch would forever remain Addison's secret. Inside the breast pocket of his suit, she had asked a silver spoon be placed. If there were ice cream in Heaven, Robert would need it.

The limousine slowly made the turn through the open iron gates leading to Highgate, and Addison briefly looked to her left. She wanted to speak, to murmur a condolence to the woman grieving next to her, but Joanna hadn't uttered a word in days.

Dressed in black and with her head bowed, Joanna sat silent, and lost in her thoughts and grief, the world around her ceased to exist. Her days had been spent weeping or staring off into space, numb and broken, so today, while different, was the same. She had become a bystander in her own life, her energy drained by the loss of the only family she ever really had. Joanna was alone now. Completely and utterly alone, and this day, like so many more to come, would slip into oblivion.

***

Christmas came and went unnoticed as it always did at The Oaks, but this year even the staff had lost some of their exuberance. While baubles decorated their own homes and shopping had been done, the joy of the holiday had been dampened. Robert's death had taken its toll on everyone, but the damage it had done to Joanna's spirit was the staff's downfall. Her smile had been replaced by an anguished grimace, masking her face with pain and sorrow, and the vitality she had once possessed had died just like her father.

There was no longer need to exercise or tend to a garden that would never be appreciated by anyone but herself, and even the taste of food had lost its appeal. Books held no interest nor did conversation, so while Joanna continued to exist in the house, she had become a living ghost, an apparition filling the space in a bedroom...but just barely.

New Year's Eve passed as well, but no mention had been made of it at the house. It was just another night that morphed into another day, another endless day where thoughts brought grief, and sleep brought even more.

At first, the drugs had helped, and Joanna had drifted into slumber, giving her body time to recover from the endless tears she had shed, but like exercise and food, Joanna's interest in sleep had waned. For her, it was merely an escape, but she didn't want to escape her father's loss. She wanted him back. She wanted to talk about football, bad calls, and crooked referees, and play endless games of Gin just to hear him swear under his breath when she won. She wanted to kiss his cheek again and feel the stubble under her lips. She wanted to feel his arms around her giving her the warmth only a father could, and she wanted to smell his aftershave...just one more time.

***

"Does she have time to see me?" Fran asked.

Millie looked up and grinned. "Yes, her diary is clear until one."

"Good. Thanks," Fran said, and spinning around, she went over and lightly tapped on Addison's door. When she didn't get a response, Fran looked over her shoulder. "Is she on the phone?"

Millie turned to her computer and brought up the application showing all the company phones that were in use. "No, she's not. She's probably just reading something. You know how she is."

Agreeing with a quick nod, Fran knocked again and then opened the door. Not at all surprised that Millie knew Addison so well, Fran took a seat opposite the executive desk and waited for Addison to stop reading the document in front of her.

One minute passed and then another before Fran's patience grew short. "Addison, I know you're probably busy, but all I need is a minute. Okay?" She waited for any sign that Addison had heard her, but when Addison didn't so much as flinch, Fran rapped on the desktop. "Addison. *Hello?*"

Addison jumped, and glowering, she looked up from the contracts she'd been hunched over. "When did you get here?"

"A few minutes ago," Fran said, and sitting a little straighter, she eyed the papers in front of Addison. "Is something wrong with the Easterbrook deal?"

"What?" Addison said, glancing at the papers. "No. Why?"

"You look worried."

"The deal is perfect," Addison said, pushing the papers away. "Like always."

Fran studied Addison for a moment. "Well, it may not be the contract, but something has put those creases on your forehead. What's going on?"

Addison sighed. "It's nothing, Fran. I'll be fine."

"Look, I know we don't always see eye to eye on things, and our friendship is...well, it's not what it used to be, but that doesn't mean I can't lend an ear or a shoulder if you need it."

Addison leaned back in her chair, rubbing her neck as she stared at the ceiling. She let out another long sigh and looked over at Fran. "It's Joanna."

If awards were given for keeping a straight face, Fran would have walked away with one plated in gold. She had expected something regarding a contract requiring a tweak or profits not up to snuff, or even a land purchase turning sour, but of all the possibilities that had popped into her head, *Joanna* hadn't made the list. Fran had attended the funeral, and she was well aware Joanna was devastated by the loss of her father, but since when did Addison care?

"What about Joanna?" Fran asked quietly.

"It's like she's died."

"Sorry?"

"I haven't seen her since the funeral. She doesn't come downstairs. Hell, she doesn't even leave her room anymore."

"And that's a problem?"

Fran watched as Addison's somber expression slowly began to change. Her lips flattened, and the veins in her temples began to strain against her skin, and Fran knew in an instant she either needed to retract...or retreat.

"I'm sorry," Fran blurted. "I just mean...I thought you preferred it that way."

"I did, but...but we've been eating dinner together for months," Addison said, playing with an invisible speck of dust on her desk. "I guess I grew accustomed to all the noise she makes when she eats, and now it's so damn bloody quiet, it's unnerving."

"You miss her, don't you?"

"No, of course not," Addison said, but as soon as she spoke the words, she let out a sigh. "Yes...yes, I do," she said, raising her eyes.

"Then tell her."

"What?"

"Tell her you miss her, and you...you like her."

"I never said I liked her!" Addison said, getting to her feet.

"No? You miss all your enemies, do you?"

A low grumble rose in Addison's throat. "I'm done with this conversation. I'll see you at one for the Easterbrook meeting."

Refusing to lose ground on a conversation that was becoming *very* interesting, Fran said, "You know, it's okay to like her. She's nice, and she's definitely not hard on the eyes. You could do worse."

"I never said I liked her, and certainly not in *that* way."

"In what way?"

"You know exactly what *way* I'm talking about," Addison said, pointing to the door. "Now get out and leave me alone."

Holding up her hands, Fran said, "Okay, so I'm wrong, but if you miss her, tell her. Tell her you miss how she chews her food with her mouth open—"

"She does *not!*"

"Well, you just said she makes noises, so I assumed—"

"Well, you assumed *wrong!* She's got better manners than most of the people I do business with. She just enjoys the food and...and comments on it. That's all."

"Oh, I see," Fran said with a gleam in her eye. "My apologies."

"Accepted. Now, get out."

"Not until you tell me you're going to talk to her."

"Since when do you barter with me?"

"This isn't about bartering, Addison," Fran said, getting to her feet. "This is about someone who's apparently really lost right now, and she needs to be found. Don't let her wither away in her room because you're too damn proud to tell her you miss her."

"I don't...I don't want her to get the wrong idea."

A sliver of a grin appeared on Fran's face. "The *wrong* idea?"

"*You* did," Addison said, glaring at Fran.

"Trust me, Addison," Fran said, walking to the door. "If you look at her the way you're looking at me right now, she will *not* get the wrong idea."

***

When Addison arrived home, she found out she'd be eating alone again, just like she had for the past four weeks. Annoyed, she picked at her food until it was a mass of unrecognizable bits and pieces, and then filling a glass with scotch, she headed to the basement gym. Working out her frustrations on the treadmill and then in the pool, when she finally found her way to bed just after midnight, her body ached from the punishment she had put it through.

The next morning, the aches and pains returned as soon as she opened her eyes and with them the memories of what brought her to this point. Before Addison's feet hit the floor, her mind was made up.

She groaned more than once taking her shower and several more times before she was dressed, but by the time she walked out of her room, her sore muscles were trivial. Addison strode to the east wing, coming to a stop in front of Joanna's door, and she was about to rap on its surface when she noticed the door was ajar. Placing a finger on the wood, she pushed it all the way open.

On the short walk from her room to Joanna's, Addison's annoyance had grown exponentially, but as soon as she set eyes on the woman, Addison's anger dissolved. Joanna's complexion had turned sallow, and the amount of weight she had lost was evident by the shadows appearing under her cheekbones.

Curled up like a baby under a mass of disheveled sheets and blankets, Joanna stared back at Addison through eyes void of life. "What do you want?" she croaked.

"I...I wanted to see how you were doing," Addison said, taking a hesitant step into the room.

"I'm fine, now leave me be."

"Pardon for me saying this, but you don't look fine."

"Not your problem," Joanna said as she rolled over and turned her back on Addison. "Now, go away."

"Evelyn says you're not eating," Addison said, taking another step closer to the bed.

"Evelyn talks too much."

Addison smiled just a tad. "Maybe so, but you still need to eat."

"I'm not hungry."

"He wouldn't want this. You know?"

Joanna whipped around, staring daggers at the woman across the way. "*What* did you say?" she shouted as she sat up. "*He* wouldn't want this? *He* as in my father? *He* as in the man you didn't even *know*!"

"Joanna—"

"Don't you ever talk like you knew anything about him. Don't you *ever*!" Joanna yelled, pounding her fists on the bed.

Addison paused to gather her thoughts. "I may not have known him, but if his daughter is any indication of the person he was, he wouldn't want this," she said, sitting on the edge of the bed. "He raised a fighter. She didn't give up when he got sick. She didn't cry poverty when the bills became too much. She stood tall and did what she had to do to give herself and her father a life. So, you tell me, would someone who raised a daughter such as yourself really want her to waste her life hiding up here starving herself?"

Joanna stared down at her hands. "I'm not starving. I'm just not that hungry."

Addison sighed, mindlessly looking around the room as she tried to think of something to say. "I have an idea," she said, focusing on Joanna. "How about we start with a change of scenery?"

"What?"

"Come downstairs for dinner tonight. Like...like you used to."

"No, I'm fine where I am," Joanna said, settling in against her pillow. "My father ate up here. So can I."

"Please?"

"What's the point?"

"Sorry?"

"What's the point of me eating down there? It's not like you can see me or...or we even talk," Joanna said as she rolled on her side, once again putting her back to Addison. "If I'm going to be lonely, it may as well be in an empty room."

Addison let out a sigh and got to her feet. Fran's suggestion echoed in her head, and she knew there were more words she could say, but to speak them was impossible. Leaving the room, she headed downstairs.

Reaching the entrance hall, Addison grabbed her attaché from the table and marched toward the front door, but as she passed the dining room, she came to a stop. She stood there, remembering Joanna's words, but as she was about to open the pocket doors she heard a noise behind her. Turning around, Addison saw a member of the staff coming out of the study carrying cleaning supplies.

"You," Addison said. "Come here."

Stuttering to a stop, Iris' eyes bulged. "M-M-Me, miss?" she squeaked.

"Do you see anyone else around?"

"Um…no, miss."

"Then come here."

Iris forced herself to take a step and then another, eventually finding herself standing in the shadow of her employer.

Addison slid the doors apart and pointed into the room. "Do you see that?"

Wide-eyed, Iris set her bucket on the floor and then looked to where Addison was pointing. "The table miss?"

Addison folded her arms as she stared blankly back at the maid. "No, not the table," she said as calmly as her anger would allow. "The bloody candelabra."

"The candle…what?"

"The *centerpiece*. Do you see the bloody centerpiece?"

"Oh, yes, miss," Iris said, smiling like she had won a prize. "Kinda hard not to, innit?"

"Exactly my point, which is why I want you to…" Addison stopped long enough to size up the twig of a woman standing next to her. "…which is why I want you to find *someone* to remove it."

"Where would you like it put?"

Addison was tempted to answer with a flippant response, but holding onto her temper, she said, "I don't care where you put it. Take it home. Give it away. Bury it in the garden or use it as a ship's anchor. I don't care. I just want it gone. Can you do that?"

"Oh, yes, miss. Of course."

"Good," Addison said, checking her watch.

Believing the conversation to be over, Iris went about gathering her bucket and rags, but before she took a step, Addison spoke again.

"One more thing."

"Yes, miss?"

"From now on, Jo—" Addison stopped, her lips pressing together in a white slash as she rethought her words. "From now on, my *wife* eats in the dining room. No more trays are to be delivered to her room unless I'm not home."

"But, miss—"

"What's your name?"

Iris swallowed hard. "I-I-I-Iris."

"Have you worked here long?"

"Almost three years, miss."

"Well, if you want to make it four, you'll do as I say. If I am in this house, my wife takes her meals down here. Do you understand?"

Unable to look the woman in the eye, Iris focused on the floor. "Yes, Mrs. Kane," she said in a whisper. "I understand."

***

Later that night, Addison returned home with a little more pep in her step. Strolling into the house, she handed off her attaché to George, removed her coat, tossing it to him just as Evelyn came out of the kitchen. Her mood being better than it had been in weeks, it showed on her face, but in a flash, Addison's expression turned menacing. Coming down the stairs was the blonde-floppy-haired maid she had spoken to earlier that morning...and she was carrying a dinner tray.

"You have just made the worst cock-up of your life," Addison bellowed, storming toward the stairs. "Consider yourself sacked!"

"Addison, wait," Evelyn said, and rushing over, she placed her hand on Addison's arm. "Let me explain."

Refusing to look away from Iris, Addison yanked her arm away from Evelyn. "There's nothing to explain!" Addison screamed as she pointed at Iris. "She is a stupid cow, and she's unemployed. End of subject!"

"No, she's not," Evelyn said as she grabbed Addison's arm again and forced her to turn around. "She's doing what I asked her to do."

Slowly, Addison faced Evelyn, and lowering her chin, she looked down her nose at the woman. "*What* did you say?"

Evelyn knew Addison was on the verge of Armageddon. Her face had turned scarlet, and every vein in her neck appeared ready to burst, so when she heard the contents of the tray in Iris' hands rattling, Evelyn decided she'd best clear the room. Daring a quick glance in the maid's direction, she said, "Iris, take that to the kitchen, please."

Iris, fearing her wobbly knees would fail, crept down the rest of the stairs, but once she reached the foyer, she scurried to the kitchen, leaving the other women locked in a staring contest.

Hearing the kitchen door swing closed, Evelyn took a breath. "Now, if you let me—"

"I specifically told her—"

"I know what you told her!" Evelyn said, raising her voice. "And we were all prepared to follow your bloody rules—"

"Then why *didn't* you?

"Because we had a slight mishap today...involving Joanna."

Chapter Twenty-Six

It took a minute for the words to register, but it was enough time for Addison's persona to change. Her posture relaxed, the fury drained from her face, and her expression went from threatening to concerned. With the volume of her voice well within normal range, she asked, "What are you talking about?"

"The reason Joanna can't come down for dinner is because she took a bit of a spill today."

"She fell?" Addison said, again raising her voice. "When? Where?"

"Just after breakfast. She came down and said she was going to go work in the gardens. She was gone for quite a while, so Noah decided to take her a flask of coffee. He found her at the bottom of the stairs. Apparently—"

"Wait. What gardens?"

Evelyn's eyes grew large. "Oh...um...Joanna's been keeping herself busy clearing the weeds from the gardens out back."

"Who in the hell gave her permission to do that?"

"Well, I...I suppose I did. I saw no harm in it, and she seems to enjoy it."

"What in the hell made you—" Addison stopped and held up her hands. "You know what? Never mind, we'll deal with that later. Just tell me that she's all right."

"Yes, she's fine," Evelyn said. "She wrenched her back a bit trying to stop herself from falling, and she's got a few bruises, but other than that, she's okay. The doctor gave her some muscle relaxants, so she's been sleeping most of the day, but she should be right as rain by tomorrow."

Addison jerked back her head. "The doctor? You called a *doctor*?"

"Why yes, but like I said she's—"

"Why the *hell* didn't you call me and let me know what had happened?"

Evelyn's stared blankly back at Addison. "Well, I-I-I don't know. Honestly, the thought never crossed my mind."

Reality checks can come at any time. They can be painful, or they can be uplifting, but despite the emotions attached, one thing is for certain. They come from the truth…the cold, hard truth.

Like a bucket of Antarctic water, reality washed over Addison. There *was* no reason to be informed of Joanna's accident because Joanna was *not* Addison's concern. She wasn't. She was a boarder. Nothing more. Nothing less. Nothing at all. Reality check.

"You know what? You're absolutely fucking right," Addison growled as she spun around and made a beeline for the cloakroom. "Just because the clumsy twat can't seem to put one foot in front of the other, it's no business of mine. As a matter of fact, I couldn't be happier. She just freed up my Friday night, and I'm planning to enjoy it. Tell David to bring the car back around. I'm going out."

***

Like with her business dealings, when it came to sex, Addison wanted all the control, and *she* chose her adversaries. They did *not* choose her.

At business meetings or cocktail gatherings, if the mood struck – which it normally did – she'd scan the room for her next victim, her eyes darting from one spangled woman to the next, looking for the haughtiest, the most untouchable. In silk or velvet, with bracelets and necklaces erupting with gemstones, they were always the ones she picked. She wasn't looking for love. Hell, she wasn't even looking for like. The name of the game was conquest. Pure and simple.

And conquer she would. In hotels all over Europe, Addison would bed the wives of financiers, fuck the girlfriends of executives, and on a few occasions, she had even shagged fellow businesswomen. Of course, many believed afterward a connection had been made, a bond of sorts that would lead to a marriage proposal or perhaps even mentoring in their own business pursuits, but they were wrong. The only guidance Addison ever gave was showing them to the door. When conducting business, there were a plethora of rules Addison followed, but when it came to her after-hours activities, there was but one. She never saw any woman more than once...until she met Luce Gainsford.

Ten years earlier, they had met at a corporate function. Working for an escort service, Luce had attended the party on the arm of a man, but she had left on the arm of a woman. She had no idea her life would change when she climbed into the back of the vintage automobile, but she did something no other woman had done before. Luce *didn't* read between the lines.

Luce didn't assume Addison wanted anything more than sex because Addison had already made it very clear she didn't. She didn't presume Addison was at all interested in Luce's background, education, or social standing, so Luce saw no need to chatter on about herself in hopes of garnering some interest. She didn't giggle or play coy. She didn't bat her eyelashes or attempt to play slap and tickle in the back of the limo. And she never once tried to stroke Addison's ego because Luce knew the night wasn't about ego or forever. It was about getting fucked by one of the richest women in the world. In other words...it was business.

And Addison did fuck Luce. There were no desires spoken in ragged gasps or breathy promises of endless love whispered under the sheets. It was exactly what Addison wanted. Unlike the other women she had taken to bed, Luce didn't hide behind bashfulness or become red-faced because of a position suggested. So, raw and hard, and anyway Addison wanted, they shagged long into the night.

Knowing her job was done, in the wee hours of the morning, Luce got dressed and left the hotel. She didn't wake Addison to say good-bye. She didn't leave a note or her phone number or even kiss the woman on the cheek as she slumbered in the bed. Luce didn't have to. This was business, and business was done, or so she thought.

Two weeks later, Luce received a phone call from Addison Kane. It was short and to the point, and later that same night Luce found herself once again in bed with Addison. Just like the first time, it was fun and definitely lucrative, so when Addison proposed an arrangement whereby she would become Luce's only client, Luce readily agreed. Luce knew it wasn't going to be a friends-with-benefits arrangement, but she wasn't looking for a friend. She was looking for a better life, and Addison Kane could afford her just that. Besides, there was something to be said for being able to give face to one of the wealthiest women in the United Kingdom.

***

"Give me my pills, will you?"

Luce opened her eyes, snickering to herself when she realized she was on the wrong side of the bed. Rolling to her side, she reached for the medicine bottle on the nightstand, wincing as her sore muscles announced themselves.

There wasn't much she hadn't done in bed with Addison, but it had been a while since they had had rough sex, and the past several hours had definitely been rough. There were no whips involved or safe words necessary, and no ropes or handcuffs had been used, but instead of their customary give and take, the night had been about Addison taking what she wanted…repeatedly.

Tapping out one of the four pills left in the bottle, Luce rolled back over and handed one to Addison. "So, care to explain what's going on?"

"I'm taking a pill," Addison said, popping it into her mouth.

"No, I mean about…well, tonight was a little above and beyond, if you know what I'm saying."

"I haven't a clue," Addison said, grabbing her glass of scotch. "And it's time for you to leave."

Luce shook her head and smiled. "I love it when you dismiss me. It's *so* you."

Placing the empty glass on the nightstand, Addison rested back on her pillow and closed her eyes. "Are you still here?"

Laughing out loud, Luce climbed out of bed. "You're seriously too much sometimes," she said, stretching toward the ceiling. Waiting as her vertebrae let out a few pops as bones and discs realigned, she moved her head one way and then the other to work out the kinks. Satisfied everything was still in working order, Luce set about gathering the sex toys strewn about and then took them into the bathroom for a much-needed cleaning.

Freshly showered, Luce reappeared a half hour later to find Addison sound asleep. Quietly opening the top drawer of the dresser, Luce placed the toys inside, and turning around, she leaned against the chest and stared at the sleeping industrialist.

Luce wasn't stupid. While it had taken her a few more years than most to get a degree, that had to do with the lack of money, not the lack of brains. Something was off about Addison and Luce knew it. Tonight, Addison had tried *too* hard.

Like a child in need of Ritalin, Addison had been amped up all night, and her approach to sex had taken on an almost adolescent enthusiasm. She had long ago proven to Luce she was an accomplished lover who knew how to please, but tonight Addison seemed almost frenzied in her approach. No sooner would an orgasm be had when Addison would change positions and start again, and when she became bored with straddling, scissoring, grinding, fingering, and tonguing, out came the toys.

It had been an almost non-stop onslaught of everything sexual. As always, Luce had been willing to receive all Addison wanted to give, but every time she caught a glimpse of Addison's icy eyes, they were distant and devoid of emotion as if instead of being a participant, Addison had become a bystander.

After spending a few more minutes replaying the night's events in her mind, Luce took a deep breath, gathered her things, shut off the lights, and went home.

***

Twice in as many days, Luce exited the lift and headed to one of three penthouse suites atop the glorious Langham hotel. She had visited the life of the opulent many times in various hotels across the continent, but while others could marvel at the dining areas, bars, and upscale shops meant to impress, Luce could not. Her admiration was limited to the suites of her clients and the hallways leading up to them.

Her steps quieted by an intricately designed hall runner, Luce meandered down the corridor. She couldn't help herself from again appreciating the artwork adorning the walls, each of which was surrounded by old-world styled frames covered in gold leaf. When she reached a small sitting area, she stopped long enough to scoop a mint out of a crystal bowl sitting on the table, and then continued on her way. Reaching her destination, Luce rapped lightly on the door, and a minute later, she rapped again. About to reach into her bag for the key card she rarely used, she jumped when the door flung open.

"You're late!"

Luce kept her eyes on Addison as she stepped into the room. Good mood or bad, Addison had always maintained an air about her. A dignity born from her surname and schooling, it never wavered. True, she could lose her temper at the drop of a hat, but when it came to her appearance, unless it was in the throes of sex, rarely was a strand of hair out of place or clothing not pressed.

The only thing Addison was wearing, her standard crisp white blouse, was neither crisp nor white any longer. The Oxford was splotched with stains of red and brown, and by the wrinkles covering almost every square inch of the fabric, it was evident the shirt had been slept in. Addison's hair seemed to be styled courtesy of an electrical shock of massive proportions, and her arctic eyes were barely visible behind lids heavy from alcohol.

Inebriated friends in pubs had often brought smiles to Luce's face, but as she gawked at Addison, Luce wasn't laughing. Like the previous night, this was yet another side of Addison she had never seen before, and Luce's forehead furrowed.

"All right, what's going on with you?" Luce said, tossing her handbag on a chair.

"I dunno what you're talking about," Addison said, staggering past.

Grabbing Addison by the arm, Luce spun her around and then gripped the woman's bicep when Addison nearly fell over.

"Last night you couldn't get enough sex, and by the way you look..." Luce stopped and wrinkled her nose. "...and *smell*, today you apparently couldn't get enough scotch. This isn't like you."

"You don't know me!" Addison said, pulling out of Luce's hold. "You're just another stupid cow inna long line o' stupid cows who thin' they know me. Well, I've got news for you. You know shit! Yarn't my friend. Yarn't my confidant, and you're certainly not my equal. You're my whore, and you'd best remember that."

Dulled by alcohol, Addison didn't have a chance to avoid Luce's stinging slap, the force of which almost sent her to the floor. A hint of metallic instantly invaded her mouth, and licking the blood that had seeped onto her lip, Addison sneered at Luce. "Hitta nerve, did I?"

Watching as Addison's cheek reddened in the shape of a handprint, Luce's shoulders dropped. Addison was holding her chin high, taking the stance of one invincible, but Luce could see a pain in her eyes that had nothing to do with the slap she had just received.

"I'm sorry," Luce said, letting out a sigh. "I shouldn't have done that."

Alcohol affects people differently. Some become chatty to the point of annoyance, while others become free, embarrassed by nothing. They gyrate on dance floors or promenade down streets during Mardi Gras sans tops and bras, oblivious to any looks they're receiving. In their fogged state nothing matters, but Luce's words lifted the impervious shroud cloaking Addison. Dropping her chin to her chest, she said, "Don't ever apologize fo' sumthin' deserved."

Luce had expected more. Something cutting and deep, befitting Addison's normal holier-than-thou attitude, so her admission of error in a tone quiet and penitent, was as sobering as it was enlightening. Under all the bravado was a woman, and she was hurting. Luce took a step in Addison's direction. "Do you want me to leave?" she said quietly.

"Depends," Addison said, lifting her head.

"On what?"

"On whether or not yo' done inflicting bodily harm."

The faintest of grins appeared on Luce's face as she stared back at Addison. "Promise me you'll never call me that again?" she said softly.

"You've my word."

"You're drunk. Who's to say you'll remember this tomorrow?"

It was Addison's turn to display a grin, albeit an incredibly lopsided one. "You're too annoying to lemme forget."

Luce smiled in return, but it quickly disappeared when she saw Addison begin to sway. "I think you need to go lie down," Luce said, taking a step in Addison's direction. "Sleep it off."

"Not tired."

"Addison—"

"I said I'm no' tired!"

Dismissing Luce with a mighty wave of her arm, Addison turned to walk away, and the combination of her movements sent her lurching across the room. Misjudging the distance to the sofa, when she grabbed out to steady herself, Addison fell flat on her face.

"Shit!" Luce said, quickly kneeling by Addison's side. "Are you all right?"

"Who moved the fuckin' sofa?"

"That would be the demon alcohol, I'm thinking," Luce said as she helped Addison roll over, but when she saw the blood streaming from Addison's nose, any hilarity Luce had found in the situation immediately disappeared. "Fuck! I think you may have just broken your nose."

"Bollocks," Addison said, and bringing her hand to her face, she found her cheeks and her chin before finally finding her nose. Flinching, she pulled her fingers away and scowled. "Zat blood?"

"Well, it sure as hell isn't Cabernet," Luce said as she got Addison to her feet. Holding onto the woman to steady her, Luce said, "You think you can make it to the bedroom?"

A lopsided leer appeared on Addison's face. "Sure...whatcha have in mind?"

***

True to her word, Addison wasn't tired, so for almost an hour she played a drunken game of grab-anything-you-can while Luce tried to clean up the blood on her face. Half-way between amused and annoyed at the woman's overactive libido, Luce decided to take a different tack. If Addison wanted sex, she'd have to shower first.

Thankful upscale hotels had bathrooms to match, in a shower large enough to hold four, Luce gave Addison a much-needed wash. Between the grab rails and a built-in seat, Addison was safe from harm, but Luce wasn't as lucky. For the next twenty minutes, Addison's libido reigned supreme again, and Luce spent as much of her time washing Addison as she did warding off the woman's sloppy gropes. The good news was after cleaning up the blood, Luce decided Addison's nose was still as straight as ever, but the bad news was Addison had suddenly gone quiet. The playful pinches had stopped, as did the lopsided drunken leers, and when they exited the shower, Addison obediently allowed Luce to towel her dry without saying a word.

She escorted Addison back to bed, and after tucking the blankets in around her, Luce said, "You ready to call it a night?"

"I'm not tired."

"Okay," Luce said, letting out a sigh. "You hungry?"

"No," Addison said, staring at the bedcovers.

"How about some tea?"

Addison mindlessly traced her finger over the floral designs on the bedspread, but after a few seconds, she raised her eyes. "Do you think I'm an uncaring bitch?"

Luce did her best to hold back a laugh. "You have your moments."

Even in Addison's drunken state, Luce thought her reply would have at the very least made the woman grin in return, but seeing a pained look cross Addison's face, Luce sat down on the edge of the bed and gently placed her hand on Addison's leg. "Why did you ask that?"

"No reason," Addison said as she returned to mindlessly picking at the blanket.

It was Luce's turn to frown. It was clear Addison didn't want to talk, and while Luce was used to the woman shutting down her questions, this was different. There was no arrogance here. No spoiled brat throwing her wealthy weight around. This was sadness, and Luce was stunned. She didn't know how to deal with a sad Addison Kane. "How about I go make that tea?" she said, getting to her feet.

Addison lifted her eyes. Watching as Luce began to walk away, she blurted, "Joanna fell the other day. No one thought to tell me."

Luce whipped around. "What? Is she okay?"

"Evelyn said she's fine," Addison said, returning her focus to the bedspread.

Worry lines creased Luce's brow, and slowly stepping over the clothes littering the floor, she sat back down on the bed. "And that bothered you? I mean, not being told."

"Yeah."

"Because?"

"I don't know," Addison said with a shrug. "Just did."

Luce leaned back as she studied Addison. Thoughts of the last two days came into her mind, and she sat quietly, processing what she knew. The only problem was, the more she processed, the more things didn't add up.

Pride could have been the basis for the frenzied sex the night before, except Addison didn't need to demonstrate her prowess in the bedroom, especially not to Luce. A bruised ego could explain the drinking, but Luce had never known Addison's skin to be that thin. Why did it matter she wasn't told about Joanna's fall? She didn't even like the woman.

Luce's head snapped up. Could it be? Did Addison actually *care* about Joanna? Did she *like* her? Did she *more* than like her? Cupping her chin in her hand, Luce debated on how to proceed. It didn't take long.

"So...I saw the pictures in the paper when you attended that party," Luce said, fixated on her target to catch even the most minor of twitches. "Your wife is beautiful."

"Yes, she is," Addison said without raising her eyes.

"Seemed quite happy, too. You make a lovely couple."

"We aren't a couple," Addison said in a whisper. "It's just for show."

Luce knew she had found her answer when, like a weight, the truth caused Addison to sink further into the bed. It wasn't ego, and it wasn't pride. It was something much more complicated than that and Luce's heart pained for the woman, who regardless of their business relationship, had become her friend.

Letting out a sigh, Luce decided the demons Addison was fighting, weren't hers to battle. Getting to her feet, she said, "I'm going to make you some tea, and then you're going to get some sleep. Okay?"

"Sure," Addison said. "Whatever you say."

***

Luce returned to the bedroom a short time later, once again stepping over discarded clothing and empty glasses scattered about the room. Surprised to see Addison still awake, Luce placed the cup on the nightstand. "Here you go. It's not too hot, in case you're interested in having some now."

"Thanks."

"If you're okay, I'm going to get dressed. It's getting late."

It was the first time Addison had looked at Luce since the shower, and seeing her still bundled in one of the hotel's bulky white courtesy robes, she said, "That's fine."

"Be back in a tick," Luce said, disappearing into the bathroom.

A couple of minutes later, Luce came back and quickly let out a sigh of relief. Not only had Addison finished her tea, but she was now softly snoring under a mound of blankets. Gathering up the empty cup and a tumbler half-filled with scotch, she swept the pill bottle back into the nightstand drawer before she turned off the light and went home.

Chapter Twenty-Seven

The doors had barely opened when she bolted from the lift and sprinted down the hallway. Mindless of the time of night, she pounded on the door as loudly as her knuckles would allow. Seconds later, it opened.

"Thank God—"

"Where is she?" Joanna said as she charged past the woman who had answered the door.

"In the bedroom," Luce said, pointing across the lounge. "Through those doors."

Joanna rushed across the room and into the bedroom, her heart dropping when she saw Addison passed out on the bed. Hearing a noise behind her, she said, "Did you manage to get her to drink any coffee?"

"No, I tried, but she kept spitting it out. Said she wanted to sleep."

"Well, that's *not* going to happen," Joanna said, jumping to her feet. "Where's the loo?"

"What?"

"The loo! Where's the bloody loo?"

"Oh, it's right in there," Luce said, watching as Joanna hurried into the bathroom. "What the hell are you doing?"

"What do you think I'm doing?" Joanna said as she ran back to the bed with the small bathroom bin in hand.

Luce tilted her head to the side, and a moment later, she blanched. "Oh my God, you're not...oh shit, you are," Luce said, closing her eyes an instant before the sound of heaving filled the room.

***

Joanna stood in front of the bathroom mirror, slowly washing her hands as she tried to get her heart rate to slow. An hour earlier, she had received a call on her mobile from Addison, but when Joanna answered, she found herself talking to a stranger out of her mind with worry. Joanna didn't know who the woman was, but she did now, and while they had yet to exchange names, more than a few *names* had already occurred to Joanna. Tossing the hand towel aside, she walked into the bedroom, barely glimpsing at Addison before heading to the lounge.

"How is she?" Luce said, placing the coffee carafe back on the serving cart.

"She passed out as soon as she stopped heaving," Joanna said. "Do you have any idea how many pills she took?"

Luce shook her head. "All I know is that last night there were three left in the bottle, and now it's empty."

"Last night?" Joanna said, crossing her arms across her chest. "So, you were here last night, *too*?"

If Luce had been closer to the door, she would have already been on the other side, but it was a dozen steps away, and Joanna was in her path. With no escape, Luce let out a long breath. "This just got really awkward, *really* quickly."

"It's awkward for you? Imagine how I feel."

"I'm sorry. I didn't know who else to call, and since I know Addison trusts you, when I saw your name come up in her contact list...well, I figured if she trusts you, so could I."

"What do mean she trusts me?"

"I...I know about your marriage."

Joanna's body stiffened, her spine stretching to its extreme as her casual perusal of the stunning redhead morphed into a glowering stare. "Pillow talk?"

"Look, this isn't what it seems."

"No?"

"I mean it is, but it's isn't."

"Have you been drinking, too?"

"No, but honestly I think I could use one," Luce said, setting down her coffee cup. Going over to the courtesy bar, she opened the cabinet and pulled out a bottle of gin. "Would you like something?"

"No, thank you. Coffee's fine for me," Joanna said as she went over and filled another cup. As she took a sip of the hotel's finest, Joanna looked over at the woman across the room and almost instantly, she felt her annoyance surge. Why in the hell did she have to be so damned attractive?

Joanna put down her cup and strode over to the bar. "I've changed my mind. Whiskey, please."

Luce grabbed a tumbler and splashed some single malt into it. Handing it to Joanna, she said, "I want you to know that if I thought she had taken any more than three, I would have called emergency services. I just didn't think—"

"No, you did the right thing. I just don't understand why you let her take them to begin with."

"I didn't!" Luce said, slamming down her glass. "I left to go home. I got halfway to the bloody lift when I remembered that yesterday there were three pills in the bottle and when I put it away tonight it was empty. I came back in, tried to wake her up, and then I called you."

"Do you think she did it intentionally?"

"Absolutely not," Luce said, shaking her head. "She was royally sloshed. I doubt she even knew her own name."

"Speaking of names," Joanna said, holding out her hand. "Joanna Kane."

Taken aback by the sign of civility, it took a few seconds before Luce extended her hand. "Luce Gainsford."

Joanna sized up Luce as they shook hands, and she liked what she saw as much as she didn't. Curvy, slender, and with flowing red hair, Luce was a beautiful woman, and the sprinkling of faint freckles across the bridge of her nose added an earthy wholesomeness that irked Joanna to no end. No sooner had their hands dropped to their sides when Joanna asked, "So, what do you mean by this isn't what it seems?"

"Sorry?"

"A few minutes ago, you said *this* isn't what it seems. Care to explain?"

"Oh," Luce said, taking a sip of her drink. "I meant me being here isn't based on...on love. I care about Addison, but I'm not in love with her."

"You're not?"

"No. I just...um...help her...help her unwind."

Joanna raised an eyebrow and placed her glass on the bar. "Is that what they're calling it nowadays? Unwinding? Why not just call it what it is...shagging." Joanna stopped long enough to give Luce a cool once-over. "Or do you prefer *fucking*?"

"Maybe I should leave," Luce said, stepping around the bar.

"How long has this been going on?" Joanna said, blocking Luce's way.

"What?"

"How *long* have you helping my wife *unwind*?"

Luce would have expected jealousy from a wife who was truly a wife, so Joanna's question gave her pause. Why was this woman jealous? Why was this woman *raging* jealous? Why did this woman even care? Thinking back to her earlier conversation with Addison, two words popped into Luce's mind. *Oh. Shit.*

Escape was only ten paces away, so sidestepping Joanna, Luce headed for the door.

"Not so fast," Joanna said, once again getting in the way of Luce's retreat. "I asked you a question, and I want an answer."

"Look, I'm not sure I should—"

"How *long* have you been helping Addison *unwind*?" Joanna barked.

Luce hesitated, running her tongue over her lips to replace the moisture that had somehow just disappeared. "Um...ten years, give or take."

Joanna's eyes bulged. "Ten *years*?"

"It really isn't what you think."

"You honestly don't want to know what I'm thinking right now," Joanna said, marching past Luce. "I'm leaving."

"Wait. What about Addison?"

Joanna spun around and glared at Luce. "You're her *unwinding* buddy. *You* take care of her."

***

Monday morning, Joanna sat at the kitchen table scanning the newspaper. Noah was busy hunched over a gourmet cookbook, and Evelyn was nibbling some toast when the quiet of the room was interrupted by Evelyn's mobile vibrating on the countertop.

Evelyn picked it up, read the message, and frowned. "That's odd."

"What?" Joanna said, looking up.

"It was text from Addison. She said she won't be home until next week. Something about a business trip to Spain."

"Thank God for small favors," Joanna said under her breath.

"And she didn't come home this weekend either. Did she?"

Joanna turned the page of her newspaper. "I didn't notice," she said without looking up.

Evelyn glanced at Noah, and he returned her confused look with one of his own. Typically, their mornings were filled with friendly banter over morning coffee, but Joanna had hardly said a word since walking into the room. Picking up her coffee, Evelyn went over and sat at the table. Noticing Joanna had turned to the classifieds, Evelyn said, "You're not looking for a job. Are you?"

"What if I am?"

"I doubt Addison would approve."

"What makes you think I *need* her approval?"

As soon as the words left her mouth, Joanna wanted to retract them. They were harsh. They were loud, and they were wrong. "I'm sorry, Evelyn," she said, raising her eyes. "That was totally uncalled for and terribly rude of me."

"Apology accepted," Evelyn said softly.

"And I'm not looking for a job," Joanna said, returning her attention to the newspaper.

Evelyn's curiosity got the best of her. Leaning forward, she squinted to read the upside-down classifieds. "Um...are those the personal ads?"

Since opening the paper, Joanna had yet to read a word. She had turned page after page because that's what you're supposed to do when you're looking through a newspaper, but the articles and sales ads had gone unnoticed. The only thing on Joanna's mind was Addison...and Luce.

Joanna glanced at the ads in front of her and shrugged. "As a matter of fact, they are. Why?"

"Joanna—"

"Relax, Evelyn. I'm not in the market for a friend with benefits," Joanna said, folding the newspaper in half. "Besides, these things creep me out."

"Then what *are* you looking for?"

Joanna leaned back and slowly exhaled. "I don't know, but I just can't..." Her words faded away as an image of Luce Gainsford began to invade her mind, and before the portrait was complete, Joanna's jaw had set. "Why does *she* get to have a life, and I don't?"

"What do you mean?"

"How come Addison gets to do whatever and *who*ever she likes, and I'm stuck here living like a cloistered nun?"

Noah's and Evelyn's heads both snapped back in unison.

"What did you just say?" Evelyn said.

"I know about Luce," Joanna said, casting a quick look in Noah's direction. "And by both of your reactions, it appears you do, too."

"How did you—"

"It doesn't matter, but if she can have a fu...a *friend* with benefits, why can't I?"

"Is that what you want?"

"No!" Joanna said, raising her voice. "But I feel like I'm atrophying. The bloody rain won't stop. I've read every book we own three sodding times, and believe it or not, there's only so much shopping I can do. Look, everyone here has been great, but you have something to do, and you have lives outside this house. I have nothing *but* this house, and I'm lonely."

A pained look crossed Evelyn's face. "I don't know what to say."

"It's okay," Joanna said, offering Evelyn a soft grin. "I'll figure something out."

Letting out a sigh, Joanna returned to the newspaper, scanning the classifieds for jobs she couldn't apply for and for dates she didn't want. Turning the page, she kept skimming the columns until an ad caught her attention. Biting the inside of her cheek, she pondered the consequences. "Do we have a driver today?" Joanna said, raising her eyes.

"Yes, George is here. Why?"

"I'm not sure where this place is," she said, getting up from the table. "Could you call him, please? Ask him to bring a car around?"

"Um...of course, but where are you going?"

Joanna smiled as she picked up a nearby pen and circled the ad. "Here," she said, tossing the pen on the table as she headed out of the room. "Please tell him I'll be down in ten minutes."

As soon as the kitchen door swung closed, Noah said, "That was a quick mood change. What'd she find?"

"Let me look," Evelyn said, turning the paper around. Taking a sip of her coffee, it promptly spewed from her mouth when she read the tiny advertisement. "Oh, no!"

***

When Addison had awoken at the Langham on Sunday morning, she had found a note from Luce. It was the first time Luce had ever felt compelled to leave a message, and as Addison sat on the edge of bed reading what

Luce had written, a torrent of emotions enveloped her. She was embarrassed she had drunk so much and stunned she had taken the pills. She was grateful Luce just didn't walk away, but the shame she felt knowing Joanna now knew about Luce was like an anvil on Addison's chest. She had never before felt so common...or so dirty.

Addison spent Sunday in a trance, sitting alone in her suite and trying her best to make excuses for her actions, but the humiliation she felt was far more painful than the pounding in her head. Every lame excuse was a lie, and she knew it. Refusing to face the truth, she did the only thing she could. She ran.

She spent a week in Spain, her days filled with work and her nights filled with rationalizations, so by the time Addison climbed out of the Rolls and walked up the steps to her home, she was as confident as confident could be. In her mind, her lies had become the truth. She answered to no one. She had no feelings for Joanna. She came and went as she pleased, and if Joanna didn't like it, that was too damn bad.

Just as Addison reached the door it swung open so quickly, she stumbled back a half-step.

"Welcome home!" Evelyn said in a tone loud enough to wake the dead.

Addison eyeballed Evelyn for a moment before walking inside. "What are you doing here?" she said as she took off her coat. "It's after eight."

"Yes, well, I had some odds and ends to take care of and...and I wanted to make sure you got home all right."

Addison narrowed her eyes and looked around the foyer. "What's wrong?"

"Wrong?" Evelyn said, her voice raising an octave. "Why would you think anything's wrong?"

"Because you're answering a question with a quest—" Addison's ability to speak came to a grinding halt when she saw what appeared to be a long-haired rodent scampering up the hall leading from the parlor, and on its heels was Joanna, laughing as she tried to catch up.

"Sorry," Joanna said, scooping up the puppy. "He's a quick little guy."

"What the *hell* is *that*?" Addison shouted.

"He's a Yorkie-Shih Tzu mix I got from the shelter. His name's Chauncey," Joanna said, holding up the puppy. "Isn't he cute?"

Addison's face turned scarlet. "His name is going to be *Haggis* unless you get him out of my house!"

"Lower your voice. You're scaring him," Joanna said, holding the pup to her chest.

"Ask me if I care? Now, get him out of here, or I will!"

In two quick steps, Joanna was within inches of Addison, and looking her in the eye, she said, "He's mine, and he's staying, and if you harm one hair on his head, the deal is off."

Addison lowered her chin and glared down her nose at Joanna. "What did you say?"

"You heard," Joanna said, never wavering from her eye lock on Addison. "I only married you because of my father, but now he's gone. I have no problem walking out that door right now and not looking back. I won't live like this, and I won't live like *you*."

"So much for your word being worth anything," Addison said with a snort as she eyed Joanna up and down.

"I don't break promises easily, Addison, but you're giving me no choice. My father's gone, so there's nothing left for me here except four walls and a roof, and that's not enough."

"Well, that's all you're going to get. Now get rid of him."

Joanna moved even closer, and when she spoke, it was in a whisper. "I think you forget who I am. I'm your wife and the woman who stuck her fingers down your throat when you took too many pills while your *mistress* looked on. Or did you forget that?"

"So I owe you. Is that what you're saying?"

"Call it whatever you'd like," Joanna said, giving a half-shrug as she took a step backward. "But I think this win is in my column, or am I wrong?"

Only minutes before, Addison had walked into her house confident Joanna meant nothing to her, but it seems distance has a way of skewing perspective. Addison couldn't help but breathe deeply the scent of the woman's perfume, and the sight of Joanna in tight-fitting jeans, her eyes smoldering with defiance, was like a match to Addison's flame, turning her single-mindedness into cinders instantly.

Addison was torn. She was bothered her backbone had weakened so easily, but after spending eight days hardly talking to anyone, she found herself enjoying the conversation no matter how heated. She already knew Joanna was going to get her way, but Addison couldn't make herself give in just yet. Squaring her shoulders, she said, "I don't like dogs."

"Why not?"

"They shed."

Joanna smiled. "He's a Yorkie mix. He shouldn't shed that much."

"They bark."

"I'll do my best to keep him quiet."

"He'll pee in the house."

"He's been here a week, and he's almost housetrained."

"Almost?"

Joanna nodded. "Yes, *almost*, but it should only take another few days."

Having refused to give the puppy even a cursory glance, Addison finally lowered her eyes and stared at the ball of fur barely filling Joanna's hand. "He's too small. He'll get stepped on."

"My problem, not yours."

Standing off to the side, Evelyn had remained quiet throughout the contest of wills, but seeing a light at the end of the tunnel, she stepped forward. "And I'll help," she said. "I'm not a stranger to dogs. Between Joanna and me, Chauncey will be walking the straight and narrow in no time. I promise he won't get in your way."

Addison looked at Evelyn and then back at Joanna before letting out a sigh and heading toward her study. "Fine," she said, turning around as she reached the door. "But I don't want to hear him, and I don't want to see him. He gets in my way, and he's gone."

***

Addison climbed the spiral stairs slowly. For the fourth night in a row, she had exercised until her muscles could take no more, but her exhaustion only added to her loneliness. Joanna had yet to say another word to her, and each time Addison had offered a "good evening" when Joanna appeared in the dining room, Joanna had ignored her, just as Addison had done to her so many times before.

The missing candelabra had gone unmentioned, and the scrumptious meals Noah prepared hadn't caused Joanna to comment, and Addison was at a loss. Stalemate was a place she'd never been before.

When she reached her study, Addison slumped into the chair behind her desk, and staring at the decanters on the credenza, she frowned. Even the taste of scotch had turned foul. Leaning back, she closed her eyes and listened to the rain beating against the windows. She was thankful for the noise it was producing, but it seemed even Mother Nature was against her as the storm suddenly went quiet. The winds died, and the rain ceased to fall and in that moment of calm Addison heard a noise nearby. It wasn't rain, and it wasn't wind, and in a flash, Addison opened her eyes.

She scanned the room only to find it empty, but then she heard the faintest of whimpers. Pursing her lips, she got to her feet without making a sound and peered over her desk. She had found the intruder.

"Get out," Addison said to the puppy sitting on the floor.

Chauncey's response was that of a happy baby canine, and his entire body wagged in time with his stumpy tail.

Addison folded her arms across her chest. "I said get out. You don't belong in here."

Lying down, Chauncey stretched to his fullest and then raised his butt in the air so it could continue to wiggle.

With a sigh, Addison walked around the desk and looked down her nose at the tiny ball of fur. "Perhaps I didn't make myself—"

"There you are!" Joanna said, rushing into the room. Scooping up Chauncey, she said, "You scared me to death."

Addison never thought she would appreciate Chauncey's existence, but her opinion changed in an instant. Intent on the well-being of her dog, Joanna hadn't paid any attention to Addison, which gave Addison all the time in the world to pay attention to Joanna.

Addison's admiration of beauty, like most, had always been based on the end result. Hair had always been styled, and makeup always applied, but it wasn't until now when Addison truly understood what beauty was. Barefoot and wearing only a plaid robe, it was obvious Joanna had just gotten out of a bath. Her hair was wet and had not yet returned to its natural waves, and void of makeup and freshly scrubbed, her face positively glowed. Never again would Addison base her definition of the word beautiful on anything else.

"Sorry, I must have left my door open," Joanna said as she hugged the pup.

Intent on giving Chauncey all her attention, it wasn't until Joanna realized Addison hadn't responded that she looked up, but whatever she was going to say, promptly got stuck in her throat. At the Langham, saturated with alcohol, Addison's face had been puffy and her hair, a mess, and beyond that, Joanna hadn't noticed. She hadn't been there to admire or to even peruse, but now, standing only a few feet from her wife, Joanna found herself doing both.

Accustomed to seeing Addison in a suit, to see her dressed so casually took Joanna by surprise. In place of pressed trousers were loose-fitting black track pants hanging low on her hips, and barely covering her torso was a nylon hoodie. Unzipped and loose, there was no need for Joanna's imagination to take charge as she could clearly see Addison's toned, flat stomach *and* a white sports bra that wasn't as opaque as the wearer probably wished.

Joanna's body reacted instantly, jolting her back to now with a jerk. "Well...um...we should be going. I hope he wasn't too much of a bother."

"He wasn't a bother. He wasn't in here long enough to—"

Addison's words were cut off by the slam of the door, leaving her feeling more alone than she had been a few minutes earlier.

Chapter Twenty-Eight

The sound from the clock chiming ten echoed through the house, and before its tolling had ended, Addison tossed the report aside. Since the night at the Langham, she had yet to take another sleeping pill, using exercise in its place. Her cigarette habit had also ceased, as had her romps with Luce. She no longer wanted either.

Addison hung her head, massaging her temples in hopes it would make her headache go away. She sighed as the pain persisted, and looking at her watch, she sighed again. She was wide awake and even though she wasn't in the mood to exercise, if she didn't hit the gym, Addison knew she wouldn't get any sleep. Her thoughts were interrupted when she heard the squeak of hinges. She looked up, and for a split-second, a vision of Robert came to mind. "Shit, she said, her shoulders sagging from the weight of reality.

"Yip."

While it was hardly booming, the small interruption to the silence surrounding her caused Addison to jump.

"Yip."

Addison scowled, and pushing herself out of her chair, she walked around the desk. "You again," she said, staring down at the puppy.

Chauncey looked up and immediately began to wag his tail. "Yip."

"I don't want you in here."

"Yip."

"You don't belong in here."

"Yip."

"Fine," Addison said, taking a step in the pup's direction. "I'll show you where you belong."

Before Addison could take another step, Chauncey dashed across the room and scrambled under the credenza. A moment later, he stuck out his nose and announced his thoughts. "Yip. Yip. Yip."

"Oh, that's just great," Addison mumbled as she got down on her hands and knees. "Come here, you little bugger. I'm not in the mood."

With his tail in full wag mode, Chauncey crawled backward under the credenza until he was out of Addison's reach. "Yip."

"Stop that blasted barking," Addison said, waving her arm under the furniture.

"Yip. Yip. Yip."

"Fuck it," Addison said, getting to her feet. "You found your way in here. Find your way out!" Stomping across the room, Addison headed to the gym without looking back.

***

It was almost midnight before Addison climbed out of the pool. She had punished her body until it would go no further and leaning on the ladder, she gasped for air so she'd have the strength to head to the shower. Finally able to slow her breathing, she stripped out of her swimsuit, but then something caught her eye in the gym. Spotting Chauncey sniffing near the treadmill, she said, "How the hell did you get down here?" Looking toward the opened door in the corner, she found her answer.

"Get out of here," she yelled, but when Chauncey continued his investigation, Addison hurled her wet swimsuit in his direction. "I said get *out* of here!"

When it landed with a loud splat inches from where he was sniffing, Chauncey let out a frightened squeak and scooted toward the stairs.

"Good riddance, you little bastard," Addison muttered as she dragged her tired self to the shower.

A short time later, exhausted but no longer smelling of chlorine, Addison donned her tracksuit and pushed the vinyl curtain aside. Noticing her black Speedo near the edge of the pool, she came to a stop. "What the hell?"

Addison looked toward the exercise area, her eyes darting back and forth as she searched for the dog. Coming up empty, she shrugged and took a few more steps, but when she reached the treadmill, her heart stopped. She spun around, and as she stared at the pool, the hair on the back of her neck instantly stood on end. Holding her breath, Addison slowly walked over to the edge.

She kept telling herself the pool would be empty, again and again in her head convincing herself there was nothing to worry about, but then she saw the dark, black spot lying on the bottom, and her blood ran cold. "Oh, Jesus Christ, *no*!"

Regenerated by the adrenaline now coursing through her veins, Addison dove into the water. Her arms and legs propelled her to the deepest end, and grabbing Chauncey, she launched herself off the bottom, breaking the surface within seconds. Placing him on the pool deck, Addison pushed herself out of the water and picked up the lifeless puppy.

"Please God, no," she said, giving Chauncey a shake. "Please, oh sweet Jesus...please."

Addison waited for a moment, but when Chauncey remained limp in her hands, she turned him upside down. "No fucking way!" she shouted, giving him a shake and then another. "Breathe, you blasted dog, breathe!" She rested on her haunches as she watched the water drain from his lungs, believing her work had been done, but when he still didn't move, Addison was transported to a place she'd never been. A place called compassion, and suddenly nothing else in the world mattered to her except for the life of this dog.

Without thinking twice, she laid him on the deck of the pool and placed her mouth over his nose. After giving him a few quick puffs of air, she waited for what seemed like an eternity, but he still didn't move. "You little bastard, you're going to wake up! Do you hear me?" she said before covering his snout again and repeating the process. Seconds later, Chauncey snorted and sprayed Addison with his spittle.

The smile that spread across her face was the largest Addison owned, and picking up the shivering puppy, she cradled him against her chest. "You stupid dog," she said in a ragged whisper. "You stupid, *stupid* dog."

She sat on the floor, rocking back and forth as she tried to keep the emotions she believed proved her weak from appearing, but when she heard Chauncey's tiny whimpers, everything Addison had locked away for so long...erupted.

The years of torment caused by a father who loathed her brought tears to her eyes. Honed by the neglect, she had turned herself into something unlikable *and* unlovable. Memories of nights spent in fear, and days spent hidden from his eyes filled her mind, and as each appeared more tears fell.

Chauncey let out another whimper, and she held him up, staring into his little dark brown eyes as she sniffled back her tears. The color reminded her of a man who she missed, and bowing her head, Addison sobbed for the loss of Robert Sheppard.

Steadfast at his funeral, her expression had remained blank, but in the damp warmth of her basement, her grief found its freedom. The only regret she had ever acknowledged was leaving her grandfather without saying good-bye, but it was a lie. Addison had many regrets, and for the next hour, they would choke her in the form of tears and wailing she could not stop.

***

After finally pulling herself together, Addison towel dried Chauncey until not an ounce of moisture remained, but when she caught a whiff of chlorine on his fur, she knew her work was not yet done. It was almost two in the morning when she climbed the stairs leading to her room, but her need for sleep was secondary to the needs of little pup she held in her hands. Carrying him into her shower, Addison tenderly gave him a bath, laughing more than once as he pranced around the shower or tried to clamber up her legs. Using every towel at her disposal, she made sure he was totally dry before she crept down the hallway to Joanna's room and set him down near the open door. She patted him lightly on the butt and smiled when he waddled in without argument. Quietly closing Joanna's door, Addison returned to her room and slept until mid-morning.

***

The clock had just finished chiming eleven when Addison came down the stairs. Ignoring the study, she kept on walking. Her mind wasn't on business. It was on Joanna and Chauncey.

It was her neglect that had caused Joanna to fall down stairs long in need of repair, and because of Addison's indifference, Chauncey had almost died simply because broken latches had never concerned her. They did now.

She strode into the kitchen, and her unexpected entrance immediately turned George and Fiona into statues. Frozen where they stood, they said not a word.

"I'd like some coffee," Addison said, breaking the silence.

"I-I-I put a carafe in your study a few minutes ago," Fiona said.

"No," Addison said, rubbing the back of her neck. "I want one of those...one of those..." Exasperated at her own ignorance, Addison blurted, "I want to go for a blasted walk and take a cup of coffee with me."

"Oh, you mean a travel mug," Fiona said, grinning.

"Yes, that's it. Can I have one of those please?"

Fiona flashed a quick look at her husband, and his face wore the same shocked expression. *Please* wasn't a word Addison ever used, at least not with them.

It took Fiona only a moment to find an insulated cup, and after filling it to the rim, she twisted on the lid and handed it to Addison. "There you go, miss. Be careful. It's hot."

"Thank you," Addison said as she headed for the door. "And I will."

***

Memories came rushing back as Addison walked outside. The last time she had set foot on the veranda was when she was a child. Running to and fro while Evelyn cast a watchful eye, Addison had twirled and tittered with the sun on her face and the wind in her hair, temporarily forgetting what lurked inside her home. It was a fleeting glimpse of youth, for her squeals of delight brought her father to the door, and from that day forward the patio would no longer be her playground, reducing the footprint of her world yet again.

Pulling the collar up on her leather coat, Addison took a deep breath of the cold air before starting her journey across the patio. More than once she hesitated when she heard the crunch of loosening slate beneath her feet, but undaunted she continued to the stairs.

Addison stopped when she reached the staircase, taking a sip of her coffee as she scanned the acreage behind the house. It was impossible not to notice the few beds now clear of brush. The bare earth and uncovered granite sharply contrasting against the tan and brown of the scrub, their reemergence reminded her of how extensive the area was.

Grabbing the iron railing, Addison gave it a tug to ensure it was secure before descending the steps, but it wasn't until she reached the bottom that she dared to raise her eyes again. When she did, she discovered she wasn't alone. Without thinking twice, she approached the figure huddled in a denim jacket.

"You need a warmer coat," Addison said.

Out of the corner of her eye, Joanna had seen Addison on the stairs, so she wasn't surprised by the interruption. She wasn't thrilled either. "The other one I have is new, and I'd hate to ruin it."

"You should be wearing gloves."

"Well, I'll put that on the bloody list," Joanna said, yanking out a handful of weeds and tossing them aside.

"It's really too cold for you to be doing this today. You'll catch a chill."

"Yeah?" Joanna said, jumping to her feet. "Well, then I guess that'll make me just like you. Won't it?" Giving Addison a quick once over, Joanna said, "Now leave me alone, Addison. I'm not in the mood."

Joanna sat back down, and when she heard the crunch of the frozen earth as Addison walked away, she let out a sigh. It was getting harder and harder to ignore a woman...she didn't want to ignore.

***

Addison had waited all day, wondering if her deception had been found out. She doubted many pups in England smelled of coconut shampoo, but by the time she sat down at the dining table, her mind was no longer on Chauncey.

Although rarely at a loss for words, when Joanna came in and sat down without uttering a sound, Addison was stumped as to how to break the ice. It wasn't going to be easy. Joanna's cold-shoulder in the garden earlier that day had proven that. Frowning as words continued to escape her, Addison settled on the simplest. "Good evening."

Joanna was trying to decide which of the paintings covering the walls she disliked the most when Addison's voice interrupted her thoughts. Slowly changing her focus, Joanna said, "Good evening."

The kitchen door swung open, and their meal began, and it wasn't until the last morsel had been consumed when Addison found the courage to say what was on her mind. "I was wondering..." she said, putting down her fork. "Do you...do you still have the corporate card Fran gave you?"

Believing it to be a stupid question, Joanna rolled her eyes and said the first thing that came to mind. "No, I gave it to a homeless man."

Addison leapt to her feet, her velocity causing her chair to tip over and bang against the floor. "*You did what?*"

Joanna tried to hold back her mirth, but unable to fight it, within seconds, she was reduced to giggles. "Oh my God, you should see your face."

The intensity of Addison's expression disappeared, and she placed her hands on her hips. "Was that some sort of joke?"

"Yep," Joanna said, wiping away a tear. "And by your reaction, it was a good one."

With her eyes remaining fixed on Joanna, Addison picked up her chair and sat back down. "All I did was ask you a question."

Joanna bristled. "And it was a stupid one," she said, putting her napkin aside. "Why the hell wouldn't I still have it, and why does it matter? It's not like I'm going to use it."

"Yes, you are. That is if you'd like to."

"What are you talking about?"

Addison took a sip of wine and then placed her glass back on the table. "That card has no limit on it."

"So?"

"If you're going to continue to work in those blasted gardens, then the stairs leading down to them need to be fixed."

"The whole bloody *patio* needs to be fixed."

"Then do it."

"What did you just say?"

"I said, *do* it," Addison said, pausing to take a drink of wine. "Hire someone in the spring and get it repaired."

"Are you serious?"

"When have you known me not to be?"

Joanna slowly picked up her glass, and taking a sip of the Cabernet, she studied the woman at the other end of the table. "Why are you doing this?"

"I told you. If you intend to keep working in the gardens, you need to get to them safely. Besides, you keep saying you have nothing to do. This should keep you busy for a while."

Joanna stared at Addison while she mulled things over until her eyes flew open wide. "Oh, now I get it!" she said, rocking back in her seat. "*I* stay busy with contractors and gardens while *you* stay busy with Luce. That's her name, right? *Luce*?"

The conversation had just taken an unexpected detour, and Addison felt her face grow warm. A few months earlier, she would have erupted with rage, but her anger had become tempered, mellowed by feelings she was trying to accept. "That's not what this is about," she said, her voice dropping almost to a whisper.

"No?"

Addison stood up, emptying the contents of the glass in her hand before placing it back on the table. "No," she said. "I was trying to be considerate."

"That'll be a first."

Joanna had no idea her barbs were penetrating Addison's walls so easily, each brusque reply causing Addison to inwardly wince at the sting. "Maybe so," Addison said, hanging her head. "But I don't want any harm to come to you or your...or to *anyone*. If you want to have it repaired, you have my permission."

"Lucky me," Joanna said, raising her arms in the air. "I've been granted the *great* Addison Kane's *permission*. When exactly am I supposed to kiss your feet?"

Unable to deal with the feeling of sadness washing over her, Addison headed to the door. "I'll have Millie send you my calendar. I have several business trips already scheduled, so if you decide to take me up on the offer, please arrange the repairs around them," Addison said as she forced herself to raise her eyes. "That's all I want."

Joanna got to her feet and threw her napkin on the table. "Trust me," she said as she marched out of the room. "That's *all* you're going to get."

Chapter Twenty-Nine

"You're awfully quiet this morning?"

"Am I?" Joanna said, looking up from her coffee.

"Well, since those are the first two words you've spoken since walking into this room fifteen minutes ago, I'd have to say yes."

"Last night, Addison told me to get the patio fixed."

Evelyn tilted her head to the side. "That's different."

"I know. She said it was because of my fall. To make sure it doesn't happen again."

"That makes sense."

"You think?"

"Don't you?"

Joanna sighed. "Honestly, I don't know."

"Well, if you ask me, maybe this is her way of...of making peace."

"How so?"

"You've barely spoken a dozen words to her since you found out about Luce—"

"This *isn't* about *Luce*! I don't give a toss about her!" Joanna said in a tone sharpened by her annoyance. "It's about Addison being allowed to have a bloody life, and I can't!"

Since Joanna's outing with Fran and her appearance at the Easterbrook party, the hubbub about the new Mrs. Kane had faded, so there was no need for Joanna to remain inside. Evelyn knew it, and she could have easily argued the point, but something told her now was not the time.

"My mistake," Evelyn said, bowing her head. "But as I was saying, you've hardly said a word to her, and those you have said were nothing more than curt. I'm not saying Addison doesn't deserve some of what she dishes out, but...but I think she was getting used to your company and now that she doesn't have it, she's trying to get it back."

"Yeah, but is she trying to make peace or just buy me off? Give me what I want so I'll come around?"

Evelyn pursed her lips as she thought over what Joanna had said. "Did she put any conditions on you getting the patio fixed?"

"No...well, yes. She said to have the work done while she wasn't here."

"Nothing else?"

"No."

"Then from where I'm sitting, I don't see a problem," Evelyn said. "She doesn't seem to have any ulterior motives, and if she does, that's on Addison. I know you're upset with her, but if I were you, I'd stop reading between the lines that aren't there. Stop questioning her motives and focus on what's important."

"What's that?"

"We're finally going to get something around this wretched place mended!"

***

Kicking a sliver of slate across the patio, Joanna hunched her shoulders against the brisk wind as she slowly walked the length and breadth of the veranda all the while thinking about the decision she needed to make. The word *permission* continued to nag at her like a toothache, but if Evelyn was right and this was Addison's way of offering an olive branch, then why not take it?

Joanna stopped at the railing and looked out over the grounds of the estate, imagining what they could look like in a year or maybe two. When the marriage had been proposed, she had weighed the good against the bad, and even though her father had died, she still believed she had made the right decision. As she stood in the grayness of the February day, Joanna decided it was time to make another.

Walking back into the house, she found Evelyn and asked to borrow her laptop, and a short time later, Joanna was ordering one of her own.

***

"I've decided to take you up on your offer."

Addison stopped mid-chew, raising her eyes to look across the table. Since their discussion the week before, Joanna had remained silent and aloof. She had returned to acknowledging Addison's "good evening" when she appeared in the dining room, but other than that, she had not spoken a word.

"About the patio?" Addison said, reaching for her wine.

"Did you make another?"

The tone of Joanna's cutting reply was not lost on Addison. While her words were few, they dripped with contempt, but in Addison's mind, it was a start. Just hearing Joanna's voice had lifted her spirits, and she wasn't about to give Joanna any ammunition to storm out of the room or cut short the conversation.

Taking a sip of wine, Addison placed the glass back on the table. "Did Millie send over my schedule?"

Joanna arched an eyebrow. She was expecting at least a hint of annoyance in Addison's reply, but instead the woman's voice was calm and respectful. "Yes, she e-mailed it to Evelyn."

"Good."

"Speaking of that, I ordered a laptop for myself, and Millie has my e-mail address. So, if any changes are made to your diary, she can send them to me directly."

"You should have let me know. I could have had the company supply you with one."

"Well, you never offered before, so there was no reason for me to bother you."

"It wouldn't have been a bother."

"No?"

"No," Addison said, shaking her head. "So...why the laptop?"

"To do research. If I'm going to hire someone to fix the slate, I need to know what questions to ask."

Research could have been Addison's middle name, and her appreciation of Joanna's thought process showed on her face. "That's an excellent idea."

"I thought so."

"So...have you contacted anyone yet?"

"Yes, I made arrangements to talk to three companies next week while you're out of town."

"Oh, I see."

"Is that a problem? You said it was up to me, or am I wrong?"

"No, you're not wrong."

"Well, imagine that," Joanna said as she leaned back in her chair and folded her arms.

Addison grimaced, and picking up her wine, she emptied it in one swallow. As she set the glass back down, she said, "Look...I know...I know you're upset about...about what happened at the Langham. I made a mistake. I was drunk—"

"You know nothing!" Joanna shouted as the vision of a slender, redheaded woman invaded her thoughts again. Jumping to her feet, she said, "And I don't want to talk about this. You have your life, and I have mine. Let's leave it at that."

"But—"

"There are no buts, Addison," Joanna said, striding to the door. "And *this* conversation is *over!*"

Seconds later, the sound of the doors slamming closed reverberated in the room.

***

Joanna had spent hours on the Internet researching not only construction companies, but also the questions she should ask when hiring one. Keeping her search within the county, she had found three local contractors that met her criteria. They all seemed reputable, and all had websites overflowing with information about their capabilities along with dozens of reviews from satisfied customers, so she called each and set up appointments for Monday. However, by Monday afternoon, Joanna believed she now knew why the word *con* was in contractor.

The first man arrived bright and early as scheduled. Appearing a bit on the scruffy side, he trudged through the house and took all of ten minutes slogging up and down the patio, dislodging loose slate and grumbling about inadequacies before his inspection was done. He pulled a wad of papers from his pocket, and without explaining his plans or his timeframe, he scratched down a price. Handing it to Joanna, he gave her a wink and made sure she understood if she didn't need a silly contract and agreed to pay him in cash, the price would go down.

The second was a half hour late. He entered the house grousing about backroads and the price of petrol as he had apparently made several wrong turns, and then clomped through the entry to the veranda. He lumbered across the slate and peered over the railing, and traveling down the stairs, he scrutinized the hill and grumbled some more. His notepad looked very professional, emblazoned with his logo and name across the top, and while he scrawled some details on the paper, he told Joanna the tunnel was at fault. The opening didn't provide the proper support for the mortar, so his plan was to fill in the tunnel and then pour concrete over the slate. It was the quickest, easiest, and cheapest answer. He jotted down his price in the total column and with a big, gap-toothed grin handed it to Joanna, but when she brought up the subject of insurance and guarantees, his grin seemed to disappear. He danced the dance of deception, trying his best to convince her insurance was overrated, and while he, indeed, could get it, it would only add to *her* expense. And as for guarantees, he would give her a whole thirty days.

By the time two o'clock rolled around, Joanna just wanted to get the day over with. Disenchanted by the two prior appointments, she had little faith that the last would end any differently, but then again, she had yet to meet Samson Dawkins.

Mr. Dawkins arrived promptly on time, and greeted at the door by Evelyn, he politely shook her hand as he introduced himself, and when Joanna appeared, he did the same. As she had done twice before, Evelyn excused herself and disappeared into the kitchen, but much to Joanna's surprise, unlike his predecessors, Mr. Dawkins didn't appear to be in a rush to get his quote into Joanna's hand.

Cordial and soft-spoken, he admitted his love for architecture before they had even taken a step, and as they meandered through the house, he couldn't stop himself from pointing out the workmanship in the plaster cornices and the detailed carvings in the plinths and blocks around the doors. He admitted all were in need of repair or refinishing, but Samson was unable to contain his smile amidst such finery. Against skin as dark as pitch, his dazzling display of straight, white teeth seemed to light up the house, and when they walked outside, the sun had found itself a competitor.

No sooner had they stepped onto the patio when Samson insisted Joanna go back inside. Dressed in a canvas, fleece-lined jacket and overalls, he was protected from the chill of the February wind, but

Joanna's hooded camel hair coat, while stylish, did not do the same. Appreciative of his chivalry, Joanna did as he asked and for the next two hours, she paced the kitchen while Samson paced the patio.

***

As soon as Joanna stepped foot in the parlor, Samson Dawkins stood up, his six-foot-five frame blocking out the streams of sunshine coming through one of the windows.

Joanna sat down and motioned for Samson to join her. "So, what do you think?"

"Your best option is to have it all jackhammered up and replaced."

"What? *Really*?"

"You seem surprised."

"Well, no...I mean...look, I'll be honest. I've already spoken to a couple of other contractors, and neither of them recommended that."

"Then they're fools," Samson said, placing his clipboard off to the side. "Mortar is nothing more than water, sand, and Portland cement mixed together, but whoever did that out there, didn't use the right ratio. That's why it's cracking and crumbling."

"So it has nothing to do with the tunnel?"

"The tunnel? Why would you think that?"

"Something one of them said. They thought it was undermining the strength of the hill."

Samson threw back his head and let out a hearty guffaw. "Oh no, miss. I don't want to speak ill of my competitors, but they don't know what they're talking about. The timbers used to build that tunnel are elm and ash, two of the hardest, most durable woods we've got, and the support columns are brick. That tunnel is as sound as it was the day it was built."

"So, the only thing you're suggesting is to remove the slate and put it back down with new mortar?"

"Well, I *could* do that if...if that's what you want?"

Noticing a hint of sadness in Samson's face, Joanna said, "What would *you* do?"

"Miss?"

"If it was up to you, and money was no object," Joanna said. Noticing

Samson's eyes instantly double in size, Joanna chuckled. "I'm fairly sure you're familiar with my last name, so hiding the fact money *isn't* a problem seems a little ridiculous. Don't you think?"

"Yes, miss," Samson said, thankful that his skin tone hid the heat now burning his cheeks.

"Then tell me, what would you do?"

Samson paused and leaned forward in his chair, resting his elbows on his knees as he looked at Joanna. "Mrs. Kane, my family has been doing this sort of thing for generations. When it comes to old homes and architecture, I guess you'd have to call me a bit of a bore. That patio out there could be fabulous, and the tunnel...my God, it's wonderful! If this place were mine, I'd make that veranda a showplace instead of an eyesore. Um...no offense."

"None taken," Joanna said, thoroughly enjoying the man's honesty. "Well, don't keep me in suspense any longer. Tell me what you'd do if it were up to you."

In an instant, Samson snatched up his aluminum clipboard and opened the storage compartment. Pulling out a tablet of graph paper, he handed it to Joanna. "I'm not an artist, but if it *were* up to me, this is what I'd do."

Joanna took the papers, and within seconds, her mouth fell open. Quickly turning page after page, the smile on her face grew until it reached her ears. "These are amazing," she said, looking up. "You...you could really do this?"

Samson's pearly whites appeared again. "Yes, I could."

Joanna scanned the sketches again. "How soon could you give me an estimate?"

"I...I could get something to you by early next week. I need to take some more measurements and then contact suppliers for pricing. Would that be okay?"

"Yes," Joanna said, handing him back the drawings. "Yes, that would be fine."

"Oh, there's one more thing," Samson said, putting the papers away. "To do some of the work, we'll need to remove a bit of the ivy. It's encroaching in some areas we'll need to get to."

"If it were up to me, you'd be taking it all down."

"It's not up to you?" Samson said, eyeing Joanna.

"No, what I meant to say was I don't have—" Joanna clamped her lips together, refusing to allow the word *permission* to escape. Taking a moment to find the words, Joanna painted on a false grin. "I'm just not sure my wife would approve."

***

"So...did you have any luck?"

Joanna slowly raised her eyes. "Not since marrying you."

Addison found herself trying not to laugh. Joanna's barb, while undoubtedly meant to harm had done just the opposite, and picking up her glass, Addison swallowed her amusement with a gulp of wine. Placing the goblet back on the table, Addison smiled. "I was *talking* about the patio."

Joanna wanted to smile, too. She wanted to chat and get back to the way they had been, but she had backed herself into a corner, and she knew it. Hostility and anger had never had a place in her life. If things went badly, she had merely turned the other cheek and moved on. She had never ridiculed or worn disdain on her sleeve as she had for the past several weeks, but to admit to Addison *why* she had been so distant and indignant would be far too telling. Jealousy was a word Joanna couldn't afford to use. It was one thing to care about someone more than you should, but it was quite another knowing that particular someone cared far less than you hoped.

Taking a deep breath, Joanna decided enough was enough. Their marriage was arranged, and in less than five years it would be dissolved, and she would be forgotten like the garden and the furniture and the walls. It was time to turn the other cheek...again.

"The patio?" Joanna said, picking up her Chardonnay. "I thought you didn't care about it. You just wanted it done."

"I wasn't asking for details. Just making conversation."

"Well, in that case, yes, I had some luck. They're going to drop off a contract early next week."

"That's excellent. If you need any help—"

"You just said—"

"If you *require* any help with the *contract*, just call Fran."

"Oh," Joanna said as blood rushed to her cheeks. "Okay, I'll keep that in mind."

"Good," Addison said as she placed her napkin on the table. "And the rest of your week? How did that go?"

The question took Joanna by surprise, and it showed on her face. Racking her brain to remember what she had done that week, she finally came up with an answer. "Um...same old. Exercised, played with Chauncey, read," she said, shrugging. "Oh, I'm ordering some books and plan to put them in the library. I hope you don't mind."

"Not at all," Addison said.

An awkward silence swept over the room as two who were strangers, yet not, tried to find common ground. One, in the midst of discovering feelings she believed she would never own, was embracing every syllable Joanna was speaking, so Addison was patiently waiting for another to slip through her lips. However, for Joanna, speech was not coming so easily.

With a hint of animosity still lurking in her brain, Joanna was seeking out a safe subject, a path she could travel without fear of being detoured by what had caused their rift. Suddenly grateful for Addison's question, Joanna looked up. "What about you? How was your week?"

Thrilled that the conversation hadn't died off, Addison beamed. "It was busy," she said, reaching for her glass. "I had meetings in Spain and France, and ended up in Germany yesterday. I think I walked off the plane last night in a trance."

Joanna had believed her question was a safe one, and she also believed her struggle to defeat a monster, green and begrudging, would be simple. She was wrong on both counts. In an instant, she discovered putting her mind over matter only works when the *matter* didn't involve another woman.

"Last...*night*?" she said, raising her chin just a tad.

Thrilled Joanna was actually talking to her Addison had missed the irritation in her voice. "Yes. The meeting in Frankfurt ran long, but I didn't want to stay there another night. Since it was so late when we landed, I just stayed at the hotel."

"You know, you should just do that more often," Joanna said, tossing her napkin aside as she got to her feet.

"What?"

"Stay at the hotel. It's not like there's any reason for you to be here. We all get along very nicely when you're not around. Trust me."

"This is my home," Addison said, her brow furrowing as she watched Joanna head for the door. "And where did that come from? We were just talking—"

"I don't *want* to talk!" Joanna yelled, spinning around. "I thought I did, but I was wrong. Just one more mistake in a long line of mistakes, but I'm stopping that now."

"What in the hell are you talking about?"

"I'm talking about bowing to you and your grandiose attitude. Do you know how many times I've second-guessed myself since I moved in? Wondering how you're going to react to something as simple as me weeding a garden or buying some books or...or getting a dog. Well, from here on out, I'm not putting *you* in the equation on any decision *I* make. As far as I'm concerned, you're just a visitor in this house. I'm the one who lives here day in and day out, so if I decide to make some changes, that's exactly what I'm going to do, and your *permission* is no longer required."

"Changes? What changes?" Addison said, standing up.

"I just told you," Joanna with a smirk. "Since your decisions don't concern me, mine most assuredly don't concern *you*. Good night, Addison. Have a nice life."

Chapter Thirty

"You can't be serious."

"Are you saying it can't be done?"

Samson heard the challenge in Joanna's voice. A gauntlet had just been thrown down, and now it was up to him to either pick it up or admit defeat. Scratching his chin, he considered his answer carefully. "No, but given the timeframe we have, in order to do what you're asking, I'll have to bring in other companies to get the job done on time. I know the money isn't an issue, but you need to understand we're talking about working around the clock for two weeks straight. That means there'll be crews here day and night, and trust me, they aren't quiet, and neither are the trucks. I'll have to arrange deliveries as soon as I can get them, which means I'll have to store all the materials here, so they'll be immediately on hand. That's a lot of disruption, not to mention the noise and the chaos. Are you really prepared to deal with all of that?"

Joanna widened her stance and held her head high. "I am if you are."

***

Noah waited until the kitchen door closed behind Joanna before he headed over to the table and slipped into a chair.

Evelyn raised her eyes. "So, what do you think?"

"Well, you're the one who told her to poke a stick."

"Yes, but this isn't a poke. This is a...a bloody stab wound," Evelyn said, pointing at the sketches Joanna had left behind. "Don't get me wrong. I'm thrilled the work is getting done and ridding the house of that blasted ivy is a godsend, but I think Joanna's timing is a bit off."

"Yeah?"

"Oh, come on. You must have noticed the change in Addison over the past several weeks. She isn't barking orders or slamming doors, and just the other day I heard her thank Fiona for bringing her coffee. So, why now, when Addison seems to have finally...well, mellowed a bit, would Joanna purposely try to make her angry?"

"You think she is?"

"You don't?"

"Oh no, I do," Noah said, smiling. "But then again, I see the forest. You're still looking at the trees."

Evelyn cocked her head to the side. "Well, I'm familiar with the saying, but I'm not sure I understand your reference."

"Well, how about this one," Noah said, his eyes twinkling as he took a sip of coffee. "Hell hath no fury...like a woman scorned."

"What in the world are you talking about, and stop talking in riddles."

"Actually, I think that was Shakespeare."

"In point of fact, it's a pared down version of a line from The Mourning Bride. A play by William Congreve."

"Seriously?"

Evelyn rolled her eyes. "Yes, seriously."

"Well, I'll be damned. I always thought—"

"Can we *please* get back on subject?"

An impish grin overtook Noah's features. "Sure. Go ahead," he said with a chuckle.

"So you're saying...you're saying Joanna is...is..."

"Jealous."

"Of what or...or of whom?"

"Luce."

"Luce?" Evelyn said, turning a one syllable word into two.

"Luce," Noah said with a nod. "Ever since Joanna found out about her—"

"Sorry, Noah, but you're wrong. I've already mentioned that to Joanna, and she said she doesn't care about Luce. It's just the fact that Addison has a life, and she doesn't."

"And you believed her?"

"Well...well, yes. Of course, I did. Why would she lie?"

"Because she's fallen for our boss," Noah said as he rested back in his chair and crossed his arms. "Think about it, Evie. Addison's always 'had a life' as Joanna calls it, but until recently Joanna didn't know Addison *also* has a mistress. And I don't know about you, but I couldn't care less who my friends are screwing, unless, of course, my feelings run a little deeper than just *friend*ship."

"So she's doing this..."

"Like I said...hell hath no fury."

Evelyn brought her fingers to her lips. "Oh my," she whispered. "Oh...my."

***

In the early hours of a Sunday morning in late March, Addison left The Oaks to start a fifteen-day business trip across Europe, and less than an hour later, flatbeds began rolling up her driveway.

Machinery was the first to arrive, and creeping down the ramps leading from the long trailers, compact backhoes and loaders were driven onto the lawns to await their need. Next were trailers complete with truck-mounted forklifts, and with the help of the Moffetts, stacks and stacks of scaffolding were offloaded and placed around the house.

Samson Dawkins had never taken on a job so large, but large or small, every project started with paperwork. He had spent weeks drawing up plans, making schedules, and signing contracts with the smaller companies he would need to finish the work. He had obtained the permits and permissions he needed, arranged for inspections, and systematically scheduled for an unbelievable amount of material to be delivered and placed exactly where he wanted it.

Before the sun had fully risen, cars and trucks filled with workers began to appear, and in no time at all, areas in the front of the estate designated for parking were filled with vehicles of every shape and size. Massive dumpsters were rolled off lorries, portable toilets were strategically placed behind trees, diesel generators were set to plan, and over a dozen light poles were put in place so when the sun eventually set, not one square inch of the house would be hidden in darkness.

Using the daylight to their advantage, the dozens of men hired to achieve the unachievable set their minds on the scaffolding while a few of Samson's most trusted workers began dismantling the patio nearest the house in preparation for the planks and frames. Promised double their rate if their work was sound and safe, not one dared to make a mistake, so once the first level was completed, safety harnesses were donned before they worked their way slowly upward. Dawkins Construction would accept nothing less. Before lunch was called, the first row of scaffolding was in place around the house, and by Sunday night, The Oaks was entirely surrounded by wooden planks, aluminum rails, and men fastened in safety harnesses.

True to Samson's word the work was noisy and dirty, but after a while, no one in the house seemed to notice. Even Chauncey, who had barked at every snippet of unknown sound during the first few days, had quieted his growls. Occasionally he'd let out a yip when something was louder than he wanted, but for the most part, he stayed snuggled on Joanna's lap while she read, oblivious to what was happening around him.

Using steel brushes, propane torches, and gloved hands, the crew of men spent eight days removing every sign of the ivy, while another group demolished the old patio and began to build the new. For the most part, there were no surprises. Loosened mortar discovered under the ivy was expected, and masons were already on call to repair it. Rotted wood around windows and flaking paint was also commonplace on homes encased with ivy, and painters and carpenters were a mere phone call away, but late Thursday afternoon, there was one surprise. As the workers were making their way across the roof, one of them concentrated on the dome directly in the middle of the house. Pulling here and there, he tore off the invasive plant, but when he took a step closer to the uppermost part of the sphere, he heard something crack. Covered in years of dirt and vines of green, the glass panels in the dome had long ago been forgotten until the worker's boot had just found them.

In an instant, the young man found himself falling into the house. The slate floor of the foyer was approaching at breakneck speed, but his safety tether stopped him twenty feet before he met his maker. It was the only day work was halted for something other than meals, but after some slaps on the back and playful teasing, everyone went back to work. There was no time to waste for their bonuses were on the line.

***

As Fran was led through the restaurant by the maître d, she grinned as she took in her surroundings. Of all the perks that came with working for Kane Holdings, accompanying Addison on business trips was at the top of Fran's list. The hotels were always five-star. The limousines were sleek and modern, and if a restaurant didn't have at least two Michelin stars, Addison wouldn't walk through their doors.

Fran slipped into the chair the maître d had pulled out for her, and after thanking him for his courtesy, as he walked away, she turned to Addison. "Isn't Millie joining us?"

"No, she was tired. Said she was planning to order room service and make it an early night. So we're on our own."

Fran nodded, giving the menu a half-hearted glance before looking back at Addison, only to see yet another smile on the woman's face. "You know, you've been doing that a lot this trip."

"Doing what?" Addison asked, waving off the waiter who approached. Reaching for the bottle of wine sitting on the table, she said, "It's a 2006 Trasnocho Rioja. Care for some?"

"Of course," Fran said, unconsciously licking her lips. "And you've been smiling since we left London five days ago."

"Have I?"

"Yes. So what's going on? And don't say it's business because I already know it's not. I've been on enough of these trips to know your moods, and no matter how successful we are, you're never *this* happy."

"You're right," Addison said, taking a sip of wine. "I finally figured out why Joanna has been in such a foul mood, but by the time I get home, she'll be back to her old self. I made sure of it."

"Okay, I'm intrigued. What did you do?"

"I gave her permission to fix the patio."

Fran scrunched up her face. "And that's supposed to help how?"

"She's bored, Fran," Addison said, leaning in closer. "If she's said it once, she's said it a hundred times. She doesn't have anything to do. A while back, Joanna got it into her head to clean up the gardens for whatever reason, but after she had fallen, I told her she wasn't allowed on the patio because it was too dangerous. After that, things went from bad to worse between us. So, by letting her get it repaired, things will get back to normal because she'll be able to rummage around in the dirt to her heart's content. Problem solved."

Fran kept her expression neutral, but on the inside, she was tickled as tickled can be. It was refreshing to know that someone as brilliant as Addison could also be seriously simpleminded at times. "Guess you figured it out."

"Of course I did," Addison said, rolling her eyes. "And you should have seen how excited she was about getting herself a laptop. Said she was going to do all this research on contractors and the like. Of course, when I get home I'll take the steps necessary to get things done properly, but there's no doubt this is keeping her busy, and that's exactly what she wanted."

"What do you mean properly? Didn't you just say she was getting it fixed?"

"Joanna won't spend a pound more than she has to. It's not in her nature. Hell, she even bought her dog from the shelter instead of from a breeder."

"There's nothing wrong with that."

"I'm not saying Chauncey isn't a cute pup, but when you have the money to buy pedigree, why not get one?" Addison said, holding her hands palms up. "Anyway, she's not used to having money, so I expect she'll have hired some handyman to glue down whatever slate's loose instead of getting it done right the first time. So, when I get home, I'll take care of it."

"She's not stupid, Addison," Fran said through a frown.

"I'm not saying she is, but she's never hired a contractor or done anything like this, and she's as frugal as the day is long. I'm telling you right now that when I get home, I'll have a lot of fires to put out, and she can't very well ask for my help and stay mad at me at the same time. Now can she?"

"And you're doing *all* of this just so you can talk over dinner?"

Addison's eyes turned to slits as she stared back at Fran. "Shut up and order your food," she said, looking down at the menu in front of her. "I don't have all night."

***

With Chauncey in her arms, Joanna came into the kitchen just as Fiona was placing a roast in the oven. Even though Joanna enjoyed every gourmet meal Noah had ever made, she looked forward to the break from bon vivant on the weekend. Fiona was a simple woman who hadn't learned how to cook from a culinary institute, but rather from her mother who had learned from her mother and so on. The meals she prepared were hearty, warm, and delicious, and in their own small way, made The Oaks feel more like home.

Putting the anxious pup on the floor, Joanna watched as Chauncey scampered over to his food bowls to finish a few bits and pieces left over from his breakfast.

"Fiona, now that dinner's in the oven, I think you should be off," Joanna said.

"Miss?"

Joanna let out a laugh. "You and I both know you don't want to be here."

"I-I-I don't know what you're talking about," Fiona said as she set the timer on the cooker.

"Yes, you do," Joanna said as her dimples appeared. "Addison will be home shortly, and we both know her reaction...well, let's just say it could be loud. You don't need to be around when that happens."

"But I don't think I should leave you—"

"Fiona, I'll be fine. I'm well versed in handling Addison's explosions, and if she has one, she has one," Joanna said with a shrug. "It's not like she can change anything, at least not for a few decades."

***

Having traveled the roads to The Oaks her entire life, as Addison looked out the window, she knew exactly where she was and how far she was from home, yet her fingers never stopped drumming against the seat of the Bentley.

Anticipation, for most, is learned at an early age. Whether it's the Easter bunny, the tooth fairy, birthday celebrations, or a holiday with presents wrapped in festive paper, the joy of what tomorrow may bring is ingrained from childhood. Lessons that, for many, carry on throughout their lives, but for Addison, anticipation was as new as it was irritating.

For two weeks she had traveled across Europe, touring factories in need of buyers, technology in need of finance, and companies on the brink of disaster desperate for a way out. She had talked and listened, wheeled and dealed, and by the time she climbed aboard her Gulfstream G650 early that Sunday morning, she knew before the year was over, Kane Holdings would be adding yet another zero to its net worth. That information would put any industrialist in high spirits, but Addison's mood had nothing to do with money. In just a few short minutes, she'd be seeing Joanna again. A new Joanna, or rather the old one returning. The one with sparkling eyes and a clever wit, but void of caustic remarks and disdain, she'd be happy and anxious to show Addison what was accomplished in her absence.

Addison was already prepared to pile on accolades for a job well done whether it was or it wasn't, and she'd wave off any problems, big or small.

She caught herself smiling again, remembering the old Joanna. Her glee during dinners and how her face lit up as she held a puppy barely bigger than her hand, and then Addison chuckled, thinking of the times the woman had become angry. Damn, angry became Joanna. It was how Addison had left her when she walked from The Oaks over a fortnight before, but it wouldn't be how she'd find her when she got home. Addison was sure of it.

George turned off the road and stopped the car long enough to press the keypad affixed to a pole near the gate. Silently saying a prayer his wife had heard the alert and had gotten out of the house, he held his breath as he steered the Bentley onto the gravel drive.

Addison's pulse began to quicken, and gathering the papers she had pulled from her briefcase, she stuffed them back inside. Slipping her mobile into her jacket pocket, she ran her hand over her hair and straightened her jacket...and then the house came into view.

Chapter Thirty-One

There are approximately one million words in the English language, but as Addison stared at her house now stripped of ivy, only one came to mind. It contained four letters...and it wasn't *nice*.

Addison slammed her hand on the button operating the privacy window, and before it had even moved an inch, she shouted, "Stop the car."

"Miss?" George said, halfway turning around.

"I said stop the fucking car *now!*"

Before George could slip the transmission into park, Addison was out of the Bentley and gawking at the house in the distance. As she stared at her home, her blood pressure began to elevate, and it took only a matter of seconds before her face was beet red, and her hands were fisted.

Climbing back inside the car, Addison closed the door so forcefully the entire car rocked. "Drive."

Replying with only a nod, George lightly stepped on the accelerator.

"I said bloody *drive*, or you'll be out of a fucking—"

Thrown back in her seat when George slammed his foot to the floor, Addison paid no attention to the sound of the pings and chinks as the gravel bounced off the chrome and polished finish of the car. In less than a minute, sending more gravel flying to and fro, George skidded to a stop in front of the house.

Addison shoved the car door open and erupted from the Bentley like lava from a volcano. Taking the stairs two at a time, she marched across the veranda and burst into the house, sending the door so wide the handle embedded in the plaster wall behind it.

Chauncey was prancing from the parlor with his favorite toy when the door swung open, and recognizing Addison, his tail began to wag, but the look on her face changed his mind. Like a metronome, his little stub slowly wound down to zero, and with the toy still in his mouth, he turned around and scampered back from where he came.

Addison didn't notice Chauncey, and she didn't notice the light now streaming into the foyer from the glass panels in the dome far above her head. The only thing she noticed was the woman standing at the top of the stairs.

"Who the *hell* do you think you are?" Addison roared, throwing her briefcase across the foyer.

"Well, hello to you, too," Joanna said, doing absolutely nothing to hide her grin.

Addison's eyes turned into slits as she charged up the stairs. "*What the fuck have you done to my house?*"

"Oh that," Joanna said with a wave of her hand. "I gave it a trim."

By the time Addison reached Joanna, the veins in her neck had swelled to their extreme. "I *never* gave you permission—"

"Oh, did I forget to tell you? That whole permission thing just doesn't work for me," Joanna said, letting out a snort as she eyeballed Addison. "Sorry."

Addison's eyes darkened, and as she moved to within a hairsbreadth of Joanna, her neck corded. "I should smack that supercilious grin right off your face."

Joanna took a step backward and crossed her arms. "You do, and you'll have a hell of a lot more to pay for than just home repair."

"You are a bitch!"

"Look who's talking."

"I've been trying my best to be—"

"Your *best*?" Joanna shouted, closing the gap between them again. "I have news for you, Addison, you wouldn't know *best* if it came up and slapped *you* in the face. The ivy's gone and all your huffing and puffing isn't going to bring it back. So, why don't you do us both a favor and just sod the fuck off?"

Joanna wasn't surprised when Addison continued to glare back at her, so shooting the woman one last cold look, Joanna turned on her heel and headed to her bedroom.

"Oh, no you don't," Addison said, running to catch up.

Just as Joanna opened her bedroom door, Addison grabbed her by the arm and spun her around. "Don't you walk away from me!"

Joanna pulled herself free. "I'll damn well do as I please. You don't own me, and you sure as *hell* don't scare me. You're nothing but a pompous, obnoxious, spoiled *cow* that's used to getting her own way. Well, I have news for you, Addison, if you want your own way, go tell your slag. She's paid to listen, and I'm sure she's *more* than willing to do *whatever* you'd like, but there's not enough money in the world to make me do the same!"

"If I'm not mistaken, I bought you as well," Addison said, giving Joanna a dismissive glance. "Although I must say, the price was outrageously high for something so cheap."

The sound of the stinging slap Joanna gave Addison echoed down the hallway.

"If you want cheap, go fuck your whore!" Joanna screamed, and placing her hand on Addison's chest, Joanna shoved her as hard as she could into the corridor before slamming the door in her face.

Throwing the bolt for good measure, Joanna stomped to the middle of her room, never in her life wanting so desperately to throw a punch at something. Spying the pillows on the bed, she took a step in their direction when the sound of her door being kicked in caused her to almost jump out of her skin.

Addison stood in the doorway with skin flushed and nostrils flaring. "I'd rather fuck *you*," she snarled as she strode across the room and pushed Joanna up against the bedpost.

They say the line between love and hate is thin, but the one between *lust* and hate is infinitesimal. Blood heated by anger and impassioned beliefs flowed like lava through their veins, desire turning molten as it searched for release.

Their eyes locked, and for a moment, time stood still. Denial had been their common ground, but Addison could no longer disavow what she wanted. Leaning in, she captured Joanna's lips in a kiss as brutal as it was intoxicating.

Addison ground her mouth against Joanna's, and feeding on the flavor of the woman like an addict for a drug, she claimed Joanna's mouth again and again. Her kisses were punishing and heated, but anger was no longer her fuel. Driven by something primitive, far beyond anything Addison had ever experienced, the more she pressed her lips against Joanna's, the more Addison needed to taste...and taste she did.

In less time than it takes to blink, Joanna went from trying to escape Addison's assault, to relishing every second of it. Addison was relentless, and Joanna was a willing victim, and when she felt Addison's tongue stab at her lips, Joanna thought she was going to die. Helpless against the desires she had kept hidden for so long, Joanna succumbed and parted her lips. In an instant, a rush of need coursed through her body, and Joanna fisted the cloth of Addison's jacket, fearing her knees were about to fail as she tasted Addison's tongue for the first time.

A primitive groan rose in Addison's throat as she plunged her tongue between Joanna's lips, and over and over again she ravished her with sweeps of a tongue, warm and wet. Control was lost, squelched by a feral need to take, and Addison did just that, pillaging and tasting until the need for air became too great. Pulling away, she greedily sucked air into her lungs.

In ragged gasps, Joanna fought for oxygen. She kept her eyes riveted on Addison, fearing if she looked away the dream would end, but when she saw the hunger etched on Addison's face, Joanna swallowed hard. The dream had only just begun.

Like fireworks lighting up the sky, Addison's mind was ablaze with conflict. Right versus wrong, good versus bad, need versus want, raw versus tender, they flashed and extinguished at a dizzying rate, but in the end, raw won out. Taking Joanna by the shoulders, Addison pushed her onto the bed.

Feeling as if the room had become a furnace, Addison wasted no time in ridding herself of her suit jacket and tie, and climbing onto the bed, she recaptured Joanna's lips. They were warm and supple and oh so delicious, Addison greedily devoured their softness before she again slipped her tongue between them. Joanna's mouth was sweet and inviting, and a surge of pleasure rushed through Addison's body when her wife's tongue began to dance with hers.

Possessed by something foreign yet so natural, Joanna's body was no longer her own, and she began to return Addison's kisses as feverishly as they were being given. Her hands traveled up Addison's arms and then to her back, feeling beneath the crisp cotton the warmth of the woman's skin as it radiated through the fabric, and the more Joanna felt, the more she wanted to touch.

Joanna wasn't the only one who wanted to touch. Although her wife's lips were divine, Addison's need to caress, to fondle, to rub, to *feel* all those parts hidden by cloth and propriety had turned her flame into a bonfire. She shifted ever so slightly and slipped her hand under Joanna's skirt. Joanna's thighs were smooth and warm, but what Addison craved to touch would be so much warmer. Wasting no time, she pushed Joanna's legs apart and cupped her sex.

Every nerve in Joanna's body seemed to explode at once. A hand, possessive and strong, was molded against her center, a palm pressing down on her juncture as fingers sought out her most secret place and as Joanna gulped for air, she prayed Addison find it soon. Never in her life had Joanna wanted something so much.

The scent of Joanna's arousal permeated Addison's senses in an instant, and when she felt the wet, slickness oozing through Joanna's silk knickers, there was no turning back. Overpowered by the most lascivious of urges, as she reclaimed Joanna's lips, devouring her in another devastating kiss, Addison hooked her fingers in the silk. Ripping it from Joanna's body, she slid her fingers through Joanna's folds and finding her entrance, drove two fingers deep inside.

Joanna cried out, digging her nails into Addison's back at the flash of pain, but then almost as quickly it was gone, and something else took its place. Something tameless and wanton, it eliminated all but the most primal, and Joanna began to rock against Addison's fingers, urging her deeper, needing her deeper...demanding her deeper.

In the very core of her being Joanna began to feel her pleasure building. Increasing with every thrust, ripples grew into swells and then morphed into waves of splendor as passion and need collided. For a split-second, Joanna froze, afraid of what was to come, afraid to give into it, afraid to lose her mind and body to Addison knowing she'd never get it back, but it was too late. Addison already owned her, and as that thought entered Joanna's mind, she opened herself up to the orgasm Addison had created, and it claimed her instantly...in spasm after spasm of pleasure.

The passage of time was lost on Joanna as she shuddered and trembled through the last throes of ecstasy, and as her breathing returned to normal, she felt the mattress dip. It took all the strength she had to open her eyes, and when she did Joanna watched as Addison walked from the room without looking back.

***

Fran followed Lydia Patel into Addison's outer office, and while the young woman returned to her desk, Fran continued to Millie's. "So, what's the emergency?" she asked. "I was in a meeting."

"Yes, I know, but I didn't think this could wait."

"What's going on?"

Millie looked past Fran to the admins sitting by the door. Keeping her voice low, she said, "Addison came in this morning and told us to cancel everything for today."

"She can't do that," Fran said through her teeth. "Ravi Nahas flew in from Dubai last night. We've been working on this for over a year."

"I know. That's why I sent Lydia to find you," Millie said, lowering her voice even more. "Fran, Addison didn't look at all well when she came in, and I could barely understand her. She was talking in whispers."

"Is she sick?"

"I don't know."

"Did you cancel the meeting with Nahas?"

"No. I thought I should talk to you first."

"Good," Fran said, glancing toward Addison's office. "Let me go see what's going on. If she's sick and we do need to cancel, I'll make the call."

"Of course."

Fran gave Millie a feeble grin and then went over and tapped lightly on Addison's door. Hearing no response, she turned the knob and walked inside. It was nine o'clock in the morning, but by the amount of light in the room, it could very well have been midnight. Peering through the shadows, she saw a figure sitting behind the desk.

"A bit dark in here, isn't it?" Fran asked as she carefully made her way across the room. Flicking on the lamp sitting atop the credenza, she turned around. "That's better. Don't you think?"

Addison didn't move. Her eyes remained focused on a desk barren of files, and since Fran couldn't hear the hum of a hard drive, she didn't need to look at the monitors to know they were blank. She kept her eyes on Addison as she went over and sat down, and crossing her legs, Fran took a slow breath. "Okay, what's going on? Millie said you wanted to cancel the appointment with Nahas."

Fran waited for Addison to respond, but when the woman remained mute, Fran's temper got the better of her, and she slammed her hand on the desk. "Damn it, Addison. I don't have time for this shit! We've worked too damn long and too damn hard on this deal to have it fucked up by one of your moods."

Addison slowly raised her head and Fran's eyebrows drew together. Even though it was minimal, Addison always wore a hint of makeup, but she wasn't wearing any, and Fran doubted that the best concealer in the world could have hidden the dark circles under her eyes. "Are you sick?"

"No," Addison said, lowering her eyes.

"Then why do you look like shit?"

"Just leave me alone, Fran," Addison said quietly. "Please, just leave me be."

For a moment, Fran stared wordlessly at Addison. The mood she was seeing wasn't one Addison had ever had in her repertoire before. "What's wrong?"

"Nothing," Addison said, slumping further into her chair. "Now go."

"Not until you tell me what's going on."

"Please, Fran—"

"We used to be friends, you and me," Fran said, leaning closer. "You used to trust me. Remember?"

"Yeah," Addison said, letting out a sigh. "I remember."

"Then talk to me. Whatever it is, we'll get it sorted."

Addison scrubbed her hand over her face, exhaling slowly as she opened her eyes. "I fucked up royally, Fran. *Really* royally."

Fran stiffened. Addison's eyes were glassy, and her expression was so pained it looked as if she had aged a decade. "What did you do? Is this about...about a contract or an acquisition?"

"No—wait. In a way I...I guess it is," Addison said, running her fingers through her hair. "It's...it's about Joanna."

"Joanna? What about Joanna?"

"Something...something happened last night..." Addison's voice trailed off as she buried her head in her hands. "Christ, what have I done?"

The color began to drain from Fran's face. "Okay, you're starting to worry me. What the hell happened last night and what's it got to do with Joanna?"

Addison looked up, shaking her head as she struggled to find the words. "Last...last night when I got home, Joanna and I got into a row. Things got...they got really heated, and we ended up..." Addison stopped, bowing her head again. "It just happened so fast. One minute we were shouting at each other and the next...the next I had her on the bed."

Fran stared blankly back at Addison. While her confession was surprising, Fran couldn't see the problem. Joanna was of consenting age, and even though she was straight, straight women had switched teams before, even if only for a night or two. Taking her time, Fran replayed Addison's words in her head, trying to find the missing piece of the puzzle, and then slowly the rest of the color drained from her face. "Wait a minute," she said, holding up her hands. "What do you mean you *had* her on the bed? Jesus Christ, Addison, please don't tell me...don't tell me you forced her."

"I...I don't know," Addison said, her voice sinking to a whisper.

"What do you mean you don't know?" Fran said, jumping to her feet. "It's a yes or no answer, Addison. Either you *did*, or you *didn't*. Now, which is it?"

Addison looked back at Fran. "I told you, it happened so fast—"

"Did she say no?"

"What?"

"Did she say *no*?" Fran yelled, pounding her hands on the desk. "Did she tell you to stop or get out or get off? Did she say no?"

"Um...I-I-I don't think so."

"You don't think so!" Fran said, rocking back on her heels. "You don't *think* so!"

"It just...it was so fast. We were angry and screaming and...and then we were on the bed. You have to believe me, Fran, if I had known...if I had thought—"

"What the hell are you going on about?"

"Fuck!" Addison said, pounding her hands on her desk. "Fuck! Fuck! *Fuck*!"

Fran's stomach began to roll. There was obviously more to the story and cringing, she said, "What aren't you telling me?"

Addison sagged her chair. "I think...I think it was her first time."

"Of course it was her first time, you bloody idiot! She was straight until she married you!"

"No, I mean...I mean when I got back to my room and...and took off my shirt, I noticed I saw a spot on my sleeve, and then I remembered she had...she had cried out when—"

"Enough!" Fran said, throwing up her hands. "Jesus Christ, Addison, what have you done? What have you bloody done?"

Addison struggled to breathe, the guilt so overwhelming it felt as if her chest was in a vice. "I...I don't...I don't know what to say. I...I don't know what to do."

"Well, I do," Fran said, going over to the credenza. Upending a tumbler, she pulled the stopper from the scotch and filled the glass.

"What the hell are you doing, Fran? It's barely nine o'clock, and that's not going to help."

Fran calmly picked up the glass and headed back to the desk. "It's not for me," she said, promptly tossing the scotch in Addison's face. "It's for you."

"What the fu—"

"Trust me. You deserve a hell of a lot more than that!" Fran said, slamming the glass on the desk. "Now, clean yourself up and pull yourself together. Nahas will be here at two, and you're going to be—"

"I canceled that."

"And I *uncanceled* it!" Fran said, leaning over so she could look Addison in the eye. "Believe it or not, you stupid cow, this company isn't just about you. We've had no less than twenty people working on this for over a year. Twenty people who were promised bonuses once the deal was made. They gave up their nights. They gave up their weekends. Hell, some of them even gave up their holidays, and I'll be damned, just because you can't keep your *fucking* hands to yourself, they're going to pay for it." Fran marched to the door. "I'll be back before two, and when I get here you sure as hell better be ready for that meeting, Addison, or as God is my witness, I'll walk away from Kane Holdings and never look back."

"Where are you going?"

Fran stopped and spun around. "I'm going to go see just how much damage you've done, and if Joanna's hurt...if you hurt her in *any* way, after the Nahas meeting, you and I are through."

Chapter Thirty-Two

Joanna listened as the rain pattered against the windows behind her. On her lap was the first of many newly-purchased novels. It had appeared on all the best seller lists, yet opened for over an hour, it still remained on the title page.

To ward off the dampness of the day, she had asked that the fireplace be lit. Unlike many of the others in the house, the hearth in the parlor had been left as originally built, so instead of the even, silent fire produced by gas, flames of orange, yellow, and red danced across logs of oak. As she sat with her feet propped on the ottoman, she stared into the blaze as if it held an answer she sought.

She shifted ever so slightly in the chair and a wince crossed her face, the pang transporting Joanna back to the night before. To a few minutes of passion infused with anger and need, and to gasps and tastes and touches. Touches she had craved for so long.

Brought out of her daydream by motion in the room, Joanna looked up and saw Fran walking toward her. "Hiya," she said, setting the book aside. "This is a surprise."

"Yes, well my day seems to be full of those," Fran said as she sat down. "How are you doing?"

"I'm fine. You?"

"I've had my moments," Fran said with a half-hearted grin. "Oh, by the way, before I forget, the house looks lovely without all the ivy."

"Thank you," Joanna said breaking into a smile. "But Addison wasn't too thrilled with it."

"Is that what caused the argument?"

"Yeah, she was...wait," Joanna said, jerking back her head. "How did you know we argued?"

"Addison told me this morning."

"Oh."

"That's not...that's not all she told me," Fran said, leaning forward and resting her elbows on her knees. "Joanna, are you really okay? I'm talking about...um..."

Joanna felt her face heat, and flustered by her own blush, it darkened even more. "Yes, Fran, I'm fine. It's not like it wasn't mutual."

Fran let out the breath she'd been holding and fell back in her chair. "So, it *was* mutual."

"Of course," Joanna said. "Did Addison think differently?"

"Honestly, she wasn't sure. She said it was...um...kind of quick, and since you're straight, she was worried she had coerced you into doing something against your...well, against your nature."

"Well, I won't argue about it being quick," Joanna said softly. She lowered her eyes, nibbling on her bottom lip as she smoothed the fabric of her unwrinkled skirt, and then taking a deep breath, Joanna looked up. "But I never said I was straight."

Fran had been having a problem looking Joanna in the eye, but that problem quickly ceased to exist as she locked eyes with Joanna. "Sorry?"

Laugh lines creased Joanna's face as she leaned toward Fran. "I never *said* I was straight."

Fran rewound the clock, back to the conversations she had had with Joanna in Burnt Oak, and coming up empty, a faint smile appeared on her face. "Why the hell didn't you tell us?"

"Because it didn't matter," Joanna said with a shrug. "And because my father was old school. He hated gays, and I couldn't risk him finding out. It would have destroyed him and destroyed us, and he was all I had."

"Jesus."

"Please don't think I married Addison believing this was going to happen. I did this to help my father, but in a small way it was also helping me."

"Helping you?"

"Fran, I never thought I'd get the chance to live my life the way I wanted, at least when it came to my sexuality, but by marrying Addison, I could. Yeah, the marriage is for show, but I can't even begin to explain how much easier it was to breathe every day. I could hold her hand in public or...or kiss her on the cheek." Joanna stopped, and all of a sudden it seemed as if sunshine was lighting up her face. "Fran, the world believes I'm gay...and I am."

"But why continue to keep it a secret after your father passed? Why didn't you tell us?"

"Knowing Addison the way you do, do you really think she wouldn't have believed I had set her up? Agreed to this marriage because I had ulterior motives?"

"Oh, good point."

"The point is that my sexuality, in the closet or out, has never defined me, so why should it now?"

***

Late in the afternoon, Joanna went to her room, and after a long, relaxing steamy bath, she puttered about deciding to what to wear for dinner. By five o'clock, her bed was littered with her first through her tenth choice, but standing in front of her mirror, she decided the eleventh was perfect.

Although it was April, spring was off to a slow start. Winter's chill continued to hang in the house, so opting for warmth as well as comfort, Joanna decided on a pair of skinny fit leggings slightly darker than rainy-day clouds and a black honeycomb knit jumper, the length of which ended just past her hips. To finish the ensemble, and adding three inches to her height, Joanna completed the look with a pair of high-heeled suede ankle boots in the color of ash.

Checking her watch, Joanna's stomach did a flip. In less than thirty minutes, she'd be facing the woman who had been in her bed the night before. Holding her chin high, Joanna headed for the dining room. Tonight she definitely needed to be early. Her hands had already begun to shake, and she was sure her knees would follow.

***

Addison wiped her palms on her trousers again. Her briefcase was on the seat next to her, filled with papers she had planned to read on the way home, but the latches on the attaché had yet to be opened.

After her anointing in scotch, Addison had used her private bathroom at work to clean herself up. Like most at her level in the world of business, appearance was important, and extra suits and shirts were always at the ready, so a change of clothes was not a problem. The problem was trying to keep her mind on business.

When Fran returned to the office, she didn't have much to say other than letting Addison know she was a very lucky woman, and Fran wouldn't be quitting anytime soon. Other than that, Fran kept the details of her conversation with Joanna to herself. It was kind of nice after all these years to see Addison finally squirm when she had made so many others do the same.

It was rare Addison took a backseat during a meeting, but more than once when facts and figures escaped her, Addison drew a breath of relief when Fran stepped in and took charge. She rattled off all the pertinent details as if they were written on her sleeve and by the time Ravi Nahas left the Kane Holdings building at five o'clock, while the deal wasn't set in stone, the etching had begun...and the carver had been Fran.

Addison looked out the window and drew a ragged breath. The meeting had run longer than expected and it was nearly half six, and Addison had a decision to make. Should she tell David to drive faster or to turn around?

***

Joanna sat alone in the dining room sipping her glass of Chardonnay and hoping the alcohol would calm her nerves. It hadn't. She had crossed and uncrossed her legs a dozen times, all the while counting the exits from the room. Should she make her escape to the kitchen, the foyer, or through the pair of doors behind her? Leading into the formal living room, she assumed they hadn't been opened for years, but with one good shove, she could make her way out. She was sure of it. Unfortunately, her decision was put on hold when she heard the pocket doors from the entrance hall slide open.

The last thing Addison wanted to do was eat. A swarm of butterflies had made a nest in her belly, and she felt like she was ready to throw up, but calling on every ounce of courage she owned she walked into the dining room and took her seat. Her fortitude remained strong until she lifted her eyes and saw Joanna looking back at her.

"Um...sorry I'm late," Addison said, picking up her linen napkin. "I had a meeting. It...it overran."

"No worries," Joanna said softly. "I was half-expecting you not to be here."

Before Addison could reply, the kitchen door swung open. Sally shuffled in with their first course, and Addison inwardly groaned when oysters Rockefeller was placed in front of her. The last thing she needed was an aphrodisiac.

Addison had never been so conscious of the staffs' existence. She wanted to continue the conversation, to say the things she practiced in her head a hundred times that day, but Sally seemed to be moving in slow motion. Finally, Addison heard the door swing closed behind her, and after taking a generous taste of her wine, she looked over at Joanna. "I just...I just want to let you know that I'm...I'm sorry. What happened last night...well, I don't know what it was, but...but if I hurt you...if I hurt you in any way, I didn't mean to, and I'm...and I'm truly sorry."

A few minutes earlier, Joanna was surprised that the paintings around the room hadn't tilted due to the pounding of her heart, but as soon as Addison spoke, Joanna's nervousness disappeared. There was a slight waver in Addison's tone, and it was as endearing as it was enlightening. The woman was obviously on edge, but while Addison's confidence had apparently tanked, Joanna's had just begun to soar.

"You didn't. Well, not really," Joanna said with a shrug.

Addison could feel her cheeks begin to burn. "Oh, Christ. I-I-I don't know...I don't know what to say."

"There's a first," Joanna said, grinning as she tasted her wine.

"I'm so sorry—"

"Stop apologizing, Addison. Nothing happened, I didn't want to happen."

Addison had been reaching for her wine, but Joanna's admission froze her in place. "Are you...are you sure?"

"Did I tell you to stop?"

All the air left Addison's body. "Honestly, I don't remember," she whispered.

"I'm that forgettable, eh?"

"No," Addison said, slightly louder than she intended. "No, that's...that's not what I meant."

Joanna smiled as she picked up her fork and dove into her appetizer. "Good to know, Addison. Now eat. It's getting cold."

While conversation was lacking through dinner, by the time the last bite of the veal cutlets drizzled in sage butter had been consumed, both women could pick up their Pinot Noir without the liquid rippling in the goblets.

Addison leaned back, and making no attempt to hide it, she gazed at Joanna and continued to do so even after Joanna's eyes met hers.

Joanna prided herself on having good eyesight, but Addison's expression was unreadable. "What?" Joanna said just before taking a sip of her wine.

"I...I..." Addison stopped and shook her head. "I still don't know what to say."

"Well, at least now I know how to shut you up."

Addison smiled, and for the first time that day, breathing came easily.

Joanna's expression mirrored Addison's, and thinking for a moment, she said, "So...how was your day?"

"Long," Addison said, letting out a sigh.

"Yeah? Mine too."

"I couldn't...um...I couldn't keep my mind on business. Thank God Fran didn't have her head up her arse or something we've been working on for over a year would have all been for naught."

"But it went okay – right?"

"Yes, I think so. These things go in stages, and I'm fairly confident we passed the first one today."

"That's great. Congratulations!"

"Thanks," Addison said picking up her glass. Discovering it was as empty as the bottle it came from, there was nothing to keep them in the room other than conversation, and that had just stalled. Racking her brain, she said, "Would you like dessert?"

While the room was cool and the air still, Joanna felt a warmth surrounding her. Born from carnal knowledge and nurtured by imagination, food was the last thing on her mind. The only thing she had yet to discover was whether Addison felt the same. Joanna's eyes began to gleam as the perfect response came into her head, and she practically purred it. "What did you have in mind?"

Addison's libido came to life with a thud and shifting in her chair, she cleared her throat. "I...um...well, we don't usually have it, but if you'd like I could ask Noah to start adding some to the menu."

"I can take it or leave it."

"Oh."

"You?"

"I enjoy it on occasion, but I usually just have a scotch after dinner."

"Well, don't let me keep you," Joanna said as her eyes met Addison's. "Would you like one?"

"No, thank you," Joanna said softly. "I'm fine."

Perception, like beauty, is owned by the beholder. An intuitive awareness overriding one's sense of sight and sound, it brings with it hope and possibilities if one dares to believe. And as Addison got to her feet, she believed.

"All right then," she said, heading to the door. "I...I guess I'll see you tomorrow."

"I guess you will."

Joanna watched as Addison left the room, and picking up her glass, she leaned back in her chair, crossed her legs, and sipped what remained until Sally came in to clear the rest of the table.

"Sally, could you do me a favor?" Joanna said as she stood up.

"Yes, miss?"

"Open another bottle of wine."

***

Addison walked to her desk, the decanter of scotch in one hand and two glasses in the other. Slowly removing the stopper, she carefully poured the single-malt into a glass, frowning when her unsteady hand caused the crystal to clank against the tumbler. Her intuition rarely failed her, at least when it came to business, but this was not business, and she was second-guessing a woman she'd yet to guess correctly. As the corners of her mouth drooped even further, she debated on whether to fill the second glass.

"I brought my own."

Joanna had whispered the words on a breath, and their effect on Addison was instantaneous. Her skin began to tingle, and her core began to throb, and it was all she could do to force herself to take a breath. Corking the decanter, Addison slowly turned around and unconsciously wet her lips.

No longer hidden behind a table that was far too long, Addison was now able to take in every one of Joanna's curves, especially those accentuated by the skin-tight leggings. The blue of her eyes darkened at the sight of calves stretched by the high heels and thighs...oh, how she remembered those thighs. Addison swallowed the moisture building in her mouth, but it returned in force as she watched Joanna saunter to the desk with a wine bottle in one hand and a goblet in the other.

"I had Sally raid the wine cellar. I hope you don't mind," Joanna said, placing the bottle on the desk.

"Not at all," Addison said, her tone lowering as her anticipation climbed.

Joanna locked eyes with Addison, and peering into the arctic blue, she brought the goblet to her mouth. She took a sip of the wine, savoring the berries and hint of licorice in its finish, and then her tongue appeared. Slowly sliding it across her lips, Joanna removed the remaining moisture in a gesture as evocative as it was sensual.

Addison glanced at the liquor in her tumbler and doubted it held the same amount of intoxication as watching Joanna drink her wine. A sudden surge of heat rushed through Addison's body and landing at her core, it was all she could do not to groan out loud at the throb.

It was a contest of wills and of wants, and Addison raised her glass to her lips to continue the game. She enjoyed the smoky apricot flavor of the single malt as it effortlessly slid down her throat, and taking a moment, she breathed in the bouquet of one of Scotland's finest before placing her glass on the table. The game was now over for what Addison wanted was *not* in a glass. Taking Joanna's goblet from her hand, she placed it next to the tumbler and in one quick step, she invaded Joanna's space.

Addison's eyes betrayed her thoughts, and Joanna felt her body respond. There was no denying their need was the same, and reaching up, Joanna loosened Addison's tie and tossed it aside.

Moving yet even closer, Addison slipped her hand behind Joanna's neck. "This means nothing more than what it is," she said, her voice thick with want.

"I agree," Joanna murmured as she leaned in close and pressed her lips to Addison's.

***

Joanna yanked the weeds from the bed, muttering to herself as she tried not to cry as she had for the past two nights. She had fallen in love with Addison, but it was becoming clearer every day, Addison didn't feel the same.

Sunday on her bed, Monday against the desk in the study, and Tuesday on the small settee in the library, Addison had taken Joanna to orgasm and then walked away without saying a word. She had never allowed Joanna to return in kind or to touch skin, bare under her clothes, and the words Addison had spoken on Monday night kept repeating in Joanna's mind. "*This means nothing more than what it is.*" Unfortunately, it meant much more to Joanna.

She knew Addison was waiting in the study on Wednesday and Thursday, but Joanna couldn't bring herself to open the door. She no longer wanted to be taken. She no longer wanted to hide her feelings. She wanted to touch. She wanted to taste. She wanted to be loved. She wanted to be held like a lover holds a lover and experience all that that four-letter word involved, and in her heart, those feelings were there, but it was quickly becoming apparent, Addison didn't feel the same. So, forgoing any more visits to the study, for the rest of the week, Joanna had retired to her bedroom and cried in the dark. She never knew love could hurt so much.

As memories of the past week swirled through her mind, Joanna sniffled back the tears she refused to let fall and got to her feet. She dusted off her hands and traipsed up the stairs Addison had yet to see. Once she reached the top, she leaned on the railing and looked out across the gardens still covered in vines and weeds. Months before Evelyn had said there were many things Addison simply didn't care about, and it was now apparent to Joanna that Evelyn wasn't just talking about the conditions of the house or the gardens.

***

Addison could hear the chime of the clock, and counting the strokes, midnight was announced as the last dong echoed through the house. This was the third night she had sat alone in her study. Her briefcase was still latched, the work inside it ignored in much the same way as she had been since Tuesday. Their talks during dinner had remained the same, filling each other in with tidbits about their days, but just as she had on the two nights previous, Joanna hadn't visited Addison's study after dinner. With every creak the old house made, Addison's eyes had darted to the door, but it had never opened, and the more she paced, the more she grumbled, the more she felt the need to numb.

Over and over Addison replayed the events of the week in her mind, trying to discover what mistake she had made, and shaking her head, she reached for the decanter again. Dulled by scotch, she misjudged the distance, and the crystal crashed to the floor. "*Fuck!*"

Addison pushed herself out of the chair. Mindless of the glass all over the floor, she trudged to the credenza for whatever liquor remained, but as she reached for another decanter, she stopped. There was no amount of alcohol that could deaden the ache in her heart. She had never felt such pain before, and she longed not to feel ever again.

For two days she had tried to erase the haunting pang of loneliness and confusion with liquor, but it hadn't worked. She didn't crave what the decanters held. What she craved existed one floor above her head. With fists clenched, Addison walked from the room and headed upstairs.

Chapter Thirty-Three

The tea on the nightstand had long since lost its heat and the book Joanna had once so anxiously wanted to read had been tossed aside. Her laptop was quiet atop the tallboy, and Chauncey laid at her feet, his little chest rising and falling as he slumbered away.

She felt so tired, but as she rested against pillows of down, sleep refused to come. Instead, as she had done for most of the week, Joanna stared off into space as if it held the answer.

Jolted from her thoughts when a growl rose in Chauncey's throat, before Joanna could stop him, he scrambled to his feet and began to bark.

"Chauncey, be quiet," Joanna whispered, but then she heard a light knock on the door and her heart stopped. Her first thought was not to respond, but when she heard another faint rap against the woodwork, Joanna groaned. "Come in."

The door swung open, and Addison filled the space. Although she was dressed as if she could return to the office at any minute, her tie was loose and slightly off-kilter.

As soon as Chauncey saw Addison, he ran to the edge of the bed, jumping around like his paws were on hot coals. Yapping, yapping, and yapping again, he didn't stop until Joanna snapped her fingers.

"Chauncey, go to your bed," Joanna said.

The pup darted over to Joanna, and clambering up her chest, gave her a few quick licks before jumping down and trotting to the corner of the room. Stepping into his fleece-lined bed, he spun around a half-dozen times before finally snuggling into the softness and closing his eyes.

Joanna let out an exaggerated sigh as she looked toward the door. "It's late, Addison. What do you want?"

Addison bowed her head and raised her eyes. "I need you," she said in a breath.

"I'm not in the mood to be manhandled or womanhandled, for that matter."

"What did I...please tell me...tell me what I did wrong."

Joanna paused when she saw Addison sway. "Have you been drinking?"

Addison bobbed her head. "Just a little."

"Then you should get some sleep."

"I can't sleep. I can't...work. I can't..." Addison stopped and let out a sigh. "Please, just tell me the truth. Tell me...tell me why you're so distant. Tell me what I did wrong."

Thoughts flooded Joanna's mind. Should she speak the truth and fear the agony of being spurned, or remain mute and forever live in a world of what ifs? She took a deep breath and gazed at the woman across the way. "Addison, I'm in love with you. I didn't plan it. I didn't want it. It just happened, but what we've had earlier this week, that's not what I want. I feel like a tart. Like something being used just because I'm there and...and if the mood strikes you're just going to toss me aside."

"I wouldn't do that."

"How do I know that?" Joanna said quietly.

Drawing in a slow breath, Addison came closer and forced the words out. "I care about you. I do, but...but I've never known this...this feeling and I can't say the words if I don't understand them. I have no reference, no definition or...or connection that makes sense for me, and I need to understand what love is before I say that word to you. I'm not stupid. I know it's a special word and not one that should be bandied about just because it's only four letters and easy to say. I just need time to...to get my head around what's going on in my heart."

Her eyes glassy with emotion, Addison sat down on the edge of the bed. Slowly reaching out, she gently ran her fingers down Joanna's face. "You're so beautiful," she whispered. "And I miss you."

It was so simple, just a tender touch, but with one caress, Joanna's heart melted. She reached over and pulled the knot from Addison's tie, and slipping it from her shirt, Joanna let it drop to the floor. "I don't need to hear the words," she said as she pushed Addison's jacket from her shoulders. "I just need you to show them to me."

Addison swallowed the moisture building in her mouth and leaning over, she placed her lips on Joanna's.

The kiss was like no other they had shared for it was tentative and gentle, and in slow motion, their heads moved this way and that. Neither feeling the need to rush, they caressed each other with their lips and their tongues, drinking in the sweetness they had both missed so much.

Joanna broke out of the kiss. The softest of smiles graced her face as her eyes met Addison's and a moment later, her fingers found the buttons on Addison's shirt.

One by one Addison could feel the fasteners giving way, and as her shirt began to gape, her heart began to pound. She had always been the seducer. Never granting anyone control over the act, she had never allowed them to strip her, but as the cool air met her heated skin, Addison couldn't help but relinquish all control.

Driven by desire and a thirst to experience all that was Addison, locked under sheets and a duvet was not where Joanna wanted to be. Quickly escaping the fortress of down and silk, Joanna wasted no time in removing Addison's shirt and a shiver of awareness fluttered through Joanna's body as Addison's torso finally came into view.

The effect from years of swimming was obvious. Addison's arms were muscled and her stomach flat and strong, but nothing could have prepared Joanna for the swells of Addison's breasts rising above a bra of lace and spandex. She couldn't prevent a low groan from escaping her lips as her center pulsed, and keeping her eyes locked on Addison's, Joanna slowly reached around and released the clasp of Addison's bra.

Drawn to what she yearned to see, Joanna fixed her eyes on breasts, creamy and plump. Tipped in rose, beaded and tight, they rose and fell in time with Addison's breathing, and Joanna didn't hesitate to reach out and cup them in her hands. Honey smooth and weighty, they filled her palms so perfectly, and for a few seconds, Joanna just held them, amazed at the sensation.

At first, the rosy centers had been taut, but when Joanna saw how hard they had become, the peaks erect and hard as pebbles, she ran her thumbs over them and watched in amazement as they grew even harder. Lowering her head, she pulled one into her mouth and tenderly ran her tongue around it.

Addison arched her spine and tipped back her head as a current of sensual need rushed through her body. Others had been at her breasts, sucking and fondling in the throes of sex, but this was something entirely different. This was something she never wanted to end, and gasping for air, she murmured, "Oh dear God, yes. Yes, Joanna...*yes*."

In the darkest recesses of Joanna's mind, there had been a fragment of worry born from a novice's concern, but Addison's raspy whisper dissolved any apprehension Joanna had. Her tender tasting turned hungrier, and sucking hard on the distended peak in front of her, she began tweaking the other with her fingers.

It took every ounce of strength Addison had not to throw Joanna onto the bed and ravage her then and there. Need coursed through Addison's body and between her legs, nectar now oozed freely, soaking through her knickers and trousers in a current born from passion. Her heart was racing, and her breathing ragged, and feeling as if her heart was going to explode from her chest, Addison tenderly urged Joanna to cease. Their eyes met for an instant before Addison wasted no time in ridding Joanna of her pajama top.

Joanna now understood why Addison had taken her so quickly those three nights because slow seemed impossible. Urged on by a hunger she had never known, while she found herself being stripped of her clothes, Joanna did the same to Addison. Coaxing her to stand, Joanna fumbled for Addison's belt, and tugging it free, she unzipped her trousers and let them fall to the floor.

Addison pulled Joanna to her feet and freed her from the pajama bottoms, but Addison didn't stop there. Hooking her fingers in the band of Joanna's knickers, Addison slowly knelt as she dragged the silk and lace down Joanna's shapely legs.

All at once, Addison was awash in the scent of Joanna's arousal. It was heady and earthy, and too enticing to ignore. Cupping Joanna's bottom in her hands, she urged her forward and then buried her face between Joanna's legs.

"Oh...Jesus," Joanna said, and unable to stop herself, she thrust her pelvis against the deliciousness of what Addison was doing. She could feel her lips and tongue greedily nibbling and licking at the juncture between her thighs, and the sensation was driving Joanna mad. Feeling as if her knees were about to give way, she threaded her fingers through Addison's hair and grabbing hold of the strands, forced Addison to stand up. As soon as she did, Joanna captured Addison in a fierce and probing kiss. Open-mouthed and demanding, Joanna ravaged Addison's mouth. She could taste her own essence on her lips, the flavor heightening the passion burning in Joanna's veins. Breaking out of the kiss, she pushed Addison's knickers over her rounded hips, and they floated silently down her legs.

Unabashedly, Joanna lowered her eyes and her breath caught in her throat. Addison was shaven and smooth, and her thighs were glistening from the wetness seeping from her.

Addison stood there naked and exposed as she gazed at Joanna, and the more she looked, the more erotic the moment became. The scent of her want became thick in the air as her walls pulsed and pushed out nectar from within, and when she felt it drip down her legs, she took a ragged breath and urged Joanna to the bed.

Joanna willingly slid onto sheets of silk and watched as Addison slowly followed her. Skin, heated and smooth, finally came into contact, and when Joanna felt Addison's knee slip between her legs, she moaned in anticipation. The touch she craved was just seconds away.

Addison claimed Joanna's mouth in another kiss, her tongue sweeping hungrily over Joanna's again and again before she began to make her way across Joanna's neck and shoulder. Her lips blazed a liquid trail of fire as she casually tasted Joanna's salty skin, but when she reached Joanna's breasts, casual was no more. Covering an engorged nipple with her lips, Addison sucked and teased, relentless in her pursuit of pleasure, while Joanna helplessly squirmed beneath her.

Joanna combed her fingers through Addison's hair and held her firmly against her breast. It was the language of lovers, a silent plea for more and Addison answered it in a heartbeat. Pulling on the bud of the other nipple with her fingers, Addison rubbed and tweaked it as she continued to feast on the one between her lips. It was taut and beaded and delicious, and she could have gone on forever, but when she felt a gentle nudge, she obeyed Joanna's silent command and rolled to her side. Joanna followed her, and as their eyes locked, their hands began to roam.

In awe of texture so incredibly divine, they lazily drew their fingers down each other's skin. It was all so new, so different than it had been before, and entranced by the touch of the other, time passed ever so slowly. The sound of their breathing was all that could be heard, its volume increasing the more their hands wandered, and when Joanna slipped hers between Addison's legs, the silence was quickly broken as a lustful moan slipped from Addison's lips.

Joanna became entranced by the petal-smooth folds slick with desire. Her hand was quickly coated in want, and driven by the arousal pumping through her body Joanna began to explore the folds beneath her fingers...and Addison began to writhe.

Pleasure and pain became one as Joanna slowly drove Addison to the brink of bliss. Unhurried in her discoveries, Joanna stroked Addison's thickened folds. Dipping between each, she slid her fingers up and down again and again until Addison suddenly rolled to her back. For an instant, Joanna's brow creased, but when she saw Addison open her legs, Joanna worried no more. Returning her hand to the warmth between Addison's thighs, Joanna guided her finger into Addison's entrance.

"Oh...Christ," Addison said, arching to meet the intrusion. "Oh...yes..."

The feel of Addison's tight, wet walls around her finger was to die for, and Joanna had to bite down on her lip to squelch her own need for release. At first, she was gentle and slow, but when Addison's moans turned guttural, and she began pushing hard against her hand, Joanna slipped out one finger and thrust in two. Filling Addison in one quick motion, Joanna wasted no time in increasing the tempo as she drove her fingers into her wife again and again, and it wasn't long before Addison matched the rhythm she had set.

The restraint Addison had always used with others disintegrated. With nameless women and even with Luce, Addison had always held back just a little, but with Joanna that was impossible. Grabbing for the sheets, Addison clutched the fabric in her hands as she finally allowed herself the freedom to let go.

Spasms of pleasure rippled from within, fluttering and pulsating through her center until they erupted from her core, her nectar flowing thick as garbled sounds of pleasure slipped from Addison's lips. Wave after wave crashed over her, and squeezing her legs tightly around Joanna's hand, Addison rode each wave to its crescendo.

Her body heated and her breaths shallow, Joanna waited in silence until she felt Addison's legs relax. Carefully removing her hand, she rested back on her haunches, softly smiling at the woman she loved.

One minute passed and then another before Addison opened her eyes, and when she did, she momentarily forgot how to breathe. Kneeling beside her was Joanna, her naked breasts heaving as she pulled in air through parted lips. Her skin was flushed and shining with sweat and tendrils of hair clung to her forehead, and Addison couldn't remember seeing anything more sensual.

She sat up and gently eased Joanna to the mattress. The flavor of the woman was still swirling in her mouth, and Addison licked her lips in anticipation as she inched downward on the bed. Leisurely kissing her way over Joanna's breasts and belly, when the divine aroma of Joanna's desire filled her nostrils, Addison breathed deeply as she parted Joanna's legs.

Earlier, Joanna had been given a hint of what Addison could do with her tongue, so when she felt her breath on her thigh, she knew the hints had ended...and ended they had.

Addison nuzzled her nose into the dark curls, and when she ran the tip of her finger up Joanna's folds, her wife's response was immediate. Raising her hips, Joanna offered Addison a sensuous invitation.

Sliding her hands under Joanna's bottom, Addison held her up as she buried her face into the pink, slippery fissures. She ran her tongue through every crevice, lapping at the need oozing from Joanna's entrance, and every now and then, she sucked against the tenderest of flesh until Joanna's squirms became frenzied.

Few words had been spoken, both using their touches, breaths, and sighs to urge the other on, but rapidly spiraling toward the sweetest of deaths, Joanna could take no more. "Please, Addison. Oh...God...please..."

It was Addison's turn to clamp her legs closed, shutting down the spasms that Joanna's words had caused. Sheathing two fingers deep inside of Joanna, Addison placed her mouth over Joanna's clit and allowed her tongue to do the rest. Between her strong, deliberate plunges and the circles she drew with her tongue, within seconds the room was filled with Joanna's cries of ecstasy.

The power of her climax caused Joanna to sit up for a moment before she fell back to the bed, welcoming spasm after delirious spasm as they rushed through her body and shuddered through her soul.

Awestruck, Addison watched Joanna's shattering release, and for the first time in her life, she climaxed without ever being touched.

It took several minutes before Joanna found the strength to open her eyes, and lifting her head, she looked down at the woman whose head was now resting on her thigh. Never in her wildest dreams had she expected something so powerful or so gloriously perfect, and even though Addison hadn't spoken the words, in every touch, in every sigh, and in every kiss...Joanna had just heard them loud and clear.

***

The wearer of thick-soled orthopedic shoes climbed the stairs, making not a sound on the carpet as she reached the top and turned toward the east wing. For the most part, Saturday mornings were like clockwork and Joanna would visit the kitchen for her cup of coffee and toast with jam, but when eight o'clock passed and nine approached, Fiona took it upon herself to load a silver tray with the makings of breakfast. After all, even she enjoyed a lie-in occasionally.

***

Sometime during the night the champagne duvet had slipped from the bed, but the heat it would have provided was not missed by the occupants. Naked and intertwined under a jumble of sheets, they slumbered unaware, warmed by the heat of the other.

Joanna was wrapped in a cocoon of sleep and comfort when a faint knocking awakened her. At first, she was going to ignore it, but when Chauncey began to yap, Joanna groaned. "Come in," she mumbled into her pillow, but a millisecond later her eyes flew open. She sat up, scrambling to pull the sheet around her as she was about to retract her offer, but before one word formed on her lips, the door swung open and in walked Fiona.

At first, Fiona was confused. Joanna looked frightened as she clutched a sheet to her chest, but when Fiona's eyes were drawn to something else, the silver tray filled with food and china slipped from her fingers and crashed to the floor.

"What the fuck!" Addison said. Turning over, she quickly sat up and gave Fiona a view neither of them would soon forget. "Jesus Christ," Addison growled, tugging with all her might to free the sheet trapped under her body to cover herself. "What the hell are you doing?"

Joanna looked at Addison and immediately grinned. She had the worst case of bedhead Joanna had ever seen, and her indignant expression caused Joanna's eyes to twinkle. "Addison, please," she whispered. "It's okay. I was the one who told her to come in. She's done nothing wrong. I'll handle it."

Addison wanted to be angry. Actually, she *really* wanted to be angry, but the gaiety in Joanna's eyes had acted like a wet blanket, extinguishing Addison's temper in an instant. Resigned to once again giving up control, Addison sighed. "All right. She's all yours."

"Good," Joanna said, giving Addison a wink. Turning back to Fiona, who now was busily picking up shattered pieces of china and coffee-soaked slices of bread, Joanna said, "It's okay, Fiona. I'll do that."

"Oh...um...no, miss...I made the mess and—"

"I think in this instance we can forget about decorum, don't you?"

Fiona raised her eyes and saw Joanna smiling back at her. "Miss?"

Joanna fought the urge to laugh when she saw the depth of the scarlet coloring Fiona's cheeks. "What I'm saying is I think you've seen enough, and since it's obvious Addison and I aren't wearing any clothes, perhaps it's best you return to the kitchen and put on another pot of coffee. And if you don't mind, please take Chauncey with you. He needs to go out."

Fiona got to her feet. "Yes, miss. Right away," she said as she snapped her fingers to get the pup's attention. Instantly springing to his feet, Chauncey darted past Fiona and scampered down the hall, and as Fiona reached for the door knob, she glanced at Joanna. "Thank you, miss."

"You're quite welcome."

Joanna waited for the door to latch before looking back at Addison, and when she saw the woman's mortified expression, Joanna began to chuckle. "Are you all right? It's not like they wouldn't have found out eventually, you know?"

"Yes, well, it's one thing for them to figure it out," Addison said, still tugging at part of the sheet lodged under Joanna's bum. "But it's quite another to be found starkers. Don't you think?"

Joanna's amusement overflowed immediately, and reduced to a fit of irrepressible giggles, she continued until her sides began to hurt.

Addison's mouth went slack as she stared at Joanna, but her momentary annoyance was no match for Joanna's laughter. True and pure, it was frivolity at its best and Addison's heart smiled. She reached over and pulled Joanna toward her, and a second before their lips met, she whispered, "Now...where were we?"

Chapter Thirty-Four

When Evelyn hired the staff for The Oaks, for the most part, her requirements matched those of other house managers except for one detail. Along with professionalism, respect, propriety, and privacy, those who worked at The Oaks could not carry with them a hint of homophobia or bias. So, while Fiona was surprised by what she had just seen, as she descended the stairs, she couldn't help but titter at the shocked look on Addison's face. It did her heart good to know the woman wasn't as icy as her eyes.

With Chauncey dancing around in urgency when they reached the foyer, Fiona opened the door and allowed the pup to visit the front lawns for a short while before she headed to the kitchen with Chauncey at her heels. Priorities being what they were, Master Chauncey received his breakfast before Fiona began preparing another tray to take upstairs; however, this time she prepared it with two in mind. Loading it with coffee, toast, and assorted nibbles, she carried it upstairs and set it on the floor outside Joanna's room. Knocking lightly on the door, Fiona hurried back to the kitchen carrying with her a smile that would last for hours.

***

Their morning and afternoon were filled with toast and jam and sex and sleep, although not necessarily in that order. They expressed their feelings in murmurs and sighs, and caresses starting as tender, ended in an urgency that took their breath away.

Guided by the love she felt, there was no hesitancy in Joanna's kisses or uncertainty in her touch, and in the warmth of her embrace, Addison discovered the difference between having sex and making love. She had always used sex as a means to an end, a pleasurable exercise resulting in a peaceful night's sleep alone in her bed, but now Addison found herself fighting exhaustion for one more taste of Joanna's luscious lips or one more touch of skin creamier than anything imaginable.

Sated, they would doze, spooned in the center of a queen size bed, oblivious to the beautiful day just outside the window, but when their eyes fluttered open, so did their hearts, and they started again.

Dressed only in a wrinkled white shirt, Addison came out of the bathroom and crept to the bed. Leaning over, she placed a light kiss on Joanna's lips and smiled when she heard Joanna's sleepy purr. "Time to wake up," Addison whispered.

Joanna grinned as she opened her eyes, but with only one button fastened on Addison's shirt, Joanna's grin quickly changed to a leer. "Nice view."

Addison looked down and snickered. "I'm glad you like it," she said, standing straight.

"And why are you wearing that? Come back to bed."

"I'm wearing it because I desperately need a shower, but all my clothes are in my room, and as much as I doubt there's anyone in the house but Fiona, I can't believe she really wants to see me naked again."

"Yeah, but I do," Joanna said, reaching out to grab Addison's shirt. "Now come here."

"You're getting bossy."

"I learn from the best."

"Yes, it seems you have," Addison said as she did her best not to focus on Joanna's breasts, which were now peeking out above the sheet.

"All I'm asking you for is one kiss."

"Is that so?"

"Lean over, and I'll show you," Joanna said, drinking in Addison with her eyes.

Addison couldn't resist the playful challenge, and bending over, she pressed her lips to Joanna's. At first, the kiss was feathery, just a slow merging of lips, but Addison couldn't help but groan when Joanna deepened the kiss. Rapidly finding out she could not deny the woman anything, Addison had no choice but to welcome Joanna's tongue inside, and as soon as she did...Joanna owned her.

When Joanna heard a throaty moan rise in Addison's throat, her body pulsed. It was a white flag signaling surrender, and Joanna wasted no time for the pillaging to begin. Slipping her hand between Addison's legs, Joanna snaked her fingers through folds already plentiful with desire.

Addison broke out of the kiss and panted for air, and as the fire inside her began to rage, she threw back the sheet covering Joanna. Raking her eyes over the naked body before her, Addison licked her lips as she reached down and cupped Joanna's sex.

For every stroke Joanna made, Addison matched her with one of her own, and when Joanna eased two fingers inside, Addison did the same, and it didn't take long before both women were on the brink of orgasm.

Captivated, neither could close her eyes, heightening the lascivious effect they were having on each other to its extreme. Skin now glistened with sweat, and breaths were short and ragged, and when Addison began to flex her pelvis, taking Joanna's fingers deep inside of her, Joanna began raising her hips to meet Addison's hand in the same tempo. They wanted the same thing. They needed the same thing, and powerless against what their love had created, they arched and sheathed until uninhibited cries slipped from their lips and glorious shudders of pleasure exploded from within.

Her knees too weak to hold her any longer, Addison collapsed over top of Joanna, but a minute later, she let out a laugh.

Joanna opened her eyes and looked at the woman lying next to her. "What's so funny?"

"If we keep this up," Addison said as she propped herself up on her elbow. "Fiona's going to find us dead."

***

Just as she placed another forkful of pot roast in her mouth, Joanna raised her eyes and discovered she was being watched. Waiting the time it took to swallow, she smiled at Addison. "You're staring."

"Was I?"

"Weren't you?"

"Maybe. Actually, I was...I was thinking about something?"

"Such as?" Joanna said, reaching for her wine.

"I was thinking this table is far too long."

Joanna's smile doubled in size. "You think?"

Before Addison could answer, Fiona entered the room to clear the dishes. As she reached for Addison's empty plate, she stopped halfway to the rim of the china when Addison said, "It was delicious."

"Oh...um...thank you," Fiona said, her eyes darting toward Joanna for a split-second. "I'm glad you enjoyed it."

"Would there be any more?"

Again, Fiona quickly looked toward the other end of the table and when she saw Joanna's eyes sparkling back at her, it was all Fiona could do not to laugh.

When she had returned in the afternoon to fix lunch, Fiona found herself to be the only occupant on the ground floor. She had tittered as she prepared a luncheon platter, but with the morning's fiasco still fresh in her mind, when she had reached Joanna's door and saw the breakfast tray sitting on the floor, Fiona had rapped lightly on the door, switched the trays, and scurried back to the kitchen. She didn't return again until shortly after four to put in a roast, and climbing the stairs, she went to retrieve the empty tray only to find the assorted lunch nibbles she had prepared had gone untouched. It had been thirty-five years since Fiona's honeymoon, but as she picked up the tray, her cheeks turned rosy, remembering the meals she had once missed as well.

"Yes, Mrs. Kane, there is," Fiona said, her face turning rosy as she picked up Addison's plate. "I'll just go fix you another serving right away."

"Thank you."

"Would you like some also?" Fiona said as she headed down the table to collect Joanna's empty plate.

Joanna's cheeks flamed crimson, and pressing her lips together, she cleared her throat. "Yes, please. If you don't mind."

"Not at all, miss," Fiona said, smiling as she picked up the plate. "Not at all."

***

A short time later, Fiona returned to gather the second round of plates, and after filling the wine glasses with what remained in the bottle, she disappeared into the kitchen to finish up for the evening.

Addison picked up her goblet, and leaning back, she crossed her legs as she gazed at Joanna. "Does Millie still send you my calendar?"

"Um...no. Why?"

"I wasn't sure if you knew I was leaving town on Tuesday."

"You are?"

"Yes, I have some meetings scheduled in Paris. I won't be back until early Friday morning."

Joanna's shoulders sagged. "Oh."

"So...do you have any plans for Friday evening?"

"I don't know," Joanna said, taking a sip of wine. "I'll have to check my diary."

"Oh, okay."

"Addison," Joanna said with a snort. "I don't *have* a diary."

Seeing the mischief in Joanna's eyes, Addison shook her head. "I have to get used to your sense of humor."

"Apparently, you do," Joanna said with a laugh. "So what's going on Friday?"

"I thought perhaps...perhaps you'd like to go out to dinner with me."

"Are you asking me for a date?"

"Well, I'm not sure *date* is the proper word, given the fact you *are* my wife."

"Oh, I don't know. I kind of like the word date," Joanna purred, running her finger along the edge of her glass.

Addison shifted in her chair. "Then yes," she said, with a nod. "I'm asking you for a date."

"Can I ask you why you're asking?"

"This is getting tedious."

"Humor me," Joanna said. "I promise. I'll make it worth it."

Addison arched an eyebrow, and slowly taking a sip of wine, her eyes locked with Joanna's. "Because things have changed and you don't deserve to be locked away in this place all day, every day. You're my wife and I...and I care about you, and I'd like to show you some finer things in life if you let me."

The sincerity of Addison's answer caused Joanna's heart to do a flip, and as goosebumps sprang to life on her arms, Joanna softly said, "In that case, I'd love to go out to dinner with you, but on one condition."

Out of Joanna's line of sight, Addison wiped her palms on her trousers. "Okay. What's that?"

"Lose the tie."

Addison reached up and fingered the Windsor knot perfectly centered in the Oxford collar. "You don't like my ties?"

"I suppose they're necessary for business, but no, I don't particularly like them," Joanna said, reaching for her drink. "They make you look...they make you look uptight and masculine, and you're anything but."

"I'm not?"

"You seem to forget. I've seen your lingerie."

All at once, Addison felt as if her face was in a furnace and after taking a moment, she cleared her throat. "Consider the tie lost."

"Good," Joanna said, but the sparkle in her eyes dimmed when she noticed Addison checking her watch. "Um...I'm not keeping you from something, am I?"

"No," Addison said, shaking her head. "I just thought since I've yet to see what you had done to the patio, we could go outside, but it's probably too dark now. That is if I'd even notice the repairs."

"Oh, you'd notice them," Joanna said, talking into her wine glass as she brought it to her lips.

Addison tilted her head to the side. "Is that so?"

"Yep," Joanna said. Placing the empty glass back on the table, she got to her feet. "Shall we?"

"The sun's already gone down. It's too dark."

"That's what you think."

***

By the time they reached the door in the parlor leading to the patio, Chauncey was doing his happy puppy dance, so Joanna quickly let him out before flipping on a series of light switches hidden behind the drapes. Flashing Addison a grin, she gestured toward the door without saying a word. With Addison's reaction to the removal of the ivy still fresh in her mind, Joanna held her breath as they stepped outside, and waiting in silence, she watched as Addison slowly took in her surroundings.

Addison's mouth fell open as she surveyed what was before her. It was the most prestigious patio she had ever seen.

Light fixtures, long since destroyed by rust and plant had been found under the ivy, and while it had been a scramble to find replicas, Samson had done just that. Six massive wall sconces, regal and old world, now hung from the house, and with the help of strips of LED lights hidden under the new railing, the entire veranda was awash in light.

Every piece of slate was gone and in its place were rectangular slabs of Yorkstone in varying sizes. Narrow and wide, short and long, while the predominant color of the natural English sandstone was blue and gray, swatches of buff could be seen throughout. In place of the antiquated iron railing, Samson and his team had installed a balustrade system constructed of precast concrete. At first, Addison believed the sculpted balusters to be a bit bulky, but as she looked across the patio, she found she was wrong. Anything less beefy would have looked minuscule.

Without so much as a glance in Joanna's direction, Addison took a few steps, but paused long enough to look down at her feet before she continued to the first of two new staircases leading to the gardens. Coming to a stop at the top of the first set of stairs, her eyes followed the steps as they gently curved toward the left, while the other, a dozen yards to her right, turned in the opposite direction. The treads were deep and covered in Yorkstone, and as she descended and ran her hand down the thick railing, she had no doubt it would stand for centuries if allowed.

The night air was cool, and while there was a slight breeze, its chill was lost on Addison as she reached the bottom step. Gone was the sound of hollow slate beneath her feet and the roughness of iron railing under her hand. Her footing was now solid, and the stone atop the banister was polished and elegant, conflicting with memories embedded from her childhood. Taking a deep breath, she sat down on the bottom step.

Addison's mind filled with the recollections of taunts and screams, and of insults and forced solitude, robbing her of a childhood and of love, but the inner sting of those memories was starting to fade. Like the familiar sounds and textures replaced by new, the future was slowly burying the past.

Joanna sat down next to Addison. "Are you all right?" she said, noticing the grim look on Addison's face.

Addison drew in another long breath, letting it out slowly as she peered through the darkness at the jumble of overgrowth on the other side of the footpath. Picking up a dried stalk of grass at her feet, she twirled it in her fingers. "Have you found the fountains yet?"

"No, but I can see—" Joanna jerked back her head. "Wait," she said, eyeballing Addison. "Fountains? As in more than one?"

"There are three actually."

"Three? How do you know that?"

Addison looked at Joanna and smiled. "Because before I was shipped off to boarding school, it's where I played when I was a child," she said, tossing the stalk of grass to the ground. "Evelyn couldn't watch me twenty-four-seven, and the rest of the staff couldn't have cared less, so whenever I could steal away, I'd come out here and play adventurer." Addison stopped, grinning as she remembered the few good memories she had. "I'd pretend I was an orphan lost in a jungle. I'd spend hours out there, making my way through the brush, memorizing everything as I went."

"Why memorize? Afraid to get lost?"

"No, I was never afraid out there," Addison said, gesturing toward the gardens. "My fears were inside the house, which is why I could never make a map. If it were ever found, my playground would have gone away, so I paced off steps and memorized the landmarks."

"Like the fountains."

"Yes. That's how I know there are three. There're also a few reflecting pools, one of which has a footbridge over it and…oh…um…statues…there are four statues of angels." Addison paused, frowning for a second as she looked across the footpath again before her lips curved upward. "And down the hill between the orchards is a greenhouse, or rather was. It was in sad shape back then, so I doubt it's still standing."

Suddenly feeling as if she was talking to herself, Addison turned her head and found Joanna staring back at her with eyes bulging. "What?"

"Orchards?"

"That's right."

"But I thought the gardens just went back to that stand of trees covered in ivy."

"No, that stand of trees is actually an overgrown privet hedge," Addison said, peering off into the darkness. "And behind it, where the property drops down, you'll find a lot of out-of-control apple and pear trees…and plums if memory serves."

Joanna drew her head back quickly. "Just how big is this bloody garden?"

"Upwards of twenty acres, give or take," Addison said with a shrug.

"Twenty acres!" Joanna said, jumping to her feet. "Well, you must have been having yourself a great laugh at my expense. Huh? Me out here on my hands and knees pulling out weeds thinking I was getting somewhere when all along you knew I wasn't even making a dent!"

Joanna turned to stomp up the stairs, but her motion was stopped when Addison grabbed her by the hand and pulled her back to the step. "If you remember," Addison said, forcing Joanna to sit. "We weren't exactly talking very much back then. Now were we?"

Joanna slouched and let out a slow breath. "No, I guess we weren't."

"But now that we are, I suggest we hire someone to clear out the mess. That way, we can see what's existing and go from there."

"We?" Joanna said, turning to face Addison.

"Sorry?"

"You said we."

"I did?"

"Yes, and I like it."

Addison's face split into a grin. "Speaking of like. I adore what you've done to the patio."

"Yeah?"

"Absolutely. It's lovely."

"I was worried you'd get angry. I went way over budget."

"I didn't give you a budget."

"I know," Joanna said, wiggling her eyebrows.

Addison let out a hearty laugh and got to her feet. Holding out her hand, she helped Joanna to do the same and then leaned in for a kiss.

Joanna sighed as their mouths met, breathing in Addison's cologne as she got lost in the feel of her lips. A hint of the essence of Cabernet remained, but the rest was a flavor Joanna had come to know as Addison's.

Pulling out of the kiss, Addison looked into Joanna's eyes and saw passion that took her breath away. "What say we go inside, and I show you just how much I appreciate what you've done with the patio?"

Joanna regarded Addison with a slow slide of her eyes, and leaning her head to the side, she snapped her fingers. In no time at all, Chauncey appeared out of the darkness, ran down the path, and scampered up the stairs.

"Now we can go to bed," Joanna said, taking hold of Addison's hand. "But I have to tell you, I'm really not that tired."

"Good, because neither am I."

Chapter Thirty-Five

"Good morning," Joanna said as she strolled into the kitchen with Chauncey on her heels.

Noah turned around just as Evelyn looked up from her notepad, and in unison, they replied, "Good morning."

While Chauncey made a mad dash to his food bowl, Joanna sat down on a stool as Noah placed a mug of coffee in front of her. "Thanks," she said, taking a sip. Swiveling to face Evelyn, she said, "So, how was your weekend?"

"It was nice, but apparently not as nice as yours."

The hint of humor in Evelyn's tone wasn't lost on Joanna, but unsure what joke she may have missed, she looked at Noah for a clue. His expression mirrored Evelyn's, but when she saw him suck in his cheeks and purse his lips, Joanna's face flamed instantly.

Amused by the color of Joanna's cheeks, Evelyn leaned in close. "It seems you may have removed the ivy covering the house, but our grapevine is still *very* much alive and well."

Noah, unable to contain his mirth any longer, exploded with a loud guffaw, the result of which added at least two more shades of red to Joanna's face.

Joanna folded her arms on the counter and quickly buried her face in them. "What did she do, put it on a bloody billboard?"

"Oh no, texting is *so* much easier," Evelyn said with a playful wave of her hand. "And it's really quite all right. It won't go beyond the walls of The Oaks, and by the staff's reaction, they couldn't be more thrilled."

Joanna popped up her head. "They *all* know?"

"Good news travels fast," Evelyn said, patting Joanna on the arm. "And since I heard just how many meals you and Addison skipped this weekend, I'm thinking *this* is definitely *good* news."

"Oh God," Joanna said, again burying her face.

Noah's laughter filled the room, and as much as she tried not to, a few titters slipped from Evelyn's lips as well.

"She's right, you know?" Noah said, wiping the tears from his eyes. "If you're happy, then we're happy." When Joanna didn't respond, he tapped her on the arm. Waiting until she raised her head, he whispered, "Are you happy?"

The radiant smile on Joanna's face brightened the room, and within seconds, the grins Noah and Evelyn displayed were of equal brilliance.

***

Joanna pulled another book from the box, and reading the title, she pondered on which empty shelf it should be placed. Before she could make up her mind, she heard the door to the library open, and looking up, she beamed. "Hi there."

"Hello," Addison said.

"You're early tonight," Joanna said, watching as Addison ambled toward her.

"With good reason," Addison said, pulling Joanna into her arms.

Like most businesses, Kane Holdings was a hectic place on Mondays. Questions or issues that had arisen in their offices across the world over the weekend would fill inboxes, and people would scurry about, putting out fires while hopefully not starting any new ones. Addison had always enjoyed the chaos, her mind so sharp that no issue was too great or question too difficult, if she had to pick a favorite day of the week, it would have been Monday. However, keeping her mind on business this particular Monday had proven difficult. Visions of the corporal delights she had shared with Joanna for three days kept intruding on her thoughts, so when quitting time approached for the rest of the people at Kane, and they scrambled to tidy their desks before walking out the door, Addison had already left the building.

Addison hadn't intended for the kiss to go on for so long, but once she tasted Joanna's lips, stopping didn't seem to be an option. The kiss ran the gamut from gossamer to voracious, and when the scale tipped toward the latter, hands began to travel.

Joanna's slipped beneath Addison's suit jacket and found their way to her back. Dragging her nails down Addison's spine, Joanna didn't think twice about the marks she might be leaving for she had left them before and Addison hadn't complained. Not even once.

Captivated by the woman in her arms, and the feel of Joanna's tongue sweeping through her mouth, the feel of the fabric of Joanna's blouse beneath her hand was not what Addison wanted. Tugging the shirt free from the waistband of Joanna's skirt, Addison's slipped her hand beneath the silk. The lace and spandex bra didn't stand a chance as Addison pushed it upward, and feeling the creamy breast now filling in her hand, Addison broke out of the kiss. Lifting Joanna's blouse, Addison gently squeezed the plump mound as she lowered her lips to the rose-red nipple craving attention.

A faint rap on the door reversed the two women's polarity instantaneously. Springing apart, Joanna jammed her shirt back into her skirt while Addison hastened to straighten her jacket. Grabbing a book from the table, Addison fell into a chair, crossed her legs, and opened the novel.

Clearing her throat, Joanna called out, "Come in."

The door opened, and Iris appeared. "Fiona thought you might like some tea before dinner," Iris said, placing the service on a small table in front of Addison. "Should I pour?"

"Um...no, that's fine, Iris. I'll do it," Joanna said. "And thank Fiona for her thoughtfulness. Will you please?"

"Of course miss," Iris said, smiling as she headed back the way she came. "I hope you enjoy your...tea."

As soon as the door closed, Addison looked over at Joanna. Chuckling to see the depth of the woman's blush, Addison said, "Don't worry. She doesn't have a clue."

"Of course she doesn't, sweetheart," Joanna said, reaching over to take the book from Addison's hand. Turning it right-side up, she handed it back. "That is unless you intended for *her* to read the book."

***

Snuggling under the sheets, Addison cradled Joanna against her. "So, what you're telling me is that they all know."

"Yes, apparently The Oaks also has a grapevine, and it's quite healthy."

Addison scowled. "Not that I care, nor is it any of their business, but how did they handle it?"

"If I'm happy, they're happy."

"Oh, so they don't care about *my* happiness."

"They don't know you. Not the way I do."

"I would think you would prefer it that way," Addison said with a laugh.

"You know what I mean. You've never been anything but an employer and a tough one, at that."

"It's the only way I know how to be."

"That's not true," Joanna said, turning her head to look at Addison. "You should give them a chance. I know they're just employees to you, but they really are a nice group of people, and they'd do anything for either one of us in a heartbeat."

"You think so?"

"I know so."

Addison drew in a breath, and as she slowly exhaled, she placed a light kiss on the top of Joanna's head. "I'll try," she whispered. "I promise."

At peace in each other's arms, for a little while neither said a word until Joanna rolled to her side to look at Addison. "Can I ask you a question?"

"You just did."

"Ha ha," Joanna said, giving Addison a playful poke. "How come we always end up in here?"

"Well, since the library was an epic fail, I think this is best. Don't you?"

"No, silly. I mean, why don't we ever go to *your* bedroom? Come to think of it, I've never even *seen* your bedroom."

Addison lowered her eyes. It was such a simple question, but it pained her to answer it. With a sigh, she looked at Joanna, but the words refused to come.

As soon as Joanna saw Addison's expression, she knew the answer to her question. "I thought you never had any...um...*guests* here."

"They never stayed the night."

Joanna rolled to her back and stared at the ceiling. "I can't tell you how much better that would have sounded if you had said *she* instead of *they*."

Propping herself up on her elbow, Addison gazed at Joanna. "If it helps, I'm sorry."

"A little, I guess."

Addison reached over, running her finger down Joanna's face until she reached her chin. Applying just enough pressure, she turned Joanna's face toward her. "Re-do it."

"What?"

"Redecorate my bedroom. Make it new. There's nothing in there of any value to me so do what you want to it."

"We don't have to do that."

"Yeah, we do. That is unless you want me to sleep in a bed where—"

"If you're wise, you won't finish that sentence."

Addison smiled. "Then is it settled?"

"Are you sure?"

"Yes. Very sure," Addison said, leaning in for a kiss. "Now, what say we seal the deal?"

***

Joanna approached Addison's bedroom, but the closer she got, the more pronounced her frown became. Stopping midway between the east wing and the master suite, for the third time in as many minutes, Joanna turned and headed back to her room.

They had been lovers for over two weeks. Passionate and uninhibited, they had touched, kissed, caressed, and loved naked and free, but entering Addison's bedroom suddenly seemed far more intimate. Even though Joanna knew Addison's offer to have the suite redecorated was heartfelt, walking into Addison's inner sanctum was proving to be difficult.

At first, Joanna told herself it was only because it was Addison's personal space, but by the time she turned back around and glared at the doors, Joanna stopped kidding herself. Behind those ornately carved slabs of walnut was a bed, and it was a bed Addison had shared with more than one woman. Setting her jaw, Joanna strode to the master suite and threw open the doors.

She ran her hand down the wall, and finding a bank of three switches, she flipped the toggles toward the ceiling. For a moment, Joanna thought she had missed a light or two, but one quick glimpse at the switches proved her wrong. Every light in the room was on, but most of the illumination had been swallowed up by its surroundings. There were, however, enough watts in the bulbs hidden behind yellowed shades to make Joanna feel a wee bit stupid.

On and off since she had arrived at The Oaks several months before, Joanna had found herself wondering just how large the master suite was, but if she had paid attention, she would have had her answer before now. There were only three sets of doors on the second floor excluding those leading to the lift. One set led to the west wing, one led to the east, and the last, the pair she just walked through, led to the gargantuan space before her.

From east to west, the bedroom was nearly thirty feet across, not including the space behind the two doors to her right, which she assumed led to a wardrobe and an en suite. The back wall jutted out like the parlor below it, and if Joanna had to guess, it would take her at least twenty-five steps to reach the heavy draperies in that area hiding what she suspected to be towering windows.

Only a thin strip of the dark oak plank flooring could be seen around the perimeter of the room, but the rest was hidden by a carpet Joanna guessed to be a few decades older than her twenty-eight years. In areas less traveled, she could still see the original green, red, and brown of the threads, but where previous occupants had walked over and over again, were now paths, worn and bland.

The room was cooler than Joanna expected and the hint of mustiness in the air told her if windows did exist behind the drapes, they hadn't been opened in a very long time. There was also an undertone of lemon-scented polish, to be expected in a room holding over a dozen pieces of furniture, but as Joanna took another breath, she grinned when she caught a whiff of Addison's cologne still hanging in the air.

Joanna looked here and there without taking a step, hoping she'd find something she liked, but other than a few pieces of furniture and the fireplace, the rest left a lot to be desired.

The bed, for the most part, was amazing. Dwarfing her own by more than two feet in width and a foot in length, it was the largest one she had ever seen. Clearly Victorian in design, the tone of the wood was much too dark for her taste, but the ornately carved headboard and four turned posts, leading to a canopy rail surrounding the bed, were as imposing as they were noble. The same intricate designs could be seen on the nightstands, armoire, tallboy, and on the chest at the foot of the bed, but a quick scan around the room showed several other accent pieces matching neither in color nor in style.

Across from the bed was a cast iron fireplace. By the lack of andirons or ash in the hearth, it was clear, that like the ones in the east wing, natural gas now provided the blaze if desired. The iron surround showed a hint of detail around its edge, adding a bit of charm to the old firebox, but even that seemed lost because of the wall in which it was housed.

Keeping with the era of the furnishings, the walls were a deep crimson, but age had brought them almost to the hue of dried blood, and tippled with forest green for a faux effect, even if Joanna added spotlights to the room, she doubted it would have brightened one watt. Joanna rubbed the back of her neck, letting out a sigh as she turned her attention to the fabrics of the room. The brocade of the curtains was thick and weighty, the garnet scroll design atop a background of hunter green, most likely opulent in its day, was now depressing and tenebrous. Given the darkness of its surroundings, Joanna was sure the chocolate brown duvet was chosen for its shade and nothing more because the faint paisley design in the fabric matched absolutely nothing in the room.

Taking a deep breath, Joanna continued her tour, and opening the first set of doors, she found herself standing in the wardrobe. L-shaped and sizable, a lone wooden rod ran down one wall and hung from its strength were numerous suits, shirts, and a few garment bags. Lined up underneath on the floor were a selection of wingtips, brogues, loafers, and ankle boots, and except for three pairs that were gray, the rest were all in tones of black. Grimacing at the drab beige walls and the three out-of-place white globe ceiling fixtures running down the center of the space, Joanna flicked off the lights and headed to what she assumed was the bathroom.

Joanna held her breath as she opened the door, and when she turned on the light, she let out an exasperated sigh. "Seriously!" she shouted. "You're a bloody billionaire for Christ's sake!"

The only thing going for the space was its size. Over ten feet in width and probably twenty feet deep, if it wasn't for the plumbing fixtures in view, the room could have easily held an entire bedroom set. The window across the far back wall allowed some natural light to stream in, but

Joanna found herself wishing it wasn't there. Halfway up the walls, and completely covering the floor, were tiles of white and black, and while the fixtures about the room were of this century, the claw-foot tub and twin porcelain pedestal sinks did their best to turn back time. Guessing that the door at the far end of the room held the loo, Joanna didn't need to look any further. Turning out the lights, she headed back to her room. She needed to call Samson...and call him now.

***

As soon as Joanna came from the parlor, her face lit up, and holding out her hand before she reached the door, she said, "Samson, I can't thank you enough for coming over on such short notice."

"The pleasure's all mine, Mrs. Kane," Samson said, shaking Joanna's hand.

Joanna's eyes were drawn to the young woman standing in Samson's shadow. A foot shorter than the man and many years younger, her tightly curled black hair was cut in a trendy, short style and the fact she wasn't wearing any makeup was a good choice. She didn't need any.

"And who's this?" Joanna said, her eyes darting back and forth between Samson and the woman.

"When we spoke on the phone earlier, you mentioned the photos on my website, so I thought I'd bring along my designer," Samson said as his toothy smile lit up the foyer. "This is my daughter, Lucinda. She's responsible for what you saw."

"Really?" Joanna said, extending her hand to the woman. "It's very nice to meet you, Lucinda. I hope you don't mind me saying this, but you look awfully young to be an interior decorator."

While Samson's skin tone was dark as night, his daughter's was far lighter, so her blush shined through immediately. "Nice to meet you, Mrs. Kane," she said softly. "And I'm not really an interior decorator yet, but I am studying to be one."

"Well, by what I saw on your father's website, you're going to have a marvelous career ahead of you."

"Thank you, Mrs. Kane."

"It's Joanna," she said, motioning toward the stairs. "Now, how about we go up, and I show you what you're facing."

As they reached the door to Addison's bedroom, Joanna stopped and looked at Lucinda. "I'm not sure what your father's told you, but I have to ask that what you see here, stays here. My wife is a very private person, and the last thing she'd want to see are photographs of her home plastered all over the Internet. After everything's finished, then, by all means, you can use it in your portfolio, but beforehand we ask for privacy."

"Of course, Mrs. Kane. My dad already told me."

"Good, and *please* call me Joanna." Pushing open the doors, she gestured for her guests to enter with a sweep of her arm. "Now, let's see if you and your father can pull off the impossible, again."

Lucinda didn't take a step until her father gave her an approving nod and then slowly walking into the room, she looked around. "Oh my," she said, looking over her shoulder. "It's a bit...um...masculine. Isn't it?"

"That's putting it mildly," Joanna said, coming in to stand alongside Lucinda.

"Can I take a minute?" Lucinda asked.

"Oh yes, of course. Take all the time you need," Joanna said.

Joanna and Samson waited patiently near the door while Lucinda looked around, taking her time as she studied the room at every angle possible. "You know," she said, rejoining Samson and Joanna. "It's definitely got possibilities."

"God, I hope so," Joanna said with a laugh. "So, where do we go from here?"

"Well, the first thing I need to ask is what you would like to keep?" Lucinda said. "Once I know that, I can work on some ideas to complement what's staying."

Joanna quickly looked around the room. "I actually like the pieces that match the bed. They are a little dark, but other than that I think they're okay."

"I couldn't agree more," Lucinda said. "So you wouldn't be opposed to losing all the odds and ends that are glaringly wrong for the room?"

"No, not at all."

"Good," Lucinda said. "And how about the sitting area by the windows?"

Joanna turned her attention to the two small chairs flanking a tiny table. "I don't know. If we get them reupholstered, they wouldn't be too terrible. I suppose."

"Have you ever sat in one of them?" Lucinda blurted.

"Lucinda," Samson said, his bass tone taking on a sudden sharpness. "Mind your manners."

"Oh, please," Joanna said with a wave of her hand. "She's fine, Samson, and she's right. I've never sat in one, but I will now."

Marching across the room with a smile on her face, Joanna plopped down on one of the chairs, emitting the tiniest of squeaks when she found herself falling a few extra inches than she expected. "Wow. They are a bit low, aren't they?" Joanna said as she leaned back to get comfortable. "And a little stiff."

"Exactly," Lucinda said, walking to the sitting area. "They are true Victorian, meaning they're shorter than what we're used to and without arms, like these two, they were called ladies' chairs. Between that and those balloon backs, they are definitely great accent pieces, but if you want comfort, you won't find it in those."

"I can see that," Joanna said, rising to her feet. "So, what are you thinking?"

"Well, we could use wing-backs, but this area is so large, I was thinking maybe a chaise or even a double with a sitting area off to the side. That way, you could enjoy breakfast, but also lounge in the sunlight if the mood struck. That is, once we get rid of those beastly curtains."

Joanna grinned. "You're hired."

Samson's pearly whites made an appearance when he glimpsed at his daughter, and as his chest swelled, he turned back to Joanna. "Well, it seems Lucinda's got her work cut out for her, but other than a bit of plaster repair, paint, and replacing some fixtures, this shouldn't take me long at all."

"That's what you think," Joanna said as she motioned toward the doors leading into the bath and wardrobe. "You ready for another challenge?"

Chapter Thirty-Six

Joanna scanned the items in her wardrobe, trying to decide which of the three little black dresses would be appropriate. The first ended just below her knee, and with long sleeves and a high neckline, it was simple and unpretentious, but convincing herself the frock would be too warm for this time of year, she pushed it aside and examined the next. The second had a bit more snap to it, and while the silk ruffled tiered skirt still ended below her knee, the halter neckline and fitted bodice added more than just a hint of sultry. The third dress, however, didn't hint at anything.

Ending slightly above the knee, and with a skin-baring v-neckline, the sheath dress was as vampish as it was alluring. With the addition of sleeves of mesh and lace, just enough sophistication was added to the form-fitting garment to tone down the steaminess caused by the off-center front slit, its placement guaranteeing to show an ample amount of the wearer's thigh every time she took a step.

Joanna pulled her selection from its hanger, and scanning the shoes lined up neatly along the wall, she picked up a pair of black patent leather with three-inch stiletto heels. With their signature red-lacquered soles, the Christian Louboutin pointed toe pumps were absolutely perfect.

***

Addison had returned from her business trip early that morning as scheduled, and heading to the office, she spent her day in anticipation of her night. Reservations had already been made, so Addison coasted through the afternoon believing she had not a care in the world. Unfortunately, when she arrived home, she discovered that wasn't entirely the case.

She wasn't surprised not to see Joanna when she walked in the door. Suspecting she was flittering about deciding what to wear, Addison handed off her briefcase to George and ascended the stairs. She disappeared into her room, stripped, and took a quick shower, and after donning a pair of lace knickers and a matching brassiere, Addison moseyed into her wardrobe. She pulled a suit from a hanger, but as she was about to step into the trousers, she stopped. They were traditional and professional, and a staple in any executive's wardrobe, but remembering Joanna's comment about ties, Addison's heart began to race. "Shit," she said, tossing the trousers aside. "If she doesn't want you to wear a tie, she probably doesn't want you to wear a suit either, you idiot!" Addison ran her fingers through her hair, snarling as she stared at the row of the suits, but then she saw the garment bags at the end of the row.

Two held tuxedos and another, a lightweight linen she had purchased in Dubai, but the last had never seen the light of day since it had left the designer's shop and was delivered to her home almost a year ago.

Addison had been in Italy, visiting the famous Via Monte Napoleone as she did twice a year, perusing the selections in the upscale shops, and finding the latest and the greatest suits to fill her wardrobes. With hotel suites in most of the major countries across Europe, not to mention the wardrobes at the Langham and in her home at The Oaks, her outing took several days to complete and on one of those days, a suit displayed on a mannequin caught her eye.

There was absolutely nothing masculine about it. Made of the finest Australian Merino wool, the fabric was soft and the drape loose. The lack of lapels and pockets on the suit jacket appealed to her, and while overall the outfit seemed relaxed in fit, it was definitely not made for casual outings.

She had purchased it on a whim, a sudden unexplained need to have something else besides lingerie to announce her gender, but until that moment, Addison had forgotten it existed. Rushing over, she held her breath as she unzipped the bag, but as soon as she eyed the contents, she smiled.

***

Addison and Joanna exited their rooms at the same time, but while Addison had somehow suddenly lost the ability to walk, Joanna had not. With her eyes riveted on Addison, Joanna slowly sashayed from the east wing on three-inch heels, and her admiration of the woman who was her wife grew every step of the way.

Joanna had expected to see Addison wearing yet another black or gray suit, but while she pegged the color, that was all she pegged. Instead of a starched and stuffy manly outfit, the one Addison was wearing was sophisticated and designed with a woman in mind. The popped collar of the jacket added attitude fitting of Addison, but by wearing the banded collared gauze shirt underneath, it transformed the attitude into something far more sensuous. As if posing for a magazine shoot, the woman stood motionless with on hand stuffed into her trouser pocket, and Joanna came to a conclusion. *If* Addison had wanted to go on the prowl, she'd be a *very* busy woman.

Addison parted her lips, sliding her tongue over them to replace moisture that had somehow just evaporated, and she found herself facing a dilemma. Enthralled, Addison couldn't decide whether to focus on the shapely thigh making an appearance with every step Joanna took or the plunge of the neckline showing just enough of Joanna's cleavage to make Addison's heart race. Doing an incredibly slow slide with her eyes, when they returned to meet Joanna's, Addison breathed, "Wow."

Joanna arched an eyebrow as she reached up and fingered the placket of Addison's velvety smooth gray shirt. Holding it between her thumb and forefinger, she slowly drew her hand downward, her knuckle barely grazing Addison's skin until she reached the first fastened mother of pearl button located almost halfway down the blouse. Raising her eyes to meet Addison's, Joanna said, "You should lose your tie more often."

"I should take you out to dinner more often," Addison said, breathing in the scent of Joanna's perfume. "You're absolutely stunning."

Addison's compliment brought a dazzling smile to Joanna's face, but when she saw the look in Addison's eyes, Joanna shook her head. "We need to go."

Again, Addison drank in the sight of Joanna as she closed the distance between them. "I know, and we will, but not until I get a kiss."

"I have a feeling if we do that, we'll miss dinner," Joanna said, placing her hand lightly on Addison's arm.

"Only one way to find out, now isn't there?" Addison said, lowering her lips to Joanna's.

The quiet of the moment was interrupted by a loud jingling chime, and taking a step backward, Joanna frowned.

"Shit," Addison said as she reached into her trouser pocket for her phone. Reading the name on the display, she sighed. "I'm sorry, but I've been waiting for this bloody call for over an hour. Do you mind if I take it in the car?"

"Of course not," Joanna said, hooking her arm into Addison's. "But after that, you're mine."

***

Since their marriage, Joanna had begun to pay more attention to articles in the papers and magazines mentioning Addison and her accomplishments, so she knew a lot more about Addison Kane than she had several months earlier. However, she had never seen the business side of Addison in action.

Sitting quietly in the back of the Rolls, Joanna watched and listened in awe as Addison spoke to the person on the phone. Her conduct was that of a consummate professional, but what impressed Joanna was the woman's knowledge. Spouting off percentages and details as if reading them from a book, it was clear Addison knew what she was talking about and how to get her point across. At times, she would gesture with her hands, and at others, she'd shake her head and look toward the heavens, all of which tickled Joanna to no end. She had just discovered another side to Addison, and while she was truly awed, she was also more than just a little proud.

The Rolls came to a stop just as Addison ended her call. "Christ, I'm sorry," she said, pocketing the mobile. "But I promise you it was important."

"You're fine," Joanna said as she leaned over to look out Addison's window. "Le Gavroche?" she said, reading the sign above the door on the unassuming brick building.

"Classically French cuisine...with a few twists," Addison said as David opened her door. "I think you'll like it."

Entranced by Addison's persona while on her call in the car, Joanna hadn't the time to get nervous, but as they walked into the upscale eatery, a swarm of butterflies began to flutter in her stomach. Her mouth went dry, and she unconsciously began searching for all the exits, but when Addison placed her hand on the small of Joanna's back, the butterflies slowed their wings. The touch was possessive and affectionate, and as they were led to their table, and Joanna noticed a few heads turning, she held her head high. She was Mrs. Addison Kane.

Joanna slipped into the half-circle booth, across the thickly-padded, olive upholstery. The design of the seating put them somewhat on display, but situated along a wall, it also guaranteed they wouldn't be distracted by the parade of white-jacketed wait staff doing their jobs. Men dressed in suits and women adorned in jewels sat at the many tables filling the room, and the sound of their hushed conversations mingled with that of cutlery being used and meals being served.

As expected their table held crystal, polished silverware, and china, the plates proudly displaying the restaurant's name written in golden scroll around the edge, but what got Joanna's attention was at the center of the table. It was a small silver sculpture of a toucan, its uniqueness found in the spoon and fork used to create it. Joanna smiled at the cleverness, but her expression wavered when she raised her eyes just as the waiter approached. For a split-second, butterflies began to flap their wings again, but when Addison took the lead, Joanna listened to the exchange and the last of her jitters faded away.

*****

After a visit by the waiter, the sommelier, and the twin assistant managers welcoming them to their establishment, the two women relaxed back and waited for their meals to arrive.

"So, did your business trip go well?" Joanna asked, taking a sip of Chardonnay.

"Yes, for the most part."

"For the most part?"

"I had a problem keeping my mind on business," Addison said as her viewpoint shifted to Joanna's cleavage. "I have no idea why."

A faint hint of red crept across Joanna's cheeks, and feeling the heat, she took another taste of her wine.

"And how about you? Did you take me up on my bedroom offer?"

"Exactly which offer was that, sweetheart," Joanna purred.

Addison shifted in her seat, clearing her throat as she leaned a bit closer to her wife. "I was talking about the redecorating, not the...um...recreation."

"Oh, that," Joanna said with a chuckle.

"Yes, that."

"Actually, I did. I called Samson on Tuesday and between him and Lucinda, I think we have it handled."

"Who's Samson?"

"He's the contractor who did the patio."

"And Lucinda?"

"She's his daughter and his interior decorator. She's young, but marvelous, and she has some great ideas."

"So what's your timeframe?"

"Why, are you anxious?"

"In more ways than one, darling," Addison said, picking up her wine glass. "In more ways than one."

Before Joanna could continue the conversation, a man approached the table and judging by his gray, pinstriped suit, he wasn't employed by the restaurant. At first, Joanna thought him somewhat handsome and distinguished for a man of his age, but she changed her mind when his expression turned smug, and his lips curled into a sneer.

"It looks like this place is lowering their standards," he said, directing his words toward Addison.

There was not a flicker of emotion on Addison's face as she slowly placed her wine glass on the table before turning to look at the man now hovering over her. She took a moment and regarded Maxwell Firth with a cool stare before she spoke. "Yes, I can see they have," she said, turning back to look at Joanna. "Pity."

Not to be denied, Maxwell bent at the waist, lowering his voice to keep their conversation private. "I have to congratulate you on that stunt you pulled off at Christmas. I underestimated the value of just how much a Pygmalion wife is worth. Perhaps you can tell me where you found yours so I can do some shopping, too. Are they as easily trained as I've heard?"

Joanna couldn't hear most of what the man was saying, but Addison was now wearing a thin-lipped snarl, and in her eyes, Joanna saw murder.

Addison's anger pounded in her ears, and the thought of pummeling Firth into a mass of unrecognizable lard crossed her mind more than once, but that's exactly what he wanted, and she knew it. His cronies had yet to best her in the board room, and Firth was no match for her when it came to business, but if he could tarnish her image, taint it with fisticuffs in the middle of a luxury restaurant, he may have limped away with a few bruises, but the damage to her reputation would be far more blemished.

Addison swiveled just enough to look the man in the eye. "I think it's time for you leave, Max," she said in an unwavering voice. "You and I have nothing to discuss, and your sour grapes is...well, it's boring."

Still close enough so only Addison could hear, Maxwell said, "You may have won this battle, Kane. Hell, you may win all of them, but in the end, I'll still win."

"Maybe you should lay off the scotch, Max," Addison said with a grunt of disgust. "You're becoming delusional."

Maxwell Firth displayed a toothy grin as he stood tall, and pulling his billfold from his pocket, he slipped a photo out of its vinyl protector. Bending down again, he showed Addison the photo. "You see this? Well, these are my sons, and all three are studying business and law. I may not be able to get my hands on your company during my lifetime, but you won't live forever, Addison, and when you die, trust me, they'll be there to scoop up your company, lock...stock...and barrel."

Firth straightened again, squaring his shoulders as he looked down his nose at Addison. "Enjoy your meal, Kane," he said as he finally acknowledged Joanna with a cursory glance, but unable to resist, he leaned in Addison's direction one more time. "Actually, Kane, enjoy them both. She does look like quite the stunning entree...or would that be dessert?"

Joanna watched as the man walked away, and when she turned back, she saw Addison empty what remained of the Chardonnay in her glass in one swallow.

"Are you all right?" Joanna said.

Addison offered the slightest of smiles. "Yes, I'm fine."

"Who was that?"

"His name's Maxwell Firth. He was the man who helped my father write such a crafty will."

"Oh, he's a lawyer."

"Was, or maybe still is. I don't know," Addison said with a shrug. "He fancies himself an industrialist now."

"Like you?"

Addison let out a snort. "Yes, but with a lot fewer hash marks in the win column."

"I see," Joanna said, looking over to where Firth was sitting. "Wasn't he at Bradley's party? He looks familiar."

"Yes, he was, for the same reason I was," Addison said with a twinkle in her eye.

"Oh, so between that and the will...no love lost?"

"None whatsoever."

"And the bit with the photo of his sons? What was that all about?"

"It was just his way of—" Addison stopped and shook her head. "You know what? It's not important. It was just Firth being Firth, and frankly, he's not worth my time."

"No?"

"No," Addison said, reaching across the table to take Joanna's hand. "Tonight, I just want to enjoy an evening with my...with my wife."

"Still having a hard time saying that?" Joanna said with a giggle as she picked up her wine.

"Less and less every day."

Chapter Thirty-Seven

Much to Addison's dismay, it was nearly two months before her bedroom could be renovated. Samson had prior commitments that filled his schedule until June, and since Joanna and Lucinda had chosen items made-to-order or not stocked locally, for the next eight weeks, Addison made the trip back to her bedroom each and every morning.

She spent her weekdays as she always did, but when Addison came home at night and saw Joanna, her tie came off, and her backbone softened. She began thanking the staff for doing their jobs and complimenting Noah on his gourmet meals, and much to Joanna's surprise, Chauncey had even taken a liking to Addison. Dancing around her feet as soon as she walked in the door, more times than not Addison would need to scoop him up and bestow on him the first kiss of the evening, while the rest belonged to Joanna.

Their conversations no longer faltered and settling into the comfortable existence that comes with love, their smiles were true...and often.

***

Having exited her bedroom, descended the stairs, and walked across the entrance hall without seeing or hearing a single person, Joanna headed into the kitchen to ask Evelyn where everyone was. The only problem was Evelyn wasn't there. "What the hell?" Joanna said as she stood in the middle of the room, and scratching her head, she turned to leave just as Evelyn came from the servant area in the back. "There you are," Joanna said. "For a minute, I thought everyone had left."

"Actually, they have, and I'm heading out now. Noah put a roast in the oven. It'll be ready just around six."

It took a second for Joanna to figure out what was going on and when she did, she laughed. "Evelyn, the mass exodus was not necessary. Addison's not going to be mad. She's the one who told me to have the master suite redecorated. You know that."

Evelyn's mouth twitched in amusement. "This isn't about her temper. This is about her being gone for over a week, and I thought perhaps you two would want some privacy. You know? So you can take your...um...*time* in showing her the bedroom."

As much as Joanna tried to prevent it, there was no stopping the scarlet invading her cheeks, and the more she felt the heat, the redder her face became.

"I may never have been married, but that doesn't mean I wasn't young once," Evelyn said, tittering at Joanna's new hue. "So, with that being said, do enjoy your evening."

Evelyn walked from the kitchen just as Addison came through the front door and when she heard Addison whistle for Chauncey, Evelyn said, "Fiona and George kidnapped Master Chauncey for the night since their grandchildren are visiting, and before you ask, Joanna's in the kitchen."

"And where are you going? Addison said as Evelyn passed her on the way out.

"I've given everyone the night off. Somehow, I didn't think we'd be needed. Good night, Addison," Evelyn said as she closed the door.

Addison scratched her head as she tried to decipher Evelyn's message, but when Joanna emerged from the kitchen, Evelyn was no longer on Addison's mind. "Hi there," she said, watching as Joanna walked toward her.

"Hi there, yourself," Joanna said as she stopped a few inches from Addison. Slipping her hand behind Addison's neck, Joanna pulled Addison's lips toward hers.

The kiss was warm and sweet, a gentle hello to start their evening, and both sighed in unison as their familiar flavors merged. One minute passed and then another before they finally separated and gazed into each other's eyes.

"I missed you," Joanna whispered.

"I missed you, too."

"Yeah?"

"Yes," Addison said in a breath. "It's becoming a habit."

"I hope that's not a bad thing."

"Not at all."

"Good trip?"

"Too long. Someone made me stay away for two days longer than I had planned."

"That's only because you said you didn't want to be disturbed by workmen, and five days wasn't enough time."

Addison looked toward the second floor. "So, is it done?"

Joanna's face creased into a smile, and grabbing Addison's hand, she pulled her toward the stairs. "Come on. Take a look for yourself."

Addison followed Joanna, all the while enjoying the view of her wife's hips, wrapped in tight denim, swaying in front of her.

When they reached the master suite, Joanna spun around. "Promise me if you don't like it, you'll tell me."

"I'm sure it's fine," Addison said, reaching for the door knob.

"Promise," Joanna said, placing her hand on Addison's.

"I *promise*," Addison said with a grin. "Now...can I see it?"

Joanna nodded, and holding her breath, watched as Addison opened the doors.

After what Joanna had done to the patio, Addison had prepared herself for changes that wouldn't be subtle, but nothing could have prepared her for the transformation in front of her. She cautiously walked into the room, her eyes darting back and forth as she tried to take in everything.

The bedroom was now awash in light, but a lamp had yet to be lit. The heavy brocade curtains across the far wall had been replaced with embroidered damask. In the shades of sand, dusty blue, and cream, they were held back by tasseled cords, revealing sheers matching the alabaster Joanna had chosen for three of the walls. Once lost in the gloom, the cast iron firebox was now framed by a surround of marble, and the sculpted white stone with its black veins contrasted perfectly against a wall now painted steel-blue.

Taking another step, Addison looked down at the plush carpet beneath her feet. Elegantly simple, it contained striations running the width of the room, the peaks and valleys repeating the colors of beige and dusty blue that appeared on the curtains and on the duvet covering the bed. A bed which now seemed much higher than it was before.

Addison walked over and ran her hand over the bedcover. The palette was the same, but amidst the dusty blue and cream was a faint paisley design stitched in threads of silver sage, and the pale green repeated in the accent pillows piled atop the bed. Sheers were now draped over the four turned posts, their elegance softening the appearance of the bulky wooden spires, and above her head, the tray ceiling, once the color of curdled cream, had been painted to match the colors in the carpet. Centered in the dome, replacing the inconsequential lamp of iron and naked bulbs was a crystal chandelier, and the finely-cut pendants and bobeches dangling from its arms reflected the afternoon light filtering through the sheers on the windows. Noticing the addition of four modern, yet understated recessed lights placed in the ceiling, each designed to cast their illumination on areas missed by the natural light, Addison looked toward the windows again and saw yet another modern touch. The two Victorian chairs and table once filling the space had been replaced by a stylish, over-stuffed gray two-seater sofa complete with a cocktail ottoman built for two.

Addison looked at the bed again before walking over to the tallboy near the door. Running her fingers across the polished rosewood, she said, "Is this new?"

"No," Joanna said, grinning. "I told Lucinda I wanted to keep the original pieces, so Samson had everything taken to a shop to be refurbished."

"It's so vibrant now."

"Yeah, I know."

Going over to the fireplace, Addison knelt down to admire the beaded detail on the arched-top cast iron firebox. "And this?" she said, running her finger over the smooth and shiny surface.

"Samson had it cleaned and polished. The details were under all the soot and dirt."

Addison got to her feet and looked around the room. "Jesus."

Joanna held her breath. "Too much?"

"No, it's marvelous," Addison said, looking toward the ceiling. "It's...it's like someone put the sun inside the room."

"And you like the colors?"

"Yes, I do," Addison said, smiling. "You've got a good eye."

"Lucinda's the one with the eye. I just told her what I liked and what I didn't."

"It's still amazing, and...and it wouldn't have happened if it hadn't been for you."

"Oh, I don't know," Joanna said, sauntering over to where Addison stood. "I'd like to think it wouldn't have happened if it hadn't been for *us*."

Addison wasted no time in pulling Joanna into her arms, but before she could pucker her lips, Joanna escaped her grasp.

"Not yet," Joanna said, waggling a finger.

"What? Why?"

"Because if you start kissing me, we both know where we're going to end up."

"Yes, I do," Addison said, pointing across the way. "On that incredibly high bed. New mattress?"

"Absolutely."

"Good idea," Addison said, reaching out to Joanna. "Now, come here."

"Not until you see the rest."

"The rest?"

Joanna playfully rolled her eyes. "Well, I couldn't very well do all of this and leave the bathroom and wardrobe looking the way they did. Now could I?"

"Oh, I see," Addison said with a laugh.

"Not yet," Joanna chirped, pointing toward the en suite.

With a playful squint, Addison went over and pulled open the doors leading into the bath. After seeing the bedroom, she expected to see another blending of old and new, but Addison had a lot to learn about Joanna.

There was something to be said for furnishings steeped in history, and with Lucinda's expert eye, centuries had been blended together seamlessly in the bedroom. Antique furniture accented by new, an old-fashioned iron firebox now surrounded by pristine marble, and current, less weighty fabrics with muted colors had turned the bedroom into a showplace. However, when it came to the bathroom, Joanna found herself at a loss, especially after traveling across London with Lucinda to view the latest and greatest in plumbing accouterments. The fixtures were sleek, the tubs trendy, and the showers were as smart as they were functional, and before they left the last showroom, Joanna's mind was made up. While the bedroom would show touches from at least two centuries, the adjoining rooms would not.

Not knowing where to look first, Addison remained in the doorway with her eyebrows raised and her eyes wide. Where once stood two pedestal sinks with boxy mirrors inset into the wall, was now a unit at least ten feet long and made entirely of marble. Two granite bowls acted as the sinks and the color of the stone repeated in the squares of granite covering the walls of the shower located directly opposite the sinks. Encased in clear glass that ran from ceiling to floor, the space could easily hold four if not five adults, and while Addison inwardly smiled at the six shower heads jutting out from the walls and ceiling, it was the four steam vents and long granite bench that made her appreciation show itself.

Taking a few steps into the room, Addison's smile grew even larger as she approached the bright white rectangular drop-in whirlpool located just past the shower. Contrasting beautifully against the granite covered deck, it was shiny and sleek, and with opposing headrests and jets throughout, it was made for comfort, and for company.

Turning around, Addison saw Joanna leaning against the doorjamb with her arms crossed and a hint of naughtiness in her eyes.

"You like?" Joanna said, all the while knowing, by Addison's expression, that she did.

"I can hardly wait to try it out," Addison said, ambling over to where Joanna stood. "Care to join me?"

A sexy chuckle slipped from Joanna's lips, but instead of walking into Addison's outstretched arms, she took a step backward. "Not until you see the wardrobe. Then I'm all yours."

Addison was thrilled with all she had seen so far, but ever since setting eyes on the bed, her concentration had wavered. The flutters of awareness between her legs had quieted while she had admired the rest of the master suite, but once Addison saw the shower, she was a goner. Her mind flooded with visions less than chaste while something else began to flood her knickers. Upon hearing Joanna's suggestion, Addison couldn't help but groan. "Seriously," she said, taking a step in Joanna's direction. "I haven't seen you in over a week. Can't the bloody wardrobe wait?"

Joanna's pout told Addison all she needed to know. Her future was going to include many arguments lost to just a look. "Fine," she said as she walked past Joanna. "But remember what you said. One more room and you're mine."

Pleased that a simple change of expressions had worked so well, Joanna practically skipped as she followed Addison to the wardrobe. Watching as she walked inside, Joanna waited for a moment before doing the same.

Again, Joanna had chosen the modern route, and a new white laminate modular closet system now lined both walls. Compartments and drawers of all shapes and sizes allowed more than enough space for

Addison's suits, shirts, and ties, and along the bottom were shelves angled to hold all the footwear Addison owned and then some.

The runner covering the center of floor matched the carpet in the bedroom, but offsetting the starkness of the cabinetry, the walls had been painted a foggy gray. Two upholstered benches sat centered in the long narrow room, and in place of the boring globular white ceiling fixtures that once existed, miniature chandeliers had been hung, their pendants just as bright as the ones in the bedroom. The finishing touch was floor to ceiling mirrors now covering the walls at both ends of the room, guaranteeing if a speck of lint existed on a piece of clothing, it would be seen.

Joanna knew by Addison's reaction to the other two rooms, she was happy with the changes, but since they had walked into the wardrobe, Addison hadn't said a word. Joanna waited and waited and waited, until she finally blurted, "Well, do you like it?"

"No, not really," Addison said, turning around. "It seems something's missing."

"What?" Joanna said, quickly looking around the room. "Addison, I promise you, Evelyn was very careful about getting all your things back where they belong. I assure you nothing's been missed."

"I wasn't talking about my things. I was talking about *yours*."

"Well, mine aren't—" Joanna stopped long enough for Addison's words to sink in, and when they did her grin overtook her features. "Really?"

"What did you think? I was going to turn the tables and have *you* prance up and down the hall in your knickers at all hours of the day and night?"

"I-I-I...I didn't think. I mean, I would never assume...you never said—" Joanna snapped her mouth shut, her eyes narrowing when she saw Addison was now chuckling. "Damn it, Addison," Joanna said, slapping her hands against her hips. "Stop laughing at me."

"Okay," Addison said as she strolled over and stood in front of Joanna. Reaching up, she pulled the band from Joanna's ponytail, and as the tresses fell free, Addison lowered her face to Joanna's. "No more...laughing."

As soon as their mouths touched, the world stood still. Lips, pink and supple, came together again and again, sending ripples of desire through their bodies. Minutes passed without notice, the intimacy of the kiss consuming their minds and their bodies as their blood began to simmer.

Joanna backed away just a bit, and without saying a word, she pushed Addison's jacket to the floor. Hungry for the feel of the woman's skin against hers, Addison's waistcoat and tie followed within seconds.

Addison found the buttons on Joanna's blouse and for each she released, Joanna returned in kind until both their shirts floated to the carpet. They came together again in a heated kiss, and while their tongues explored, so did their hands. Fingers danced over skin now peppered with goosebumps, and both smiled into the kiss when each found what they sought. Fasteners were undone, and bras fell to the floor, and breasts naked and heaving came into view.

It took all Addison could do not to ravage her wife right then and there. Rising and falling in time with her breathing, Joanna's pert, rounded breasts were displaying a salacious invitation that if Addison accepted, they'd never get out of the wardrobe.

"Bed...now," Addison groaned as she slipped her fingers through Joanna's and led her into the bedroom. Pushing aside the pillows and duvet, Addison turned back to Joanna, and when their eyes met, Addison unzipped her trousers and dropped them to the floor.

A shiver of want fluttered its way through Joanna's body, ending at the apex of her legs. In an instant, she was fumbling with the fasteners on her jeans. It seemed like forever before she was free of the denim, but as soon as she kicked them aside, she climbed onto the bed, and Addison followed.

Addison slowly slid herself over Joanna, allowing nipples hard and erect to scrape against Joanna's belly and breasts, her lips placing feathery kisses every inch of the way until she found Joanna's luscious mouth. Capturing it in a demanding and ravenous kiss, when at last their lips parted, Joanna's were swollen and wet.

It was domination of the sweetest kind, and Joanna surrendered to it. Throwing one leg over Addison's hip, Joanna silently pleaded for what she wanted, but then sighed when Addison didn't appear to want to listen.

It had been seven long days. Seven days to dream about skin, tender and warm. Seven days of feral thoughts forcing Addison to take more showers than a human being needed, and seven days spent hungry for the eighth, so when Addison moved to Joanna's breasts, she began to feast. Cupping one in her hand, she kneaded and caressed the ripe flesh while her tongue tortured the other. She circled the tip with her tongue, teasing it until it was pebbled and tight, and then placing it between her lips, she tugged at the bud before sucking it into her mouth.

"Oh, God," Joanna said, threading her fingers through Addison's hair. "Oh...yes..."

Driven by the sound of Joanna's throaty gasp, Addison tweaked the other nipple until it was just as hard as the one she was torturing with her tongue, but when she felt Joanna urge her downward, Addison stopped her delicious assault and raised her head.

Joanna looked into Addison's eyes. "I need you. I need you so much."

A sexy growl slipped from Addison's lips, and slowly she made her way down Joanna's body toward where they both wanted her to be. The smell of Joanna's sex was amazing. Provocative and plentiful, the scent made Addison's mouth water, and gently lowering herself between Joanna's legs, Addison finally tasted the nectar she had craved for seven long days.

Divine and addicting, Addison couldn't get enough of the ambrosial slickness seeping from Joanna's core. Drawing her tongue through the thickened folds, Addison reveled in the flavor until Joanna began to squirm.

Addison was certain more lessons would be learned in time. More erogenous zones would be discovered, and more acts enhanced by location or perhaps by toy, but at the moment Addison didn't need to be taught. While they only had been lovers for a short time, Addison knew what would turn Joanna's squirms into bucks. Using her thumbs to expose Joanna's clit, Addison began to circle the engorged flesh with her tongue, applying more pressure with each delicate rotation until Joanna's undulations became frenzied.

Clutching at the sheets, Joanna gasped for air. She had become a slave to what Addison had created, and the most primitive need untethered her inhibitions. Arching to meet Addison's assault, she began to gyrate against Addison's tongue, but when Addison stilled her motion and sucked Joanna's clit into her mouth, Joanna lost the ability to breathe. Seconds later, the murmurs and moans spilling from Joanna's lips filled the room.

Addison crept up the bed, and resting on her elbow, she watched as Joanna slowly came back to earth. Although she had an ache between her legs, Addison refused to acknowledge it, much preferring the view before her.

Joanna inhaled slowly, and opening her eyes, she smiled up at Addison. "Hiya."

Addison reached over to push a few strands of hair from Joanna's brow. "Hi, yourself. You okay?"

"Wonderful," Joanna purred as she pushed Addison onto her back. "How about you?"

"I won't lie. I almost came watching you, so...this isn't going to take very long," Addison said, spreading her legs. "Come here."

It was rapidly becoming one of Joanna's favorite positions, and she didn't have to be asked twice. Placing herself between Addison's legs, Joanna arched her back and rubbed her sex against Addison's. Amazed at the copious amount of wetness that coated her in an instant, Joanna rubbed again...and then again.

"Oh yes..." Addison said as she placed her hands on Joanna's bottom. Urging her forward again, Addison opened her legs to their widest, and when she felt Joanna's clit against her own, Addison pulled Joanna hard against her.

The intimate melding of their sexes continued for only a few minutes longer before Joanna knew Addison was close to release. Her breathing was shallow and fast, and her movements had turned frantic, so reaching down, Joanna exposed Addison's clit and then rubbed her sex hard against it. The result was as instant as it was raw.

Grabbing Joanna's bottom, Addison held her in place as the spasms began to rock her body, her core pulsing out nectar that coated their thighs with the heady slickness of her climax. Her words were lost in shuddering breaths and cries of pleasure as tremor after tremor erupted from within until finally her hands fell away, and the room went quiet.

***

"Sorry, it's a little dry."

"It's as much my fault as it is yours," Addison said, looking up.

"Yes, it is," Joanna said as she rested back in her chair. "I think I'm rubbing off on you."

Addison raised her eyebrows, and a grin slowly grew on her face. "Sorry?"

"I'm not talking about *that*," Joanna said with a little laugh. "I'm talking about the fact that what you're wearing doesn't *exactly* fall under the heading of being properly dressed, or does going without knickers not count?"

Their afternoon had been lost to a feast of sensual pleasures and delectable flavors, but with their appetites temporarily sated, when the sun went down, they dozed without a care in the world. A short time later, Addison was awoken when Joanna had scrambled out of bed yelling something about a roast. After watching her wife hastily dress and dash from the room like a banshee on fire, Addison climbed out of bed and chuckled her way to the wardrobe. Grimacing at her lack of casual attire, she remembered the house was void of staff, so she did something she'd never done before. Passing over her trousers, pressed shirts, and suit jackets, she donned a loose-fitting track top and a pair of spandex leggings that hugged her like a thin coating of paint. A very *thin* coating of paint.

Reminded of her attire, Addison looked down and noticed the zip on her top revealed much more than she had intended. Tugging it up a few inches, when she raised her eyes, they were glinting with amusement. "Nor bra, for that matter.

"I noticed," Joanna said. "Trust me."

Addison smiled. She had never felt so content. It was as if everything had finally fallen into place and it was all because of the woman at the other end of the table. A woman who she had once thought stupid, a woman who she had once found repulsive, and a woman who she had once tried to avoid at all costs, was now the woman who owned her heart. Addison ran her hands over her arms, quieting the goosebumps she knew now prickled at her skin. "I really did miss you, by the way," she said quietly. "Just in case you think I didn't."

"I missed you, too."

"But I also have to thank you for insisting I take those two extra days. It gave me time to work out all the details."

"Oh yeah?" Joanna said, leaning her head to the side. "Let me guess. Another feather in Kane Holdings' cap?"

"Oh, no, this wasn't a business trip for the company."

Every muscle in Joanna's body tightened. "Oh, I see," she said, grabbing her wine glass. Slamming back the contents in one gulp, she put the goblet on the table and got to her feet. "You know what?" she said as she stormed to the door. "I think I need something stronger!"

Addison stared at the space Joanna had once occupied, scratching her cheek as she mulled over what had just happened, and then she began to snicker. Tossing her napkin on the table, she got up and went in search of her wife whose skin tone, apparently, had just turned green.

The crystal of the decanter clanked against the rim of the tumbler as Joanna tried to rein in her temper. "What the hell was I thinking?" she mumbled to herself, putting the bottle on the credenza.

"I'm actually wondering the same thing," Addison said, coming into the room. "Because if you think I was holed up in a hotel shagging my brains out with some...some tart, you're wrong."

Joanna whipped around. "Am I now?"

"Yes, you are," Addison said as she walked over and took Joanna by the shoulders. "And if you had let me finish, instead of storming out of the room, you'd have known I was there for business."

"You just said you weren't."

"I said it wasn't *company* business," Addison said, as she released Joanna from her hold. Picking up the decanter, Addison poured some scotch into a glass. "A long time ago my grandfather started up a small company for me in order to prove myself to him."

"Prove?"

"That I could take his place at Kane when the time came."

"Okay?"

Addison motioned toward the chairs in front of the desk, and once they both were settled, she continued. "After I had proved my worth, he signed the company over to me, and when he died, he left me a significant inheritance, and over the years, I've used the money from both for my own investments. Since I can't ethically delve into areas where Kane Holdings may hold an interest since I was old enough to invest, I've chosen paths outside their norm, so this past week I purchased a vineyard."

Joanna flinched back her head ever so slightly. "Did you...did you just say a vineyard?"

"Yes, near a city called Burgos in northern Spain," Addison said, and pausing, she took a sip of her drink. "Several years ago, I began buying up properties in the area. The region's been producing wines for centuries, but over the years, some of the smaller vineyards had run into financial troubles due to weather conditions or their own bad choices. So, I've been buying up properties as they came along and letting them stand as is until an opportunity presented itself, which it did a few months ago. I was contacted by a realtor who told me about a small vineyard producing award-winning wines. The patriarch died last year, but the sons and daughter, who inherited the company, while extremely knowledgeable in what it takes to make fine wine, were less than knowledgeable when it came to finances."

"So you bought them out?"

"Not exactly," Addison said, resting back in her chair. "I did purchase their vineyard, but contractually, until the day they die, they're to run it and produce the wines like their ancestors have done for hundreds of years. The only difference is my company will oversee the financial aspects and instead of having fifteen acres under their watchful eyes, combined with the land I already own, they now have over a hundred. And since we're splitting the profits right down the middle, it assures them not only security, but protects their heritage as well."

"That sounds like a great plan, but isn't it going to take you some time to get a return on your investment? I mean, I thought Kane was all about high-risk and quick dividends," Joanna said, but when Addison tilted her head, Joanna blushed. "I've been doing some reading."

"Yes, I *see* that," Addison said, her eyes widening in surprise. "And you're right. When it comes to Kane Holdings, we prefer our portfolio to be fluid, ever-changing, and to do that, we invest in higher-risk avenues, and if successful—"

"If?"

"Very good," Addison said with a grin. "*When* successful, the dividends will speak for themselves, but when it comes to my personal business, I prefer a little less risk knowing that, in the future, if I played my cards right, I'll get my return." Addison got up to refill her glass, and as she pulled the stopper from the decanter, she looked back at Joanna. "Would you like some more?"

"No, I'm good," Joanna said. "Thanks."

Addison returned to her seat, and after drinking an ample amount of the single malt, she placed her glass on the desk. "And speaking of the future, I know given our relationship now, this is something I should have talked to you about before tonight, but...um...I didn't make up my mind until this past week, and it's...it's definitely something you need to know."

"Oh yeah," Joanna said, lifting her glass to her lips. "What's that?"

"Well, I hope you don't mind, but...um...I'm going to have a baby."

Chapter Thirty-Eight

The smile on Joanna's face slowly faded as she gawked at Addison. Her mouth opened and then closed, and then opened again. She jumbled the words in her head like a puzzle believing she hadn't heard them correctly, but the anxious look on Addison's face told Joanna she had. "Did you just say...did you just say you're having a *baby*?"

"Well, technically it'll be a surrogate, but yes."

"A *baby*?" Joanna said, cocking her head to the side.

Addison nodded. "Yes."

Joanna kept her eyes on Addison as she got to her feet and headed straight to the liquor decanters. She took her time as she filled her glass allowing her mind to sift through all that had transpired since she had met Addison, and before she placed the stopper in the bottle, Joanna knew the subject of children had only come up once. Returning to her seat, she sat down, crossed her legs, and took a swig of her scotch. "This is about what that man, Firth, said at dinner, isn't it?" she said, setting her glass aside. "The one who showed you the photo of his sons."

"How did you—"

"I overheard more than you thought."

"Oh."

"So, am I right? Is this about winning some sort of corporate contest of wills?"

"No, it's not, but Firth in his infinite stupidity made me aware of something I hadn't really thought about."

"Such as?"

"When my father's will was read there were two points that Fran and I brought to mediation in hopes of overturning. One was the fact I had to get married, and you already know how that ended up."

"Yes, I do," Joanna said, giving the rings on her left hand a quick glance.

"The other...well, the other had to do with producing an heir. The bylaws stated it must be done, but when Fran argued that point a few weeks after you and I were married, she won. Apparently, the mediators believed they didn't have the right to act as God, nor did the company's ancestors."

"So if you won the point, why suddenly do you want a baby?"

"When the idea of having to be forced to have a child came up, I was adamant about never allowing that to happen—"

"Imagine that," Joanna said under her breath.

A hint of amusement crossed Addison's Face. "Yes, well, anyway, what Firth made me realize was that if I don't have an heir, then everything I've accomplished or will accomplish will be for naught, and before I'm cold in the crypt, the company and the Kanes will be gone. I have no sisters. I have no brothers or cousins or aunts or uncles, so I'm it. If I don't do this, the Kane bloodline ends with me and so does the company, and I don't want that to happen."

"Addison, tell me the truth. If you weren't the only Kane, would you still want a child?"

"I honestly don't know. I never wanted a dog, but I'm kind of used to him now," Addison said with a half-hearted grin.

"There's a big difference."

"I know, but that's all I can give you," Addison said as her grin disappeared. "I don't know the first bloody thing about children, but I can afford as many nannies as it would take and the best boarding schools and universities, and they'd never want for anything. That shouldn't be such a bad life, should it?"

"You tell me, because you just described *your* childhood."

Addison's brow wrinkled as Joanna's words sunk in, and she hung her head. "Christ, you're right."

"I'm not saying it was the worst childhood in the world, Addison, but it wasn't the best either."

"I know."

Joanna reached for her glass and took a sip of her drink while Addison, seemingly lost in her thoughts, rested her elbows on her thighs and stared at the floor.

Putting down her glass, Joanna reached over and placed her hand on Addison's knee. "So, I have a question for you, and you have to promise me to be completely honest when you answer it. All right?"

Addison lifted her eyes. "Okay."

"Do you want a divorce?"

"What?" Addison said, instantly sitting straight in her chair.

"In four years, when this *arrangement* of ours is over, do you want a divorce?"

"I'm not sure I understand—"

"Yes, you do," Joanna said, rolling her eyes. "You understand the question perfectly, but you're afraid to answer it because of one bloody four-letter word. Well, I told you before I don't need to hear the word, so just answer the question. Are you going to want a divorce in four years?"

"No," Addison said softly. "No, I don't want a divorce.

Joanna's entire face spread into a smile. "Then I think I should be the one who carries the child."

"What?"

"Addison, I'm not saying I wouldn't love a child of yours, whether or not I gave birth to him or her, but if you don't want a divorce, if you want *us* to build a life together, which, by the way, so do I, then let me carry our child because then it truly will be *our* child."

"No. Absolutely not," Addison said, shaking her head. "I won't let you do that."

"Why not? You just said you don't want a divorce and whether you can ever say the words or not, I know how you feel about me. I'm not going anywhere, and if you want a child, if you want a *family*, then let's *be* a family."

"It's too dangerous."

"It is not!" Joanna said with a laugh. "I'm young, and if you read that blasted doctor's report you made me get months ago, you know I'm healthy. I love children, and if we're being honest here, I wouldn't mind having more than just one."

"I...I didn't even know you liked children."

"That's because you never asked, and it's not like we've been...um...together for that long for the subject to come up, but yes, I like them a lot."

"I still don't think I want you to...to do this. Something could go wrong."

"Addison, I could fall down the stairs tomorrow and break my bloody neck."

"Don't say that."

"Sweetheart, I'm young, and I'm healthy, and I love you," Joanna said, touching Addison on the arm. "There's nothing more I want than to have your child...*our* child, but I'm telling you right now there won't be a hoard of nannies or boarding schools in his or her future. I won't stand for it."

Joanna's words were articulate, and her voice, steady and calm, and the corners of Addison's mouth arched upward when she saw the determination now etched on her wife's face. "Making rules already?" Addison said with a twinkle in her eye.

"Yes," Joanna said, getting to her feet. "And if you agree to follow them, I suggest we go upstairs and start working on making a baby."

Addison let out a snort. "We don't have the right equipment."

Joanna leaned down, drawing her tongue across Addison's lips before she looked her in the eye. "We'll improvise," she said in a breath.

***

"Do you want a boy or a girl?"

Surprised by the question, Addison laughed as she rolled onto her side. "I don't know," she said, reaching up to brush away a few strands of hair clinging to Joanna's face. "I suppose a boy, to carry on the name."

"*You're* carrying on the name," Joanna said, tugging up the sheet when she noticed where Addison's focus was riveted.

"True," Addison said, raising her eyes to meet Joanna's. "But unless we can guarantee our daughter is a lesbian, a boy is a safer bet."

"It's more than carrying on the name."

"I know it is," Addison said, frowning. "But you asked me a question, and I answered it honestly."

"Okay," Joanna said, looking down at the sheets. "So, I have another question."

"All right?"

"Last week when you worked so late and...and had to stay at the hotel—"

"I know where this is going," Addison said as she propped herself up on her elbow. "I didn't know I married such a jealous wench."

"Well, if I'm going to have your baby—"

"Joanna, I haven't seen her in months, and, as a matter of fact, the agreement with the hotel is coming due, and I was thinking about not extending it."

"Really?" Joanna squeaked.

"Yes, *really.*"

Joanna could not contain her smile, and doing a slow slide with her eyes, she stopped their advance when Addison's breasts came into view. Letting out a sensual purr, Joanna pushed Addison onto her back and then climbed on top. "So...you don't want anyone else in your bed?" she asked, placing her leg between Addison's.

"Can't you tell?" Addison said knowing the evidence of her arousal was now coating Joanna's well-placed knee.

A devilish gleam appeared in Joanna's eyes, and licking her lips, she slowly slid herself downward. "I think I need a closer look."

Addison let out a sigh as she felt Joanna's hair on her belly, and with each butterfly kiss Joanna bestowed on her skin, Addison felt her libido lurch. Closing her eyes, the air rushed from her lungs when she felt Joanna's hands on her bottom, lifting her ever so slightly...for a better view.

Although Joanna had yet to follow suit, a Brazilian wax was definitely on her to-do list. With no curls blocking her view or errant strands to tickle her tongue, Joanna was about to take pleasure in tasting her wife. Slow...delirious...pleasure.

Breathing in the aroma of Addison's excitement, Joanna leaned closer and blew warm air across folds glistening with want. Taking her time, she explored the furrows with the tip of her tongue, nudging into crevices as if looking for a pearl buried deep, and the more she tasted, the more Addison began to squirm.

Joanna adored Addison's flavor. Lapping at the nectar oozing from her wife's core, she feasted again and again, drawing her tongue over the feminine petals until they were engorged with blood on the verge of boiling.

Addison had been with many women, but none had ever stripped her of her inhibitions so easily. None had ever caused her to *want* to be exposed in such a manner, but with her knees raised and her legs spread, Addison savored every stroke of Joanna's tongue. She couldn't help but lift her hips if Joanna strayed too far away, and when Joanna circled Addison's entrance with her tongue, Addison found herself grinding against it, begging it to enter.

With Addison's movements becoming more frenzied by the minute, Joanna removed her tongue just long enough to ease two fingers into Addison's entrance. Burying them to the hilt, she slowly began to draw them in and out while she returned to circling Addison's clit with her tongue.

Addison's reaction was as involuntary as it was feral. Arching her back as she fought for air, her body ceased to belong to her. Controlled by the rapidly approaching orgasm Joanna had created, Addison sucked in a quick breath and held it, waiting for the crescendo to wash over her.

Tasting and then sucking and then tasting again, Joanna was relentless in her pursuit to take Addison to ecstasy, and by Addison's writhing, Joanna knew her climax was quickly approaching...so Joanna tasted some more.

With her fingers sheathed in her wife's wetness, Joanna lapped at Addison's clit, flicking her tongue against the swollen pearl until she felt Addison's fingers in her hair. It was a silent appeal for mercy, and Joanna stilled, and seconds later, Addison stiffened as guttural cries of pleasure slipped from her lips.

Joanna rested her head on Addison's thigh, taking the time to catch her breath before slowly making her way back up Addison's body. "You okay?" she whispered.

Addison took a deep breath and opened her eyes. The words were right there. In her mind and in her heart, they screamed to be spoken, but deep down inside of her was fear. Put there by a man who scorned her, who rebutted her love with ugliness and hatred, the pain of which scarred her soul and erected walls Addison wasn't sure she'd ever be able to scale. To show love was easy. In a touch, in a breath, in a kiss gentle and soft she could display the feelings she had for Joanna, but each time she had spoken those words to the man who was her father, they had been tossed back in her face with a slap that sent her young body spiraling across a room.

"Hey, you in there?" Joanna said, placing her hand gently on Addison's chest.

"What?" Addison said, blankly looking back at Joanna.

"You were a million miles away."

"Sorry," Addison said with a shake of her head. "Just lost in my thoughts."

"Good thoughts?"

It was neither the time nor the place, and Addison wasn't sure if there'd ever be a time she could share the nightmare of her youth, so she shoved the memories aside and replaced it with something far more pleasant. As a hearty chuckle rose in her throat, she rolled Joanna to the mattress, and climbing on top of her, Addison said, "I'll leave that up to you to decide."

Chapter Thirty-Nine

Two months later...

Joanna looked at her watch and couldn't suppress a giggle as she remembered Addison's disapproval when *she* had been late for dinner so many months before. Debating on whether she should turn the tables, she lost her train of thought when Addison rushed into the room.

"The bloody meeting ran long," Addison said as she went over and gave Joanna a light kiss on the lips. "Sorry, I'm late."

"You're not the only one," Joanna said, watching as Addison went to take her place at the other end of the table.

Addison made it halfway to her chair before she stopped and slowly turned around. Joanna's eyes were sparkling, and in an instant, all the air rushed from Addison's lungs. Returning to Joanna's side, Addison knelt down, unconsciously lowering her eyes to Joanna's belly. "Are you sure?"

Joanna bobbed her head. "Yes, I'm sure. I didn't want you to know until I was positive, but the ultrasound today confirmed it."

"Are you okay?"

"Yes, I'm fine. A little queasy this morning, but I'm good," Joanna said. "How about you? You look a little pasty."

"Yeah...um...I just...I just didn't think it would happen on the first try. I mean you always read about people trying and trying and trying again."

"Well, it doesn't seem we have a problem in that department."

"No, I guess not," Addison said as she stood up.

Joanna pursed her lips. She had expected to see joy on Addison's face or at the very least a smile, but her expression had yet to change from shock. "I thought you'd be happy."

"I am. I just...I just need some time to let this sink in," she said as she leaned over and placed a light kiss on Joanna's cheek. "Okay?"

Joanna weighed the question and then pushed aside her worries. "Okay, that's fair. Take all the time you need."

***

Joanna had intended for Addison to be the first to know, but her joy at finding out she was carrying Addison's child apparently was something she couldn't hide. Feeling as if she was floating on a euphoric cloud, when she had walked into the house earlier that day, as soon as Evelyn saw her face, she pulled Joanna into a hug which seemed to go on for forever. Quickly following suit, every member of the staff congratulated her with hugs and faces crinkled with laugh lines, and like her, they floated too.

A contagion made its way into The Oaks that day, an infection of happiness and joy that Joanna was sure would last for a very long time, but one it seemed Addison was immune to.

During dinner, Addison had gone quiet, but keeping her promise to give the woman time, Joanna harnessed her glee. Refusing to allow it to bubble over at dinner, they ate in silence until Addison excused herself to fetch her nightly glass of scotch.

For a while, Joanna busied herself around the house. She played with Chauncey and gave him his evening romp across the lawns, but when she finally settled in the parlor and picked up her book, she tossed it aside just as quickly. In her mind was an image she couldn't erase. The image was of Addison the moment she found out Joanna was pregnant, and that image showed not one ounce of joy. Joanna drew in a quick breath and stood up. Reaching down, she scratched Chauncey's head as he snoozed on a chair, and then she went in search of Addison.

***

It had been months since Addison had last sat alone in her study, but tonight her mind was not consumed by business, and it hadn't been for quite some time. She stared at the green-shaded lamp on her desk wondering how many times over the years the bulb had been replaced. It had burned so brightly through all those nights in the west wing, lighting her way to a better place. A place containing success and money, power and influence, it was all she had ever wanted. It was the force behind her drive...and it was slipping away.

Her routine had changed ever so slowly. Her nightly visits to the gym were now shared by Joanna, and the time spent on weekends studying the latest in possible takeovers now waited until Monday. More than once she had forgotten her briefcase and more than twice she hadn't cared, but as she looked away from the lamp to the shelves filled with books and to the laptop sitting closed on her desk, Addison felt lost.

Hearing a light rapping on the door, she looked up just as Joanna walked into the room.

"Hi there," Joanna said.

"Hi."

"I know you said you need some time, so I guess I'm breaking my promise, but I'm worried."

"About what?"

"You," Joanna said, taking a seat. "Addison, what's wrong? I thought you wanted this."

"I do."

"You haven't even smiled, and I know you went through the process, too, but I thought at the very least I'd get a congratulations or a well done or...or something."

"I'm sorry."

"Don't be sorry, just talk to me. Tell me what you're thinking. Why are you so quiet? What's on your mind?"

Addison fell back in her chair. "It's just...it's just my life has changed so much since I met you. I mean, sometimes I look in the mirror, and I'm not sure it's me anymore. I used to be so...so focused on work and doing what I do best, but now it seems that's slipping away, and I'm not sure I want it to."

Joanna leaned back, her lips drawing into a straight line as she looked at Addison. "What's that mean? Are you telling me you don't want this child because it's a little late for that?"

"No. No, that's not what I mean," Addison said, running her fingers through her hair. "I-I-I don't think that's what I mean."

"You don't *think* it's what you mean?"

"It's not," Addison said, raising her voice. "Joanna, I wouldn't have gone through what we've gone through these past few months if I didn't want a child. It's just...it's just now that it's happening, it's...well, it's a shock. Okay? It's a shock, and it's going to further change my life and...and I just need to sort that out in my head."

Joanna opened her mouth, but she uttered not a sound. They had spent endless hours talking about a having a baby and had spent countless afternoons visiting clinics and doctors. Weekends had been devoted to poring over sperm donor reports trying to find just the right bloke to help them out, and through it all, Joanna had never once doubted Addison's sincerity. There had never been a reason to, but now there was.

"Well, I'll tell you what," Joanna said as she stood up. "When you get it *sorted*, you let me know."

"Please don't get angry," Addison said, getting to her feet. "I have a business to run—"

"I don't give a fuck about your business!"

"No?" Addison shouted. "Well, it's that bloody *business* that afforded you this *life!*"

As soon as the words spilled from her lips, creases of regret carved themselves into Addison's face, but Joanna hadn't seen them. She had already stormed from the room and slammed the door.

***

Joanna walked from the en suite, but came to a stop when she saw Addison sitting on the edge of the bed. It had been the first time in months they hadn't slept together, and by the appearance of Addison's clothes, if she had gotten any sleep the night before, it was in a chair or on a sofa.

"Are you all right?" Addison asked, but when the only response she received was Joanna's cold stare, she said, "I heard you in there. It sounded like you were sick."

"I was. It's to be expected," Joanna said as she headed to the wardrobe.

"I'm sorry."

"For what? For me throwing up or...or for you being such a bitch last night?" Joanna said, turning around. "Because that's exactly what you were. We talked about this. We planned this. We went through tests and procedures for *this*, and now all of a sudden, *you* need to sort it out." Joanna paused and shook her head. "No, wait. That's wrong, isn't it? You don't need to sort *this* out. It's your bloody business you're worried about, isn't it? Well, guess what, Addison? You take care of your business, and I'll take care of myself."

"Jesus Christ!" Addison said, jumping off the bed. "Yes, we talked about it, and yes, we did the tests, but there's a difference. You didn't have my child inside of you then, and now you do and...and it's bloody, fucking scary!"

Addison moved across the room and stood in front of Joanna. Bowing her head, Addison raised her eyes. "I'm sorry my reaction last night wasn't what you expected, but honestly, it wasn't what I expected either. I want to be happy. Actually, I think I am or...or I will be once the shock wears off. My head feels like it's about to explode with all the thoughts running through it. Thinking about the future, about that baby inside of you, about where you and I will be in five years or in ten. Will I be a good mum or a tyrant like my father? Will it be a struggle for me to find the time the child needs or will everything else cease to matter? I've only ever had one thing driving me in my life, Joanna. Only one thing that held any importance, but then you came along and changed everything. I adapted to that change, and I'll adapt to this one. I just need you to be patient. Please, just give me a bit more time."

The last few words Addison spoke were barely audible, but while they were hushed, they held the love Joanna needed to hear. With tears filling her eyes, she placed her hand on Addison's face. "Sometimes I really wish you could say the words," she said in a breath. "But I love you, and I know you love me, and I'll give you until June. How's that?"

"June?"

"Yeah," Joanna said, her face lighting up with brilliance. "That's when our baby is due."

***

Evelyn smiled when she noticed Joanna coming down the stairs. "How are you feeling?"

"The crackers helped," Joanna said as she reached the bottom. "Thanks."

"You're welcome. I've never had the...um...*pleasure* of having morning sickness, but I remember both of my sisters having a devil of a time with it."

"Yeah, I figured I wasn't the first," Joanna said with a weak grin.

"No, but from what I remember, it doesn't last forever. You'll feel much better soon. I'm sure of it."

"It won't be soon enough for Addison."

"It's been two weeks since she found out. Is she still having trouble with it?"

"Just a little."

"I thought she wanted the child."

"She did...she *does*, it's just I think she's having a problem wrapping her head around it all. It's not *real* yet. You know?"

"Well, it will be soon enough."

"I know," Joanna said, resting her hand on her stomach.

"So, are you planning on doing some more decorating?" Evelyn said, pointing at the paint cards and magazines Joanna was holding.

"Lucinda dropped these off the other day. I know I have plenty of time to get the nursery ready, but I just feel like I need to get everything done right now," Joanna said with a shrug. "I have no idea why."

"I believe they call that nesting."

"Well, it's annoying," Joanna said with a laugh. "I started out with a small list of things we'll need for the nursery, but the more I think about it, the longer the list gets."

"Wait until we have to start childproofing this place for a two-year-old," Evelyn said with a snicker. "Oh, and I should warn you—if that baby is anything like Addison was when she was young, we are all going to have our hands full."

"Really?" Joanna said, her shoulders dropping just a bit.

"Oh, my God, yes. She was an absolute terror," Evelyn said, throwing her hands up in the air. "As soon as she learned to crawl, she began grabbing at cords and curtains, and when she started walking...well, let's just say I wore trainers for a few years just to keep up." Evelyn smiled as the memories came rushing back. "Wait, would you like to see her playroom?"

"I would love it!" Joanna said as she quickly turned to head back upstairs.

"Oh, no, it's not up there."

"It's not?"

"No," Evelyn said, motioning to a set of doors Joanna had never traveled through. "It's in there."

Joanna followed Evelyn across the entrance hall. "I don't understand. You told me these doors led to the formal living room."

"They do, but I had to become creative when it came to Addison. When the weather permitted, and her father wasn't home, she played on the front lawns, but if it was too cold or raining, she played in here," Evelyn said as she pushed the two towering doors open.

"Oh my God," Joanna said as she stared into the cavernous space. "It's huge!"

The room was impressive, if only for its size. Matching the dining room in width, its length appeared almost double that of the master suite, but contrary to the other rooms where sunlight was defeated by heavy curtains, the formal living area wasn't that lucky. Across the front wall, running just shy of the floor to the ceiling, were six windows framed by draperies, which had been left open, and the light streaming in only enhanced the damage done by time and neglect.

The center of the room was covered by a tremendous Persian carpet, but around the entire perimeter was the same dark, dreary slate that covered most of the ground floor. The vivid purples, blues, and greens of the wool rug could be seen in areas untouched by the brilliance of the sun, but those in line with the windows had faded to various shades of gray, creating a striped effect across the once impressive carpeting. Also washed out by the sun were the walls. Now the color of cantaloupe, the original shade of terracotta could be seen in the dark square and oval ghosts left behind by paintings long since removed.

The fireplace at the far end of the room was more imposing than any other in the house, and the twin chandeliers were magnificent even though their crystal pendants were hazy with dust, but other than that, the room was completely empty.

"Where's all the furniture?" Joanna said, turning to Evelyn.

"Remember, this was Addison's playroom, and I couldn't chance her being injured. The upholstered pieces were so old, I had them discarded, and the rest I had stored in the west wing for safekeeping."

"And she really played in here?"

"Yes, she loved it actually," Evelyn said, looking around the room. "Granted, it's not much, but with nothing for her to break, she was basically free to run about and do what children do. We had a couple of close calls with the windows, but thankfully she never broke the glass."

Joanna noticed a football off to the side, and going over, she picked it up. "Is this hers?"

Evelyn could not contain her toothy smile. "Yes, like I said she had lots of energy."

Joanna looked out over the room and imagined a little girl running here and there, no doubt coming up with games she could play by herself. Glancing at Evelyn, she said, "I'm glad she had you."

"Thank you. I tried my best to give her *some* sort of normal childhood."

"I'm sure you did," Joanna said, aimlessly spinning the ball in her hands, but then something caught her eye, and she stilled the football. "I recognize that. It's still as hideous as I remember."

Evelyn followed Joanna's line of sight and scowled when she saw the Gorgon head candelabra sitting on the floor in the corner of the room. "I couldn't agree with you more."

"Why would anyone ever own something like that?"

"To further make a point."

"What do you mean?"

"When Addison was nineteen, she came home from school on holiday. Since she obviously didn't need a nanny any longer, I had returned to my duties around the house years before, and that night I was serving her and her father dinner. Oliver didn't allow talking of any kind during meals, and God forbid if Addison made a sound while she ate, but as I was about to clear the dishes, Addison spoke. I can still remember struggling to hold onto the plates in my hand. I was so stunned."

She hadn't thought of that day for so long, so as the memories came rushing back, they ensnared Evelyn in their net. She remembered how Addison had sat tall in her chair, proud to be what she was. How she had jutted out her chin and held her head high, and when she had spoken the words, Evelyn could still see the smirk on her face and the defiance her eyes. That was the day Addison Kane became the woman the world would eventually know.

"Evelyn, are you okay?"

The sound of Joanna's voice jerked Evelyn from her thoughts, and giving the woman an apologetic grin, Evelyn said, "I'm sorry. Where was I?"

"You were talking about Addison speaking at dinner, and you were shocked."

"Yes, of course," Evelyn said with a nod. "Anyway...that was the night Addison told her father she was gay. It was no surprise to me, but it should have been to Oliver, yet he didn't even blink. Not a flicker of emotion showed on his face. It was as if he had suddenly gone deaf, but the very next day he had that candelabra delivered and placed in the middle of the table with orders that it never be moved. I'd have to think it was his way of telling her she didn't exist."

"Jesus," Joanna said, shaking her head. "Wait, I'm confused. Why didn't Addison have it removed after he died?"

A sly smile crossed Evelyn's face. "She did, but she told me to put it back the day she married you."

For a split-second, Joanna's expression didn't change, but then she burst out laughing. "Oh my God, that's too funny."

"It is now, but at the time I hated having to do it."

"Well, at the time she hated *me*."

"I'm glad that's changed."

"Me, too."

Together, they strolled further into the room, their footsteps echoing in the cavernous empty space.

"Well, this is certainly large enough, but I think it's a bit over the top to use as a playroom again. Don't you?" Joanna said, glancing at Evelyn.

"Probably," Evelyn said, looking up at the intricate ceiling and chandeliers. "But it's a thought."

As Joanna turned to leave, she noticed a stack of boxes neatly tucked into an alcove near the wall that held the fireplace. "What's in those?"

Evelyn's eyes flew open seeing the pile. "My God, I forgot all about these," she said as she hurried over to the boxes. Without thinking, she opened the one on top and immediately regretted her decision when a plume of dust rose in the air. Coughing as she waved her hands to disperse the cloud, she said, "Remind me not to do that again."

"I will," Joanna said, waiting until the dust had settled before joining Evelyn near the cartons. "So, what's in the boxes?"

"Things belonging to Xavier."

"Who's Xavier?"

"He was Oliver's father. Addison's grandfather."

"Oh," Joanna said, looking at the cartons again. "So why are his things stored in here?"

"I hid them," Evelyn said, her memories once again rushing back as she turned to Joanna. "There was no love lost between Oliver and his father, so when Xavier died, Oliver sold everything the man owned. His house, his car, his clothes...it all went in a matter of weeks, but one afternoon a few of Xavier's most-trusted staff brought these over. I didn't think twice about telling Oliver, assuming he would want them, but instead he ordered me to throw it all out, but I just couldn't do it. So, knowing that this room had all but been forgotten by everyone except for me, and Addison was no longer using it as a playroom, I had them put in here."

"So..." Joanna said, eyeing the cartons again. "Don't keep me in suspense. What's in them?"

"Family documents," Evelyn said. "Bibles, ledgers, and histories in one form or another. Basically everything there is to know about the lineage of the Kanes over the past few centuries."

Joanna's mouth went slack. "And he wanted to throw it all *out*?"

"Oh, the depth of that man's hatred was only equaled by his stupidity," Evelyn said as she reached into the box. Carefully pulling out a Bible bound in red goatskin, she ran her fingers over the "Kane" name impressed into the surface in gold. "Thank God, I didn't listen to him."

Joanna eyed the volume in Evelyn's hands. Excessive handling had worn the binding at the edges and rounded the corners disproportionately, but the detail of the embossing was still clear and rich. "That looks very old."

Evelyn nodded as she carefully opened the Bible to the ribbon in the middle. "Yes...1814, by the date."

"Date?"

Evelyn turned the Bible around and showed Joanna the page marked by the ribbon. Inscribed on the parchment in quill pen was *Cedric and Lavinia Kane 1814*.

"Wow!"

"Yes, it's marvelous, isn't it?" Evelyn said. "And that bastard wanted to toss it out."

"I'm glad you didn't listen to him," Joanna said as she stood on tip-toes to peer into the box. "Does Addison know about these?"

"No, actually she doesn't," Evelyn said, placing the holy book back into the box. "Like I said, I totally forgot about them."

Joanna was about to pull another Bible from the box when she stopped and looked around the room. "You know what? Would you mind if we moved these into the library? That way, we can get them out of these boxes and display them properly."

Evelyn beamed. "I think that's a fantastic idea. I'm sure Addison will be thrilled to see them."

Chapter Forty

Saturday morning, Addison, again, found herself sitting on the bed waiting for Joanna to emerge from the master bathroom. Each morning had been a carbon copy of the previous day, and before Addison could fully open her eyes, Joanna was rushing to the loo to empty her stomach. Hanging her head, Addison let out a long breath, silently cursing herself for being so selfish.

Joanna stood in front of the sink, holding a wet washcloth to her neck to cool her heated skin. Morning sickness would definitely not appear on her highlight reel when it came to being pregnant, but spending the first few minutes of her day bent over a toilet seemed a small price to pay for the tiny human growing inside of her. She took a few more slow, steady breaths before rinsing out the cloth and putting it aside.

When Addison heard the door open, she jumped off the bed. "Are you okay?"

"Do you have any idea how many times you ask me that?" Joanna said as she climbed back into bed. "I'm fine. I just need a minute to cool down."

"You don't look fine."

"Yes, well that would be because I just threw up, now wouldn't it?"

"You're doing that a lot."

"Addison, it's to be expected. It's called morning sickness, in case you didn't know."

"I know what it's called, and if it were *just* in the morning I wouldn't be as concerned, but apparently it's happening throughout the day." Seeing the surprised look on Joanna's face, Addison said, "Fran told me when she met you for lunch, you had to run to the ladies' twice and Evelyn told me that you're doing the same thing at home."

"Fran and Evelyn talk too much, and every woman is different. I spoke to my doctor, and she says I'm fine. Some women get sick more than others, and I guess I'm one of the lucky ones," Joanna said with a weak grin.

"You're losing weight, too."

Joanna let out a sigh and sat up in bed. "That's because I keep getting sick, but again the doctor says I'm fine. I'm taking my vitamins and following her orders to the letter. And from what she tells me, I'll be plumping up in no time."

"I should have never allowed you to do this," Addison said, staring at the floor. "We should have hired a surrogate."

"What? Why?"

"Because you shouldn't have to be sick every day—"

"I thought you *wanted* a child."

"I-I-I do, but I can't handle seeing you like this, Joanna. You're pale, and you aren't eating properly!"

"How would you know?"

"What?"

"Unless I'm mistaken, you weren't at dinner last night. Come to think of it, you've missed three in the past week."

"I know, and I'm sorry."

"Don't be," Joanna said as she shifted on the bed. Rearranging the pillows behind her back, she gave the one on top a swift, solid punch before turning back around. "I'm becoming used to it."

Addison sighed, hanging her head for a moment before she approached the bed. "Look, I *am* sorry, but it seems like everything I've been working on for the past year is all coming to a head at the same time. Imagine a...a car crash with the occupants being contracts and negotiations because that's exactly what I'm going through right now."

"Sounds hectic."

"It is," Addison said, sitting on the edge of the bed. "But it's what I do."

"I know. It's just that you've been doing it a lot lately."

"I don't know what else to say other than I'm sorry," Addison said. "But I'm here now, and we have the weekend together. That should count for something, shouldn't it?"

"You said that last weekend, but you spent half of Sunday on a conference call."

Addison let out a sigh. "I know, but it was important."

"Of course, it was," Joanna said, crossing her arms.

"Joanna, please, it's Saturday, and we have the entire weekend ahead of us." When Joanna's pout didn't waver, Addison took her hand. "I know I've been a bit distant, but I'm just worried about you. That's all."

"You sure you're not worried about what you're going to do when the baby's born?"

"It's on my mind, yes."

"Jesus Christ," Joanna said under her breath.

"I'm being honest, damn it. You can't have it both ways, woman. If you want me to be honest, then you need to be prepared for just that, but I've got the weekend off with no calls scheduled. So, we can either spend two days arguing...or two days shopping."

"What?"

"I've lost count of the hints you've dropped about the nursery, so why don't we go shopping. If I know you, you've got a list of places you'd like to visit, so why don't we?"

"Do you mean it?" Joanna said as she sat upright.

"Yes, we'll make a day of it. How's that?"

Joanna scrambled to get out of bed. "I need twenty minutes."

Addison looked over at the clock on the nightstand and laughed. "It's only seven. I think we have time."

***

Their day almost ended before it began because, much to Addison's dismay, when Fiona brought Addison her poached eggs and bacon, the smell instantly caused Joanna's stomach to roll. Running from the room, Joanna sequestered herself in the parlor to munch on dry toast until her stomach finally settled while Addison ate alone in the dining room. Meeting up an hour later, they climbed into the Rolls, and George drove them into London, and they spent the day crisscrossing the city visiting every shop Joanna could pull up on her mobile.

Addison had the wisdom and experience to run Kane Holdings and run it well. Between schooling and her tenure at the company, her qualifications were exemplary and her confidence lofty, but thirty-six years of being female did absolutely nothing to prepare her when she walked over the threshold of the first shop.

Women with baby bumps and basketballs waddled about, cooing and awing at the frills, lace, and cutesy baubles displayed on walls, shelves, and floor. They tittered and buzzed, trading stories with whoever would listen, and joyfully rubbing their stomachs as they filled their baskets with pink and blue.

Joanna's face lit up as soon as she stepped into the shop, and like a beacon, it attracted the clerks like flames did moths. Salespeople quickly swarmed around her, pausing only to inquire about a due date before their recommendations began.

Addison tried to participate, tried to display a toothy grin that matched her wife's, but the more she listened, the more incompetent she felt. Why the need for a crib *and* a bassinet, and why wouldn't a baby require a pillow for its head? It seemed sensible to buy blankets to keep the child warm, but the ones they were shown were thin and light, and what the hell was a swaddle wrap? She was shown nursery sets and changing tables, pads for mattresses and syringes for noses, one-piece rompers and stocking caps, dribble bibs and nappies of every size and style, and by the time they walked from the shop, three words kept repeating in Addison's head. What. The. Fuck.

Like an obedient puppy, Addison followed Joanna into the next store, and her eyes grew wide. More upscale than the last, the shop offered luxury furniture for a luxury price, and all their tiny bedroom sets seemed to be designed with future kings and queens in mind. She did her best to be patient while Joanna browsed diminutive armoires, four-poster cribs, and swinging cradles draped in delicate sheers, all the while forcing a smile whenever Joanna looked in her direction. Price had never mattered to Addison, but bunny night lights, fairy wall stickers, intricately stitched teddy bears, and gilded mobiles for above the cribs all selling for well over a hundred pounds each had caused her eyebrows to raise more than once.

After visiting all the shops on Joanna's list, Addison suggested an early dinner, and Joanna happily agreed. Unfortunately, no sooner had they sat down in the upscale Indian restaurant when the smell of the spices wafting through the eatery made Joanna's stomach lurch, causing her to make a mad dash to the loo. Taking it in stride, Addison had George drive them to one of her favorite French restaurants, but again, when they walked through the door, Joanna went gray.

Hoping the third try was the charm. Addison held her breath as they entered Balthazar. The restaurant's menu was inspired by the French, but the aromas filling the brasserie were not overpowering, and in less than no time, the two women were sitting in a red leather half-round booth scanning their menus. One sipped wine and the other tea, and when the waiter returned, they placed their orders. Dover sole with parsley for one, and pancakes with bananas and maple syrup for the other.

***

Addison had never been so happy to see Chauncey. After spending the entire day dealing with all things baby, when the pup demanded Joanna's attention, and she took him outside for exercise, Addison escaped to her study for a much-needed drink. Standing at the credenza, she stared off into space, trying to come to terms with what she felt, which was nothing.

Ambivalence had replaced her feeling of incompetence before they had left the second shop and as much as she tried not to, Addison carried that attitude like luggage wherever they went. She had no connection to match Joanna's. No maternal link that caused her skin to glow or her face to brighten at the mere mention of the word *baby*...and she was scared.

Unlike in business when Addison would spend months or even years planning out her moves in advance, this one had been put into motion in only a few short weeks. Had that been enough time to fully understand that her life would truly change forever? Was that the problem? Was she so selfish in her own wants and desires that resentment now lurked in the shadows of her psyche, smothering the maternal jubilation Joanna showed so effortlessly?

Addison closed her eyes and took a deep breath, hoping it would rid her mind of the thoughts poisoning her, but after a few minutes, she gave up. She picked up the glasses and left the room just as Joanna and Chauncey came through the front door.

"I poured you a drink," Addison said.

"Thanks, but I can't have that. It's not safe for the baby."

"Oh, right. I forgot," Addison said with a frown, placing the other glass on a nearby table. In silence, she stood and watched as Joanna squatted down and played with the pup until he scampered up the stairs.

"I think I'm going to follow his lead," Joanna said as she stood up.

"What do you mean?"

"I'm tired. I'm going to go bed."

Addison looked at her watch. "But it's not even eight o'clock yet."

"I know," Joanna said, and walking over she wrapped her arms around Addison's waist and rested her head against her shoulder. Joanna relished the familiar warmth, but after a few seconds, she pulled away and gazed at her wife. "I'm sorry. I'm just tired. Busy day and all that."

"All right," Addison said, looking toward the upper floor. "I'd offer to join you, but I'm not at all sleepy."

Joanna tried not to let her disappointment show. Addison hadn't touched her since she had been told about the baby, and while Joanna was truly exhausted, for Addison not to even hint at things delightfully carnal wasn't like her. It wasn't like her at all.

Joanna pulled out of their embrace and headed to the stairs. "Sorry, but you can always work or go for a swim."

Addison let out a sigh as she watched Joanna climb the stairs. "Believe it or not, I didn't bring anything home with me," she said as she looked toward the study. "Maybe I'll check out some of those books you bought. Find something to read."

Joanna jerked to a stop at the top of the stairs and spun around. "*Shit!*"

In an instant, Addison was taking the steps two at a time and in no time flat she was holding Joanna by the shoulders. "What's wrong?" she said, eyeing Joanna's belly. "Are you all right? Do I need to call a doctor?"

Joanna pressed her lips together, preventing her laugh from escaping. Other than the annoyingly repetitive questions Addison plagued her with over morning sickness, the woman had yet to act like an expectant parent so the panic in Addison's eyes, while unnecessary, warmed Joanna's heart. With a chuckle, she said, "Relax, sweetheart. I'm fine. I just forgot to tell you something. That's all."

"Seriously woman, you just scared the shit out of me," Addison said, dropping her hands to the side.

"I'm sorry," Joanna said, reaching out to place her hand on Addison's arm. "But it's nice to know you care."

"Of course, I care," Addison said. "If...if something happened to you, I don't know what I'd do."

"Well, the only thing happening to me tonight is a quick shower and then bed, but you, on the other hand, have some reading to do."

"That's what I just said."

"No, I'm not talking fiction. I'm talking fact."

"Sorry?"

"I didn't get a chance to talk to you last night because you came home so late, and I forgot all about it until just now."

"About what?"

"There are now three shelves in the library filled with information on your family."

"What?"

"To make a long story, short, Evelyn had some boxes hidden away that belonged to your grandfather. Family history, Bibles, old ledgers, some photographs, things like that, and yesterday I sorted it all out and put everything in the library for you."

"*Three* shelves?" Addison said, a grin overtaking her features in an instant.

Joanna adored hearing the excitement in Addison's tone. "Yes, you can't miss them," she said, leaning in for a quick kiss. "Now go enjoy your family, sweetheart. I'm going to get some sleep."

As soon as Joanna walked into the bedroom, Addison trotted down the stairs, stopping long enough to grab the second scotch from the table before striding to the library.

***

Addison stood before the bookcase, running her fingers over the Bibles bound in cowhide and goatskin. In every shape, size, and color, they filled one shelf and overflowed onto another, leaving the rest of the space for historical ledgers, journals, and dilapidated photo albums.

She pulled a long, narrow ledger from the row and carefully opening its pages, she scanned the cursive written with quill and ink. Smiling as she read the ridiculously low prices listed for items purchased, Addison pulled a few more ledgers from the case and sat down. Propping her feet on an ottoman, she took a sip of her drink and then became lost in time.

Three hours later, Addison returned from her study carrying a decanter of scotch. She refilled her glass, and putting the bottle aside, she turned and stared at the row of Bibles across the way.

Addison had learned about Christ from Evelyn. Through Sunday morning games and puzzles, quizzes and discussion, they would hunker over her desk, reading from an annotated children's Bible overflowing with pictures meant to keep a child's attention. She was taught God was good. Unwavering in his love, sinners were forgiven, and those who had wandered were welcomed back into the fold without question, and Addison believed. She believed in goodness and faith, and hope and love, but on one heinous night when she was eleven, one night of terror that still haunted her dreams, God ceased to exist for Addison.

Drunk and raging her father had stormed into the west wing. Bellowing his hatred as spittle sprayed from his lips, he burst into her room and almost pulled her arm off as he yanked her from under the bed. Expletives flowed like vomit from his mouth as he stood there and shook her and shook her and shook her some more, calling her words she had never heard before. She had no idea it was her mother's birthday. She had no idea his fury was born from a soul twisted by loss. All she knew was on that night, on the night he nearly broke her jaw with a slap that sent her flying over her bed, she'd always remember the feeling of warm urine soaking through her knickers and the last prayer she uttered before turning her back on God. He should have saved her, and He didn't.

Addison was not a connoisseur of vintage biblical volumes, but by the appearance of their bindings, it was easy to tell which was old and which was not. Going over, she pulled the most pristine from the row.

Its leather was thick and embossed, and still carried the shine of polished calf, but already knowing the fiction it contained, she was about to return it to the shelf when she noticed a thin red silk marker nestled between the pages toward the center of the Bible. Opening it to the ribbon, she found herself looking at facing pages displaying the Kane family crest at the top, and beneath it, under the heading of *Marriage* was written *Oliver and Alena Kane 1978.*

Addison stared at the handwriting. Large and loopy, it was definitely written by a woman. A woman who had been her mother, and according to the foulness her father had spewed throughout her life, a woman who Addison had killed. She ran her fingertip over the ink, and her emotions began to stir. Had she ever touched anything belonging to her mother before?

She blinked, clearing the moisture that had formed, and trying to get her mind off of the memories she didn't have, Addison looked to the other page, and her gasp broke the silence of the night. Under the heading of *Births* was not only her name, but that of her brother's. "Christ," she said, seeing the birth and death dates of a boy who was to be called Alastair.

It had been years since she had thought of her twin. In her youth, there had been times when her mind had wandered, and lying in bed, she'd stare at the ceiling and think about a brother she didn't have. Would they have been the same height? Would his hair have been the same color or his eyes as blue? Would he have grown up to be a businessman like their father or would his wants take him in a different direction?

She hadn't known his name until now and in a way, she wished she hadn't. Now he was real, named and dated, he had existed if only for a short while, but he *had* existed, and tears welled again. Annoyed that her emotions now seemed to lie just under the surface, she brushed her tears away and was about to close the Bible when she realized she recognized the printed, strong block letters tilting slightly to the left. While her father may not have cared to record the event of the birth of his children, her grandfather apparently had.

With a sigh, Addison set the Bible aside and grabbed the next in the row, expecting by its fairly unblemished condition that it had belonged to her grandfather, but when she opened it to the page marked with the red silk, her eyebrows drew together. She had no idea who Samuel and Cordelia Kane were, but when she looked at the list of births and saw her grandfather's name, she smiled.

Xavier had never talked about his parents or spoken of his wife. Like Addison, his world revolved around the present, not the past. There had been a few times when Addison was young and inquisitive when she asked about her grandmother, but dismissed with a wave of her grandfather's knobby hand, eventually she stopped asking.

Addison had never thought herself to be a curious person. She had the passion it took to learn, investigate, and explore anything that had to do with business, but when it came to everyday life, to the rooms in her home or the cars in her garage, she had always doubted she possessed the gene containing curiosity. However, intrigued by the information the Bibles may contain, she put aside the volume belonging to Samuel Kane and studied the ones remaining. Having already been proven wrong that condition determined age, Addison chose a different tack. Noticing that one stood out among all the others, its height and girth much larger than the rest, she pulled the Bible from the shelf. Misjudging its weight, it immediately slipped from her fingers and when it hit the floor, a wad of papers that had been lodged in its pages scattered across the library.

"Shit!" she said, and letting out an exaggerated sigh, Addison knelt down to clean up the mess.

With its rounded corners and cracked spine, Addison had assumed it was one of the older Bibles, but as she began gathering the papers on the floor, she noticed the same bold, block letters covering every sheet. Curious to see what her grandfather had written, Addison scooped up the Bible and notes, tipped a bit more scotch in her glass, and settled back for a read.

Four hours later, the library was littered with journals and Bibles, and the ashtray overflowed with a habit Addison had once quit, but now craved. The decanter was almost empty and the room smelled of stale smoke and old books, but she didn't notice. She must have read his pages a hundred times, over and over and over again trying to find some hint of insanity in his writing, but there was none. His words were precise. His thoughts were clear, and his findings could not be argued...and Addison had never been so scared.

Why hadn't he told her? Why hadn't he told his son? How could someone allow others to die?

Chapter Forty-One

"I thought you quit."

Addison flinched at the sound of Joanna's voice, and keeping her head bowed, she quietly said, "I did." Fixated on the overflowing ashtray on the table in front of her, it took Addison well over a minute before she raised her eyes. "Joanna...we need to talk."

The hair stood up on the back of Joanna's neck. Addison's voice was flat and void of even the slightest inflection, and she was still dressed in the suit she had worn the day before. The room reeked of smoke, and journals and Bibles once aligned neatly on the shelves were now scattered about the library. Some were on the floor, fanned open to pages of interest, while others had somehow managed to find the four corners of the room.

"Okay, but if it's about cleaning up this room, that's on you," Joanna said, attempting a grin.

It took all the strength Addison had to look Joanna in the eye, but taking a deep breath, she did just that. "Tomorrow you need...you need to call the doctor and...and make arrangements to terminate the pregnancy."

Joanna jerked back her head, and taking a step into the room, she said, "What did you just say?"

"You have to lose the baby. If you don't, you'll die."

Noticing the empty decanter on the table, Joanna picked it up. "Are you pissed?"

"No. Tired, but not drunk."

"Well, then go get some sleep because you're obviously not thinking straight."

"Yes, I am," Addison said, getting to her feet. "I know exactly what I'm saying and why I'm saying it. You need to call the doctor and—"

"I will do no such thing!" Joanna said as she strode over and stood in front of Addison. "I don't know what this is all about—"

"It's about these," Addison said as she snatched up some papers from the table. "It's about the fact that no wife of a Kane has ever survived childbirth. They all *died*, Joanna. My mother, my grandmother, my great-grandmother—"

"You're here."

"You're not *listening*!" Addison said, grabbing a Bible off the floor. "The *wives* died. Every fucking one of them and my grandfather knew it. The son-of-a-bitch knew my mother was going to die, and he didn't do anything about it. He even says so in his notes. He knew that in three hundred years, not one Kane woman survived after their child was born. Not *one*."

"Oh, that's impossible," Joanna said, shaking her head.

"No, it's not!" Addison said. Tossing the papers on the coffee table, she began scrambling to gather the Bibles and notes from the floor. "Read them," she said, stacking everything on the table. "Joanna, please, I'm begging you. Just read his notes, look at the Bibles. There are family trees started in every one of them, but they all end at the birth of the child and the *death* of its mother...on the same day."

"Addison, you're tired, and you're not thinking clearly."

"Jesus Christ!" Addison said, running her fingers through her hair. "Will you please just read his bloody notes? Can you do that? Can you do that for *me*?"

Joanna looked at the stack of books and papers. "Addison, this is ridiculous. I don't want to spend my Sunday in here reading a bunch of...a bunch of crap."

"It's not crap!" Addison screamed. "It's the history of my fucking family, and you need to read it!"

Addison's face had turned scarlet, and her eyes were opened so far that the white almost overtook the blue. Whether it was crap or not, it was obvious to Joanna that Addison believed whatever she had read, and it terrified her.

"Okay. Okay," Joanna said, holding up her hands. "I'll read it, but on one condition."

"What's that?"

"You don't hover," Joanna said, and dropping into a chair, she reached for Xavier's notes. "Meaning you go get a shower or something. I'll come find you when I'm done."

"I'd rather—"

"This isn't up for discussion," Joanna said, glaring at Addison. "You're tired, and you need a shower, and I need a clear mind for all of this. I can't do that if you're going to be pacing back and forth watching every page I turn."

"You'll find me when you're done?"

Joanna took a slow, steady breath, and as she exhaled, her annoyance escaped with the air. "Yes, I'll find you when I'm done."

***

The shower had washed away the scent of liquor, sweat, and smoke, and not one to own many clothes falling under the heading of casual, Addison pulled on a pair of dress trousers and an Oxford shirt. Forgoing a belt, tie, or tucking in her shirttails, she sat on the bed drumming her fingers on her knee.

She had told Joanna she needed to understand the word love before saying it, but now Addison believed she had finally grasped the meaning, so the decision to have Joanna end the pregnancy, while tragic, made perfect sense to Addison. The child Joanna was carrying was a stranger. A nameless, faceless, sexless stranger with no qualities other than a heartbeat, but Joanna was real. She was breathing and smiling, loving and feisty, and she had become a part of Addison's world, a part that Addison was not willing to lose...for anything.

The door to the master suite had barely opened when Addison leapt off the bed. "Did you read them?"

"I told you I would," Joanna said, coming into the room.

"Thank God," Addison said in a breath. "I'm sure if you call the doctor first thing in the morning—"

"I have no intention of calling the doctor."

"What? But you just said—"

"I said I read your grandfather's notes and looked at the Bibles, but Addison, I have no intention of aborting this child."

Addison rocked back on her heels. "You have to!"

As she had promised, Joanna had spent over an hour reading through Xavier's notes and looking at the information written in the Bibles.

Although it was hard to believe, Addison was right. Every Kane wife had died in childbirth, and on the three instances of fraternal twins prior to Addison and her brother, while both children had survived their birth, only the boy had lived a long and prosperous life. All three girls reached maturity and then married, but died giving birth to stillborn children, confirming what Addison had said. She had no cousins, aunts, or uncles. Her lineage was a very thin, straight line, and the baby Joanna was carrying was at the end of it.

Sadness was the prevailing emotion Joanna felt while reading what Xavier had written. She had no idea why the women had died or why the Kane family had such a tragic history, but there was nothing written on those pages that could have changed Joanna's mind...for her instinct was maternal and unwavering.

"No, I don't," Joanna said calmly. "There's nothing to say those women were in the best of health, or if they weren't, and medicine back then was...well, it isn't what it is now."

"Stop being so bloody stupid about this!"

Joanna's entire body went rigid. "Don't you *ever* call me stupid."

"Then stop acting like it!" Addison shouted. "It's clear my family is cursed and—"

"Cursed?" Joanna said, scrunching up her face. "Jesus Christ, do you hear what you're saying?"

"I know exactly what I'm saying, and I know why I'm saying it. I read my grandfather's notes and the Bibles and the bits and pieces in those sodding journals, and they all say the same thing, which is why you *are* going to call the doctor tomorrow and *do* what needs to be *done!*"

Joanna crossed her arms and took a slow, deep breath. "Listen carefully because I'm not going to say this again. I *am* going to have this child, and whether or not I die doing it does not matter."

Addison paled, and rushed to stand in front of Joanna. "Don't say that. You have a way out, and you need to take it."

"No, Addison, it's not a way out for me. It's a way out for *you!*" Joanna yelled. "Since the day you found out I was pregnant, you've been a changed person, and I don't mean that in a good way. You started working longer hours, coming home late, missing dinner, and hardly talking to me when we did have a few minutes alone. You haven't touched me in weeks other than an occasional kiss on the cheek, and the only attention you've given me is when you're *complaining* that I'm getting sick too much or losing too much weight."

"I'm just worried."

"Yes, you are, but you're *not* worried about *having* a family. You're worried about finding a way *out* of having a family."

"That's not true," Addison said, furrowing her brow.

"Yes, it is, and that's what this is all about," Joanna said, waving her arms in the air. "You're scared, and suddenly you realize that your life *is* going to change, and you don't want it to, do you? So you took your family's history, blew it out of proportion and decided to use it as the excuse to make me kill our child. Well, I have news for you. That's *not* going to happen!"

"It's not an excuse."

"Yes, it bloody well is!" Joanna screamed. "Jesus Christ, Addison, get your head out of your arse! You're a daughter of a Kane, and you survived well past childhood, so whatever you think about all those women who died, it's not some sort of...some sort of family curse. It just happened. That's all."

"It's too much of a coincidence, Joanna."

"I don't bloody care!" Joanna said, getting in Addison's face. "I don't care what you think. I don't care what you want. You made it crystal clear yesterday that you're not interested in being someone's parent, so stop with all of this crap before you go too far."

"What the hell are you talking about?"

"Do you honestly think I'm blind? You weren't the least bit interested in anything we were shown in the shops, and you continually and *arrogantly* proved it by walking away while the clerk was talking."

"They were selling. Not talking."

Joanna's nostrils flared. "It's their bloody job to sell and I, for one, wanted to hear what they had to say, but you didn't care about that, did you? How many times did I ask for your opinion, and you just shrugged and said it didn't matter. Silly me...I *thought* you were talking about baby furniture."

"I care about *you*."

"Oh, that's a bunch of crap. If you cared about me, you wouldn't be asking me to kill my child just because...just because *you're* a coward."

"I am *not* a fucking coward. I just didn't think this decision through and—"

"And now you regret it. Right?"

"I didn't say that."

"You didn't have to."

"I just don't want you to *die!*"

"I'm *not* going to die," Joanna said, rolling her eyes. "And if, by chance, I do, that's my decision. Now, as far as I'm concerned, this discussion is over."

Watching as Joanna headed to the wardrobe, Addison blurted, "I love you!"

Joanna spun around, waiting only for a second before she took four long strides to reach her target. Not holding back one ounce of strength, she slapped Addison across the face, splitting her lip in the process. "*How dare you try to use that to change my mind!*" Joanna shrieked. "After all these bloody months of you not being able to speak those words, you suddenly understand what they mean? Well, fuck you, Addison, because they're too late! They mean nothing to me now because you've shown your true colors, and they are *ugly!*"

"Can't you see I'm trying to save your life?" Addison said, wiping the blood from her lip.

"I honestly don't think you really want to know what I see right now," Joanna said, giving Addison the once over. "But I can tell you this, you and I are done."

"Don't say that."

"Do you really believe after all of this, I'd want to stay with you?"

"I just...Joanna, I can't bear the thought of losing you. Can't you see that?"

"No, all I can see is someone who's selfish and confused and jumping to conclusions because they give her the easy way out, but you don't have to worry about that any longer, Addison, because I'm going to give you your way out. We're done. I'll be moving back to the east wing today. We go back to the way we were. We don't speak. We don't eat meals together...and we sure as hell will never sleep in the same bed again."

***

Throughout history, the impossible has been proved possible. From a man walking on the moon to harnessing nuclear energy, the unimaginable has occurred, but that wasn't the case when it came to Joanna and Addison.

The mood inside The Oaks was palpable. The staff had left on Friday, smiling and euphoric about Joanna's condition, but when they returned on Monday, their mood turned somber and quiet.

For reasons unknown to them, Addison had returned to barking out orders and slamming doors, stomping around the house and staring daggers at anyone who came too close, while Joanna had become introverted and reserved. Offering only the smallest expression of acknowledgment as she passed the staff in the corridors or kitchen, they had no idea her familiar smile and friendly banter had been smothered by her annoyance.

True to her word, Joanna moved back into her room in the east wing, but the transition hadn't been as easy as she thought. Mourning the loss of the woman she undeniably loved, she cried herself to sleep night after night until one morning bent over the toilet as another wave of nausea washed over her, the blurred lines of her emotions became crisp. In her belly was a child she already loved more than life itself, and that was all that mattered. She knew in her heart she would always love Addison, but they had reached a stalemate Joanna felt insurmountable.

While Joanna cried alone in the darkness, Addison spent her time pacing her bedroom, chain-smoking and sipping scotch until the wee hours of the morning for two weeks straight. Not entirely without heart, she understood the seriousness of what she was asking, and it gnawed at her like a rabid dog, but she was convinced history would repeat itself, and she'd lose the love of her life just like her father had lost his. Unfortunately, the chasm she had caused by demanding Joanna abort their child had created a rift a canyon wide. Joanna had become a ghost in the house, no longer appearing in the dining room for meals or in the hallways, and when Addison had heard doors open and close late in the night, and she rushed to catch a glimpse of Joanna, she had already vanished into the shadows.

***

Addison ran her fingers through her hair, staring mindlessly at the Bibles and journals on her desk as she had done so many times before. She had looked for the gray, the sliver of hope or doubt in the words written by her ancestors, but the pages only contained black-and-white. So, when she heard a door open, she jumped from her chair and bolted from the study. Her vision was still as tunneled, and in the light at the very end, she only saw Joanna, so when Addison reached the foyer and spotted Joanna on the stairs her mind was on only one thing.

"Joanna, please, we need to talk," she called out.

Addison waited to be acknowledged, but when Joanna continued her climb, Addison's temper got the best of her. "*God damn it, woman!* We need to *talk!*"

Joanna stiffened, and coming to a stop, she slowly turned around and looked down at Addison. "No, we do *not!*"

Addison had hoped that time had eased Joanna's anger, but the expression on her wife's face proved her wrong. Stern and filled with contempt, Addison paled at the rage etched on Joanna's face. One moment passed and then another before Addison found the courage to approach the staircase. "Look, I know...I know you're angry, and you think I'm a cold-hearted bitch—"

"Among other things."

"But...but I do love you—"

"Oh, you can go to hell!" Joanna said as she spun around and ran up the stairs.

Love can mask faults and cloak imperfections, but it can also blind one to the peripheral. As Addison looked up at Joanna, she lost sight of the child in her belly. All she saw was the woman who had stolen her heart, and to imagine the world without Joanna was unfathomable.

Addison charged up the steps, catching up to Joanna before she reached the east wing. Grabbing her arm, she spun Joanna around. "Will you please stop being so fucking pigheaded and just give me a chance to explain myself."

Joanna pulled out of Addison's hold. "What's there to explain? You think your family is cursed, and you want me to kill our child. Did I miss anything?"

Addison took a half-step backward, her face paling at Joanna's brutal interpretation. "It...it sounds so wrong when you say it."

"Because it *is* wrong, Addison! It's wrong, and it's cruel."

"I'm trying to save your life, damn it! Can't you see that? And I think I can if you let me."

"What the hell are you talking about?"

"We hire a surrogate. Hell, we can hire five surrogates. I don't care, but since they wouldn't be my wife, the family history wouldn't come into play. We have children. I'll have an heir...and you'll live."

Joanna rocked back on her heels, the blood in her veins turning cold as she glowered at Addison. "And the baby I'm carrying?"

Addison bowed her head. "We make arrangements—"

"Like hell, we will!" Joanna said as she got into Addison's face. "We will do no such thing because we aren't a *we* anymore. Now, for the last bloody time, I am done with this conversation!" For a split-second, Joanna sneered at Addison before she turned around and marched into the east wing.

Addison trotted to catch up, and stepping in front of Joanna, she blocked her path to her bedroom door. "Please don't do this."

"Get the hell out of my way."

"I'm begging you, please...please reconsider."

"Get...out...of...my...*way*!"

"Joanna, can't you see that I love you? Doesn't what I'm asking you to do, prove I love you? I know there's a child inside of you. I know it's my child, and if there were any other way to save both of your lives, I would. I swear to God, I would, but there isn't. Please, Joanna, I'm begging. I'll do anything you want. We can hire as many surrogates as you'd like. Just please don't do this out of...out of spite."

"Spite?" Joanna blurted. "You think I'm doing this out of *spite*? Jesus, Addison, it's not spite! It's called love, but you can't understand that, can you? How someone can give up everything, even their life, for the person they love, and trust me, I love this baby more than I can put into words." Poking her finger into Addison's chest, Joanna said, "If it's the last thing I ever do, I will go to my grave content and happy because my child *lived*. A child who will have a future because as cold-hearted as you are, I know somewhere deep inside of you, you'll make that happen, and a child who will know love, because as long as Evelyn and Fran and Noah and the staff are around, that *will* happen. Now, for the last bloody time, leave me the fuck alone. We have nothing more to say, and this house is large enough that if I'm lucky, I'll never have to see you again!"

"You won't if you go through with this."

"Sorry?"

"If you do this, I'm leaving. I can't ...I *won't* come home every night knowing that you're living with a time bomb."

"Jesus Christ," Joanna said under her breath.

"I mean it, Joanna," Addison said softly, placing her hands on Joanna's arms. "I can't just stand around and...and watch you die."

Joanna took a step backward. "Who's asking you to?"

"What?"

"Who's *asking* you to stay?" Joanna said, putting her hands on her hips. "Maybe it hasn't sunk in yet, but you and I are finished, and if you don't want to *watch* me die, feel free to get the fuck out. Go back to your hotel and your whore and your *precious* sodding company and let me worry about my child and me because *we* are no longer *your* concern. That is...if we ever were."

***

The thought of losing Joanna ate at Addison like a cancer, destroying her sensibilities and obliterating the line between right and wrong. Unable to stop herself, for the next two weeks Addison tried to champion her cause again and again. Her mindset was granite and her insistence concrete, but with every word she spoke, every syllable she yelled, and every plea she screamed, she drove an even larger wedge between her and Joanna.

They had become opposing forces; headstrong and insistent each held her ground, and arguments began to break out if one so much as glanced at the other. The staff made themselves scarce. Disappearing into the kitchen or finding the furthest corner to clean, they hunched their shoulders, shook their heads, and prayed to God for détente, but peace did not come.

Fourteen days after Joanna had first told Addison to leave The Oaks, Addison did just that. With her head bowed and her heart broken, Addison climbed aboard her corporate jet fighting back tears as she left her homeland and the woman she loved behind, but before the plane had landed, her emotions had solidified into a rage bordering on an inferno.

Chapter Forty-Two

Six months later...

Joanna opened her eyes and smiled. When Addison had left The Oaks months before, Joanna had suffered through more than a few sleepless, teary-eyed nights before one morning her tears refused to fall any longer. Staring at her naked self in the bathroom mirror, she noticed the smallest of baby bumps, and suddenly things became clear. She had survived after the loss of her father...and she would survive now.

A month after Addison abandoned Joanna, the staunch walls of foreboding she had erected within The Oaks with her attitude began to crumble, and soon music could be heard throughout the house. Drapes and windows were opened to allow fresh air to enter, but with air came sunlight and before too long Joanna decided changes needed to be made. She didn't know how long she'd live at The Oaks, and technically it wasn't her house, but while she lived under Addison's roof, while she and her *child* lived under Addison's roof, it would be a place bright and cheerful where no shadow would ever lurk again.

Familiar with all the areas of the house save one, one dreary, rainy morning Joanna walked to the west wing and opened the doors, the hinges causing her to hunch her shoulders as they screeched for oil. Just as Evelyn had told her so many months before, the layout seemed identical to that of the east wing. Yet even though the placement of the rooms appeared to be the same, Joanna paused. During one of her many conversations with Evelyn over morning coffee, Joanna had found out that it had taken Evelyn and the staff only two days to prepare the east wing for the arrival of her and her father. As Joanna stood in the doorway, something seemed off. There was no way anyone could have cleaned *this* wing in two days, let alone a month.

Joanna made her way slowly down the lengthy corridor. Most of the rooms were packed with furniture, and by the amount of the dust covering everything, it had been there for decades. Boxes of odds and ends long since forgotten were also stacked here and there, but knowing the wing had been used for storage, Joanna paid it no mind. She was more interested in the little touches that *weren't* there.

The windows had no drapes to block the sun and the floors, no rugs to warm one's feet. One quick look at the lighting fixtures above her head proved their dimness wasn't due to burned-out bulbs, but rather the lack of them as their sockets were empty. There was no artwork on the walls or shades on the crooked sconces, and the plaster was in far worse shape than anywhere else in the house. A chill ran down Joanna's spine, and she leaned her head to the side. Why was it so much colder in here? She knew, at times, the east wing could be drafty, but this wasn't a draft. It was a breeze.

The mass of tables, chairs, and accent pieces stuffed into the rooms prevented Joanna from easily entering any of them, but when she reached the end of the hallway and opened the last door on the right, sadness swept over her.

The room had been left untouched, and Joanna knew in an instant this was where Addison lived as a child. The bed was small, barely large enough to hold one person and the armoire, while providing a place to hang clothes, offered nothing else for the mirrors on the doors were cracked or shattered. Again, there were no curtains or carpets, but there was another piece of furniture in the room, and it drew Joanna to it like a magnet to steel.

With four legs, one drawer for pencils, and a surface on which to write, it was the simplest of desks, and absentmindedly Joanna ran her finger across the top leaving behind a track in the dust. She looked around the barren room again, trying to imagine a child living within its walls and tears sprung to her eyes. There was no love here. No hope or promise of the future amidst the gray and the brown and the bleak. There was only sadness and despair, invisible stifling blankets that had smothered a child's need for love, or worse yet, the ability to open her heart and let her love out.

Joanna took a ragged breath, choking back the tears and shaking her head at the inhumanity of a parent who didn't deserve that title. Without so much as another glance at her surroundings, Joanna went back to her room and picked up her mobile, and after placing a call to Samson and Lucinda, she pulled the corporate card from her nightstand drawer...and then began to make a list.

***

The following day, Samson, Lucinda, and Joanna toured The Oaks together, discussing colors, repairs, and furnishings required to make the house a home for a mother and her child, but when they reached the study, Joanna denied them entry. It had always been Addison's bastion, and it would remain that way. She had entered it only once since becoming the sole occupant of the house, but the smell of cigarettes and a hint of Addison's cologne still hung in the air, causing Joanna to run from the room with tears streaming down her face. Eventually, she knew she'd try again because within its walls were memories Joanna could not imagine living without.

Her morning sickness finally came to an end, and her appetite increased just as her doctor said it would, and when the baby began to move halfway through her second trimester, the magnitude of love coursing through Joanna's being was incredible. Most of the time she felt like she was floating on a euphoric, fluffy white cloud of enchantment and dreams, yet there were still days when smiles were hard to come by, and that's when Joanna's friends took over.

While her circle of friends was small, it didn't take long for Joanna to know she needed no others. The staff was happy to serve a woman who appreciated them for all they were worth, and their glee at the upcoming arrival of Joanna's child matched that of Fran's and Millie's. Visiting every chance they got, Fran and Millie would stay for dinner and over scrumptious meals lovingly prepared by Noah, they'd giggle and coo about a baby they couldn't wait to hold. Millie knitted and crocheted like there was no tomorrow, and Fran became an expert on the location of every baby store in London, and all was right in Joanna's world, except for only one thing. Sometimes, late at night in the quiet of her room, her mind would drift to a woman with blue eyes and honey smooth skin, and Joanna's heart would break all over again. She damned herself and muttered expletives, trying to convince her heart to ache no more, but she doubted the pang would ever really go away.

Joanna took a moment to rid her mind of all things Addison before tossing aside the sheets and attempting to sit up. She felt weak this morning, heavy with child and water yet to be shed, her arms and legs felt weighted, but that didn't prevent a laugh from escaping when she saw the size of her belly. It was absolutely huge, and its circumference had prevented her from seeing her feet for weeks. Chuckling, Joanna struggled to sit up, but her strength disappeared in an instant when she saw blood on the sheets.

***

Addison refused to open her eyes. The ice picks of pain boring their way through her head confirmed she had consumed far too much alcohol the night before, but when she inhaled, and the hotel's familiar aroma invaded her senses, she breathed a bit easier. At least she had made it back to the suite that had become her home.

Like a nomad, Addison had traveled across Europe, visiting one Kane office and then another while she debated on which would fill her needs. She created havoc in each and every one as she bellowed and scowled about the amenities until she finally settled in Spain...with her new PA in tow.

When Addison left England, she had done it alone. Refusing to relocate, Millie had stayed behind, but not before subjecting herself to one of Addison's temper tantrums. Vases were broken, and foul language was spewed, but in the end, beaten down by her endless arguments with Joanna, Addison folded her hand, and a deal was struck. Millie would remain in the London office and act as a conduit for Addison while she was abroad, and taking her place as Addison's personal assistant would be Lydia Patel.

Lydia had begun to thrive at Kane Holdings and while Addison was clueless, Millie was not. The tears once shed by the novice junior secretary had long ago dried up and in their place was a blend of confidence and willingness to learn, which reminded Millie of her younger self. Early to work and eager to take on more than her fair share, Millie saw the younger woman as her eventual replacement, so when Addison announced her relocation, Lydia was the obvious choice.

Stepping up and stepping up nicely, Lydia had learned from the best when it came to handling Addison. When the woman howled, Lydia turned a deaf ear, and when employees were sacked for no reason other than Addison's foul mood, Lydia countermanded the order, gave them a day off, and calmed the feathers of her ruffled employer just as Millie had done for her so many months before. Whatever hours were needed, Lydia worked, and no matter the task, Lydia accomplished it, and in less than two short months, before Addison could reach for a pen, Lydia was handing her one.

Addison had never included Millie when invitations for business lunches or dinners were made, but as time went on Addison found herself craving Lydia's companionship. There was comfort in having the woman with black hair, fair skin, and green eyes sitting to her left, and while no notes were ever taken or meetings scheduled, more times than not Lydia found herself enjoying Addison's company at almost every meal.

During the day, Addison was all about business. Diligent and focused, she immersed herself in files, reports, prospectuses, and finance, but when the sun came down it brought with it a sadness that enveloped her. Addison never spoke of Joanna, never hinted at the life she had left behind in England and Lydia had never asked. At times, she could see the pain in Addison's eyes as they ate their meals. Lost in her thoughts Addison would stare across the restaurant, the sorrow creasing her brow and adding years to her face. Lydia soon noticed that scotch was gulped more than it was sipped and cigarettes were now aplenty, and as weeks turned into months, the once perfectly tailored suits Addison wore began to hang from her frame.

Many a night Lydia found herself guiding Addison back to her suite. Her balance and decorum eradicated by some of the finest single-malt money could buy, Addison would sway and swear her way through the hotel, oblivious to the stares and the whispers, and to the paparazzi hiding behind columns of marble and stone.

Early on, there had been a few stories about the rift between the billionaire and her wife, tales of betrayal and indiscretions, but built on nothing more than assumptions, the articles eventually faded away. After all, Addison and Joanna weren't the first married couple to have problems, and they certainly wouldn't be the last, but when Lydia noticed the photographers hiding in the shadows outside restaurants or the hotel, she quickly added damage control to her list of duties. Pulling every Euro from her handbag, she bought back the memory cards containing images of Addison unraveled and unruly, and the next day, she called Millie to ask her advice. After explaining the situation, Lydia began leaving the office each night with a wad of Euros courtesy of the office's petty cash, guaranteeing that not one hint of Addison's behavior would ever make it into the tabloids, and it hadn't.

So, to the world, Addison Kane now lived and worked in Spain, doing what she did best and never missing a step as her company's coffers continued to fill. There were no pictures showing her in a drunken state. None showing the weight she had lost or the way her hair had begun to gray at the temples. Those closest to her had noticed her ice blue eyes had lost their luster, and her posture had weakened, but her thirst to succeed in business had remained the same. It truly was her life's blood, and without it, she would have surely gone insane with the thoughts of dread constantly whirling around in her head. The woman she loved was going to die, and it was Addison's fault, and every morning when she opened her eyes, Addison damned herself for being a Kane.

Addison swallowed once and then again, trying to replace the moisture in her mouth that had been sucked away by the scotch. Her muscles ached, and her head pounded, but after wetting her lips with a slow slide of her tongue, she forced herself to open her eyes. Running her fingers through her hair, she worked out the kinks in her neck before stretching her arms to the extreme, but when she felt a lump under the sheets next to her, she exploded from the bed as if shot from a cannon.

Instantly recognizing the long, black hair sweeping across the other pillow, Addison stumbled back a step. "*What the fuck are you doing in my bed?*"

Lydia grabbed her head, clamping it between her hands as she tried to keep her skull from splitting open. "For Christ's sake, stop screaming," she hissed as shards of pain stabbed at her brain. "My head's going to burst."

"I don't bloody care!" Addison said, keeping her voice at the same volume. "What the *hell* are you doing in *my* room?"

Unwilling to yet open her eyes for fear even the lowest wattage would laser into her head, Lydia reached out, grabbed Addison's pillow and covered her face. Through the satin-covered down, she mumbled, "Just give me a minute. Okay?"

"Not on your life," Addison said, snatching the pillow away from Lydia. "Now what the fuck—"

"Jesus Christ, I heard you already!" Lydia growled as she tossed back the sheets and got to her feet. "I'm in your *room*, and I'm in your *bed* because we both had too much to drink last night and unlike you, I had no one to help *me* back to my bloody room!"

Addison's jaw dropped open at the sight of Lydia wearing the clothes she had worn the day before, albeit the pencil skirt was now terribly wrinkled, and the silk blouse was rumpled and skewed. "Wait. Do you mean...do you mean we didn't...we didn't—"

"Oh, *please* give me a break," Lydia said, rolling her eyes. "You may be the be-all and end-all to lots of women, but I'm *hetero*sexual and have no interest in jumping the fence, thank you very much. Besides, if I was so inclined, I sure as hell would pick someone sober, single, and not head over bloody heels in love with her wife."

Addison couldn't argue two of the points, but one she refused to ignore. "I'm not a drunk."

For months, Lydia had wanted to talk to Addison as a friend, to voice her concern and perhaps offer a shoulder to cry if the need arose, but the time never seemed right. Days always revolved around business and nights always revolved around scotch, so when Lydia heard the sadness creep into Addison's voice, she decided to finally speak her mind.

"I didn't say you were, but you can't go on like this. Okay?" Lydia walked around the bed and stopped in front of Addison. "Look, I don't know the particulars of what's going on with you and your wife, and it's certainly not my place to ask, but it's bloody obvious you're in love with her, and this..." Lydia paused, gesturing with a sweep of her arm. "*This* isn't what you need. Hiding away in hotels, working yourself to death during the day and then drinking yourself into a stupor every night isn't going to cure the problem. You've got to see that."

"You're right. It's not your place to say," Addison snapped as she stepped around Lydia. "Now get out so I can get cleaned up."

Lydia sighed, hanging her head for a moment before she did as she was told. Slipping on her open-toed pumps, she grabbed her suit jacket from a chair and started to leave the room when she came to a sudden stop. "Oh, by the way," she said, turning around. "If you're looking for your mobile, it's in the nightstand. I got up last night to use the loo, and the bloody thing was vibrating all over the place. I got tired of hearing it, so I put it in the drawer."

Addison watched as Lydia left the suite, and scrubbing her hand over her face, she made her way to the loo to empty her bladder and brush her teeth. A short time later she emerged and headed straight for the hotel phone, and after ordering up a pot of strong coffee, she grabbed a pack of cigarettes from a nearby table and headed to the balcony. Opening the doors, she breathed in the balmy air of May and looked down at the row of motor scooters lined up along the curb. The hotel was located on a quiet street, so the only sound interrupting Addison's morning was the jabbering of guests enjoying their breakfast on the veranda below her and the occasional honk of a car horn in the distance. Sinking into one of the ornately decorated iron chairs at her disposal, Addison was about to light her cigarette when she remembered what Lydia had said. With a sigh, she went back inside long enough to fetch her mobile.

Returning to the balcony, she got comfortable and lit a cigarette. She stared at the phone in her hand, but accustomed to receiving messages about so-called emergencies happening throughout the company, it wasn't until she lit her next cigarette when she tapped on the mobile's screen. It came to life instantly, and when it did, Addison frowned. She had six missed calls, one message, and one text, all of which had come from Fran. Not in the mood to listen to her lawyer chatter in her ear about contracts and deadlines, she passed over the voice mail and went straight to her text...and seconds later all the blood drained from Addison's face.

"You need to come home. It's Joanna. Something's wrong."

Chapter Forty-Three

George escorted Addison back to the limo, doing his best to protect her from the onslaught of rain that had been falling for days. With the handle of the black brolly so secure in his hand his knuckles had turned white, he fought against the wind as best he could, but when he momentarily lost control and Addison got drenched in an instant, she didn't seem to notice. Actually, she didn't care.

Others around her cowered at the sound of the thunder or flinched at the arcs of lightning as they split the sky again and again, but Addison was in a world of her own. A world that contained only darkness and sorrow, and the bleakness of its catacombs were lonely and barren. Echoing through the tunnels were the mistakes she had made out of anger or pride or stubbornness, and like stalactites, she was sure they would hang over her head for years to come.

She climbed into the car, unconcerned about the rain soaking through her suit, and when the passenger door opened, and the Rolls dipped ever so slightly, Addison's eyes remained focused on the floor.

Fran uncrumpled the tissue in her hand and tried to repair the damage her tears had done to her makeup, but quickly giving up, she wiped away the remaining mascara. She opened her handbag and retrieved another tissue, and after blowing her nose, she sat back in the seat and turned to Addison. "I think I should call the board. There's no need to do this today."

Fran waited for Addison to say something, but when she remained silent, Fran pulled out her mobile, but before she could press one button, Addison broke the silence.

"No. We do it now," Addison said flatly. "If they felt the need to interrupt me today, it must be important."

"It can wait," Fran said, leaning down to look Addison in the eye. "They'd understand."

"There's no reason to wait, Fran," Addison said as she turned to look out the window. "No reason at all."

***

Addison didn't notice the puffy faces or reddened eyes of her employees as she walked the hallways of Kane Holdings. She didn't hear the sniffles or the whispers, and while there were many who wished to offer condolences, none dared to approach. The wound of Addison's loss was far too gaping for that.

She stepped into the room and looked around. There were two conference areas at Kane. The larger being modern and containing the biggest flat-screen television available, it was used for video conferencing and brainstorming sessions and easily could hold twenty or thirty people if chairs were brought in, but the smaller one – this one – was what most referred to as the old board room. It was rarely used now, but given its age and that of the men who made up the board, it made sense. The room smelled of leather, polish, and cigar smoke, the latter clinging to the jackets of the men surrounding the table, and like the furniture, they were old and polished, too. Wearing ties announcing their university in colors and sporting lapel pins for their causes, all but one had skin the color of a ghost.

Reece Somersby had been on the board as long as Addison could remember, but unlike his colleagues, who preferred to spend their time at clubs smoking cigars and drinking brandy, Reece loved the outdoors, and it showed. His skin was dark and leathery from years spent on sailboats and golf courses, and the paunch worn by all the others was non-existent on the man. Trim and fit, he was out of place at the table in more ways than one for he was a friend...and the rest had become enemies.

When Addison took over the company, Reece couldn't have been more thrilled, and at first, the others had felt the same way. Like Xavier, Addison was taking the company upward, and the dividends proved it, so there were no complaints until Firth and her father had replaced some of the board with those more like-minded to a greedier end game. Whispered promises about bank accounts overflowing if the company was sold outright had caused several of the other board members to lean toward the left. After all, they weren't getting any younger and being rich was worthless if you were dead.

Out of the corner of her eye, Addison noticed someone approaching, and she offered a weak smile when she saw Reece walking toward her.

His face mirrored Addison's, but as heavy as his heart was at her loss, the remainder of the burden was due to the meeting he had been forced to call.

"I'm sorry about this, but they insisted. Apparently, Calvert and Gladstone are going on holiday, and couldn't give a good goddamn about what you're going through."

"It's all right, Reece," Addison said as she shifted her viewpoint to the dumpy men straining the construction of their chairs. "I don't know what's going on, but I know you wouldn't do this today unless it were important. So let's get it over with. Shall we?"

Before Reece could reply, Addison walked to the chair at the end of the table, and slipping into it, she looked up at the men watching her with keen, beady eyes. "Now, what's this all about?"

Raised to be a gentleman, Reece did not take his seat until Fran settled in a chair in the corner of the room, and then sinking into his own, he opened the folder in front of him and pulled out a piece of paper. Letting out a sigh, he raised his eyes and looked at Addison as he motioned to the man on his right to pass the paper to her. As soon as it was in her hands, he said, "That was sent to us by a Miss Prudence Craddick a few weeks ago. She states that she was one of the nurses caring for Robert Sheppard. Is that true?"

Intent on trying to decipher the sloppy handwriting on the paper, it took a moment before Addison looked up. "Sorry, but that name doesn't ring a bell."

Reece looked at his notes. "She states here that you fired her."

A few seconds had passed before Addison nodded. "Yes, I remember her now. She was sleeping on the job."

"Well, she says that when she left your home, she inadvertently took some items that didn't belong to her, one of which is that paper you have in your hands."

"Inadvertently?"

Reece knew where Addison was going, and his sadness showed on his face. "Yes," he said quietly. "That's what she says."

Addison looked at the scribble again, but this time she gave it her full attention, and before she was halfway down the page, she knew who the author was. She continued to read his words, and when she reached the end, she handed the paper to Fran and then turned her attention to Reece.

It took Fran only a few minutes to read the note, and before she read the last word, the color had drained from her face. Resting back in the chair, she closed her eyes and tried desperately to think of a way out...for them both.

Intent on protecting themselves from Maxwell Firth, Addison and Fran had both forgotten that enemies can come in all shapes and sizes, and an angry nurse with vengeance in her heart had been one of them.

Prudence had watched Robert Sheppard write in his diaries so many times that on the night when she was sacked, she grabbed the notebooks stacked toward the front of the nightstand drawer. At the time, it was simply out of spite. Having worked the morning shift on more than one occasion, she knew if he didn't have them at his fingertips, Robert would awaken screaming and ranting and turning the house into turmoil. It was petty and childish, but most paybacks are.

By the time she had reached her flat, she was more concerned with how much liquor was in her cabinet than what Robert had written, so stuffing the notebooks into her wardrobe, she drank herself to sleep. They would remain there for months, settled in between scuffed shoes and empty boxes until one day while rummaging through her closet for something to wear, a blouse fell off a hanger. When she picked it up, she saw Robert's diaries. Tittering under breath at her deviousness, she gathered them up and headed to the rubbish bin, only to stop before she dropped them inside. What could a feeble-minded stroke victim possibly have to say that would have filled so many pages?

She went to work as she always did, but later that night, with fuzzy slippers warming her feet and port warming her belly, she settled into her favorite overstuffed recliner, opened one of the notebooks and immediately became entranced. Robert's words spoke of an arranged marriage and secrets built on handshakes. He spoke of restitution and the price Addison Kane would pay if discovered, and for a few hours, blackmail crossed Prudence's mind, but Addison frightened her. She was a powerful woman with powerful people at her fingertips, but even Addison Kane couldn't stop the post from making their deliveries. In the wee hours of the next morning, Prudence began writing a letter to the board of Kane Holdings.

If someone had dropped a pin on the carpet, it would have been heard for all eyes were on Addison, but refusing to say a word, she continued to stare at Reece. It was no longer her place to speak. It was his.

"All right, enough of this," Reece stated, rocking forward in his chair. "Addison, investigations have already been made, and it's been confirmed that the handwriting on that paper belongs to Robert Sheppard, but it's bollocks, and you and I both know it. From what I hear the man suffered several strokes, so it goes without saying he was most likely not in his right mind when he scrawled that story. So, just tell us he was daft, and this is all over. The company remains yours, and we go about business as usual."

It had always been the single most important thing in her life. She had lived it, breathed it, and nurtured it for endless days and endless nights, never regretting one minute she had spent on the company bearing her name, and with one lie, it could remain hers. One untruth, while sullying the name of someone buried months before, was all she had to utter and things would remain status quo with no questions asked. It was her word against a man who was at times confused and scared. Puzzled by his surroundings, his knees would shake, and his voice would tremble, but he was also a man who over pints of ice cream had become her friend...but he was dead. Gone from the earth to the heavens above, what harm would a lie do now? He was an unknown so why would it matter if those around the table thought him a fool? Why would it matter at all?

Addison cleared her throat, prepared to speak the fiction that once and for all would assure her that Kane Holdings would be forever hers, but as she looked up at the men staring back at her, their eyes dark with greed and their lips glistening with anticipation, she was transported back in time. To a time when angry words were spewed and when Joanna told her that she'd never understand how someone could give up everything in their life...for someone they loved.

Swiveling in her chair, Addison held out her hand to Fran, silently requesting the return of the paper that had damned her. Turning back around, she met the steely gaze of the Board of Directors of Kane Holdings with one of her own. "It's true," she said, pushing the paper across the table.

Their heads popped from their collars like moles in a carnival game, and if any blood had remained in Fran's face, it was gone.

Reece's eyebrows disappeared into his hairline, his eyes shifting from one board member to the next before his focus fixed on Addison. "Damn it, girl, do you know what you're saying?"

"I know exactly what I'm saying, Reece," Addison said as she got to her feet. "I can't speak for the rest of the men in this room, but Robert Sheppard was no more daft than you are. His body may have been weak, but his mind was sharp, and what he wrote on that piece of paper is the truth." Addison glanced at Fran before she looked at the ones who were about to tear her company to shreds. "And unless I'm mistaken, my services are no longer required here. Good day, gentlemen. I'd like to wish you luck, but my heart wouldn't be in it. I'm sure you understand."

***

Addison entered a house now void of people and of life. No one greeted her at the door. No little dog scampered frantically to welcome her, and no one was there to take her briefcase, but then again, she no longer had a need for one.

If it had been up to her, Addison would have never returned to The Oaks, but owning no luggage she had had no choice. She had flown back to England with nothing but the clothes on her back, and since she had given up her suite at the Langham, and shopping was unimaginable, four hours after the wheels of her jet touched the runway in London, she returned home with her face stained with tears and her mood foul. She wanted heads to roll and other people to hurt as much as she did, and they would have if it hadn't been for Evelyn.

Having already received numerous scathing texts from Addison, Evelyn knew what her staff would be facing if they were anywhere near The Oaks. So, giving the majority of them extended holidays, she offered Fiona and George a bonus if they'd stay on, stay out of the way, and do what they could to help. They agreed without blinking an eye, and became very, *very* covert.

As she had done for the past ten days, as Addison placed her briefcase on the table in the foyer, she became engrossed by her surroundings. On her first night home, the things she saw caused her tears to flow uncontrollably, and on the second night, she fell to the floor and wept some more. On the third and fourth she fared no better, but on the fifth, she began treasuring what was around her...for it was the only thing left of Joanna.

Floors once slate were now marble and walls once cracked were now patched and painted. Molding surrounding doors, floors, and ceilings had either been repainted or stripped, and with the oily, old varnish removed, the grains of cherry and walnut finally saw the light of day. The black iron lamps and dingy shades once casting their lackluster light over the space had been replaced, and the balustrade leading up the stairs and surrounding the octagonal opening in the ceiling had been modernized with glass and polished steel. The carpet covering the steps had also been replaced, and the threads of vibrant blues, maroons, and greens were richer than any Addison had ever seen before.

She couldn't help herself from wandering over and peering into the formal living room now deserved of its name. Again, walls and moldings had been restored, and slate had been replaced with marble, but clueless as to what the west wing had contained, Addison had no idea that most of the furniture she could see had been in the house for decades. Hauled out by the truckload, it all had been taken to artisans across the county who had worked on restoring the antiques to their glory, and they *were* glorious now. Grains rich with history and elegance announced themselves through coats of modern finish, and the settees in front of two of the windows, once covered with thick brocade had been reupholstered with fabrics, light, velvety, and feminine.

The overstuffed sofas and chairs had been purchased new, as had the area rugs, but unbeknownst to Addison, Joanna had kept a child's comfort in mind when choosing both. The deep sofas complete with a dozen throw pillows would give a toddler a place to snuggle and play, and while the carpeting was indeed stylish, the thickness and padding sewn beneath the surface would protect a youngster from a fall onto a floor of metamorphic rock.

Hearing a noise, Addison looked toward the kitchen and saw Fiona staring back at her. Addison nodded, and Fiona disappeared, and taking a deep breath, Addison headed to the dining room. She wasn't hungry, but then again...she never was anymore.

***

An hour later, Addison walked toward the library with wine bottle in hand. Like her father, the space had become her bedroom of sorts. The sofa was small, but with the help of alcohol, Addison's discomfort was minimal. Finding it impossible to sleep in the room where she and Joanna once shared a bed, other than showers and visits to the wardrobe, Addison avoided the master suite like the plague.

Her legs were heavy as she aimlessly walked through the study. Her thoughts spun like a tornado through her mind, berating her with regrets, chastising her for her stupidity, and cackling at her for the overwhelming grief she had brought on herself. So, by the time she reached the leather sofa, she no longer was interested in the wine. Stretching across its cushions, she hoped sleep would find her; a deep slumber that would encase her mind in a thick, inky blackness, smothering her anguish and easing her pain, if only for a few hours. It had yet to come in oh so many days, but perhaps tonight Joanna wouldn't visit Addison in her dreams. Perhaps tonight, Addison wouldn't be reminded of Joanna's smile or her laughter or her beauty...or her love.

***

Habits, like autopilots, plot your path. From the moment your feet hit the floor in the morning until you rest your head on the pillow at night, unconscious patterns are formed by time and necessity, and as Addison stared at herself in the mirror and adjusted her tie, she sighed.

There was no need for a business dress any longer. No need to parade about in tailored suits, neckties of silk, and shirts, refined and crisp, and for a moment, Addison stood frozen. Other than a few sets of workout clothes, she had no garments fit for relaxation, no shoes with soft soles or shirts of jersey to putter around the house in, and trousers of denim had never been bought. Had she ever relaxed?

Addison hung her head as the answer came rushing back to her. Over dinner conversations and whispers in the dark, tranquility had found her. In the arms of Joanna, there had been a peace she had never known. For a brief blip of time, Addison had been able to make a truce with her past and embrace the serenity Joanna had given her, but that was gone now. Addison had destroyed it with her arrogance and her fear.

She fisted her hands as she felt her emotions begin to rise again. She had shed more tears in the past two weeks than she had done throughout her entire life. Backhands had caused sniffles, and a father's condemnation had caused sadness and confusion, but this grief controlled her. It pumped her blood. It expanded her lungs, and it had become her shadow. Following her through every minute of her day, Addison could not escape it, but she continued to try. She dashed from the wardrobe, trying to outrun her tears, and refusing to acknowledge there was a bed in the room, Addison ran out the door and slammed it shut. Stomping down the stairs, she looked at her watch and sighed. It was only six o'clock, so there was no coffee yet made, but then an aroma wafted from the kitchen, and Addison breathed easier. Fiona was early...for once.

***

"What are you doing here?"

Evelyn looked up from the coffee maker. "I thought you could use a friend and...um...a good cup of coffee. Fiona, bless her heart, has never gotten the hang of this machine."

"I hadn't noticed," Addison said as she sat down.

Evelyn remained quiet as she filled two mugs and walked over to the island. "There you go," she said, sliding one in front of Addison.

Addison wrapped her hands around the mug. "Long way to drive to make a pot of coffee."

"Yes, well, there's also that thing called friendship, unless you no longer believe I fall under that heading?" Evelyn said as she dropped two cubes of sugar into her cup.

"We all do things we believe are right at the time," Addison said quietly as she breathed in the aroma of the French Roast. "Spilt milk."

Evelyn raised her chin just a tad, studying the woman across the counter. Addison had lost weight, weight she couldn't afford to lose, and her expression was blank, devoid of even the smallest hint of life. Hunched over on the stool, she had yet to make eye contact with Evelyn, and when Addison had reached for her coffee, Evelyn saw her hands tremble. This was not the same woman who had marched away from The Oaks so many months before.

They sipped their coffee in silence until Evelyn thought it time to break the ice. "Fran called me yesterday." Evelyn waited patiently for a response, but when Addison finally raised her eyes, Evelyn's heart broke. They were bloodshot and filled with more pain than she had ever seen.

"So, you know?" Addison said in a breath.

"Yes, and to put it mildly, I was shocked. Here I thought you didn't even remember his name."

"I remember a lot more than that."

"What's that supposed to mean?"

Addison hung her head. "It doesn't matter."

"Spilt milk?"

"Something like that," Addison mumbled.

A dozen questions came to mind, but considering the defeated woman in front of her, Evelyn took her time when deciding which to ask. "So what now? Where do you go from here?"

"I don't know," Addison said, looking up. "Sell this place and move somewhere...somewhere that doesn't remind me of...that doesn't remind me...that doesn't...damn it!" Addison said, choking back her tears as she jumped to her feet. "Sorry, but this isn't working, Evelyn. You need to leave. You need to leave right now!"

***

Later that afternoon, Addison emerged from the master suite after taking her second shower of the day. Before the mug of coffee Evelyn had given her had cooled, Addison had poured herself a scotch, and by noon, she had passed out on the sofa in the library only to wake up a few hours later feeling worse than she had that morning. She heard Fiona puttering in the kitchen on her way up the stairs, so when Addison came back down, she headed into the dining room for her sandwich without crust.

The bread was soft and the meat moist, yet even with a pungent cheese, her palate sensed no flavor. There was a texture, a need to chew and swallow, yet like the water she drank in hopes of repairing the effects of dehydration, the food was tasteless, but autopilot kicked in, so she ate it.

It wasn't long before Addison found herself back in the library, the air thick with the smell of the cigarettes she had smoked that morning. The decanter was still on the table, the level of single-malt more than enough to take her to oblivion again, but she had lost the desire to drink it.

She ran her fingers through her hair as she wondered if anything would ever hold her interest again. Neatly folded newspapers were stacked on her desk in the study, and her laptop was at the ready, connecting her to all that used to be important, but her definition of importance had somehow changed. Kindness was important. Compassion was important. Standing by those you love was important and speaking the words was *important*, but her epiphany had come too late, and as that thought crossed her mind, the veins in her temples began to bulge.

Addison reached for the decanter, yet she didn't thirst for its contents. She wanted to hear the crystal shatter against the wall. She wanted to rip the books from the shelves, tearing their pages and their spines until only tatters remained, and those filled with her family's history, the Bibles emblazoned with the name she was once proud to call her own, Addison wanted to burn. She wanted their pages turned to char, sending her past up the flue in bits and pieces of smoke and ash, but as she brought back her arm with crystal in hand, the distant sound of a door slamming caught her attention.

Fiona was there for only one reason, and it had nothing to do with anything upstairs. It had been made very clear to her that her duties were to cook and provide drink when needed, so when Addison heard the door, she launched herself off the sofa. Propelled by her rage, she made it through two rooms in a flash, but when she reached the foyer, it was as if she had hit an invisible wall, her stop so abrupt she stumbled back a step. The air rushed from her lungs, carrying with it only one word. "Joanna."

"Hello, Addison."

Chapter Forty-Four

The house was so silent that each could hear the other breathe, the mantle clock in the drawing room adding to the cadence as it ticked and tocked its way to the next minute.

If Fran and Evelyn hadn't warned her, Joanna wouldn't have been able to hold back her shock at Addison's appearance. She was pale and thin, her cheekbones now casting shadows almost to her jawline, and the icy brilliance of her eyes had melted into pools of pale blue filled with anguish.

There was no longer a contest of wills as they each gazed at the other. Both had words to speak, but forming a sentence, or even a word, was proving difficult. It had been nearly seven months since they had last seen each other, so time ceased to matter as Joanna and Addison just allowed the moment to penetrate their souls.

After taking a deep, stuttering breath, Addison finally found her voice. "I...I thought...I thought I'd see you at the...at the funeral."

"Something else took precedence," Joanna said, slowly moving down a step. "I'll pay my respects later this week. Knowing Millie, I'm sure she would have understood."

"They said her heart just stopped in her sleep."

"I know."

A cloud of uneasiness washed over Addison. Joanna's expression was unreadable, and fearing if she said the wrong thing, Joanna would bolt, Addison grimaced as she struggled to find the right words. Taking a step toward the staircase, she said, "I...I tried to see you. You know? I tried, but no one...they wouldn't even return my calls or texts."

Joanna nodded as she switched the small bag she was carrying to her other hand. Unsure she could make her way safely down the stairs on knees now weakened by the sight of Addison, Joanna placed her hand on the railing before daring to take another step. "I know. I told them not to."

"Why?"

"Because I was angry," Joanna said, taking another step. "And I wanted you to know what it was like to feel helpless. I wanted you to feel like I felt when you walked out on me. I wanted you to feel like I felt when you gave me a choice impossible to make, and I wanted you to feel as alone as I've felt...for month after month after month." Joanna moved to the next step. "Long before I was due, I made everyone promise that no matter what happened, you were not to know where I was until it was done. If I were to die, then I would die the way you left me...alone. Just before they put me in the ambulance, I found out what Fran had done, so I made her swear, I made her swear, and Evelyn swear and Millie, poor, sweet Millie swear that they wouldn't tell you anything else."

"They didn't, and I had no idea where you were."

"I know, and trust me I had plenty of time to put everything into place. My doctor knew of a private hospital, and once I bought them a much-needed MRI machine, my privacy was guaranteed. Not even the damn reporters could find me. The only people who knew where I was were Fran, Millie, and Evelyn, so sacking David was uncalled for."

Addison scowled as she remembered that night. After reading Fran's text and discovering that her voice mail was one she had left the day before, Addison had placed a dozen calls to Fran as she rushed to the airport, but all had gone unanswered. During the flight back to England, she had placed even more calls to Evelyn and Millie, and texts by the dozens had been sent, but when no replies were received, by the time Addison stepped foot on the tarmac in London, her temper was far beyond simmering.

Climbing into her waiting limo, Addison ordered David to take her to the hospital, but when she found out that none of the staff were privy to Joanna's location, she took out her mobile and began calling Evelyn, Millie, and Fran again. For two hours, she paced around the car, sending text after text as her blood pressure continued to rise until finally, she had no choice but to tell David to take her to The Oaks. Just before they reached the gated entrance to her estate, Addison's phone finally chimed with a text message from Fran. It was short. It was *not* sweet...and Addison's tempered boiled over.

"I panicked and shouldn't have texted. She's fine, but doesn't want to see you. She's made sure you can't find her. Sorry, Addison. That's all I'm allowed to say."

Dynamite had nothing on Addison when she climbed from the car. After taking out her frustrations on the pristine exterior of the 1972 Rolls-Royce Phantom VI, she fired David on the spot and then went into the house and drowned her anger with scotch.

It was not one of her finer moments, and as Addison thought about it, she sighed. "You know about that, do you?"

"I know more than you think."

It was one of the hardest things Joanna had ever done, but during the renovations and repair of The Oaks, she had returned to her father's room for the first time since his death. Refusing to live in the past like her wife, although she had shed buckets of tears as she gathered his things, it was time to move on. She tenderly packed up his clothes, methodically going from one drawer to the next, but when Joanna opened his nightstand drawer, she found a thick wad of papers covered in her father's left-handed sloppy scrawl.

Prudence Craddick had stolen what she believed to be important, but she had left behind the scribbles of a rambling man. A man who spoke of a woman with piercing blue eyes and a kindness he felt served his daughter well. He wrote about ice cream and secrets, about assumptions and judgments, and about how wrong he had been.

Joanna had sat on the edge of the bed for hours, squinting as she tried to decode her father's erratic handwriting, and as each word was uncovered and each meaning became clear, she cried again. People change, he said. Pressure removed by new surroundings had cleared his mind and friendships born over ice cream had erased his prejudices. Horizons expanded, and acceptance blossomed in a kitchen where two people enjoyed their dessert...and where one hid behind the presumptions of another.

On the night he had first met Addison, Robert was indeed confused, but as Prudence had gathered her things, she had made enough noise to wake the dead. So, after she left his room, he opened his eyes, opened his nightstand, and quickly jotted down his thoughts while the taste of his coconut and lime dessert was still fresh on his palate. Yes, he was confused on the first night they met, but he was never confused again. He knew who Addison was. He knew her connection with Joanna, and on the night he died, on the night Joanna walked into his room appearing more beautiful than he had ever seen her before, he knew the look in her eyes. She was in love...and she was in love with Addison Kane.

Lost in her memories, Joanna stared off into space, giving Addison a chance to steal a few glances. She could see that Joanna had gained a wee bit of weight, and the bodice of her shirt now seemed stretched to its maximum, but Addison couldn't have cared less. Joanna was still the most beautiful woman she had ever seen, and that thought put a ghost of a smile on her face.

"Something funny?"

Addison jerked out of her thoughts. "What? No...no, nothing's funny," Addison said, shaking her head. "It's just...it's just you look good."

It was unexpected, and Joanna silently damned herself for how it made her feel. Holding her head high, she said, "I'd say the same to you, but I'd be lying."

"I've had better days, I guess."

"Yeah?"

"Yes," Addison whispered. "Days spent with you that I never wanted to end, but now every day seems to go on forever."

"I know the feeling."

"You do?"

"Yes, I do," Joanna said, making her way down the rest of the stairs.

The kitchen door swung open, and Evelyn appeared, and even though Addison was surprised the woman was still in the house, she didn't say a word.

"I'm sorry. I was doing some work in my office and didn't know you...you were out here."

"That's fine, Evelyn. I've got what I need for now. I was just leaving," Joanna said as she headed toward the front door with suitcase in hand.

"Wait," Addison called out, taking three long strides to reach the door. "I-I-I don't...I don't even know if...if the baby lived."

"Do you care?" Joanna said, locking eyes with Addison.

"Of course, I care."

"Funny...you didn't seven months ago," Joanna said, and turning on her heel, she walked out of the house and slammed the door.

Before she reached the car, Joanna was fighting the urge to run back into the house. She had tried for months to convince herself she no longer loved Addison, but it had all been lies. Lies to cover up the pain and the hurt, and lies to cover up desire so strong it took her breath away; she had lived them for months until the truth finally slapped her in the face one

Saturday afternoon. Standing in the middle of a shop filled with nursery furniture, trying to decide what would go best in the room adjacent the master suite at The Oaks, Joanna suddenly realized the future she was planning still contained Addison. From the style of the furnishings to the colors of the room, Joanna had unconsciously chosen everything she knew Addison would like.

As George opened the door to the limo, Joanna looked back at the house, inhaling slowly as she took in all she could see. Behind the front door was the woman she would always love, and it took all the strength she had to climb into the back seat of the limousine, but Joanna's future now contained more than Addison, and if Addison wanted to be a part of it, she'd have to prove it.

***

Evelyn winced when the door slammed, but then quickly turned her attention to Addison, who was standing motionless in the center of the foyer. "What are you waiting for?"

Addison looked at Evelyn. "What do you mean?"

Marching over to Addison, Evelyn placed her hands on her hips. "If you don't go after her, you are by far the largest imbecile on this planet."

"She hates me."

"She hates what you *did*. She hates what you *said*, and she hates that you ran *away* and left her alone, but look around, Addison. Look around at this once gloomy, dreadful house. Can't you see that Joanna has made it into a home? If she had any intention of walking out that door and never coming back, why would she have done all of this?"

"I don't know," Addison said in a breath as she shook her head.

"Damn it all to hell, stop being a stupid cow! You gave up your bloody company because you apparently cared about Robert a hell of a lot more than any of us imagined, but now you're just going to let the love of your life leave without a fight?"

"I'm all fought out."

"Bollocks!" Evelyn said as she grabbed Addison's arm to get her attention. "Addison, let it all go. Let go of your past. Let go of your father's words because they were the words of an idiot, and they sure as hell weren't a prophecy. She's alive, and she's right out there. Fight like you've never fought before, Addison! Tear down the rest of the walls around your goddamned, bloody heart and tell her you love her."

"I have!" Addison shouted, pulling out of Evelyn's grasp.

"Then tell it to her again and *mean* it, but don't just *use* the word. Breathe the word. Live the word. Show the word. *Promise* the word! Tell her what that word means to you, because that's what she needs to hear. That's what she needs to see."

"I-I-I don't know how—"

"Yes, you do," Evelyn said as she poked her finger against Addison's chest. "It's right in there. You just need to let it speak for itself. Tell her the truth, Addison, or you'll regret it until the day you die."

Frozen in place, seconds ticked by as Addison stared at Evelyn. The last seven months had been filled with days that seemed to go on forever and drunken nights that blurred, but did not erase. Consumed by so much anguish and loneliness, even after returning to England she felt as if each breath was a struggle...and the cure was driving away.

Addison bolted for the door, her feet barely touching the patio and steps as she made her way to the drive, and seeing the sleek, black stretch limo meandering down the gravel fifty yards in the distance, she dashed across the lawns.

The June sun was shining brightly, the day warmer than any so far, and beads of sweat began to appear on Addison's brow as she made her way across her property. Having not run on a treadmill for months, the muscles in her thighs and calves began to tighten, but instead of slowing to a jog to ease the ache forming in her legs, she lengthened her stride and pushed the pain aside.

For three years, George and his wife had put up with Addison's antics and her attitude. They had been yelled at and ignored, and he had spent countless days repairing panels on collectible cars when Addison's foot had found their paint, so when he spied her in the side-view mirror his reaction was instinctive. He had traveled the drive hundreds of times, and he knew exactly the speed needed to prevent damage to the car, but as memories invaded his mind, George applied a bit more pressure to the accelerator. His eyes were glued to the mirror, the smallest of grins appearing on his face as Addison's reflection reduced in size. When he saw her trip and fall, face planting into the grass like a sack of seed, it was all he could do not to laugh out loud, but then he looked in the rearview mirror and saw Joanna crying.

She had always been so kind, and over the past few months, he had seen her grieve for a love lost. The sparkle in her eyes had dimmed at times, and the easiness of her smile had waned, and it was all because of the woman now lying like a heap in the grass behind them. A woman who, several months earlier, had stopped barking orders. A woman who had begun to notice them, thank them, and at times had even smiled at them. Addison *had* started to change, and it was all because of love, and George knew love. Thirty-five years together and going strong, he couldn't imagine a life without Fiona in it. She was his everything, and as God was his witness, he knew Addison was Joanna's, so lifting his foot off the pedal, the car slowed to a crawl.

Addison pushed herself off the ground, and feeling as if she was on fire, she stripped off her jacket and tie before taking chase again. Sprinting like a deer across grass, thick and green, she gulped for air and prayed for surefootedness, and a minute later she reached the limo which had stopped only a few yards from the gate.

Joanna felt the car slow to a stop, and peering through the side window, she saw the gates were open. Pressing the button for the intercom, she said, "Why are we stopping, George?"

Before George could say a word, Joanna's door opened. Sunlight poured in, and for an instant, Joanna leaned toward the passenger side as instincts took over.

"Please...Joanna, please...please get out...get out of the car," Addison said, gasping for air.

"No!" Joanna said, reaching for the door handle.

A crowbar couldn't have broken Addison's grip on the door, and holding it firmly, she said, "Please just...just give me five minutes. Five minutes, that's all I ask."

Chapter Forty-Five

Joanna closed her eyes. Was she stupid to have hope? Was she stupid to love the woman standing outside the car even after all she had done? With a heavy sigh, Joanna opened her eyes and slowly climbed from the limo. Closing the door, she turned to face Addison, but immediately lost her train of thought when she saw Addison's appearance. Beads of perspiration were rolling down her face, and the knees of her trousers and front of her shirt were stained with grass. Narrowing her eyes, Joanna leaned slightly to the right to look past Addison. She could see a faint track of bent grass not yet having time to find the sun again, and the path ran from the front of the house to where Addison now stood.

Joanna scowled as she focused on Addison. "What's this all about?"

Addison drew in a breath, filling her lungs to their maximum before she let the air out slowly and with it, her ego, her pride, and her past. "I was a fool."

"Why, because I lived?"

"No, because Millie died."

"What?"

"When I got off that plane, and David didn't know where you were, I went crazy. I called Fran and Millie and Evelyn, and none of them would tell me anything. Three people I thought were my friends turned their backs on me, and all I saw was red."

"Why am I not surprised?" Joanna said, folding her arms.

Addison knew she deserved every ounce of contempt Joanna could throw her way. She was more than willing to take it, but while repentant, she forced herself to look Joanna in the eye. She needed for Joanna to see that the words she was about to speak were heartfelt, and she prayed that in the misted-over crystalline blue of her eyes, Joanna would see just that.

"For four days I drank myself stupid and then Evelyn walked into the library and told me that Millie had...Millie had passed in her sleep, and all of a sudden everything came crashing down around me. Millie was gone. The woman who had been my right and left hand for years was *gone*. The woman who had never uttered a harsh word about anyone was gone. She'll never know that I loved her. She'll never know how I adored that pinched, peeved look she'd get when I'd do something she didn't like, and she'll never know that sometimes, sometimes I'd do something just...just to see that look. And she'll never know how it made me smile on the inside because I never realized just how precious time was until now."

Joanna had her own secret smile forming, but while Addison's words seemed sincere, Joanna's heart had yet to melt completely. There was more she needed to hear, so she casually looked at her watch. "Speaking of time, I have someplace to be, so if you're through—"

"I'm not," Addison said, taking a step in Joanna's direction. "Joanna, I'm sorry. Seven months ago, I was a fool. Seven months ago, I was terrified that my father's words were true. That I was a murderer, and... and you were going to be my next victim. I was so bloody scared of losing you, I couldn't see straight. All I knew is that I had finally found someone who gave meaning to my life, someone who made sense out of the senseless and light out of the dark, and made my nights so blissful, so exquisitely alive, my heart felt like it was going to explode. Joanna, you have more courage than I will ever have, and convictions I can only pray one day to attain, and whether you drive through that gate right now or remain by my side, I will love you for the rest of my life."

Addison paused and took a ragged breath as her emotions began to get the better of her. "I can never apologize enough for the hell I've put you through, but I promise you, Joanna, I promise you, as God is my witness, I will spend the rest of my days loving you like no one else ever could. Please, please just give me another chance. I'll do anything you want. I swear to God...I'll do *anything* you want."

Joanna lifted her chin and re-crossing her arms, she gave herself the time she needed to harness the emotions she knew would leak out in her tone. Clearing her throat, she said, "Is that so?"

A shiver ran down Addison's spine. She had spoken the truth in the only way she knew how. She had opened her heart and confessed her mistakes, her fears, and her undying love, but Joanna's tone had remained cold and flat, and feeling like she had just been sucker punched, Addison fell to her knees, bowing her head seconds before her tears overflowed.

With her vision blurred by emotion, she hadn't seen the hint of a smile in Joanna's eyes, so when Addison heard her walk away, her shoulders began to quake as she tried to smother her cries. Kneeling in the grass, she listened as the car door opened, and then a minute later it closed, but just as she felt herself suffocating from her sobs, a pair of feet came into view. Feet wearing trainers Addison knew belonged to Joanna. Drawing in a shuddering breath, Addison looked up.

"How are you at changing nappies?" Joanna said, her smile no longer hidden.

Blinded by the sun, Addison raised her hand to block its brilliance just as George appeared with an umbrella, casting a shadow, large and round, over both the women.

Addison blinked to clear the spots left from the sun, and then she blinked again. Enough time had passed since her sprint across the lawns for her heart rate to return to normal, but it slowly began to increase again when she blinked one more time.

Joanna stood patiently waiting for Addison to get to her feet, but when the woman remained squatted on the ground, Joanna decided a nudge was in order. "Are you planning to stay down there all day or would you like to come up here and meet your daughter?"

Addison's mouth dropped open, the blood slowly siphoning from her face as she stared up at Joanna.

"You really shouldn't keep her waiting. Trust me, she won't be this quiet for long."

Addison rested back on her haunches as her breath was knocked from her body, and sniffling back her tears, she wiped the remainder from her face and got to her feet.

The birds in the trees ceased to chirp, the sun ceased to heat, and the breeze ceased to blow as Addison gazed at the slumbering baby in Joanna's arms. All of a sudden, she felt dizzy, and her heart began to race, but then Addison felt something else, something she had never felt before. A sense of purpose that far outreached any she could have ever imagined. A sense of pride, of hope, of miracles, and of love, it was so overwhelming that while she believed her tears had dried up, Addison was wrong.

Overcome, tears welled in her eyes as they remained locked on the babe swaddled in a pink blanket.

"Her name's Sheridan. It means bright and untamed...just like her mother," Joanna said quietly, her eyes fixed on the woman she loved.

"She's so...she's so tiny," Addison said in a whisper.

"Yeah, that she is," Joanna said. "She came a bit early."

Addison stared at the baby in Joanna's arms, and in awe, time stood still as she burned the moment into her memory. Her daughter's cheeks were rosy and round, and her lips so pink and full that Addison knew if Sheridan ever pouted, she'd own Addison in an instant. Entranced by the child, Addison's expression remained frozen until she saw a few wisps of thin hair sprouting from the baby's head. They were the color of cinnamon, just like Joanna's.

"She's...she's beautiful," Addison said, raising her eyes. "She's...she's *so* beautiful."

"Yeah, she takes after her mum."

"Which one?" Addison said, a glint of humor appearing on her face as she looked at Joanna.

"You'll see when she opens her eyes."

Addison grew an inch taller. "Yeah?"

Joanna nodded, preferring to remain quiet as she watched Addison fall in love with their daughter, but when Addison reached out toward the baby, Joanna took a quick step backward and bumped right into George. Even though she probably owed George an apology, Joanna was more concerned about Addison's reaction. She had snatched her hand back as if it had been hit by a ruler, and her head now hung like that of a penitent child's.

Joanna sighed. "Christ, I'm sorry."

"No, I'm...I'm sorry," Addison said as she looked up. "I just...I just wanted to touch her."

"And you can," Joanna said, taking a step closer. "Blame it on me being a new mum, Addison, but your hands, they're filthy."

Addison looked down at her hands, and seeing the grass stains and dirt covering both, she paled. "Shit," she said, wiping them on her trousers. "I'm sorry. I didn't know."

"I know you didn't, and I'm sorry I pulled her away."

"No," Addison blurted, squaring her shoulders. "Don't you *ever* be sorry for protecting our daughter."

Joanna's heart did a flip as the last sliver of her doubt about Addison's sincerity disappeared. Her response had been natural and that of a parent, and with words spoken not by thought, but by instinct, Joanna now knew she'd be Addison's wife until the day she died.

Addison was having a hard time reading Joanna's expression, but as she looked at her holding their child, Addison said the first thing that came to her mind. "I love her...and I love you."

Joanna gazed at Addison. "I know you do."

"And I'll never run away again."

"No?"

"No," Addison said, but as she opened her mouth to continue, she heard the sound of bells coming from Joanna's pocket.

"Crap," Joanna said, pulling her mobile from her jeans. "I need to go," she said, shutting off the alarm before carefully moving around the car to place Sheridan back into her car seat.

A shadow of sadness swept over Addison's face as she watched in silence while Joanna put their daughter in the car. "Wait. Joanna, I thought...I mean...didn't anything I said make a difference? I thought we were..." Addison stopped and stared at the ground. "Never mind. I guess I was wrong."

"I could get used to you admitting you were wrong," Joanna said as she rounded the car. "But this isn't one of those times." Leaning in, Joanna placed a small kiss on Addison's cheek. "I love you, and we have a lot of things to talk about, but right now I have somewhere else I need to be."

"But...but when will I see you again?"

Joanna let out a small laugh. "In an hour, that is if you let me leave right now."

"An hour? You're...you're coming back here?"

"Well, the last time I checked, it was my home."

"But I thought...you've not been here so...so I thought...I thought you moved out."

"Like I said, we have lots to talk about, but now isn't the time," Joanna said as she placed her hand on Addison's arm. "Go get yourself cleaned up, and I'll be back before you know it."

"Promise?"

A dazzling smile spread across Joanna's face. "Absolutely."

***

Joanna chuckled as she watched Addison dash across the front lawns. After swiveling around to make sure Sheridan was still asleep, Joanna pressed the intercom button. "We can go now, George."

"Why didn't you tell her?"

Joanna looked over as Fran made her way from the furthest seat to the one nearest Joanna. "I thought you were on the phone with that Reece fellow."

"I was, but afterward I...um..." Fran pointed to a nearby window, now partially cracked open.

"You were eavesdropping?"

"Well, I didn't want to interrupt."

"So, you listened instead?"

"It's what lawyers do," Fran said, grinning back at Joanna. "Besides, when I heard you not mention a certain something, I thought I'd best stay in the shadows. It would be kind of hard to explain why I'm driving around with you if she saw me."

"True. I didn't think of that."

"Oh, and by the way, congratulations on the reconciliation. I couldn't be more thrilled."

"Thank you," Joanna said, her eyes creasing at the corners.

"So...why didn't you tell her?"

A sly smile slowly made its way across Joanna's face. "Would you?"

Fran's expression remained neutral for only a moment before she let loose with a loud guffaw. "Not on your life!"

Amused, Joanna joined in Fran's merriment until Sheridan began to cry.

"Shit, I'm sorry," Fran said, leaning forward to take a peek at the baby. "I woke her up."

"No, you didn't," Joanna said, checking her watch. "She's hungry."

"Oh my," Fran said with a snicker as she relaxed back on the seat. "Guess I'm going to see your tits again, huh?"

Joanna's life had changed drastically since meeting Addison, but six weeks shy of her thirtieth birthday, she knew she could add another change to the list. Joanna now had a best friend, and she was one who had unselfishly stood in for Addison for the past seven months.

Shocked and angry when she found out Addison had fled to Spain, Fran was at Joanna's side before the corporate jet had landed in Madrid, and she remained there throughout Joanna's pregnancy.

Their friendship had started in a house in Burnt Oak, but it blossomed as Joanna's belly began to grow. In the beginning, Fran's intent had only been to lend a shoulder to lean on, but when Joanna's tears eventually dried up, and she finally wanted to get out of the house, who better to go shopping with than Fran.

With two sisters, both of whom had children, Fran was well versed with what shops catering to babies and expectant mothers contained, so when they entered the first, Joanna was tickled with Fran's enjoyment of her surroundings. She tinkered with mobiles, played with baubles, tittered at the tiny shoes lined up in a row, and pulled outfit after outfit from the racks, eagerly stating she adored each and every one. She chatted with the clerks as if she was the one expecting, asking all the things Joanna had forgotten to ask, and by the end of the day, Joanna felt better than she had in weeks.

It was nice to have someone to talk to, and even though Evelyn had always been there for her, having a friend closer to her own age made Joanna feel less alone. So, a few days later, feeling slightly nervous about her upcoming twelfth-week prenatal appointment, Joanna called Fran and asked if she would be willing to go with her, and Fran didn't have to think twice before she answered.

One appointment led to two and then to three, until Fran took it upon herself to coordinate her schedule with that of Joanna's. They spent their weekends shopping until the nursery was complete and Joanna's wardrobe overflowed with maternity clothes, and afterward, they met for lunches in the city and dinner at The Oaks with Millie. And when Joanna's due date approached, Fran was honored when Joanna asked for her help again.

Acting as her coach, Fran sat by Joanna's side during four weeks of natural childbirth classes, and then again, at ones involving the basics of babies, infant CPR, and how to nurse your child, and when Joanna was brought into the delivery room, bleeding and afraid, Fran was there to hold her hand through it all.

She had stumbled only once in their friendship when she had tried to get a hold of Addison, but the misstep had come from love and concern, and it was quickly excused by the woman who had become Fran's best friend as well.

"Sorry, no tit viewing in the car," Joanna said, chuckling as she opened the bag to her side and pulled out a baby bottle. "That's why I had George stop at the house. I can't believe I forgot to do it, but I knew she wasn't going to last and I sure as hell wasn't going to make it back to the hotel."

"Oh, you pumped."

"It was either that, or I was going to explode," Joanna said as she began to feed Sheridan.

"Funny how things work, isn't it?"

"What do you mean?"

"Well, if I'm not mistaken, you had no intention of coming home as long as Addison was here, yet something you *never* forgot before...you did today. Now, here you are, your life forever changed because you produce milk like a Holstein."

In an instant, Joanna was reduced to a fit of giggles, and unable to hold the bottle still, Sheridan began to squawk almost instantly.

"Oh bugger, slide a cheek," Fran said, slipping between Sheridan and Joanna. Placing the nipple back into Sheridan's mouth, within seconds the only sound in the limo was Joanna, who was still trying to rein in her amusement.

"You know, it's amazing how much I know about babies now," Fran said as she adjusted Sheridan's blanket. "I mean, I learned a fair bit with my nieces and nephews, but nothing like this."

"That's not necessarily a bad thing," Joanna said as she wiped away her tears of laughter. "That way you'll be prepared when it happens to you."

"I'm not sure that day's going to come."

"No? But you love children. That's obvious."

"I do, but Connie...well, if you think Addison is a workaholic, you need to meet my partner," Fran said with a snort. "Not that we've never talked about it, especially once you got preggers, but she's just not parent material. She loves her work, and I think she loves me, but children, they're not in the cards. She's much too single-minded for that."

"That's a shame."

Fran shrugged. "It is what it is, and besides it gives me the chance to spoil everyone else's children and still go home to a quiet house."

"I don't know, after all these months of quiet, I think I'm going to like a little noise."

"*You're* not the one we need to worry about."

Joanna gave the woman a side-eyed glance. "Give her a little credit, Fran. Addison may not know a lot about babies, but she knows they cry." Seeing Fran's eyes instantly grow larger, Joanna let out a snort. "Okay, well if not, she's in for a surprise."

Fran smiled, and as she did, she spied her mobile still sitting on the seat across the way. "Oh, speaking of surprises, I have another to add to your list."

Chapter Forty-Six

Evelyn came out of the kitchen and sighed. After rushing into the house for a much-needed shower, Addison ran back down the stairs and planted herself on the step third from the bottom, where she had remained for the last half hour. "You really need to learn some patience."

"I thought I had, but..." Addison stopped and scowled. "Where the *hell* did she go?"

"That's not for me to say," Evelyn said, keeping her grin to a minimum.

"And why did she rent a bloody limo? It's almost as if she was planning to...well, to run away."

Evelyn rolled her eyes. "She's not planning to do what you did, and she rented the limo because nothing in your garage is equipped with seat belts. Something that's necessary when you have an infant carrier."

"Oh," Addison said, and staring at the floor, she began to ramble. "But she said she'd be back in an hour, and she's not here. Maybe she's not coming back. Maybe she...maybe she lied just so...just so she could get away from me."

Evelyn felt her mobile vibrating in her pocket again, and hiding her excitement at the message she knew it contained, she crept toward the front door, thankful Addison wasn't paying attention.

Unable to rid herself of the insecurities whirling around in her head, Addison furrowed her brow. There were still so many things she needed to say to Joanna, but because of some errand, Addison was put on the back burner. It wasn't a good feeling, yet how many times had she done the same thing to Joanna? Working too late, traveling the continent...running away.

Addison drew in a long breath, and pushing her anxieties aside, she raised her eyes to continue her conversation with Evelyn. Discovering Evelyn was no longer standing next to her, Addison flinched back her head, and as she quickly looked around, she saw Joanna standing just inside the front door with a baby carrier in her hand.

"Joanna," Addison said, jumping to her feet. "I didn't hear you come in."

"I know. We planned it that way," Joanna said, stepping aside to allow Fran to enter.

Having not seen Fran since the board meeting, Addison smiled at her friend, but as she rounded the table to greet them both, Addison came to a stuttered stop when she noticed Fran was holding an identical carrier. "Fran, you...you had a baby?"

Fran pressed her lips together for a moment, and casting a quick wink in Joanna's direction, she said, "It wasn't me."

Addison's eyes darted back and forth between Joanna and Fran as she tried to find a clue to the amusement showing on both of their faces, but coming up empty, she honed in on the two carriers the women were holding. Both were black, and both had gray trim, but while one had a blanket of pink...the other had a blanket of blue.

Addison's mouth dropped open, and stumbling back a half-step, she fixed her eyes on Joanna. "You...you had twins?"

Joanna beamed. "Yes, *we* did."

"You...we...we have twins?" Addison said, taking another half-step backward.

Evelyn saw Addison begin to sway a half-second before Joanna did, and rushing to her side, she wrapped an arm around her waist. "I think you need to sit down."

Addison stared blankly at Evelyn. "We...we have twins."

"Yes, I know," Evelyn said, her eyes creasing at the corners. "But you're not going to be able to enjoy them if you faint in the middle of the foyer."

"I'm...I'm not going to faint," Addison said as she stepped away from Evelyn. "I'm just...I'm just shocked."

"So was Joanna when she found out," Fran said, snickering. "I squealed, and she went pale."

"Wait...what?" Addison said, looking at Fran.

"While you were...um...*away*, I stood in for you."

"You did?"

When she saw Fran nod, Addison bowed her head, paused, and then raised her eyes. "Thank you."

"You're quite welcome, and I'd like to say I'd do it again, but..." Fran stopped and eyed Joanna. "Hell, I'd do it again in a heartbeat, but I don't think there'll be a need. Do you?"

"None whatsoever," Addison said as she gazed at Joanna. "If we have more children, I'll be there for them from start to finish. I promise."

Joanna smiled, and taking a few steps, she placed the carrier on the table in the center of the foyer. "Well, before we discuss having any more, would you like to meet your son?"

"Very much," Addison said, moving to stand by Joanna's side.

Addison held her breath as Joanna moved aside the blue blanket and when her son came into view, wearing the tiniest of blue stocking caps, Addison's eyes filled with tears. "Oh my God," she said in a breath. "He's...he's beautiful, but...but he's so small. Smaller than Sheridan."

"That he is. It's why he couldn't come home until today. He had a few issues—"

"Issues?" Addison blurted.

"His lungs were congested, but he's fine now. He was given a clean bill of health earlier today."

Addison looked at her son again, marveling at his angelic face and the dark brown threads of hair escaping his cap. "And his name?"

"Well, I hope you don't mind, but I named him Robert Sheppard Kane. Once it came into my head, nothing else seemed to fit."

Addison's skin prickled as goosebumps sprouted on her skin, and fighting to restrain the tears threatening to escape, she looked at Joanna. "No, I don't mind at all. It's a good name, and it's an honest name, and I'll make sure he does it proud."

"*You* will, will you?"

The corners of Addison's mouth arched upward. "*We* will."

"I'm glad you agree," Joanna said, her eyes creasing at the corners as she picked up the carrier. "Now, if you ladies don't mind, how about we get these two settled in the nursery, so I have a few minutes to relax before they're hungry again."

"Wait," Addison said as she looked from Fran to Evelyn and then back to Joanna. "We have a nursery?"

Joanna snickered and motioned toward the stairs, and one by one the women followed her. As they came to a stop at the doors leading into the east wing, Joanna reached into her pocket and pulled out a key, and noticing Addison immediately arch an eyebrow, she grinned. "I'm sorry, but if you saw this...well, I'd have shown my hand, and I wasn't yet prepared to do that."

Unlocking the doors, everyone followed Joanna to the first door on the left, and unlocking it as well, she said, "And to answer your question, yes, we have a nursery."

***

An hour later, the babies were comfortable in their cots and Addison was in awe. Yet to have learned what apparently they already knew, Addison had stood back and watched as Fran, Evelyn, and Joanna extracted the twins from their carriers, changed their nappies, and got the babies settled into the cribs, all the while cooing at the sleepy infants or chattering to each other like it was just another day.

They had no idea Addison was memorizing their movements, pressing into the recesses of her brain every word spoken, every smile displayed, and every gurgle bubbling from the pouty lips of her children. They had no idea she would never forget this day, and they had no idea just how close she was to crying...again.

Addison cleared her throat, and blinking back her tears of joy, she focused on her surroundings in hopes of getting her emotions in check.

Joanna had turned yet another place in the house into something to talk about. The walls of the nursery had been painted a pale, blue-green, and the draperies were the color of ivory. The wood moldings were now white to match the furniture filling the room, and while the dark tones of the oak planking could be seen around the edge, a thick carpet matching the hue of the drapes covered the floor. In the far corner was an L-shaped crib made for two, and to the left and right of it were identical changing tables and tall, narrow wardrobes, all displaying hardware of either pink or blue. Along the wall nearest the doorways were two matching cushioned rockers and between them, a small table holding a lamp decorated with baby animals. But of all the items in the room, the ones that caught Addison's attention and held it was the two mobiles hanging above the cribs. Spinning ever so slowly were butterflies hanging from threads dangling from plastic rainbows of red, orange, yellow, green, blue, and purple.

Hearing a slight hum, Addison scanned the room, and noticing the tiniest of refrigerators just off to her right, she frowned as she tried to discern its purpose.

Joanna, concerned Addison hadn't seemed interested in helping with their children's care, left Evelyn and Fran to chatter quietly near the cribs while she went over and stood by Addison's side. "You know, I'm not opposed to hiring a nanny to help out, but she won't be here twenty-four-seven. So, you really need to learn how to do some of these things."

"I know," Addison said, rubbing the back of her neck. "I just...I just feel so inadequate right now.

Joanna sighed. "Addison, I have over a dozen books you can read if you'd like, and the classes I took meet every month so if you want to attend a few, I wouldn't mind."

"Classes?"

"Yeah," Joanna said, bobbing her head. "Baby basics, infant CPR—"

"*CPR!*"

"Ssshh," Joanna said, holding a finger to her lips as she tried not to laugh "You're going to wake them up."

"Sorry," Addison said, lowering her voice. "But CPR? You said they were fine."

"It's just precautionary for *all* parents, not just us."

"Oh, thank God," Addison said, placing her hand over her heart.

"Anyway, if you'd like to go to some of them, we can. I don't mind."

"I'd like that, but can we bring the teacher here instead? I think I'd be a little bit more comfortable if...um...it was more private. I mean, I'm still Addison Kane. You know?"

"Yes, you certainly are," Joanna said, smiling as she reached down and threaded her fingers through Addison's. "And I'll call them tomorrow and see what we can arrange. How's that?"

"That would be great. Thanks."

"Ladies, I hate to disturb you, but dinner is ready," Fiona said quietly as she stood in the doorway. "I can prepare trays and bring them up if you'd like?"

"No, that won't be necessary, Fiona," Joanna said. "We'll be right down. Thank you."

Without having to be asked, Fran and Evelyn followed Fiona from the room, but as Joanna was about to do the same, she noticed Addison hadn't moved. "You coming?"

"No, I thought perhaps I'd stay here, just to keep an eye on them. The dining room is a fair distance away, and I wouldn't want them to wake up and be scared."

Joanna's heart melted into a puddle again. Taking Addison by the arms, she spun her around and pointed toward the ceiling. "You see those?"

Addison squinted. "Is that a camera?"

"It's actually a dock of three, all of which are controlled by the state-of-the-art monitoring system I had installed," Joanna said as she picked up two hand-held units sitting on the table by the door. "No matter where we are in the house, with these, you not only can see the babies, but you can also hear them. So, if they so much as pass gas, we'll know it."

"I'm not sure I'm going to like *that*," Addison said, arching an eyebrow as she studied the monitor in her hand.

Joanna's dimples quickly appeared. "There's also an app. It's already on my phone and Evelyn's, and I can put it on yours if you'd like. That way, no matter where we are, we can always look into this room, which means we can even go *out* to dinner and still keep an eye on them. Well, as long as we have a nanny, that is."

"I thought you didn't want one of those. Nannies, I mean."

"That was before I had twins."

"Are two that much harder than one?"

Joanna cocked back her head. "Um...how about you ask me that again in a couple of hours."

***

After dinner was over, Joanna was not surprised in the least when Fran and Evelyn both offered to spend the night. She knew they had also noticed Addison's reluctance earlier in the nursery when it came to tending to the babies, but Joanna also knew the best way to learn how to swim...was to be thrown into the deep end.

Hugs and well wishes were exchanged at the front door, and waves were given as the two women drove away, and no sooner had Joanna closed the door when the sound of their children's cries came over the hand-held monitors.

"Looks like that's our cue," Joanna said, heading to the stairs. "Time to be mums."

Addison scrubbed her hand over her face. Taking a deep breath, she followed Joanna up the steps, and into a room filled with the sound of hungry babies.

"Christ, what's wrong with them?" Addison said, rushing over to the cribs.

Joanna suppressed a giggle as she opened the tiny fridge and placed a bottle in a warmer. "They're hungry and probably wet, but the wet can wait," she said as she went over and lifted Sheridan from the cot. "And since I haven't yet mastered the art of feeding two at once, you get her, and I'll get him."

"Oh, no, I—" Addison's words were cut off when Joanna placed the wailing infant against her chest.

"Just cradle her in your arms and keep her head supported. It's easy."

Addison stared at Sheridan as if she had come from another planet. "But...but she's crying."

"Yes, and she will continue to do so until she gets fed," Joanna said, stifling a grin. "Now, go sit down and just try to relax. Her bottle will be ready in a tick."

Joanna picked up Robert, and cradling him in her arms, she turned around only to discover Addison was walking slower than a turtle across the room. This time there was no stopping Joanna's grin and catching up to Addison with one step, she said, "I'm almost positive she's not carrying nitro, Addison, so she won't explode if jostled."

Sniggering to herself, Joanna grabbed the bottle from the warmer and then sat down. Waiting until Addison took a seat, Joanna handed her the bottle. "Just tilt it slightly, put the nipple in her mouth, and she'll do the rest."

Addison held her breath as she followed Joanna's instructions and when Sheridan wrapped her lips around the bottle's nipple and began to suckle, a smile spread across Addison's face. "She's eating."

"Yes, I had no doubt she would."

Entranced with the baby in her arms, a few minutes passed before Addison raised her eyes, and when she did, she froze. Unlike Sheridan, who was happily consuming her bottled dinner, Robert was enjoying his straight from his mother's breast.

Joanna gently ran her finger down Robert's face as he suckled. Preoccupied with feeding her son, it wasn't until she noticed that the room had gone curiously silent when she raised her eyes and found Addison staring back at her. "What's wrong?"

"Oh...um...nothing," Addison said as her focus kept changing from Joanna's eyes to her breast. "I just...I just never saw anything so incredibly breathtaking as that." Raising her eyes, she said, "You're amazing."

"I'm just a mum," Joanna said, looking down at the baby at her breast. "And this comes with the territory."

"So, how come she gets a bottle and he gets the real thing? Playing favorites already?"

"No, silly," Joanna said, shaking her head. "They're both getting the real thing. Like I said, I haven't really had time to learn how to comfortably feed them together, and since I have help, why struggle?"

"What do you mean they're both getting the real thing?" The look Joanna gave her was one Addison had seen before, and if her count was correct, it was the sixth time she had seen it that day. "What?"

"I didn't say anything."

"You didn't have to. You have *dolt* written all over your face."

"I do not," Joanna said as merriment danced in her eyes.

"Yes, you do, and I can't blame you. I'm probably asking really stupid questions, but it's better than asking none at all. Isn't it?"

"You're absolutely right, so to answer your question, I pumped," she said, pointing across the room.

Addison followed Joanna's finger, and seeing what looked like a ray gun sitting atop a cabinet, Addison tilted her head to the side. A second later, the penny dropped. "Oh, right," she said, looking back at Joanna. "You used a...um...a breast pump."

"Exactly."

"Does it hurt?"

Joanna's dimples sprang to life. "No, it doesn't."

"Good," Addison said, returning her attention to Sheridan.

It was the first time they had truly been alone all day, and while Addison remained focused on the baby in her arms, Joanna remained focused on Addison. Her loss of weight couldn't be missed, but it wasn't until just then when Joanna began to notice the other changes in her wife. Threads of gray now intertwined with those of dark brown and laugh lines once appearing only when Addison smiled, now seemed to be permanent. Yet, the most drastic change was that the hardness which had once enveloped Addison, the stern look, the rigid jaw, the sculpted marble of her façade that had remained in place for years, was gone. To Joanna, Addison appeared to be at peace now. Comfortable in her skin, in her life, and in her love, her features had calmed, adding more to her beauty than Joanna ever thought possible.

As she continued to covertly stare at her wife, Joanna noticed Addison seem enthralled with something in the corner of the room, and following her line of sight, Joanna grinned as she turned back to Addison. "You know, I bought those mobiles to entertain the babies, not you."

Caught in the act, Addison gazed at her wife. "I know it's going to sound odd, but the butterflies kind of remind me of...well, of me, although I'm not that colorful."

"As long as we're not talking about language, I'd have to agree," Joanna said, smiling. "But I don't see the connection."

Addison took a moment to get her thoughts together. "Butterflies start their lives in a cocoon, and protected from things that could harm them, they grow into adulthood and then emerge, spread their wings and fly away. Away from their past and toward their present, never looking back, never caring where they come from, almost like me. Except, you see, I could never stop looking back and remembering how...how painful it was to love someone who never returned that love.

"When I was young...when I was a child, I loved my father. I mean, that's what you're supposed to do, right? Love your parents? But all that brought me was pain and rejection, nasty words, and nastier looks, and an overwhelming feeling of being so worthless that more than once I wished I was the one who had died at birth instead of my brother. Why was I even alive? After all, if your father doesn't love you, how could anyone else? So, I didn't even try. It was easier that way, and to make sure I never got hurt again, I built this fortress, this cocoon, and I wouldn't let anyone in. Not Evelyn, not Fran, not even my grandfather.

"I sometimes question whether he actually loved me, or did he just see in me something my father didn't possess, so he took me under his wing to hone me until I fit the mold he needed, a mold he knew my father would never fit into. I can't tell you how many nights I've lain awake trying to remember if he ever *said* he loved me. He said I was a good girl, and I was smart. He said I was sharp, and...and I was pretty, but...but love? Love was a word I can't remember him ever uttering. Yeah, from his actions you would think that he did love me, but then again, who knows? Maybe he just saw me as a means to an end," Addison said with a shrug. "Anyway, I lived in my self-made cocoon, safe from harm and safe from words I would never have believed if they *had* been spoken...and then you came along, and everything changed.

"You forced me to emerge from that fortress of mine. No..." Addison said, shaking her head. "You made me want to. You made me want to trust and to believe, and to spread my wings and escape that safe place I had built for myself. The only difference between butterflies and me is that they are born from cocoons, and I was..." Addison stopped and chuckled under her breath. "I was...born out of wedlock."

Joanna raised her eyebrows and grinned. "I'm fairly certain that's not the correct connotation for that particular saying."

"Well, maybe it should be. If I can be sitting here today with my wife and my children, looking forward to a future filled with love and family, why can't something else change, too? If there's one thing I've learned is that seeing the good in something is so much better than seeing the bad."

"Yeah?"

"Yes," Addison said with a nod. "Having meals with those you love is more important than the clothes they wear at the dinner table. Appreciating someone's need to be vital, to work with their hands, to create something that all can enjoy is better than condemning them for something you're not yet able to see. And instead of fearing the future, you need to remember there's no guarantee any of us will have tomorrow. If you walk away...if you *run* away, you're losing time you can't get back. So, instead of worrying about what lies ahead, cherish what you have, while you have it."

Addison looked down at the baby in her arms. Sheridan seemed quite content sucking down her dinner, so taking a deep breath and holding it, Addison gingerly got to her feet. Pleased that her movements hadn't disturbed Sheridan, Addison carefully knelt down in front of Joanna. "I'd like to say something. It's something I've said to you before, and I'm not really sure if I can remember exactly how it goes, but I'd like to try. That is if you don't mind."

There was no reason to feel anxious. Addison's tone was soft and her expression, loving and kind, but that didn't stop Joanna's stomach from fluttering. "Um...okay?"

Sensing Joanna's nervousness, Addison offered her a warm smile before she began to speak. "From this day forward, for better or for worse, for richer or poorer, in sickness and in health, and 'til death do us part, I'll love you with all my heart...and I'll never leave your side again."

Joanna's eyes overflowed with tears, and leaning forward she met Addison half-way so they could share a kiss. It was gentle and tentative, lasting for only a moment, and even though it wasn't meant to arouse...it did.

"I love you," Joanna whispered as she rested back in her chair.

"I love you, too," Addison said, returning to her seat.

"And I know you meant what you said, but eventually you will have to go back to work."

Addison lowered her chin, and letting out a sigh, she looked over at Joanna. "There's...um...there's something else I need to tell you."

"Will it make me cry again?"

"I don't know," Addison said as her eyes met Joanna's.

Once again, Joanna's stomach fluttered seeing the sadness in Addison's eyes. "Okay, what is it?"

"I...um...I walked away from the company yesterday. I'm no longer its president or CEO, and AK Investments doesn't take very much of my time, so as far as work's concerned, I really don't have any."

Joanna paused, holding back her grin as best she could. "You owe Fran a raise."

Addison jerked back her head. "What are you talking about? I just told you—"

"I know what you told me. It's the same thing Fran told me yesterday when she called me after the board meeting."

"You knew?"

"Yes."

"Oh," Addison said, hanging her head.

"But today in the car while we were going to get Robert, Fran told me something else. Something you don't know."

"Such as?"

"After you walked out of the meeting, the board went after Fran. They sacked her and threatened to get her disbarred because of her part in our...in our marriage of convenience."

Like a deflated balloon, Addison sagged in her chair. "Oh, Jesus Christ, no."

"Unfortunately for the board, Fran knows a bit more about Kane Holdings and its bylaws than anyone gave her credit for...including you."

Addison's head snapped up. "What do you mean?"

Joanna gave Robert a quick glance before she continued. "It seems that while they were going after you, Fran was spending her time rehashing what she remembered about the company's bylaws. Apparently, she knows them backward and forward."

"Yes, she can almost quote them by section and article. It was truly aggravating at times."

"Well, I don't think you'll find it aggravating any longer," Joanna said, her eyes creasing at the corners. "It seems that the article *following* the one stating that you had to be married by the age of thirty-six is all about what happens if the president is found to be *unable* to continue their position...for whatever reason."

"Okay...?"

"Fran believes it was written to protect the company in case the person in charge fell ill or became incapacitated or perhaps died without a will, but what it states is that if you, for instance, are found unable to continue as president of Kane Holdings, your stock isn't absorbed by the company. It's handed down to your heirs."

Addison sat straight in her chair. "One more time?"

"Sweetheart, Sheridan and Robert are now the majority stockholders of Kane Holdings."

"Are you serious?" Addison said as a smile began to form.

"Yes, and since Sheridan and Robert are a *little* too young to take the helm, and as their parent, you'd be their proxy and represent the majority stockholders of Kane Holdings, the board decided to cut their losses. They voted this morning to keep you as president and CEO of Kane until the time comes for one or both of our children to take your place. It seems they'd prefer to have you on their side, rather than you turning AK Investments into a force to be reckoned with. Oh, and the board also reversed their decision regarding Fran and won't be taking any legal action. Again, they know they'd be facing your wrath and, well...we've all been there."

Addison had listened intently to every word Joanna had said, but when the last slipped from her lips, Addison laughed. "My wrath, eh?"

"Yes, and I...I hope I'm not going to face it now."

"What do you mean?"

"Addison, our children are...are new and these times we won't get back. So, even though you *do* have a job to go to, I'd still like you to take some time off to be a family, even if it's just for a couple of weeks."

Addison gazed at Joanna and then to the children they held in their arms. It had only been a few hours since she'd been introduced to her son and daughter, but in that short amount of time, Addison swore they had changed. Had Robert's chin been that square earlier in the day? Had Sheridan's cheeks suddenly developed the tiniest of dimples or had Addison somehow missed them? Were her eyelashes always that long...or her fingers? Addison stared in wonderment at her daughter, and when Sheridan opened her eyes, the palest of blues met the palest of blues. Tears began to well as the emotion rushing through Addison's body overwhelmed her, and taking a ragged breath, she looked over at Joanna.

"I was thinking months. One, two, six...you name it," Addison said softly. "It's time for me to start trusting people. There are quite a few at Kane worthy of handling projects without me and my wrath, as you so eloquently put it, and Fran is at the top of the list. She knows what I do and how I do it, so along with that raise you insist I owe her, she's going to get a promotion and start pulling a bit more weight. I've got a family to think of now, and they come first."

***

Once the babies were done with their meal, Joanna gave Addison a crash course on how to change a nappy, and Addison's horrified expression at seeing the goopy poo her daughter had produced caused Joanna to giggle more than once. However, resolute in learning the rights and wrongs, Addison scrunched up her nose and got the job done...eventually.

Shortly after that, with the infants again snoozing in their cots, Joanna settled in for a much-needed kip, and Addison happily returned to the nursery to hover over the babies again. Fascinated by the tiny humans clothed in footed sleepsuits covered in pink and blue bunnies, Addison lost track of time until the ache in her back forced her to straighten. Unwilling to leave her children alone, she looked around, and for the next hour, Addison spent her time memorizing all the instructions on every bottle, box, and jar in the room.

Nearly three hours had passed before Addison returned to the master suite, and sitting on the edge of the bed, she placed a light kiss on Joanna's forehead. "Time to get up, darling," she whispered.

A content moan slipped from Joanna's lips as she opened her eyes. "Are they awake?"

"Just beginning to stir, so I thought I'd give you a few minutes to wake up before all hell breaks loose again."

Joanna smiled as she pushed herself into a sitting position. Since that afternoon, a surreal warmth had enveloped her, and gazing at Addison, Joanna knew it would never wane. "I love you."

"You've been saying that a lot today."

"I've been saving up."

"Me, too," Addison said, waggling her eyebrows.

Joanna chuckled and was just about to toss aside the sheets when something caught her eye. "What's that all over your shirt?"

Addison looked down at the stains on the fabric and chuckled. "Robert. He started squirming about an hour ago, so I checked his nappy like you showed me and he was soaked, so I decided to do the deed, but someone forgot to tell me that I needed a shield. I almost grabbed the breast pump, but it was far too small."

Joanna burst out laughing. "Oh my God, I'm sorry! Little boys are different."

"Yes, well I do know that little boys are different from little girls. I just wasn't privy to the distance and arc at which their pee can fly."

Joanna had seen many sides to Addison over the past two years. The good, the bad, the angry, the headstrong, and the intelligent, but this side was as new as it was refreshing.

"Who *are* you and what have you done with the real Addison Kane?" Joanna said with a sparkle in her eye.

"I'm just a woman in love with a woman," Addison said, smiling as she reached over Joanna's hand. "A woman who has given me two beautiful children, and whether they throw up on me a hundred times or pee on me a thousand, I'd rather have that than not have them...or have her." Noticing how Joanna's mouth had gone slack, Addison squeezed her hand as she gazed into her eyes. "I told you, I've changed."

Joanna could feel the goosebumps as they covered her arms, and giving Addison the once over, Joanna leaned her head to the side. "Born out of wedlock – eh?"

Addison grinned. "Growing on you, is it?"

"Yes," Joanna said in a breath as she leaned in for another kiss. "Yes, I think it is."

The End

Thank you for reading *Born Out of Wedlock*. As an Independent author, I have no publicity department or publishing company to depend on to spread the word about my books, so if you liked *Born Out of Wedlock*, I hope you can find a few minutes in your day to return to where you purchased it and leave a comment or a review. If you want to contact me personally, please drop me a line at Lyng227@gmail.com or catch me on Facebook https://www.facebook.com/lyn.gardner.587

Lyn

<u>Acknowledgements</u>

I like to give a tremendously large "thank you" to those who have spent their days, nights, and weekends reading my words. Some may label them editors and others may label them betas or proofreaders, but they are so much more than that. They are my friends. So, to Susan, Marian, Mike, Joyce, Bron, Boni, and Marion...I simply could not have done this without you. You kept me true. You kept me sane. You are utterly amazing!

Other Titles by Author

Give Me A Reason

- Winner of the 2015 National Indie Excellence Awards – LGBT Fiction
- Finalist in the 2015 International Book Awards – Fiction: Gay & Lesbian
- Winner of the Silver Medal 2014 Global Ebook Awards – LGBT Fiction
- Winner of the Silver Medal 2014 eLit Book Awards – Gay/Lesbian Fiction
- Finalist in the GCLS Ann Bannon Popular Choice Awards – 2014
- Finalist in the GCLS Awards for Contemporary Lesbian Fiction – 2014

Intelligent, confident and beautiful, Antoinette Vaughn had it all until one night she went to help a friend and paid for it...with a life sentence in hell.

Four years later, Toni's judgment is overturned, but the damage is already done. She walks from the prison a free woman, but she's hardly free. Actually, she's hardly alive. A prison without rules can do that to a person.

She was raised amidst garden parties, stables and tennis courts, but now a dingy flat in a decrepit building is what Toni calls home. It's cold, dark and barren just like her heart, but it suits her. She doesn't want to leave much behind when she's gone, but the simplicity of her sheltered existence begins to unravel when a beautiful stranger comes into her life.

How does anyone survive in a world that terrifies them? How do you learn to trust again when everyone is your enemy? How do you take your next breath and not wish it were your last? And if your past returned...what would you do

***

Ice

- Finalist – 2015 National Indie Excellence Book Awards for LGBT Fiction
- Winner of the Gold Medal 2014 Global Ebook Awards – LGBT Fiction
- Winner – Indie Book of the Day – April 19, 2013

Ice begins when a boy is kidnapped from a London park and Detective Inspectors Alex Blake and Maggie Campbell are brought together to work on the case. While their goal is the same, their work ethics are not. Intelligent, perceptive and at times disobedient, Alex Blake does what she believes it takes to do her job. Maggie Campbell has a slightly different approach. She believes that rule books were written for a reason.

Unexpectedly, their dynamics mesh, but when her feelings for Alex become stronger than she wants to admit, Maggie provokes the worst in Alex to ensure that they will never be partners again.

Three years later, fate brings them together again. Their assignment is simple, but a plane crash gets in their way. Now, in the middle of a blizzard, they have to try to survive...and fight the feelings that refuse to die.

***

Mistletoe

- Winner – Indie Book of the Day – December 28, 2013

Four-year-old Diana Clarke sends her wish to Santa Claus, but lost in the lining of a sack, it isn't discovered for thirty years. Now, Santa has a problem. No child's wish has ever gone unanswered, but the child isn't a child anymore.

Believing there is nothing in Santa's Village to satisfy the little girl's wish now that she's an adult, he calls on a Higher Power and is given a suggestion. Although most of Santa's workshops contain only toys for boys and girls, there is one that holds a possible solution to his problem. Learning that Diana will be attending three upcoming Christmas parties, Santa calls on his lead elf to deliver three sprigs of mistletoe, hoping that under one, Diana Clarke will find what she asked for thirty years before.

Made in the USA
Middletown, DE
20 February 2017